A GATHERING OF EVIL

A GATHERING OF EVIL

WALT OXER

JanWal Publications

A GATHERING OF EVIL

A JanWal Publications book
First published in Great Britain in 2023
Copyright © Walt Oxer 2023
All rights reserved.

No part of this publication may be reproduced by any means, nor transmitted, nor translated into a machine language, without the written permission of the publisher.

The right of Walt Oxer to be identified as the author of this work has been asserted in accordance with sections 77 and 78 of the Copyright, Designs and Patents Act 1988.

Condition of sale
This book is sold subject to the condition that it shall not by way of trade or otherwise be lent, re-sold, hired out or otherwise circulated in any form of binding or cover other than that in which it is published and without a similar condition including this condition being imposed on the subsequent publisher.

JanWal Publications
Lancashire, Great Britain

ISBN: 978-1-9160819-9-4

ACKNOWLEDGMENTS

To my most trusted friend Duncan Mangham, photographer and lyricist.
'Flying Tigers'
An enormous thank you to Duncan for his help and support.
Also Birgit Gurtier for the book's brilliant cover artwork
bg-coverdesign@gmx-topmail.de
Peter John Wootton for his sponsorship, and Alan Whelan for his formatting.

A reminder of the ending of book 1, DOONATA...

In a large house in the picturesque town town of Colmar on the French- German border, Conrad Wolff sat dinking coffee with his personal aide, Ferdinand Cortez. They were putting together final plans for their next money-making scheme, one negotiated with the Russian Bratva that involved stealing nuclear torpedoes from the storage facilities at Pantex, South Carolina, after which there would be just one more operation to finalise: the execution of agent Joc Delph.

In a quiet MI6 office in Vauxhall, Anton Spicer received a crimson call asking of him a favour. To agree, he would after bring Joe back from leave.

So begins A GATHERING OF EVIL...

1
A COLD EXCHANGE

Anton Spicer gave a deep sigh before replacing the phone back on its cradle. He needed a drink, needed to take a quite undisturbed moment to gather his thoughts on sister Rachel's phone call. It was nine years since the abduction of brother-in-law Gordon Cummings off the streets of Saint Petersburg,Twelve years since he had given her away, standing in for their deceased father Ray, with Joe Delph acting best man for Gordon on that wonderful summers day.

Gordon and Joe being probably the only link to his past life in terms of friendship, Anton didn't have too many friends in his chosen business; being head of MI6 United Kingdom. The few friends he had then now regarded him with suspicion.

Rachel's phone call had put the seal on recent rumours, Gordon was to be released from a Russian Siberian dungeon and returned to the UK. Nine years had passed from the day they'd grabbed and imprisoned him without trial on charges of espionage. Rachel with two-year-old son Jason was left stranded, frightened, before being rescued by the British Consulate and brought home.

It was only after the recent capture of a Russian spy, Neil Boswell, alias Tiko Gregoravich, that had brought about a Russian offer of a swap; Boswell for Gordon.

Rachel asked Anton for Joe Delph's help, hoping to ensure the changeover would go according to plan with no sudden Russian trickery. Anton had given his word, promised his sister that Joe would supervise the English handover operation.

A date was set for the coming Friday at 6am on the Vartius border crossing between Finland and Russia, with all normal crossing procedures to cease for two hours to allow this delicate operation to take place.

Joe had replied to Antons code crimson call of a return to base knowing the urgency and high importance this must have for his chief to end Joe's Cuban holiday leave.

Joe replied. 'See you Wednesday.' He would remind his chief he was still owed a further two and a half week's furlough.

Wednesday came with a gathering of storm clouds darkening the early evening sky over Vauxhall. Flashes of lightening, followed by the sound of rolling thunder brought a heavy torrential downpour causing Joe to race from his Range Rover, across the open paved area and into the sectioned offices of MI6. Giving a nod and a wave to security he entered the lift-elevator that would take him to level three and the office of Anton Spicer. He exited and checked his dress in a mirror before knocking and entering the chief's outer office where Secretary Monica Turner was busy making fresh ground French coffee. She smiled saying 'Best you go in Joe he's expecting you, I'll follow with coffee. He's asked me to bring in a packet of sour cream Pringles says they're your favourites. I thought you'd be a beef flavoured man myself.'

Joe said. 'I like them all sour creams were a favourite of a friend.'

Monica sighs.. 'Friend no longer with you, Joe?'

Joe. 'Sadly yes, Stacy Kilmer has passed...but seems she's still in the thoughts of Anton....I appreciate that.'

Joe proceeded into the main chamber where Anton was rising to greet him. He holds out his arms in a welcoming gesture.

Anton shrugs and apologises, 'Thought I could hear your voice conversing with Monica.'

He sighs. 'Sorry about the holiday Joe but an old friend has asked for your presence in a forthcoming delicate operation.'

Joe holding up a palm asks. 'And who might this old friend be Ant?'

Anton waits, allowing Monica to enter with the tray of coffee. She looks to them, saying 'I've left it black for you to pour and fix to your likes.'

Anton smile's and nods 'Thank you Monica you needn't hang around, you're free to finish for the day, Joe and I could be quite a while yet.'

Monica 'You sure Sir?'

Anton nods following with, 'Have a good evening.'

She turns and leaves the office.

Joe- 'Seems a nice girl you've got yourself there Anton.'

Anton rubs his face. 'Monica fits my needs, Joe....But I don't let them get too close these days, especially after the Naomi Randell episode.'

He sighs. 'God I couldn't go through all that shite again.'

Joe laughs. 'Come to that, me neither. So who's the friend in need Ant?'

Anton offers Joe a chair and passes over a black coffee to him. He shakes his head whilst stirring his cup and allowing a spoonful of cream to enter the pool. He looks up and shrugs.'Its Rachel, Joe.'

Joe squirming. 'Rachel?...I don't think.... Rachel Ant?'

He blinks. 'Your...our..Rachel Ant. Your sister Rachel?'

He looks at Ants face and can see, it's his sister Rachel who he's referring too. 'Rachel...our Rachel?'

From their early upbringing, Joe had always treated Anton's sister like his own and it was only fair to say at one youthful time it could have developed into a serious romantic affair.

Joe gasps. 'What's happened?..No don't say it...'

Anton is quick to interrupt. 'She's OK, Joe ...it's Gordon, she's worried sick.'

Joe gives a head shake. 'Gordon, but ain't he in Russia... he's not?'

Anton. 'No thank God, he could be on his way home, the Russians they want to exchange him for spy Boswell that MI5 caught in Oxford.'

Joe sighs. 'Jesus, you sure had me worried for a moment there.' He holds up his hand. 'But ain't that good news? Rachel must be over the moon that he's coming home.'

Anton shrugs. 'Oh, she is Joe, but that's if the Russians are going to play by Geneva rules.' He shrugs, 'You and I know what happened in their last exchange. United States pilot Grant Stevens, a few years back. ...Rachel remembers that too. The Yanks gave Alex Churinko back to them, a rose, they returned Stevens, a cabbage.'

Joe. 'I remember.'

He shakes and nods his head. 'So Rachel's thinking that Gordon's return could be somewhat similar to that incident?'

Anton nodding. 'Exactly, Joe, and we can't allow that to happen to Gordon. She's hoping, praying, that you can take charge by going over to Finland and overseeing this exchange.'

Outside there's a flash of lightning and a heavy thunder-roll. Joe smiles at his chief saying.

'She knows I'd never refuse her, so who's with me on this Ant?'

Anton claps a hand. 'Thank you Joe, you know I'd promised her you'd never refuse her. She happened to shed tears on hearing that.'

Anton waves Joe over to a side table where a map of the Finnish/Russian border lies. He points at a pencil circle around the border town of Vartius.

'This is where the exchange is scheduled to take place, 6am Friday morning at the main border crossing point.' He shrugs. The Fins have allowed us two hours to complete the exchange. There will be the expected Finnish border guards on duty along with your old friend Norman Aimes and four of his marine commandos.'

Joe stares, Anton smiles. 'I was having lunch with Admiral Mathews and on him hearing of the operation he suggested I use Major Aimes who is in Norway on some training exercises.'

Shrugs. 'Of course I took his kind offer of assistance.'

Joe pats Anton on the shoulder. 'With Norman we have the best of support, that man, I'd trust my life with, nice one Ant.'

Anton nods. 'Thought you'd be pleased, be like old times you two back working together.'

Joe laughs. 'Not that old Anton, three months at the most.'

Anton wagging a finger. 'In our business three months is a long time, Joe.'

Joe. 'In that case let's get this motor running and get Gordon Cummings back to Rachel alive and in one piece, a rose.'

Anton. 'They have one Colonel Zenakoff doing their negotiating. You heard of him Joe?'

Joe slowly nodding. 'Oh, we know each other, the Colonel and I have had a few close encounters. He's what you might call an old sparring partner. Tell him Joe Delph's the man he'll be dealing with.'

Joe smiles. 'Lets give his tree a shake.'

Anton nods. 'I'll give their representative Mikel Travinski your message. Like you say let's shake their tree.'

4.30 am Finnish time. The Finland-Russian Border Crossing at Vartius.

Joe, with Norman and his Commandos had arrived early. They were being taken along with traitor Neil Boswell by the Finnish border guards to the place where the exchange would go down. Joe had been told their two hours would start at 6am.

It was apparent to Joe that the Finnish guards were somewhat nervous about this operation taking place on their patch. Although not a Nato country Finland held a rain check on some future entry and so allowed this swap-over to take place. Also there was an added fear of a Russian invasion. This fear being the only reason that they'd not joined Nato.

With the temperature showing minus 20 and no sign of getting any warmer, the party was held up at a point where bright overhead spotlights shone down on a well travelled road. The guards indicated to the two timber log houses that stood facing each other on either side of the road. An electrical obstruction vehicle barrier spanned the road's width.One guard held up his gloved hands showing Joe two fingers. Then both guards turned and walked away. Not surprisingly they carried on down the road away from the crossing.

Norman shouted after them. 'Oh, thank you very fucking much.' One guard without turning, gives an over the head wave.

Joe pointed to a few shadowed sections, a small clump of pines. One with a large wood pile stacked near to the roadside. He nodded to Norman.

'OK, Norm, pair the guys in a crossfire position. One pair behind that wood pile is ideal and the the others directly opposite, in the shadows.'

Norman nods. 'Where you're wanting me, Joe?'

Joe smiles. 'You're with me old buddy in the fucking firing line standing right behind the traitor. Just you make sure your boys don't freeze up if action is called for. Keep them warmer-covers over their weapons.'

'I've brought a strong team, Joe, they'll go the distance, I dare say they're as good as me when it comes to shooting the iron.'

Joe. 'They'll need to be, we have an old enemy bringing Gordon, Colonel Fredrik Zenakoff. He's known for the odd dirty trick or two.'

Norman shake of the head. 'Can't say I've ever heard of him, Joe.'

Joe grinds his teeth. 'You don't ever want to Norm he's not a nice chap.'

Joe stabs a finger. 'But he knows me and what I'm capable of, and that will worry him.'

Joe, looks to his watch, rubs his hands together. 'We have around an hour, so let's retire.' He points at the outgoing house. 'That outgoing hut and take a warm cup of Bovril while we wait.'

Norman goes to Boswell taking his arm. Joe holds up a hand, saying.

'He stays here Norm on his knees.' Joe points to a bright central spotlight.

'Under that bright warm spot. Tape his ankles Norm while I put a collar on our dog.'

Norman asks 'Collar, Joe?'

Joe fixes a thick leather Collar around Boswells neck then attaches a grenade to it, he then puts a cord through its pin and unwinds it taking it away towards the log-house. He returns to jangle the cord in front of Boswell.

Joe shouts at the now terrified spy, 'One false action by your Colonel Zenakoff and the cord gets pulled and blows you to hell. I will give you the time to tell him this, furthermore my man Cummings I want to see fit and well and able to answer any questions I may ask of him.' He snarls 'You got my drift traitor?'

Boswell spits. Norman gives him a hard stab with his rifle butt. Boswell lifts his head giving Joe a smile. He spits again before saying.

'Delph, ...you're marked for an overdue call my friend... Your six feet has already been dug, your days are numbered.'

He gives a sick looking smile.'My advice Joe Delph is don't attack our fire with an empty extinguisher for Zenakoff is only one of many who want you fucking dead.' He begins to laugh hysterically.

Norman throws a canvas sheet over him and looks to Joe. 'We all finished here, Joe?'

Joe nods. 'Never make time with a nobody Norm, he's no good to their future plans. They want him dead his time is served, his king in check-mate.

That final hour seemed like a lifetime for Joe, he was thinking of his coming encounter with Zenakoff, making sure he kept control over this wise Russian opponent. He looked at Norman and his hand picked Commandos, who sat around the stove burning fire, drinking their hot Bovril, seemingly unconcerned of what this next hour would bring. Laughing and joking. Like their Major Norman Aimes showing no sense of fear. They had supplied Joe with a large thermos of hot Bovril. Just one tiny but essential item that Joe hadn't given thought to. Thank God Norman had remembered the Finnish climate and its minus temperatures. Joe looked for the umpteenth time at his watch, turning to Norman saying.

'It's quarter to six Norm, time for the guys to get into position.' Norman nods, stands and addresses his men.

'Take your positions boys, it's showtime. Remember to cover all the field of play. If you see me raise a hand then take whoever's out on the Russian side down. Suppressors fixed, head shots with the exploder bullet. I don't want any fuck-up.'

He turns to Joe. 'You OK with that Colonel?'

Joe shrugs. 'We have no other choice Norm, just make sure your guys don't hit Cummings, and don't go scratching your ear.'

Norm laughs. 'Oh, see what you mean Joe, now that would cause some international upset.'

Joe claps his hands. 'Ok, let's do this.' He follows the men out of the wood house door, he exits feeling the bitter cold getting into his body, the warmth leaving it. Somewhat suprised he notices the Finnish guards have not returned from their walkabout. This leads Joe into thinking, do they know something he doesn't, are they expecting something they don't want to put witness to. The guards non appearance was worrisome. He looked down the eastern approach road and the avenue of pine trees that ran either side on a heading towards the Russian border point that lay some quarter mile away out of vision.

Joe turns to see Norman cutting Boswells ankle tapes, pulling the spy to his feet. His Marine's have taken up their positions. Joe comes out of the shadow and stands besides Norman. Joe goes up to Boswell and whispers in the spy's ear. 'Remember traitor?' Boswell spits.

They didn't get to hear the sound of any vehicle's engine on the Russian approach to the crossing. What they did hear was the crunching sound coming from the marching boots of what turned out to be six paratroopers, walking in from the east. To their rear a frail looking, head shaven, Gordon Cummings, finding it difficult to walk in unlaced boots. Shabbily dressed in clothes unbefitting for the weather.

Joe couldn't recognise him from the man he once knew, the husband of Rachel Spicer. The Russians halted and formed a half moon across the width of the road. The cradled their automatic Kalashnikov rifles and stared at Joe and Norman, ignoring Boswell completely.

Boswell, his voice a tremble began his speech, relaying what Joe had asked. What followed was a period of silence, with no response.

Joe was just about to call out for Zenakoff when the Russian Colonel's voice comes screaming out from somewhere a little way behind his troopers, directly behind the swaying Cummings.

'Tell Delph it is I, Fredrik Zenakoff who issues the fucking orders, my first being for you Delph to stand with Boswell. Let me see your sick English face. You see, Delph, I don't converse with shadows. You will stand with Boswell and I will approach with your Cummings.' He laughs, 'Just like the proper gentlemen we are.'

Norman whispers to Joe. 'This is going to be shit Joe, stalemate, you move up to Boswell and they'll blow you away, Boswell too.'

Joe nods, asking. 'Those guys of yours Norm they got their night-views on?'

Norman. 'You bet, Joe.'

Joe nudges him. 'Then why don't you give that ear of yours a scratch.' Norman smiles, raising his hand. 'I thought you were never going to ask Colonel.'

Normans arm action brings an immediate response from his hidden: Commandos. The Russian troopers too late to respond are cut down each with a hole in their head the size of a golf ball, that came from the contact exploding bullets.

A shocked Zenakoff stands in the open, his guard gone. He rushes up to Cummings and puts a pistol to his head. He shouts half screaming at Joe.

'You're a no good fucking double crossing English bastard Delph. OK you win, I take Boswell, I give you Cummings and we leave. We finish this play some other time, agreed?'

Joe laughs. 'Now come on Fredrik, it's me that's in control, but OK, let's do this. Isn't that what this party is what we've come for, a swap?' He sighs. 'But then, I'm giving you a fit and healthy Boswell. My man Cummings well he didn't look too good on his feet, like he was in pain.'

Zenakoff shrugs, 'Cummings he's OK, he's good, he was silly boy he got put into solitary. He's getting better every day stronger.'

Joe. 'Like the American pilot Grant Stevens, Colonel?'

Joe shouts over at Gordon, 'You OK Gordon?'

Gordon slowly nodding his head says. 'Get me home, Joe. Get me the fuck away from these animals.'

Joe takes the collar off Boswell but leaves him tied behind his back. He pushes the spy forward, saying. 'On your bike traitor.'

Zenakoff releases Gordon, the two cross. With Norman rushing forward helping Gordon over the line. In doing so he smells the clothes that are stiff and soaked in urine. He holds up a blanket and covers the shivering Cummings. Turning to Joe.

'He needs a fresh warm change of clothes, Joe and a hot shower, he's needing hospitalisation.'

Joe watches the laughing pair. Zenakoff and Boswell walking arm in arm away from the crossing. He nudges Norman and points to them, winks.

'Ain't that ear of yours itching Norm?'

Norman holds up a hand, a volley of rifle fire follows, Joe watches the laughing couple fall.

Joe, 'Let's get Gordon into that house and that fire, get his circulation moving, some of that fine hot Bovril into him. Tell the guys fine job, to get those bodies of the road, take them into the forest, the Finnish side.'

He sighs. 'See they're well covered till we can get the removers to clean up.' He shakes his head. 'We need time to fabricate some kind of story, otherwise we'll have a International incident at our door.'

Norman nods. 'Consider it done, Joe.'

Joe continues to say 'The last thing Anton would want is further Russian involvement.'

He looks at his watch and sees the time of the whole incident at the Vartius border crossing has taken exactly 35 minutes. He tells Norman that they have around 1 hour 20 minutes, maybe less, to get the bodies away. That it was all depending on how keen those two guards were in returning, probably with others, to open up the road. The Russian rifles and any other arms, they would conceal and take away in their vehicle. Everything must be cleared of any conflict taking place.

Norman, shrugs saying. 'Let's hope those border guards haven't heard the gunfire, Joe? and, come to think, what about the Russian border guards, they still back there? Because if they are, they've heard all.'

Joe smiles. 'They've not ventured forward Norm. The pop, popping, coming out through the fitted suppressors. We just have to like you say, hope. It's a risk we've got to take. I need to get Gordon dressed into the spare uniform, some clean clothes I've brought along with me. Get those stinking rags off him.

We get him to lie flat to the boards in our retreat vehicle. I don't want those guards to suspect anything, if they ask, the Russians didn't turn up.' He shrugs. 'Best get Anton on crimson and tell him we need cleaners here. One of your guys will have to meet-up and show them the cemetery.'

Norman smiles. 'Sounds good, Joe. So fucking good it could well work out like a merry Christmas.' With that Norman waves for his men to come out. He then sets them to task.

Some 30 minutes later five border guards return, the road is clear, Norman and his men sitting in the army's vehicle, it's engine running ready to leave. Joe stands explaining to the most senior officer that the Russians didn't show.

Back in London it's Monday morning and Joe Delph is sitting in Ronnie's barge floating restaurant taking an early breakfast, one of Ronnie's special Banjos. He's listening to a few of the early birds, street cleaners and bin men who are discussing the weather. There's apparently flooding in most parts of the south-west with rivers overflowing turning pastures into lakes. Some towns and villages, being hit for the third time in a year, and, what with the huge ice mountains breaking away in the Polar regions, a definite climate change was happening on a world-wide scale. Joe sat thinking. 'When will we ever learn?'

He could hear one guy saying thank God he lived in London, that he couldn't take what was happening to some; raw sewerage flooding into their homes. Going on to say 'Bet these million pound cottages were finding a value drop. Three times in the past year and the year wasn't over yet.'

Ten minutes later and Joe entered the outer office of MI6 and saw the smiling face of Anton's Girl Friday, Monica Turner. Anton had called him, to give a verbal report on the weekends swap operation. Anton wanted no written account. Not until a great deal of thought was given to a most delicate situation.

Joe, whispering, asks. 'How's our chief?' Monica smiles and replies.

'You fetched a bone for him Joe?' Joe, shrugs. 'That bad, eh?'

Monica gives him a wobble wave with a hand. Joe nods.'Best I knock first then.'

Monica. 'I don't think it's that bad, Joe. Just go in.'

Anton seated, motions for Joe to take a seat, giving him a moment to settle before holding up a palm, saying. 'Rachel has asked me to thank you, Joe, for returning Gordon to her safe and sound.'

He nods. 'I must say it's taken nine years to see a smile back on my sister's face and I thank you for that.'

Joe shrugs. 'No problem Ant, tell her it's the least I could do for a dear friend.'

Anton goes on to say that it's going to take time for Gordon to return to something like normal but he was sure he'd make it. He had the best of care tending to his needs. Anton leans back in his seat, holds out a hand.

'So tell me, Joe. What the fuck happened? I've been working all weekend rushing around getting the cleaners over there and those bodies out of the way.' He sighs. 'Sending that team into Finland did not go unnoticed. Those cleaners put those bodies so deep they struck a fucking coal seam.' Anton shakes his head. 'The Foreign Secretary tells me the Russians are giving the Finnish government grief over their loss.' He gives a deep sigh. 'OK, I know a good soldier never looks behind in this case we've a Russian deployment on our tails, looking for answers. All I'm asking you, Joe, was it necessary?'

Joe slaps Anton's desk top. 'It was a case of them or us, Ant. For fucks sake I had to decide.' He, again slaps the desk.

'I'm sorry, Ant, but what with the weather 20 below at 6 am in a open environment, with six fucking Russian Paratroopers standing over us armed to the bollocks with their Kalashnikov automatics awaiting the signal to cut us down.'

Joe shakes his head. 'Let me tell you this brother, you don't give it a second thought, it's an immediate decision, like I said it's them or us. I happened to choose us.'

Anton with arms spread. ' OK, I was just asking, Joe. It's important we don't lose the plot on this, one slip-up and the Russians are going to take revenge. I'm hoping that we are shut tight all down the line.'

He gives a deep sigh. 'I know Major Aimes has been told and that he's wise to this. But what's it with his commando team, they good, Joe?'

Joe shrugs. 'Both Norman and I have already instructed the team, that it's a closed curtain in regard to discussion on the Finland incident. They know the score Ant.'

Joe, puts up a finger, jabs it. 'Norm, he brought professional soldiers, hand picked Marines.'

Gives a shake of his head. 'Leaks, I've no worries in Norman's department, I can sleep soundly knowing that.'

Anton seemingly relieved. 'That's good to hear, Joe. You understand I need to ask these questions.'

Joe, nods. 'We've just got to see how far the Red Army are wanting to go with it, Ant.'

'Anton sighs. 'They'll take it to the wire, Joe, you know that but at least we can breathe a little easier.'

He nods, claps his hands. 'So how about lunch you fancy a pint at the Kings Arms?' Smiles. 'There's something else I need to talk to you about.'

Joe gives a laugh. 'Hope it's a return to my Cuban holiday.'

He looks at Anton's face.'But that look, Tells me it's not.'

Shake of the head. 'No, you wouldn't be taking me to lunch, if I was that lucky.'

Anton and Joe seemed somewhat surprised on entering the Kings Arms public house. The place was overflowing, with most of its customers huddled over by a blazing log fire. Outside the rain had returned and thunder could be heard rolling overhead. Joe spotted a table unoccupied over by the toilet area, he looked at Anton, shrugs and made for it. With Anton making for the bar. On taking up the seating it suddenly occurred to him why the table had been free.

Two old timers were at each other's throats on an argument about football. The Spurs, Tottenham we're playing the Hammers West Ham and although the pair of elderlies were friends, it was plain to see they each had a different view when it came to football. The East Ender quite adamant that the Hammers were going to blow the Spurs apart.

Joe smiled on hearing the bet of a pint being offered as to the result, thoughts that William Hill would be shaking in their boots on such a wagering.

Finally Anton returned with two pints of Guinness, shrugs, saying that all the steak, the cheese and onion pies, with the usual mash and mushy peas were sold out. So he'd ordered baked potatoes with salad, both with a Tuna and Mayonnaise filling. Joe gave him a thumbs-up to the substitute lunch, thinking: should have gone to Ronnie's.

Anton leans over and whispers 'What's those two silly old sods arguing about?'

Joe shakes his head. 'The great game, football. They've got a pint going on a result.' Anton smiles. 'Such high stakes, shame there's got to be a loser.'

Joe. 'Could be a draw.' Lifts up his glass.

'Cheers.' Anton, with his touches Joe's . 'Cheers, Joe'

Anton takes in the surroundings, eyeing the pub's customers. He smiles at the many standing before nudging Joe. He nods to the two empty chairs that are still vacant at their table.

'Think they know we're Police, Joe?' Joe smiles.

'If you've anything private to tell me, better say it now, Ant. because I'm sure those seats are not going to be empty for too long, coppers or not.'

He winks. 'I noticed a couple of old birds eyeing them up. I think they're working out if we're sex maniacs, if it's safe to join us.' Anton laughs.

'So, if we are they'll join us, Joe.'

Joe puts up a finger. 'It's been known, Ant, if some women are lonely and desperate they'll risk it.'

Anton smiles, 'Best give you the griff on a call I received this morning from Berlin, General Porter, Norbert.' Takes a swallow of his Guinness. 'Seems the CIA have a problem. One that has cost and lost them three top agents in trying to find an answer.'

Joe. 'Cost, lost, Ant?'

Anton, nodding his head. 'That's right, Joe. Three top A's having been sent to investigate haven't returned or been heard or seen since.' Joe holds up a hand. 'So, what are you saying, Ant. Norbert s asking for SIS 's help and you're offering me?'

Anton shakes his head, replies. 'Not so brother, he, Norbert asked for you. His actual words were. Do you think Joe would help us. and could I spare you. My reply was, that

I'd ask you. I then added that what with the Finland no show fiasco, you were contemplating a break, a holiday.'

Joe smiles, shake of the head. 'No show fiasco, how come no show,Ant. When we have Gordon back home. How are we going to cover that up?'

Anton smiles. 'Already taken care of, Joe, we've done a little shuffling in giving Gordon a new ID, along with Rachel and the boy. They're up north, not too far from our neck of the woods. All's cool, Joe.'

Joe nods. 'Good, I don't want to know anymore....So getting back to Norbert, what's the General's problem?'

Anton shaking his head.

'OK, Joe, this is what he's told me. Reports are coming into Berlin's CIA headquarters of a build up of Wolves gathering in Bavaria about 40 kilometres east of Munich. The local government are allowing it with caution. Hoping that this so called rally is only a one-off event.'

Joe. 'Seems like a bit of an Isle of Man TT cover. They got racing Ant?'

Anton shrugs. 'Nothing on that from Norbert, it's all rock and roll,...a beer festival is what he's given me.'

Joe. 'Suppose it could be nothing, but the missing agents that's a no, no,' Anton. 'Not only that but it's by invitation only, these Wolves are coming from all over the globe on an invited ticket. The Alphas and their Zeta Generals are attending.'

He sighs. 'It's a main event, Joe.'

Joe, with a suspicious look. 'So Norbert is asking Joe Delph to walk into the fire.' He shrugs, 'He's not asking for much, Ant. They running out of staff over in Berlin?'

Anton replies, 'Like I've told him, I'd ask you, no guarantees that you'll accept.'

Joe. 'If I go I pick my own team. I'd ask Norm. But with no Ryona or Roberto anymore it's a case of who's the best for entering what could well be a snake pit.'

Anton smiles. 'Oh, I can tell you Norbert's already wired Roberto. He and Ryona are in England doing a summer vacation in North Yorkshire and like you, they're wanting to know more on the intended mission before considering it.'

Joe gasps. ' You saying Ryona is in with Roberto on this?'

Anton laughs. 'You know the score, Joe. Where Batman goes, Robin goes with him. There ain't no way Ryona's letting Roberto enter the arena alone.'

Joe smiles. 'I hope to God they come in on this, nobody knows those Wolves like Roberto.'

Anton lifts up his glass with a toast of let's hope. Then goes on to say that their business detection services had really prospered, that it was touch and go they'd return to the more dangerous side of crime. Joe reminded Anton that had always been the plan of Stacy's to settle into something similar..

Joe pauses for a moment and sighs.

Anto could see that the death of Joe's only real love of his life, Stacy Kilmer was still haunting him. Joe finished with saying that if Roberto had any sense in that Italian brain of his then he'd stay away. Anton added that he thought Roberto had a little of Joe about him. A seeker of adventure and all that it brought, win or lose. Just maybe, Joe's involvement would sway the decision for them.

Outside the sound of thunder rolling like some omen, whilst inside the two elderly ladies had returned and were standing over Anton and Joe, wearing a looks of Cuckoos seeking a nest, with one enquiring if the seats were vacant.

Joe looks at Anton and winks. He smiles and rubbing his hands together, replies to her. 'They're yours for the taking, being men of the road ourselves, in need of female company.'

The other lady says '

Oh, come on Mavis.' She nudges her friend.

'You know what these two pair of cocks are after.'

She snarls at Joe. 'Sexy Northerner's .'

Anton stands. 'I can assure you ladies, that such thoughts never entered either of us.' He holds out a hand presenting it to the chairs. Mavis tells him to bugger off and taking, her friends elbow, walks away from the table uttering.

'You were right Janet, I could see it in those two's eyes, why, they'd would have had us.'

Janet gives a nudge and giggles saying. ' In that case, shouldn't we go back?'

The thunder and lightning although moving East, sounded and looked like a panoramic artists dream. The sky over the great city had darkened and over its rooftops the lightning forked like some skeleton hand crawling across the heavens. As for the rain, it had eased off slightly, so making it easier for Anton and Joe to leave the Kings Arms public house.

Joe, who had decided to find out more on this Wolf motorcycle clan gathering was accompanying Anton back to their Vauxhall Base. His thoughts on General Porter losing three Agents , top A's, worried him. But then if Roberto and the old team got back together, then who knows. He'd need to know more on the CIA's presumed dead agents. Of course Roberto would know of them, he being one time head of the American top CIA, A's.

One thing Joe didn't want to happen, was mistakes going down, by not giving situations enough thought. He was thinking on the Doonata mission, when their dear friend Major Tony Ford was killed because of a jacket he was wearing in a hundred degree temperature. A jacket that marked him mistakenly as FBI.

All such thoughts were running through Joe's brain like a fast flowing river as they entered the office of Anton Spicer. With Anton checking that the heating systems radiators was on fully. He turns to Joe whilst setting the systems thermostat. 'Sorry there's no Guinness, Joe, but I've got Jameson if you fancy a short.'

Joe shrugs 'I'm more for a hot coffee Ant, if that's OK?'

Anton nods 'Yes, I'll see to it when we get a little more heat into this place, I've put the stat up to twenty four. Soon be like a furnace in here.'

Joe. 'This rain, when's it gonna stop, floods all over the UK, fires raging in the Australian bush , America with California burning, wonder what's happening in Bavaria besides a motorcycle rally. Snow, wouldn't surprise me.' Anton shouts. 'Mud slides in Peru, Antarctica crumbling, don't forget those, Joe.' He sighs.

'Best organise the coffee, you still taking it black Joe?' Joe nods.

'I only take milk if it's instant Ant.'

Ant, nods. 'I like to add cream and a shot of Jameson's with my French blend, makes for a sound sleep.'

Joe, laughs. 'With what's on the cards, I'm thinking you're going to need a bucket full and don't be surprised if I don't join you.' He shrugs.

'Best you give Norbert a bell, tell him I'll help, but only if I can use my own team. Explain that I like to know the horse I'm riding.'

Anton making the coffee smiles. 'With three down I'm thinking he's not wanting to lose anymore.' Shake of the head.

'Can't see you having a problem with that request, Joe.'

Joe puts up a finger. 'No disrespect to the General, but it's either my team or it's a no go, Ant.'

Anton nods bringing over the coffee. 'Understood, Joe, no problem.'

It was sometime later that Anton put through a call to Norbert Porter, giving him the conditions that had been requested by Joe. Norbert seemed somewhat relieved by the news, more so on hearing that Roberto could be included in Joe's line-up. Anton explaining that they were waiting confirmation from the ex Berlin head of CIA European Field Activities. That he would keep him informed on developments regarding Roberto and Ryona. Now known by their married name of Roberto and Mari Veneto.

Norbert told Anton, hearing Joe and Roberto joining, was the best news he'd heard in the past month. Adding to tell Joe to just ask if he needed anything. Anything at all. Anton relayed Norbert's message to Joe.

Joe was sitting back going through how the operation would work out. It's main objective would be to get an invite to this motorcycle gathering. Whilst Anton was making arrangements on transport and costumes, leathers with the right insignias, ppweapons, and a complete silence black-out on the operation.

Joe's cell phone began to screech with the name of Norman Aimes appearing on the display. Joe answers.

'Hi, Norm, what's with you?'

Norman. ' Is there any chance, Joe, on including my Sergeant, David Frazier in the team?' Joe could hear a sigh, before Norman continues. 'I was thinking as a replacement for Major Ford...Tony, Joe?'

Joe didn't give too long a thought in replying.

'Fine by me, Norm. I've a liking and trust in Frazier. He can only make our team stronger.

Norman. 'Great, Joe, we will fly into Heathrow this evening, if that's OK with you?'

Joe answers. 'I'd sooner you'd fly into Leeds Bradford or, better still, Doncaster, but in thinking that, Doncaster would probably have no scheduled in flights from Oslo. You'd have to check that out.'

Norman chuckles. 'Am I right in thinking we're to make your Yorkshire base, Joe. If so, Frazier, he's gonna love those fish and chips. Although we've been sampling your Currywurst here in Norway I must say they come a close second to that Chippy of yours. They've got sausages here as long as a donkeys dick.'

Joe. 'Oh, can either you or Frazier handle a motorcycle?'

Norman. 'Jesus, Joe last time I sat on a bike was on my Norton Dominator, some fifteen years back, but yes I can kick one up. Frazier I'll ask....Motorbike, Joe?'

Joe. 'You get yourselves to Doncaster. You may find Ryona and Roberto already in the house, but if not the keys in the usual place in the wall box. Numbers 9648.'

Norman seems surprised on hearing Ryona and Roberto were back. Hadn't they married and were living in America, was told running a prosperous business, investigating company fraud. Them leaving to return to a world of life and death situations. Are they mad, lost it upstairs? Probably, but he wasn't going to knock them, there must be a reason.

'Ryona, Roberto, Joe?'

Joe told Norman that he was still waiting for confirmation, but felt sure they'd be joining up, that he'd know before the night was through. Also, that he himself was flying to Berlin for a CIA meet and should be back the following evening and would join them at the South Yorkshire base.

Norman finished by saying Frazier would be pleased and thanked Joe.

2
HOWLING GIG IN BAVARIA

It was 9pm when Joe boarded the flight leaving Heathrow for Berlin, he'd received a call from Roberto to say that they were on their way to Donny. With Joe asking if they were sure in coming back, that the drum was beating louder than the Doonata mission. Roberto told him that he'd already contacted General Porter and informed him of their decision. Only to add that this would be their last time. That they'd always thought the battle with the Fly was not at an end, and until it was, with feelings for Tony, finalisation, a Sicilian vendetta. They had a notion that the Fly was somehow involved in this Bavarian gathering. Joe gave him the code to the key box saying to expect Norman and Frazier arriving. Roberto had laughed saying in a broad Yorkshire accent that he'd put kettle on.

The flight to Berlin gave Joe time to ponder on the coming situation which was the reason for the gathering, especially the attending Alpha and the Zetas. Also to make the event more authentic specially invited female Vixens had been allowed to accompany their male Wolves. This Joe thought could be a weakness on the organisers part. Definitely a path for Ryona to venture down. It was almost midnight when, Joe had been met and taken to the Prestige Hotel for what had been booked as an overnight stay. He entered to see the solitary figure of a man behind reception. Joe carrying an over the shoulder leather Fossil bag which contained the bare essentials, toiletries and nothing more for his over night stay. On his pick up he'd been handed a Glock pistol with a full clip of bullets. It seemed that security had definitely been tightened since his last stay. Furthermore he'd been booked in as one Marvin Tate. He'd been advised to use one of his many alias. Joe was a marked man .He was given room eleven. He looked all around the foyer. Satisfied that there were no peeping Toms he made for the lift that would take him up to the first floor. It was late and he took straight to his bed setting the alarm for 8 am. His meeting with the General was scheduled for ten. The Glock automatic he slid under his pillow. He had put a chair with a large flower vase up against the door as a precaution. The vase was so finely balanced that the slightest movement against the chair would send it crashing to the room's part tiled floor.

The CIA taxi service would come for him at 9. 30 hours. Revealing the name Tom Sawyer.

The sound of the alarm brought Joe up out and under the shower. The night thankfully, much to Joe's relief, had ended without incident. He'd take breakfast in the hotel before embarking to the office of General Norbert Porter. Although not really a fan of the continental breakfasts of Ham, Jam, and other ingredients he'd give it a go, but really hot coffee, black, was an early morning must.

It was bang on 9.30am and the taxi arrived that would take Joe to CIA headquarters. The password Tom Sawyer was given and all was good. Some ten minutes later and Joe was being escorted to the office of General Norbert Porter.

Joe felt he was getting the all-star treatment with Norbert pouring the coffee and asking if he'd had breakfast. He could see that Norbert was more than pleased to see him. Joe politely refused saying he'd already eaten back at the hotel.

Norbert smiled, saying. 'I was going to offer you a full English, Joe, not that continental, how you say, jam butty.' He shrugged. 'Still we can have lunch here in the office as I know you're eager to get back and prepare.' He walks over tapping Joe on the shoulder. 'Can I first thank you for giving your time to the CIA on what has become a complete fucking nightmare. Three of our top agents, Joe, missing without a clue as to where, how, or when.' He shakes his head. 'One, Sam Grainger, top man ex Major Delta Force, Roberto knows him well, Sam had been working undercover for the last twelfth months. His abductors would have had to be good to take him down.'

'What of the others, Sir?'

'Curtis and Patterson...Top A's, Joe...I've given all to Roberto.'

Joe, shrugs. 'Seems this enemy are no longer making mistakes, General. Unlike the Doonata killings they're covering up and are wise to your movement's. Leaving you nothing but a mystery to solve.' He sighs.

'But they underestimate my team. We brought them down once and we'll do so again.' He taps Norbert's desktop.

'I think it's the Bratva that we are dealing with and calling on their worldwide army to come in on something big.'

Norbert, 'You thinking like Roberto, Joe, that the Fly is still on the wing?' Joe replies. 'A partnership General, the Fly and the Bratva? I very much doubt, after what the Fly administered in Sicily to the Russian Pakham.'

He shrugs. 'But then again the Russians are the complete artists when it comes down to the art of deception. One can only guess whether they'd go so far as to lure the Fly into their sticky web by offering a partnership.'

The session with Norbert was highlighted when they both settled for lunch. Unknowing to Joe, an earlier conversation had taken place between Norbert and Roberto. The ex CIA man had answered Norbert's call about the deadly situation that had arisen. The three, missing, believed to be dead agents. Roberto was shocked to hear that his old friend Sam Grainger was one of the three. Norbert adding that Joe Delph was being called upon to get some answers. Roberto had promised to get back to the General after consulting his wife Mari, alias Ryona Steel.

Norbert, told Roberto of the day's meeting with Joe. That he'd be giving the MI6 double - O man full control over the mystery.

Roberto, on a parting note had suggested that he give Joe a lunch of Currywurst with fries. Norbert had taken Roberto's advice and noted Joe's eyes light up on his Currywurst lunchbox. Roberto had also suggested apple pie with custard as a desert. This the headquarters chef provided, with a cinnamon and nutmeg topping that he'd sparingly sprinkled over the custard. All washed down with fine French coffee.

Joe smiled licking his lips, saying. 'Roberto, you've been talking to him, wait till I see that one in a million Sicilian. He knows how to get into my good books.'

Norbert laughed before giving Joe news that the Bavaria was due to start this coming weekend leaving Joe with only four days to come up with a plan.

With no time to lose Joe's brain was going through several ideas of what was needed, getting the required information, on what he knew to be a most dangerous and delicate situation.

It was well after midnight when Joe, after eight hours of non stop travel that had included a flight from Berlin into London's Heathrow.

Then driving his Land Rover around the M.25 onto the M.11 then the A1. finally reaching Doncaster and his rural, detached South Yorkshire home.

As he entered its long driveway, the house looked dark, bleak, and somewhat gothic in the 4x4's headlights. Reminding Joe of some Hollywood movie, it could well have been the setting for an Edgar Alan Poe drama, with the Vincent Price ready to step out of the darkness to welcome him.

He could see the Saab of Ryonas parked up. They had arrived and retired, Norman and Frazier, he felt sure, along with them.

Joe entered and could immediately smell the perfume of Ryonas Joe Malone. He yawned, tired and ready for the old four legged friend, his comfy bed, to wake refreshed and see what the new day would bring. He took to the stairs trying hard not to disturb his sleeping guests, trying harder to put aside his thoughts on the three missing agents.

He'd get Roberto's thoughts on how they'd been taken. He was hoping that they'd not got another mole in the hole.This being the main reason he would not disclose his plan outside of the team. That he'd asked for complete control of Norbert, with no questions asked.

Those Wolves he knew would be waiting, having already been alerted to the CIA presence they'd expect the CIA to retaliate. This mission was going to be far from easy. The Alpha Wolf had called for and gathered an invited strong pack. Whatever he'd planned was big, Joe, smelt money along with power had to be its main gain, money and lots of it.

This festival could only be a front for what was really going down. Joe was thinking on why the Alpha had gathered such a large pack when sleep overcame him.

He awoke to the smell of bacon and a clattering of pans, with the time showing 9am. Voices, laughter was coming from downstairs. Joe slipped out from his sheets and made for the rooms en- suite shower. Ten minutes later he entered the dining room to four smiling, good morning wishing faces. He smiled, nodded to his assembled team, Ryona, Roberto, Norman and Dave Frazier.

Ryona pointed to a covered fry pan, saying. 'There's a full English keeping warm for one hungry man over there, Joe.'

'We decided to leave you be, not to wake you, that's after hearing you arrive in the early hours.'

Joe replies. 'Yes, that's much appreciated. I was completely knackered after travelling some eight, nine hours coming in from Berlin.'

He looks at each face in turn before saying. 'You just don't know, how pleased I am to see you all again. Seems like yesterday. It's good to see Dave joining us, keeping the memories of Major Tony Ford alive and in all our thoughts.' He sighs.

'Jesus, I fucking miss that guy.' Turns to Norman. 'I know Norm does to, if ever he had a friend, then it was Tony.'

Norman with his head down just nods.

Joe smiles. 'Can't tell you how surprised and pleased I am to see Mr. and Mrs. Veneto coming in, leaving what I've heard to be a profitable business, returning into a world where profit isn't the dollar bill but one more nail driven into the coffin of international crime.' Joe shrugs. 'I love all you fucking guys.'

He points to the table and their unfinished breakfasts. 'With what I've got to go over with you, leaves us with little time. So   let's finish breakfast before getting our heads together on General Porter's problem.'

Roberto looks at Ryona smiles, saying. 'These company fraud case files are so boring, my wife and I needed a change, a need to sharpen up.' Ryona laughs. 'In other words stop us from falling asleep.'

Joe. 'Nice to hear, but I know just where your coming from. There's other ways to stop you both from falling asleep, but laying your lives on the line ain't in the top one hundred.' He smiles.

'I've got to thank you for offering your help.' He claps them all.

'I applaud you all, let's eat before I get my hanky out.'

With breakfast over Joe takes his team into the lounge and asks them to sit while he remains standing. He goes on to tell them about his meeting with Norbert Porter, of the CIAs problem about the loss of three of their top agents. Missing or dead no bodies had been found. It was like they'd just walked off the planet, leaving no clues to investigate. Adding that these agents were top A's and would have been difficult to take down. This giving his team an insight on what they were dealing with, a dangerous unit that he thought could only be Zetas, the Alpha's Generals. The cream of the Pack, highly trained killers.

Roberto interrupts Joe saying. 'I worked with one of the missing three, Sam Grainger, he was a trained ace card.' He sighs.

'These Zetas have to be good to take down Sam, a man who has worked undercover all over the globe for numerous years.'

Joe nodding. 'So that brings us to the question, how do we get into this, by the invitation only arena?' He points a finger at them.

'Remember they are now wise to the CIA coming in seeking answers. The Wolves will be howling, guarding, like demons at the gates of hell.' He shrugs. 'We have to find their weakness, a point of safely penetrating their armour without losses.'

Norman nods. 'They'll have a hole in their blanket, I'm thinking of their women, their Vixens. Surely they'll be accompanying their men. Could we find a weakness in that department?'

Roberto. 'Good idea Norm but they'll not be carrying the information we require. A Wolf soldier wouldn't either. We've got to take and break a Zeta.' He sighs. 'It's not going to be easy, I'm thinking, we have only one go at it.'

Joe. 'What we're all forgetting is our need to get in amongst them. Getting an invite, a ticket, or whatever gets us through that door.'

He gives a shake of his head. 'I have brought with me from Berlin a selection of leather jackets with the Wolf insignia on them. Curtesy of the CIA's Berlin prison connections.'

He looks at Roberto. 'My initial thought was that we somehow capture an Italian Soldier and his Vixen. Taking their invites and letting Roberto and Ryona get into the festivities.' Sighs. 'But it's high risk, I can't order them to do this.'

He shakes his head. 'No, no fucking no. I'm wanting another option. So come on now guys let's sort this.'

Roberto. 'Thanks, Joe for thinking of us.' They all laugh, including, Joe.

Roberto goes on. 'It seems to me, it's all on these invites. But there is another way.' He smiles. 'You know what I'm thinking?' They all look at each other. Ryona gives a shrug, saying. 'We don't, so please tell us husband of mine.'

Joe tells Roberto they're all ears. Roberto puts up a hand.

'We're looking at this like those three CIA agents looked at it, the need to get hold of an invite.' He sighs. 'I really believe that may have cost them their lives.' He winks.

'But what if we gained entrance as inspectors, local government environmental dudes. A team like us that required assurances on safety, toilet facilities.'

Norman smiles adding. 'A ticket to say that the festival had all the boxes ticked to allow the festival to take place.' He looks to, Joe.

'Think Roberto's idea is feasible, Joe?'

Joe shrugs. 'We'd have to let General Porter in on it, he's the only one who could find this information for us, that this inspection procedure is called upon by local councils.'

Joe takes out his cell and puts in the number for General Porter. Norbert replies. 'Yes, Joe?'

Joe goes on to ask him what Roberto had put forward. The way to gain entry to the by invitation only festival. Would the organisers need some kind of safety documentation, issued by the local government that allowed the gig to take place. If so, what were the chances of the General getting a docket made up for Joe and his team to enter. Made-up Inspectors Fire and Safety or whatever.

Norbert had taken time in replying to Joe's question. Firstly he told him that he honestly didn't know, in fact had never thought of entry by that official door. He added his thoughts that it was a risky move. That he didn't know of anyone in Bavaria, that he could safely address on the subject.

His nearest contact would be, in that department, an ex police officer, Gustav Muller.

The retired Muller would know, from a police point of view, just what would be required. But then your 'keep it in house' door would be open. And that would create a problem. Questions would be asked, documents would need to be forged and that brought in others. Norbert went on to say that such an operation needed more time than the three days they had left. He advised Joe to think again.

Joe thanked the General then cut the call. He looked at his team who he could see were deep in thought. Joe gives a sweep of his hand, saying.

'So that puts that plan in the shredder. Norbert's right, for it to have worked we would have needed more of what, we haven't got, time.'

Roberto nods in agreement, jabbing his finger. ...'Not getting in may leave us with no knowledge of what's going down, but then isn't that exactly what these Wolf soldiers know? They know, like us, nothing.' Still jabbing. 'They are waiting instructions coming from their Zeta, who in turn are waiting for the Alpha to tell them.'

Joe. 'So what you are saying Roberto, is, that we are next in line gaining the knowledge, that we take a Zeta after the event?'

Roberto smiles. 'How you say, nail on the head Joe, exactly.'

Ryona adds. 'We don't have to enter, we find out when it's over. We don't need that wishful time you speak of Joe.'

Frazier, for the first time, speaks. 'Maybe we could enter into Bavaria as tourists. We'd not be alone, they'd be hundreds of happy holidaymakers all around, drinking their steins, having a good time.'

Joe. 'That's not a bad idea that David's suggested. Tourists, could be the way to go, it's a beautiful area, with green valleys and a walker's paradise. Ideal holiday location for the South Yorkshire Hikers Association.'

Norman slaps Frazier on the back, puts up a thumb to Joe. 'Didn't I tell you Colonel? my man here's got a brain.' They all laugh.

Joe smiles, nodding. 'Best Ryona gets us some flights booked. Pack your flight bags with casual clothing. I'll nip into Doncaster to purchase everything a camper carries tents hand cooking pots along with boots, so give me your sizes.'

Norman. 'Give me the list, Joe. Dave and I will go round the charity shops, they'll be plenty in Donny. If we're going to do this right then we're going to need worn items. Giving the right impression is a must if we're ever going to pull this off we have to look the part.'

Joe. 'At least we seem to be getting there with this, nice work team.'

Roberto. 'I'll get the General to sort out some weapons for us knives, and automatic pistols for us on arrival in Bavaria....Be probably Munich we fly into.'

Joe nods. 'We go as tourists on a cheap charter flight, we look like tourists, talk and think like hikers. Watching our every step of the way. Knowing one mistake could be fatal, our last. I don't want any more Tony Fords.'

He shakes his head. 'God bless him.' He sighs. 'Wearing a jacket cost him his life.'

Ryona smiles. ' South Yorkshire Hikers Association, that's cool, brothers, I think we're getting there. All we need is a little luck and the jigsaw will be complete.' She turns to, Joe. 'Think the Fly's in with all this, Joe?'

Joe. 'Could be, but somehow I don't think so.'

Roberto asks. 'What makes you think that, Joe?'

Joe. 'It's just a gut feeling, look at the invites to this piss-up, it's a Wolves only show, with one big Alpha in command. Could well be the Russian Pakham, and if it is then is he going to allow another Sicilian horror to happen. He's still looking for his vendetta and wants that Fly no more.'

Roberto nods. 'You could be right Joe, but I'm inclined to believe that Flys still buzzing around out there. He his seeking a vendetta he wants Joe Delph dead.'

Joe smiles, gives a wink. 'He can only dream, Roberto, he must join the queue.'

Ryona had booked an early morning flight, Manchester to Munich that was leaving by Lufthansa AG arriving 3.30 pm. The cost was two and and fifty pounds Sterling per person, a two hour journey.

Three hours later and all was ready. A message had arrived from Norbert to say all would be waiting for them on their arrival in Munich.

It was just left for the team to pick up their luggage and clear customs before being approached by a representative of Norbert Porter and ushered into a 4x4 Jeep, that would take them to their hotel. One rural, away from the city hostel that the General had booked.

It was early morning 2 am, they'd finally been shown to their rooms. Norbert's man, a middle aged, tall, slim looking character whose name was Jordan had handed the keys of the Jeep over to Joe, telling him that their weapons were concealed in a large hold-all in the back of the vehicle. Joe thanked the man who simply nodded and left.

It had been one hectic day and Joe told his team to take to their beds. He had ordered an early breakfast after being told, by the hostel night Porter, that breakfast was from 6.30am to nine. He told his team that he was looking for an early breakfast and departure. Hoping to be away by 8 am.

Joe had taken the hold-all out of the Jeep, taking it and his team to his room, he'd set it down on his bed. He then opened it to disclose five Glock automatic fully loaded pistols and knives which he distributed to the team. Also a tourists road map. That had their destination marked by a circle around it. He handed it to Roberto, telling him he'd be taking the wheel. With that he dismissed them. Saying he'd see them all up, and ready to go for eight-o-clock sharp.

Norman reminded Joe that they were already into German-Bavarian-European time. That the clocks had moved forward by one hour. Joe told Roberto that their destination was a town some 60 kilometres from Munch called Waldkraiburg. The festival itself was set to take place a little further east, in a rural remote area. Their rock and roll festivals were a long on-going happening with many of Germany's top Heavy Metal bands performing.

But this Alpha organisation was not one of them. Nor advertised, and with a ticket only admission, with a visiting Russian band 'Pile Driver' headlining. This information Norbert had received from one of the agents. The last message to come back into CIA Berlin. The information line then suddenly cut, with three agents, not responding, missing.

Joe on their approach to the hostel couldn't fail to notice a line-up of parked high powered motorcycles, indicating Wolves were staying in the lodge.

Joe asked his team to converse in German. All but Frazier knew a little, enough to get by.

Roberto adding, especially when running into a Zeta that these Alphas Generals, highly trained killing machines, were most likely to stop and question any suspicious unknown face. After the CIA failed attempts, the Zetas would be on their guard.

Joe. 'Don't let them get close, any sign, you take them down.'

Breakfast was a somewhat cheap deal of twelve euros. Then again it was the usual jam and ham, continental, with accompanying cold bread rolls. Only thing that was going for it was the coffee, which was good. The restaurant was half full of leather clad Wolves sitting with their Vixens, preferring to forsake coffee for beer. Shouting and using bad language after every second spoken word. This surely the reason for the non appearance of the tourist hikers. Not one single one in sight.

Joe had split the team up to enter at different times, each member would carry their pistols concealed. He and Norman would go first followed by Ryona, Roberto and Frazier. They would occupy the same table. Joe would look and hope to gain one with his back to the wall, allowing an all round observation of the comings and goings of the morning's clientele.

The breakfast had been pre-set with a selection of jams, meats and cheeses to suit all individual tastes. Coffee, although freshly ground was a weak substitute for the popular best of French, Italian, Columbian blends. The only good thing about it, on a cold morning, it was hot.

Joe and the team sat somewhat distanced from the Wolves, showing no concern. Joe began by asking Roberto on his thoughts.

Roberto in a low voice whispers. 'The Wolves here they're just soldiers, there's no Zeta present so they're taking advantage of this by drinking and rebel rousing.' He raises a finger, gives a light tap to the table. 'But don't underestimate them, as a gang they remain deadly, it's only once alone they weaken.' He smiles. 'That's why they'll always be soldiers '

Norman asks. 'The Zeta, Roberto, what's his strength, his weakness?'

Roberto. 'Zetas are a different kettle of fish, being Generals to the Alpha. Not easy to break, we would need some powerful means to get through their guard.'

Norman nods. 'Like Joe's interrogation methods, by knowledge of their families?'

Roberto sighs. 'When the time comes, then we will see.'

Joe, smiles, saying. 'Seems to me it's a case of finding the weakest of the Zetas.'

Ryona adds. 'We've got a weekend to find one and break him.'

Frazier nods his head. 'If there's one we'll find him or her.'

He turns to Roberto. 'These women they have with them, Vixens, would the Zeta have a woman with him and if so would she share his knowledge of why the meeting had been called?'

Roberto smiles 'That's good thinking Dave but to be honest with you all they probably have but I just don't know.'

Joe nods. 'I'm sure they'll have a woman.' He chuckles.

'They can't be all gay.' Looks to Roberto. Shrugs.. 'Well can they?' The team all chuckle among themselves.

Roberto. 'We laugh but we must never forget, never let our guard down, these Zetas will have, attached to their jackets, an emblem of some kind, a sign, a recognition of their status.'

Joe. 'Then we've got to take a soldier to find out what the emblem is, if like our army they carry a ranking.'

Roberto nods. 'Yes, but we take a soldier that's without a Vixen, we cannot afford too much interference. We have to do the job professionally.'

It's then a slurred voice interrupting in German with. 'Who the fuck are you?'

The team look at one swaying, looking to be in his mid twenties. A disheveled soldier Wolf being supported by his Vixen. Both looking to be high on drink or drugs. He's carrying a bottled beer and drinking from it, his Vixen grabbing his arm to take gulps from the bottle.

The Vixen slurping. 'They're fucking trotters, Hans, foot sloggers, fucking hikers.'

Joe answers. 'We're climbers, rocks and mountains.' He shrugs, looks to the Vixen, who reminded him of rock vocalist Susie Quatro in her black shining leathers, a cigarette hanging from her dark ruby lips.

The Wolf snarls. 'You done Everest?'

Joe smiles. 'Not as yet, but maybe one day.'

The Wolf laughs. 'In your fucking dreams man, what you doing here, this ain't Tibet?'

Joe nods. 'True, but then, we ain't on a climbing weekend. We're taking in this beautiful countryside on a few days hike.

The Vixen smiles. 'So are we, hiker man, but we ride the stallions of the highway. Walking is for idiots, and boy do we get high.'

The Wolf laughs. 'We go fucking higher than your fucking Everest man, we got rock too.' Shouts. 'Yeh, Rock and Roll.'

From across the room an older middle aged Wolf shouts out. 'Hans you get your fucking arse back here, you're letting that mouth of yours stray too much, so shut it, you hearing me?'

Hans waves a hand to a long bearded Wolf, snarling. 'I'm with you Twister, I fucking hear you.' He holds out his hand letting the beer bottle go crashing to the floor.

He looks at Joe still snarling. 'Now see what you made me do, think you owe me a beer brother.'

Joe, stands. Roberto holds him back, whispering.'Easy cowboy.' Norman takes an under coat grip on his pistol looks to Frazier who's doing likewise.

Joe smiles as the snarl leaves Hans the Wolfs face. 'No problem biker man, sorry I've upset you, one beer coming up.'

Again the bearded Wolf shouts. 'He's had enough beer, he's a bike to ride and a schedule to keep. So no beer for him, hiker man.' He points to the Vixen, his bag partner. ' Give her the beer, she can have it.'

The Vixen turns and shouts back. 'You don't speak for me Twister, so go play with yourself.'

Twister replies. 'Shall I tell our friend Corneille how you've both been talking free mouth to the hikers?' A moment's silence relapses before the Vixen drags the wobbly Hans away from the team and over to Twister. She sits him alongside the bearded Wolf. With her fisted hands on hips she stands scowling at Twister.

'You want him to ride, then get him sober, freshen him up.' She jabs a finger at the middle-aged biker. 'Oh, let me just remind you, that sicko Corneille ain't our Zeta.' She winks. 'Hans and I are Berlin, we have Thomas Kline, he's our General.'

Twister laughs. 'Maybe, but Corneille he's above your Thomas Kline, you remember that.' He shrugs. 'You're so fucking lucky I'm not reporting the two of you. Best you remember that you owe me. Perhaps a shag,' He winks. 'Now wouldn't that be nice?'

She winks back, laughs. 'In your dreams Twister, I'd sooner lay under a fucking express train than lie under you.'

Twister turns back to the table and picking out two of its seated Wolves, gives an over the shoulder nod, saying. 'Get that fucking Hans Christian Andersen storyteller under a cold shower. Corneille will be arriving soon, he better be good to ride.'

He points up at the restaurant wall clock that's showing eight-fifteen.

'He expects us packed and ready for nine.' He shakes his head.

'Don't need to tell you what will happen if we're not.'

He turns back to the Vixen. 'Your Kline, he's probably coming in with Corneille so be warned bitch!'

He points to the falling-asleep Hans. 'Better make sure your story teller's ready to ride.' He laughs. 'Cause if he isn't.' He shakes his head, winks.

Without more of the Vixen-Twister slagging the bikers begin to exit the restaurant, with a coming awake Hans, snarling, shouting, asking, what the hell was happening before being told he was going for a bath, that Corneille was due. This definitely having an immediate effect on Hans who was trying his hardest to stop himself from stumbling into the furniture, causing bottles and crockery to fall onto the stone tiled floor. Resulting in quite a few breakages.

Joe and the team watched them all leave and waited whilst the owner and two staff cleaners had swept and mopped the floor clean. The apologising owner clearly upset by the bikers actions. Still swearing under his breath as he ushered his staff out.

Only when all was back to normal, the restaurant now empty, the Wolves, with the last roaring sounds of their bikes fading into the distance, did Joe quietly begins to discuss his plan for the coming weekend operation.

He said ' I'm thinking let's move and observe from a distance, much too early for confronting the enemy.'

With a shake of his head. 'Saying that, I'm sure they'd like to meet up with us.'

Ryona adds. 'When we find our Zeta, Joe, I'm thinking it's gotta be on the last night of the festival. A last minute night snatch, what's your thoughts?'

Roberto nodding. 'My wife's right with that, Joe.' He shrugs. 'By that time the Zetas will have instruction on just why the Alpha has summoned the gathering and what he requires of them.'

Norman says. 'We must take the first opportunity that comes, we may not get a second chance.' He looks to Ryona.

'Although I feel, like Ryona and Roberto, it's got to happen on their last night.'

Frazier smiles. 'I imagine they'll be as pissed as farts by then.'

Joe. 'Let's hope so, and I do agree with Ryona's views.' He looks at his team, each face in thought. 'I take it we all agree, that it's a last night at the Proms action?'

It's then Roberto tells them that he's had dealings in the past, whilst serving in CIA, Berlin, with the Zeta Thomas Kline, that Kline had passed through countless interrogations, suspected involvement in robbery and murder. He added that a record was on file in CIA headquarters Berlin, going on to say that General Porter could forward on crimson, details on the life of Thomas Kline.

Joe. Then asks Roberto. 'What about this other Zeta, Corneille. You got anything on him?'

Roberto. 'I don't think he's from our neck of the woods, doesn't ring any bells, best see if Norbert's anything on him.'

Norman. 'According to Twister he's a station above the Berliner Kline.'

Joe shrugs. 'That doesn't mean Kline won't be in on whatever's going down.' He taps Norman's shoulder.

'But as you say brother we have to grab at any opportunity that happens to fall our way. Could be Kline, or any Zeta come to think.'

Joe's thoughts were to go for the Berliner Kline, he was a known by Roberto to be a hardened criminal, suspected of major robbery and murder. Major Norman Aimes was correct to remind them that they would have to take any opportunity that came into play, to be ready to change horses if Kline became a no go.

Frazier had suggested that they take two Zetas, with support for this coming from Ryona, saying that it would double their chance of success.

Joe reminded the team that there would be a thousand eyes and ears at the gig. That security would be top notch as three CIA agents had already found to their ultimate cost, the score being already three to nothing in the Wolves favour. He suggested that they take it to three-three.

Ryona. 'Three, three, Joe?'

Joe smiles, nods. 'Yes, two Zetas and one Alpha, would be a good final result.' He shrugs. 'But I'd still settle for three to one, with all of us safe.'

Less than an hour later the team walked through a now empty hostel car park to where their 4x4 stood. Joe throwing its keys to Roberto and telling him that he'd have the wheels and to head for their already agreed bivouac, a secluded forest area that lay some 3 kilometres from the festival site.

Joe had contacted CIA's General Porter to arranged a helicopter pick-up time, at a given map reference point. Telling Norbert that Norman Frazier and himself would board with one captured Zeta. Leaving Roberto and Ryona to drive the 4x4 back to Munich.

He was hoping on a very early morning getaway immediately after the festivals Sunday night finish, which would be the on the Monday before dawn, this was always assuming all went to plan.

Joe asked Frazier if he was enjoying his adventure of being part of a special operation team. Frazier smiled before replying, saying that he'd come from a military family, his father, Alister MacGregor served as sergeant in the infamous Black Watch. He had always had a deep love of the sea, his grandfather Willy was a long serving merchant navy engineer. He was born David Frazier MacGregor and schooled in Aberdeen. He had passed through his Navy career going from the Marine Commandos to the special Marine Task Force. He looked at the teams interest in his given profile before finishing with...

'Yes, Joe, I'm honoured to be on the team that my late, but never to be forgotten chief, Major Tony Ford belonged to.'

He gave a deep sigh. 'God bless him.'

He nods. 'To be here with my new mentor Major Norman Aimes is a real pleasure.'

Norman nods, 'So right Dave, Tony was a man to be remembered, he was my friend.' He whispers. 'I'll never forget him.'

He shakes his head, gives a pat to Frazier's shoulder, 'Not that I'd ever want to.'

It was late afternoon when Roberto pulled the Jeep off the motorway driving it through an open gateway onto a cart track which led them, across an open field into a dense pine forest. Norman indicating the track had not been used for some time. The rest of the team were busy going through the various tourist leaflets that they'd acquired from the hostel. Small booklets that listed all the hotels, guest houses and restaurants in the Bavarian countryside, along with historical sites and beauty spots, Maps showing road routes for vehicles and pathways for the hiker.

Ryona began waving a leaflet at the team. 'Here's what we want , it's a guesthouse for rent that accommodates up to eight people. It's just a kilometre from the festival site. It's self catering.'

Joe shrugs. 'It's more than likely to be occupied Ryona' with one house full of Wolves.'

Roberto. 'That's always depending on the owners allowing these unfavourably guests to take residency.'

He takes the leaflet from Ryona looking at a picture of a most traditional type, log built, detached hunting lodge. Then turning to Joe.

'Just for one moment ask yourself Joe, would you as the owner of this beautiful lodge hand over the keys to some drunken leather pirates?'

He shakes his head. 'Me, I think not, if truth be knowing, the owners would sit in with a double-barrel shotgun whilst this gig was over and away.'

Frazier asks if the lodge could already be occupied by hikers, people not unlike themselves, hikers they were hoping to portray?

Joe answers. ' Going on what Roberto has just been saying I'm doubting that hikers would stay so close to a pack of prowling Wolves.' He smiles.'It's something that only nutters like us would risk.'

Joe had already made a crimson call to Norbert on what would be their location, the helicopter pick-up point should everything go according to plan. Where Norman, Frazier and himself would board with their captive and fly to Berlin. Roberto and Ryona would take the Jeep back to Munich, then a flight back to Berlin and rejoin the team.

But first thing was to find if the Lodge was vacant and if possible, whether the owner could give them any information on its last occupancy. Was it at all possible that the missing agents had stayed there? Joe instructing Ryona with her most fluent German to get these questions answered. His thoughts being that a woman's enquiring would be best served in mind finding this out.

In the meantime, Norman along with Frazier, began to set up camp close to the camouflaged jeep. Three two-man tents with a sleeping bag that would remain in the jeep for guard duty. The days light was fading and after a small brunch of chicken sandwiches, followed by hot, out of the flask tea, Joe decided to go for an evening stroll; this would take them close to an hillside view of the festival site.

Frazier would remain with the Jeep, keeping a close eye on the camp. Though a little disappointed, Frazier knew that it was a job that someone had to do. His small knowledge of the German language was also a reason he'd been picked.

Ryonas phone suddenly beeped. She looked at its display screen, a call coming in from the lodge, from a Frau Walter. She explained that the lodge was indeed vacant, before going on to say that a period of one week was required with monies, euros, to be paid in advance. This was a most recent request after three male occupants had absconded. They'd left a deposit but failed to pay the full amount. She was very annoyed, adding, That if they were in any way involved with the festival and the bikers then she would not accommodate them.

Joe told Ryona to go ahead and book it, to explain to Frau Walter that they were tourists, hikers, and would pay the rent in cash for one week to commence this very evening. Norman giving a sigh motions for Frazier to help him take down the camp and be prepared to drive the team to the lodge. Roberto suggests that they'd best arrive in the morning light, that a night arrival could be cause for concern, especially with them not doing a survey over the area. Besides, wasn't it better to enter the lodge with the Wolves already pre-occupied with the festival going on....Dave, could stay with the jeep, I'm hoping to make that lodge and a warm bed tonight.'

One hour later and with the forest thinning out, the team found themselves looking down into the level base of the valley floor. Bright lights, spots, had already been erected shining down onto the main concert area. They could see that this section with its stage in darkness was a permanent fixture. A stadium for many previous events. That somehow brought a small Glastonbury to mind.

It was then a gasp came from Roberto, followed by him uttering. 'Oh, my God.'

Joe looks to him for an explanation.'What gives, something not right?' Roberto points to a flag that's caught in a spot, flying above the stage area. It depicts the cross of Christ upside down. The emblem is pictured burning with the figure of an Angel, who's wings are hung it triumph over the cross. The Angel is all in black, hooded with a goat horn face.

Roberto shaking his head. 'I never thought I'd get to see this, Joe. It's so fucking heavy duty man...The elite, the Black Angel, he's here!'

Joe holds up a palm. 'Black Angel, Roberto, please explain man?'

Roberto gives a deep sigh. 'I, the CIA, have little if anything at all on them. What little we have is that the Black Angel is one of six elite, most feared activists of crime on the planet. Known as Satan's overlords. They are the exterminators.'

He shrugs. 'Gods if you like, hooded, nameless, not unlike America's Ku Klux Klan, a secret society with the six overlords. Nameless men who strike terror throughout the world.' He nods.

'Forget about the Alphas, Joe they're just servants here. I can honestly say without any doubts a Black Angel is top of the bill at this gig.'

Joe. 'But he's only skin and bone Roberto, he's only human. He's no fucking superman. He's vulnerable, he's here to be taken if need be.'

Roberto shrugs. 'I'm beginning to think that's the reason top of the tree CIA agents like Sam Grainger are missing....One thing to remember, Joe, don't underestimate these Angel's.' He shakes his head puts up a finger. 'It'll be a sad day for us all if we do.'

Norman asks. ' How come you know all this Robbie, About there being six elite secret society members. This comes entirely new to me and I'm sure Joe too?'

He shrugs, looks at Joe. 'Where we been living these last ten years, Joe, that we've never come across these creeps?'

Joe smiles. 'Could be we're a little behind on information held by the CIA. Norm.'

Ryona hands over her night view binoculars, points out to a section that's displaying several long rows of Motorcycles. 'There must be around 200 bikes parked up, surely you'd have expected more.'

Norman adds. 'There's a few Mercedes, BMWs sitting rear of the stage, 4x4s, probably Zeta transportation vehicles

She points. 'If you look over to the right of that platform. Then there's four large motorhomes.' She asks. 'Am I thinking Zeta residencies?'

Joe,nods. 'Definitely, they'd never bunk-up with their soldiers, Too high up in the ladder for that, I should think.'

He turns to Roberto. 'Your thoughts please, Roberto.'

Roberto nods. Saying. 'Your all more than likely to be right, with the Alpha or Alphas sharing. These Wolves follow their order in the pack...Soldier being the lowest taking orders from their Zeta Generals. The Generals serving Alphas.'

Joe. 'What about these Wolves, are they the top dog?. I'm thinking what part do the Bandido, the Middle Eastern gangs have to play in all this.' He shakes his head. 'These gangs are at war with each other. Surely they don't fall under the Black Angel ruling.'

Roberto follows with. 'Wish I knew, Joe. The Russian Pakham, the Bratva. I'd think being all now under the same roof....The Fly is the loner in this. Oh, but he's still buzzing, he's out there somewhere regrouping. He's certainly not one that's finished with that's for sure.'

Ryona. 'Seems to me that these Angels have had a meet and decided to send an envoy out to control whatever it is that's planned, that they're looking to recoup their losses in a major operation.'

She holds up her hand to Roberto, who smiles.

'Your guess is as good as mine sweetheart, but whatever is planned has to be big. There's no way an Angel from hell would oversee anything less.' He shrugs. 'Yes, whatever is going down is mountainous.'

Norman. 'Then we've got a serious problem.' He looks at Joe. 'We can't afford any mistakes on our planning, Joe.'

Joe. 'That's why we need a Zeta a fucking Alpha to capture and find out.' He looks to them all. 'We have one night, the last night to take and break our prisoner.' He sighs. 'Like Norman says. we cannot afford to make any mistakes. I don't want to lose any of you guys, so keep alert and be on your guard.'

He turns to Norman. 'Frazier, let him know what we've found in regard to the Black Angels, he's got to be in tow on everything. Because he's a sergeant means we don't pull rank on him. He's part of the team and of equal standing.' He sighs. 'So best we return to base and prepare for tomorrow and the lodge. We need to plan, come up with a good idea on how to proceed.'

Roberto adds. 'Looks like we're in a David and Goliath situation and will be needing more than a sling shot stone to get through and win.'

Joe. 'Ok, we have two days to put together a plan. This operation is one that can't afford to fail.' He points a finger at the festival site, that's now in semi darkness, showing only a ring of spots around its circumference. 'We have to get in there and take out a Zeta and I feel it's not going to be easy.'

Norman. 'But have we, Joe?'   Joe. 'Have we what, Norm?'

Norman answers by asking if the really need to enter the arena. Why can't they take a Zeta or better still an Alpha on the festival's closure. On their leaving, their departure, take them on their way home?

Roberto nodding. 'That could be a better plan, Joe...We already have a name.'

He smiles. 'One Thomas Kline, and we know where he'll be heading, back to Berlin.'

Joe shrugs. 'That's all very well, but what if he's given a task by his Alpha, that prevents this home to Berlin journey happening?'

He sighs. 'Then we miss out.'

Ryona winks, saying. 'Then we would hit some other bod. There must be quite a few rocking the night away...We would of course have to find another face, a substitute.'

Norman. 'The lady's right, Joe. We could do this, take another face.'

He smiles 'Personally, I'd like to take down and capture an Alpha. He'd be sure to hold all of the operation plan given by this Black Angel.' He adds. 'A Zeta, I feel would only know his part, not the whole of the enterprise. What Ryona has suggested is well worth thinking about.'

Joe nods. 'Let's make our way back to Dave, we move into the lodge. Like I say, we've two full days on the clock to plan this.' Shake of the head. 'From this moment on it's high alert.'

What Joe and the team were unaware was that the rear of the stage, stood a luxurious RV Winnebago. Inside,taking place, was a meeting. Six Alphas were sitting listening to the voice of a Black Angel that was coming from the mouth hole of a back hood, through its eye slits could be seen two dark brown eyes. The voice told them that beneath his full length black cloak was a man of middle age. He spoke in English, in a tone so powerful, it sent fear through its listeners.

It spoke of the organisations losses, failed attempts that had been far to many. He talked of the interference of the enemy, namely the United States of America of Europe's international crime fighters CIA, MI6, and various Middle Eastern blocks. Citing the dreaded Israeli Secret Forces.

He told them that these terrorists organisations had done nothing but strengthen the enemy doubling their guard, having more success in breaking through, punching holes through the organisations defences. They had in fact lost millions of Dollars, Euros, Sterling.

He snarled, telling them that these losses had to be recuperated. No more mistakes because what was planned, any failure would result in a virtual sentence of death. So make sure you pick your Zeta well. Make sure he knows his soldiers. Because your lives depend on your army.

What was planned would shake the very foundations of the crime fighters, would make the organisation billions. A glorious day was on the cards.

Joe had meanwhile returned to camp finding all had been quiet with no incidents. There'd been the usual expected animal movements but other than that, nothing. Joe could see Frazier was eager for news on their exploration of the Festival site, he explained that Norman would go through everything with him.

Joe went on to tell the team that an all night watch would begin. He looked at his watch, it was showing nine pm. Saying he'd take first watch till midnight, then Norman would take the next three hours, followed by Roberto.

Frazier elected to follow Roberto allowing, Ryona to miss out but be available for preparing a breakfast of hot porridge oats and coffee. Come just after nine, Joe wanted to move. Frau Walter had arranged for the key to be left in a key box, securely fixed onto the outer stone of a ground to roof chimney stack. The box number was given as 1708.

She would herself send her husband Herman to pick up the rent around 11 am. She added that some bare essentials such as milk, tea, coffee along with fresh eggs and home baked bread, would be left. Sufficient to serve a family of five adults for two days. A small covering charge of 30 euros would be asked.

A bottle of the area's fine hock with accompanying cheese biscuits would come as a free welcoming gift.

The team took to the main highway with the sat-nav showing they were only a distance of two kilometres from their destination. A small slip road would take them up onto the valley shoulder where the Kaiser Lodge was sitting, one kilometre away from the festival site, that lay well hidden in a pine forest clearing.

The site area looked to be in a well established arena, fenced and obviously used for numerous festivals and country fairs. A beautiful panoramic location.

Abundant varieties of wild flowers covering green patchwork quilt fields. A bouquet a la carte for the grazing cattle. Large sections of pine forest woodland adding to what could only be described as a landscape painter's dream setting.

With a happy Herman Walter receiving the rent, and satisfied that he could return to his wife with the good news that their guests were indeed tourist hikers and not the feared Wolves, Herman said that they would find everything, food wise, at a nearby garage that had a convenience store that stayed open 24/7 stocking just about anything in regard of food, drink and fuel.

Joe thought it better to let Ryona and Roberto do the shopping, enough to last them three days. He stressed that they should avoid,at all costs, any contact with the Wolves. Joe explaining, that to go in heavy handed, could give some curious brain a reason for wanting to know who and why a team of hikers was still around, when all other's had left the area.

It was Friday night, the opening of the festival. This, Joe thought, being a time to buy their supplies. A good chance that the pack would be all occupied, getting pissed, rocking the night away. Like prisoners in the securely fenced arena.

The need was to do a reconnaissance, view from a distance through their night scopes, on any unusual activities. Getting nearer to finding out the enemy's strength. But first they would eat, work on a plan that would safely take a prisoner. The one thing, Joe did not want was casualties.

His leadership in the specialist Pathfinders had put keeping his team safe the first priority. The days of the First World War trench attacks of going over the top was not going to happen. His thoughts on that being that if you cannot win, then don't lose, a draw being better than a loss if such situations arise.

11pm. The Rock band Pile Driver had finished and 'left the building; to give a well known Elvis quote. With the crowd slowly dispersing, the stage now in darkness,leaving only the fence spots and tented accommodation area, a section that had been prepared especially for the soldier Wolf, remained lit. This area being just off to the right of the arena, but still inside, allowing for no exit. This being simply a once-in-you- stay till the end, ruling. This included Pile Driver and its entourage. With men every twenty metres on guard inside the site's circumference, each with a Doberman or German Shepard to accompany him, the site looked to be inaccessible.

Joe and his team had eaten, been out surveying, and having returned to the lodge began to finalise a plan. As they warmed around a crackling log fire, each holding a mug of hot chocolate, carrying thoughts on how they could accomplish what they knew to be one difficult operation, it was Joe who broke into the silence by asking for any ideas.

Norman spoke saying there was just no way they could enter that compound without them walking into a high risk situation. His thoughts were to hit after the final curtain, if at all possible, early Monday morning. Always assuming their selected Zeta, Alpha target was on his way. Traveling without an escort would be nice.

This, coming from Norman, Joe thought feasible, having high possibility. Even more so on seeing the team's nodding heads.

Joe, 'Let's just give Norm's suggestion some thought...I'm thinking we'd need to have a certain amount of luck; like our target leaving unaccompanied, in a vehicle carrying no more than four.'

Roberto was quick to jump in with.

'The Zeta I'm sure would be riding in his usual Mercedes saloon. The Alphas could well be airborne.' He shrugs. 'But then again one can never be sure.'

Ryona turning to Norman asks, 'OK, Norm, so we hit them on the road...A major highway then we'd have problems.'

She sighs. 'There's bound to be packs of these Wolves travelling; the gig it's finished, they're making for home. Our attack could become messy, don't you think?'

Norman smiles saying. 'I never said it was going to be easy.'

Puts up a hand. 'However, I agree we've got to pick our spot, a quiet, if possible off road area... If he's travelling to Berlin, then I'd assume he's going to stop somewhere, fuel, toilet, cafeteria.'

Roberto. 'What if he doesn't, which I feel highly unlikely, but could happen?'

Norman. 'Then we pop him while he's rolling, take out a tyre on his vehicle. A rifle shot with a suppressor attachment, we force the stop. He's thinking he's got a blow out. Someone's going to exit that motor to exchange the tyre.'

Joe smiles, nods. 'That could well work, if not then we have no option but to follow the Wolf to its final destination, his lair.'

He gives a head shake before adding. 'Whichever way we go on this it's got to be a clean, with no mistakes, take.' He looks to Frazier. 'Dave, get those maps out and let's try to figure out what routes our Wolf would take.'

Roberto tells Joe that he'll crimson General Porter to find out what the CIA have on file for Thomas Kline.

3
THE BILL TOPPING BLACK ANGEL MASS

It was Sunday 8 30pm last night of the festival and with a darkening sky, Joe sat with his team in the closest cover to the festival site, a proceeding finger of forest, that edged downwards stopping some 100 metres from the site's main entry gates. Their elevated position giving the team a bird's eye view over the whole concert area. Through their night-view helmets they could see the crowd of soldier Wolves that had gathered, an estimated guess of around three hundred. Most had a Vixen for company.

The Wolves were standing in unexpected well organised rows addressing the stage, down the middle a corridor had been created, not unlike the boxer's passageway from dressing room to ring. With Zetas keeping the walkway clear, not allowing this 5 metre wide tunnel to overspill and close. The stage itself in complete darkness.

Music was coming out of two columns of stacked speakers with the band 'Red Herring driving out their biker anthem of 'Flying Tigers' the listeners were whooping and cheering each verse, swaying and head shaking to its driving rhythm. Suddenly a black people carrier enters the gates, stopping directly below Joe and the team.

Four Wolves step from the vehicle followed by three men who are cuffed and blindfolded. Joe points to the men being led by one Wolf, with the other three taking the arms of the blindfolded men and leading them down the corridor heading towards the stage.

Joe turns to Roberto, asking. 'What the fucks going on man?'

Roberto gasps. 'They, the CIA agents...they're alive, Joe....The man leading he's an Alpha, the others Zetas.' He sighs. 'That first agent is Sam Grainger, that blindfold doesn't stop me from recognising him. His height his red hair, that's Sam.'

Ryona to Roberto 'What's going down baby, what's happening down there?' It's Norman that answers with. 'It's a ceremony of some kind. Those guys have been saved for this. It's a fucking last night top of the bill. A Black Mass.'

As the possession nears the platform the curtain begins to open. To show a single blue spot light, shining down on a plinth, where a full black cloak, hooded figure stands.

Roberto gasps, whispers. 'He's here, oh my God the Black Angel.'

He turns to the team uttering. 'We have to stop this, our agents, he's going to sacrifice them, show his fucking power.'

He makes to rise. Joe pulls him back. Roberto pleads. 'We have to stop this, Joe'

Joe. 'If we try, then I'm sorry Robbie, then we all die.' Norman puts his hand gently on Roberto's shoulder squeezing it.

'It's too late man, those guys they're already lost, like the chief says, we try then we die too.'

He shakes his head. 'We have to stick with our job.'

Again he squeezes Roberto's shoulder. 'But don't you worry brother, our day is near. It is said, in the old country.....If the cause is wanting, then vengeance be ours for the taking.'

Joe, giving a deep sigh. 'Is there nothing we can do to rescue those guys , Norm?'

Shrugs, looks to Roberto, Ryona, finally Frazier.

Norman, nodding winks. 'I could put a hole into their electricity supply.'   He points to a overhead cable that's running in to the box complex via a nearby tower.

'Put the whole site in darkness, then looking through my night view, pop a hole into that Black Angels head. Rifle with suppression attachment.'

Joe. 'That you could, but it wouldn't get us in there, we'd never reach them to obtain a rescue.'   He sighs. 'I like the idea, but it's a very high risk situation you're asking, Norm, a play that would take us further off our goal and likely cost us our lives.'

There followed a prolonged silence with the team watching a back curtain fall showing a large 12x12 foot image of a rearing Horned Goat with yellow blazing eyes. The Satanic form of Satan.

The Black Angel mumbling into the microphone strange text, that Ryona thought was a mixture of Latin and Hebrew, with unheard of words coming from some book of ancient witchcraft.

The bikers all kneeling with heads bowed while the Black Angel began pointing, shouting at the three CIA agents. A moment when two Alphas appeared on stage uncovering a white Satanic Altar With the agents positioned to it's right. Still blindfolded they were made to kneel their bodies facing the Goat image.

Frazier, through clenched teeth was hissing. 'For fuck's sake Joe, let's shoot the bastard.'

Norman shaking his head, telling the upset Frazier to calm himself down. Frazier nodding, saying sorry, but it was going to be hard for him to watch what was coming next, their execution.

The next hour was to be one of the hardest the team had to go through, to witness the execution of the CIA agents. Harder still for Roberto who had known and worked with Sam Grainger. Having to watch the Black Angel piercing their hearts with a long silver dagger. Then to cut out each heart from its body cage and hold it up triumphantly to the cheering bikers.

He then dropped the hearts down into a large dogs feeding bowl before a chained tamed wolf was brought on to feed, gobbling it down. Again to rapturous cheering and applause.

Joe, sickened by this barbarism, nudges Norman, saying. 'Take out the power and hit that bastard, Angel, put a fucking hole in his head.'

Norman nods. 'Consider it done Joe, but first get the team and yourself back to the chopper's pick-up point. You'll need to crimson him in earlier than we thought. Meanwhile, I'm on to this, I'll catch up with you later after delivering the Jeep back to Munich.' He taps Joe's arm. 'Load the jeep...So what you waiting for, get the fuck out of here.'

Joe along with Ryona and Roberto exits leaving Frazier to assist Norman.

A little later and the festival was going in full swing with drinking, dancing, a theatre of merriment. Meatloaf was giving his all with the bikers anthem 'Bat out of Hell' blasting out, echoing across the valley.

Norman smiled on hearing the faint sound of the helicopter, first coming in and then leaving. Meatloaf was certainly blocking any sound of it reaching the Wolves. Both Norman and Frazier are armed with powerful sniper rifles with attached suppressors.

They looked down upon the scene. The Black Angel was now sitting front stage in a high chair, a throne, observing this spectacle, this merriment of the soldiers celebrating with their Zetas.

Norman winked at Frazier before saying. 'Time for you to cut the power Dave, I'll see to the Angel.'

He puts up a finger points to a large junction box that was held to a 20 foot pole. The box had a cable running out and over into the festival arena.

'You settle shoot a spreader and hit that box. We go on the count of three, ready?'

Frazier settling into position, sights up the box and says he's ready on three.

Norman begins the count on putting his sighting on the hooded Angel. 'One, two, three.' The suppressed pops of the rifles go off simultaneously. The arena, it's power cut, falls into darkness a shattered junction box with it's cable cut, whilst on his throne the Black Angel is slumped with a hole the size of a golf ball, mashed inside a black hood that's now smoking with blood free flowing, coming down his cloak, dripping onto his knees.

Norman and Frazier are quick to silently disappear back into the forest on a pathway back to the pre-loaded, ready to roll, Jeep.

Behind, they've left a concert of gathered biker Wolves in disarray, confused, running around like headless chickens, with no idea on what has happened. Only that the Black Angel is dead. The frightened Alpha's shouting out instructions, to look amongst their own for these traitorous assassins.

Screaming for some emergency power to be put on, for the Zeta to collect their soldiers and find these culprits. To guard the exit gate, to see no one leaves the arena.

It had taken another hour for limited power to be reinstalled by the use of a generator. All to no avail, for the assassins were now some sixty miles away on the main autobahn that would take them into Munich. The Alphas begin to clean the site, with the bodies of the three CIA agents cremated, burnt along with the weekends rubbish, their ashes thrown unceremoniously down the toilet pan then flushed away with the excrement.

The Black Angel's body remained hooded, covered, and destined to be returned in his de-lux Winnebago. Then back to a small remote village in the Transylvanian mountainous region of Romania. There to be received and entombed in an unchristian place. A private ceremony attended only by members of the Black Angel secret society.

With the Alphas being ordered to find the assassins, the hunt was given to one Henri Mossette who was recognised as a number one Alpha. This native of Tangier was not unknown by Europe's crime fighting forces. Known as the feared 'Axeman,' he had continually evaded police arrest.

It was the following evening after the shootings that Henri arrived on the festival site to take over. He'd been told that all the soldiers and Zetas had been eliminated from the enquiries. That the Alphas had all come to the agreement that the killing of the Angel had been an outside job. It was on this information that Henri had brought with him two top forensic experts. These two men ex French police investigations operators had been told to sort out the whos, whys, and wherefores of the killer or killers who had penetrated the Wolves guard.

They were to inspect, the bullets directions, was it a inside hit or from long range. Some identification of the weapon that had fired them. Then Henri issued orders for the Alphas to collect all the soldiers, cell phones and inspect their content. He also instructed that no Alpha and their Zetas would be allowed to leave the site. Unless they were part of the oncoming operation code named PA. 'Pakhams Angels' those that had been hand picked would be allowed to leave, and that being only for them to proceed to their allotted duties.

He went on to explain to his most trusted Alphas that the Black Angels Satanic Brotherhood had heavy moneyl invested in this operation and to cancel or pull out would be one high costing failure. He had before him the names of all who had attended the last discussion on PA. He would interview each name on his list personally. The Black Angel known only as 'Claw' was dead and somebody had to pay.

He looked at the faces that had been invited to sit at his table. He spat and snarled at the assembled Alphas. Seeing the fear in their eyes. He growled, 'Check your soldiers, your Zetas, their Vixens . Because somewhere in amongst them there sits a traitor.'

With a gauntlet leather studded hand he violently slams down on the table a shining, silver, finely sharpened short handle battle axe. He looks out from the RV. Window, points to the confined to festival Wolf packs. ' Go out there, bring me that fucking traitor.'

Meanwhile Joe had received news from Norbert on the Wolf Thomas Kline. The Zeta was using an address in central Alexander, Berlin. A place already well known to Joe and his team. One no-go tourist area. Where gang warfare were currently producing more murders than the police could handle.

Bodies filling the city's morgues fished out of the rivers Spree. Unclaimed John Does, buried in their unmarked graves. Those identified and claimed given incite for a revengeful vendetta. There was once a time when the Wolf packs had strayed away from the Russian Pakham, their Godfather.

Pulling away with a feeling that this new messiah, the Fly would eventually take over the world of crime. That the Russian dynasty had finally come to its extinction.

But after a series of failed operations put down to the Fly's miss management and costing Russian and Albanian Alpha lives. The pack had crawled their way back to the Pakham. With the Fly becoming top of the Russian Bratva's most wanted list.

4
THE TAKING OF THOMAS KLINE

In a large house that was overlooking the French-German border town of Colmar a white haired man, in his sixties, Conrad Wolff sat in a silken embroidered smokers jacket with a royal blue cravat tucked neatly into his open neck aqua blue shirt. He smiled at his two dinner guests. Ferdinand Cortez and Sergio Romano. The only two people that knew Conrad as being the Fly.

Sergio, who single handedly successfully torn the Russian Pakham's world to pieces by extermination of the Sicilian Silent ones, so opening a doorway for the Fly to take over his international crime organisation. All that had been going to Wolff's plan till Joe Delph entered stopping operations, driving his Russian and Albanian wolverines back home to Pakham control.

This Conrad had felt unexpectedly, causing him to reluctantly call on, and persuade the Wolf's known enemies the Bandido's and the Iraqi Al'Salam 313, to join forces. along with the Arab Hezbolla, and take a share of any future spoils. Sitting with his two friends, and with the knowledge of the Pakhams future, a solid gold operation, with minimum cost to him.

A well thought out plan, obtained by Ferdinand from a Wolf Alpha, was an absolute bonus. This time, no mistakes.

He laughs, saying to his guests. 'No mistakes..... That's only if they make them.'

Sergio. 'Conrad, are we good with this mixture?'

Conrad Smiles. 'We let the Pakham wolverines do the work, then my friends, we simply take over the treasure.' Again he laughs. 'When they return to base, I know where they'll be heading, we intercept.'

He gives them a sad face, shrugs. 'They work, we just take away from them.'

Sergio putting up a finger. 'We must be sure of our army, Conrad, Ferdinand has acquired this information though a leak in theirs, we must have no such holes in our bucket.'

Conrad nods. 'A good point Sergio, I totally agree.'

He turns to Ferdinand. 'See this is done Ferdinand....See that the Bandido and 313 leaders, the Arabs. know nothing of our plans, till the very last minute. Again he laughs. 'After which we massacre our enemy, for we leave no wolverine alive to tell the tale.'

He holds up his hands to them. 'Why it will be a new era for us, what was lost, returned.'

He points to Ferdinand. 'Ferdinand has negotiated a new partnership with these highly rated crime families.'

Sergio asks. 'The Hezbolla, Conrad?'

Conrad begins nodding enthusiastically. 'Yes, Sergio my friend....OK, they are new, but eager to enter the premier league of International crime nobility.' He laughs. 'I welcome them wholeheartedly, for they will be an unexpected surprise for the Pakham army.'

Ferdinand adds, 'Also feared by the Saudi Sheik oil barons. Word as come to our notice that soon they will be as strong a force as the most feared; the Taliban.' He winks. 'I'm hoping too strong for the Pakham the Bratva and these hooded Black Angel idiots to handle.'

Conrad smiles. 'The Pakham the great Tyrannosaurus and his Dinosaur empire will become one of total extinction.'

Sergio claps his hands, shakes his head, saying. 'Wow!, the Wolf pack extinct, I tell you Conrad, I can't wait for that day.'

Ferdinand looks at his friend and asks. 'Sergio my brother, I've never asked you, but how come you hate these Wolves so much?'

Sergio sighs. 'It all stems back to my early years In Sicily. I'd always been close to Angelo Rosario.' He sighs. 'Thirty years, my best friend...That was util I found he had raped my twin sister Corina and left her open to the rest of his Silent Ones to have their way with. He gives a deeper sigh, ' This led to her taking her own life, by hanging herself in my fathers barn. He then had the audacity to attend her funeral all tears and innocence showing.'

There's a moment of silence before Sergio continues, truly affected by his disclosure. He shrugs. 'I'd been having thoughts on how to get my revenge, Sicilian style.'

He turns to Conrad. 'That's before I became friends with Ferdinand and yourself on that holiday week in Naples, You knew who I worked for and offered me a chance to complete the vendetta. Your offer of a new life and a sincere friendship would be the turning point away from my sad old life.'

Conrad nods. Asks. 'How did you get to know of that bastard Angelo's rape of your sister Sergio?'

Sergio holds up a hand. 'The night when the Silent Ones had gathered to discuss business. I was about to bring in more wine when I heard Jaques Hardie shouting in his drunken stupor for my sister....Saying he wanted Corina, his exact words being 'I want to empty my balls into her.'

'Then they all laughed. I wanted to kill the French frog there and then...But I knew deep in my heart it wasn't the right time, besides I wanted them all.'

Conrad nodding his head looking to Ferdinand and uttering. 'Understandable.'

Sergio sighing continues. 'It was the following day that I consulted Corina on what I'd heard, she broke down and told me she was frightened of our father getting to know that he would take his gun and enter the home of Angelo, and she feared for his life....She also believed she was pregnant. That they had all violated her, that the father could be any one of them.

Sergio sobs. Conrad puts up a hand to Ferdinand asking he give their friend a moment. Sergio with tears in his eyes.

'Four hours later and my father found her hanging from a timber beam in our barn....Corina was dead.'

Ferdinand hugs Sergio whispering. 'We are not done with these animals my friend...You will be here to witness their deaths, the promise you made, over the grave of Corina, the wheels are in motion for their annihilation.'

Conrad raising his glass. 'So my friends let us drink to our new family...For the want of a name I'm calling us the SS.'

Ferdinand, the SS Conrad? Is this some Nazi coming out that's been hidden in you?'

Conrad laughs. 'Maybe that's what people will think, but my SS simply means 'Silent Savage.'

Sergio nodding, shrugs. 'So I move from a Silent One to a Silent Savage, Conrad?'

Conrad winks. 'Yes, Sergio, but don't fucking poison your new found workmates, eh.' They all three laugh.

It's hours later that Joe and the team are safely back together in the office of General Norbert Porter in Berlin with Joe coming to the end of his report on the Wolves festival, describing the butchered satanic deaths of the CIA agents to Norbert Porter.

Joe shakes his head. 'So you see General, we are still no nearer to finding out what operation the Wolves are planing.'

Norbert shrugs. 'Seems this Zeta, Thomas Kline, could be our way of getting some answers....I'm thinking of another of your find and grab operations, Joe.'

Joe nods. 'Could be Sir, but getting our hands on an Alpha, would be better because Klines not certain to know.'

Roberto. 'We could always get a grip on Kline, get him to give us a name of an Alpha...One who attended the gig, one that would know.'

Norman nodding. 'I think Roberto's right, we have to go easy on this. Think of non disclosure. Don't leave our door open, we can't let them know we're still on to them, that it was us that took out the Black Angel.' He sighs.'Whatever they've got planned it's going to be big....We've got to sort it we cannot afford another session like the one we had with the Fly.'

Ryona nods her agreement. 'Somehow I'm tending to believe that the Fly,...Well he's just as interested in what's going down. He's still out there guys...Could well be involved.'

Joe wanting to involve Frazier in the discussion. 'Any thoughts on this Dave?'

Frazier scratching his chin. 'Oh, I'm thinking like Ryona that the Fly is involved in some way...But he's a lone shark and known enemy of the Pakham..Didn't he have the Pakham generals murdered? The Albanian Wolves, they have by now, I'm sure, deserted him.'

Norbert coughs. 'Let's not just surmise on this. Let's go and catch Thomas Kline and go from there. I have his address, his whereabouts... Shouldn't take us too long to bring him in. But like, Norman was saying, let's not leave our door open.'

Joe claps his hands. 'OK, we survey the area and plan our attack. Once satisfied we go in and take Kline ….We can't allow any witnesses to the abduction. It's got to be a clean take of the Zeta….Any questions?'

There was a long silence in the Russian home of the Pakham after his right hand advisers the Black Angels sat at his table. The Pakham was angry, he'd lost a little of his supremacy on being told of the infiltration and death of an Angel. What was it coming down to. Who the fuck, after the Fly episodes, would dare to upset his apple cart again.

Although he knew every face under their hoods, they, his Black Angels remained anonymous to each other. It was a ruling that he'd insisted upon. A what you might call. Whats not seen, remains hidden. A complete new outlook after the episode of murder in the Sicilian villa of Angelo Rosario.

Meanwhile back in the office of General Porter. Joe could see that Norbert was deeply saddened on hearing of the executions of the CIA agents.

Joe, gave a deep sigh before expressing for the team, his sorrow that they could do nothing to stop these executions. The killings had come as a complete and unexpected surprise. That the taking out of a Black Angel would give little compensation.

Norbert nodding. 'So what are your thoughts, Joe?'

Joe shrugs. 'What we do have is the address and known haunts of Thomas Kline. We know of his whereabouts, his wife Turid, and their three year old son Thor.'

He smiles. 'What will happen next is his abduction. What Kline knows, I promise so will we…The name of an acting Alpha and whatever plans that were issued.'

Norbert. 'So you're thinking robbery of some kind, Joe?'

The General shakes his head,sighs. 'What is it they're after....Fort Knox?'

Roberto utters. 'They wouldn't dare.'

Joe. 'We will find out, that's for sure...You and Ryona can do a stake-out, bring whatever's plausible back to us and we will plan, green light go.'

He claps his hands, looks to them all. 'It's showtime, you all ready to rumble?

It was late afternoon when Ryona and Roberto found themselves walking the Alexander plaza. They'd already viewed his apartment in a highly populated area of central city Berlin. It's Venetian blinds showing a light on in its first floor location. Now it was time for them to visit his favourite haunt, a sex den called The Blow Hole.

Joe had already stressed that this was a surveillance operation and to go no further. To stay safe and phone back to base every two hours..

They had found the plaza, a Mecca for the tourist, it's cafes, it's music clubs with their flashing beckoning lights, like moths to the flame. Warning posters telling of pickpocketing, burglaries and gang rape. Even with a heavy police attendance crime had skyrocketed out of control. The known amateur thieves were regularly being pulled with pockets bulging, full of the days takings; Rolex gents and ladies watches, gold body ornaments, necklaces, bracelets. The small back-packs that held camera's and cell phones were a favourite target.

Ryona and Roberto hand,in hand, were now walking the street of a well known no go area. Where prostitution was ripe. Each of these ladies of the night parading their patch. The street was one sex den after another.

Roberto nudged Ryona to indicate the flashing neons over the door of one called 'The Blow Hole' he whisperers. 'Looks like we've arrived baby, keep a hand on your purse.'

She surveyed the scene of the sex den with its rather small entrance door, a solid wood with eye hole. Outside two gorilla bouncers in similar attire of jeans and sailor shirts under leather jackets. They seemed to be being entertained by three of the pro's. girls that looked to be sixteen,if that, and one that looked no older than thirteen. Music was blaring out with the sound of Iron Maiden's 'Run to the Hill's'

With smiling faces they made for the door. The bouncers just stood back, and surprisingly, without any confrontation, bowed and allowed them to enter. Ryona nodded a thank you but could hear the girls hissing her entry. They closed in, giving a nudge and a wink, a come and fuck me eye contact, to Roberto, who just smiled, squeezing through the heavy perfumed passage.

Inside was as dark as a dungeon the only lighting coming from a semi circle of booth's orange and blue wall lights. A single blue spot shone down on to a small square dance floor, but the place was hardly half full and its dance floor empty. Ryona and Roberto stood for a moment allowing their sight to adapt to this gloom. She stiffened, feeling a hand that was not Roberto's touching her elbow.

She turned to see a smiling waitress with her breasts, naked and on display, urging her over to an empty booth. She nodded and followed with her husband in tow. They were no sooner sat when the topless waitress was asking for a drink order. Ryona replies asking for the wine list. The waitress speeding off like some rabbit chasing greyhound to fetch one. She was certainly a fast working chick,returning with a wine list, producing a pen and pad from the pocket in her short skirt, most eager for their order.

Roberto took a look at the menu. He smiles at the prices saying. 'Fancy a Pilsner or a Bud darling yours at 15 euro a bottle or champagne, that's running at 250?'

She smiles replying. 'Haven't they anything a little more expensive darling, the champagne can't be a Dom Perignon....surely not.'

Roberto shrugs. 'It isn't, with the name I'd say it's from Italy, a Prosecco.'

The waitress interrupts saying the fizz is Italian and is very good.

Ryona smiles, gives her a wink before saying. '250 euros for a bottle of Spumante, I see it's a Rose Brut...much too cheap.' She sighs. 'Sorry dear, we'll have two Buds.'

A look of expectation leaves the girls face, she quickly spins and walks away. Thinking is that woman mad or what? I can buy that Prosecco at my supermarket for something like 14 euros. and she's thinking 250 is too cheap. She gives a laugh and heads direction bar for their cheap Pilsner. Another supermarket buy at 16 euros for a six pack. Are these two for real or what?

Roberto holding out a small sound detector, carefully does a check on the booths seating and table setting for any listening bugs. He'd remembered in his past there being several bars rigged with listening devices. He whispers. 'We're good,'

Ryona asks. 'So what do you think, are we ever likely to catch our prey in this den?'

Roberto shrugs. 'According to Norbert this is his favourite haunt...Then again is Kline at home, he's Zeta and could well be involved in a role, having a part, always surmising their plan has been started.'

Ryona. 'So how we going to find out if our man is at home? ..knock on his door?'

Roberto winks, kisses the back of her hand, saying. 'Something like that my love. Let's think about it. We must be careful by being above any suspicion.' With that in mind the two sat back and began to take in the whole club's interior, its customers were all becoming much clearer, with their eyes getting more accustomed to the dim lighting.

The waitress had appeared and brought the Buds. She'd asked if they'd like to dine and was told maybe later that they weren't hungry and were on a tour of the area for some future entertainment. Ryona adding a little sarcasm by asking if their food al a carte, was as cheap as their wine.'

The waitress answered that their food rated favourably with customers, having no cause for complaint. Roberto, meanwhile was taking in a nearby booth conversation were a stout looking bull necked man was asking for companionship. Asking for some girl called Annegret and being told by a heavy set floor madam that the girl was not available. That there were others just as appealing .

The man snarled that he wanted Annegret and he would wait till she became free. He turned to look at Roberto who gives him a shrug.

Looking at Ryona the man smiles saying. 'Now if your girl there is free then I'd make an exception.'

Roberto. 'We'll she isn't better for your health that you wait for your Annegret mister.'

The man turns away, their waitress winks. 'He's got a long wait, Annegret she isn't back on till ten .'

She looks to her watch and smiles. 'Hope he can hold back for another three hours.' She turns and walks away.

Ryona whispers. 'Can we afford to hang around much longer, we need news on Kline?'

She smiles. 'Let's go knock on his door.'

Roberto, with the Bud to his mouth, gulps, splutters. 'You can't be serious?'

She giggles. 'Well not actually knock, silly, but I've an idea that could well give us the answers to our problem.'

Roberto nods. 'Go on, I'm listening.'

She looks all about, and due to the crescendo coming from the overhead speakers blasting out a track from Guns and Roses, with Axl Rose giving his dynamic all. Ryona finds that she would have to shout.

She shook her head, shouting into Roberto's ear. 'Let's get out of here,'

Roberto nods, saying. 'Ok, looks up at the speakers, adding. 'Sorry Axl.'

They both stand, with Roberto throwing a 50 euro note onto the table and make for the club's exit. Ryona saying that they had passed a nice little cafe called 'The Welcome All' a short distance down from the Blow Hole, ideal for what she had in mind.

On going through the clubs exit doors they find the strong muscular arm of a bouncer barring their way, stretched out and across them like some car park exit barrier. The other gorilla re-entering the club only to emerge moments later with a nod to the barrier boy, saying. 'Ok, their tab's paid, free to go.'

The barrier gorilla's arm drops, he smiles.saying. 'Have a good evening.' Roberto nods, looks back at the club and says to him. 'Blow Hole ...that dive ought to be re-named 'Dead Hole.'

The other gorilla taps Roberto's shoulder and whispers.

'It don't pick-up till after ten.' He smirks. 'But that'll be far past your bedtime I take it?'

Ryona winks at him. 'Oh, it's more than an hour over mate, we're in bed for nine.'

With that they both turn and walk away. But not before hearing one gorilla remark. 'If I had her in my bed, I'd never get out of it.' They laugh.

The Welcome All was one of Berlin's many fine delicatessens of fresh ground coffee and supreme bakery. Magnificent arrays of cakes and pastries and seating for just ten people. Ryona could see it was half full, with a lone back wall table for two that was unoccupied. Ideal for what she was about to suggest to Roberto, getting his thoughts on her proposal of a way of finding an answer to the Thomas Kline problem.

The coffee had been served along with what could only be described as a wonderful cream tea. Giving Ryona thoughts of England and Yorkshire's Aunt Betty's. 'So what's this idea of yours sweetheart?'

He looked at the seated customers and was picking out the tourists from the locals. French and Italian was being spoken along with German. No Baltic, no English. Ryona gives a tug on his sleeve.

'I think it's Ok, There's no interest in us. So here's what I'm suggesting.'

She begins by keeping her voice low. 'We go to that apartment of Klien's, make like we're looking to buy that number eleven that Norbert told us was vacant and up for sale. It's on the same floor.'

Roberto is all ears urging her on by saying. 'I'm listening baby.'

'We begin to argue in the hallway near to their number seven. With me not wanting to buy and you going for it...the argument, we hope, will bring someone out of that door and, if he's there, then I'm sure it will be him that opens up. A woman with a young child, never.'

Roberto nods. 'Just one thing baby...What if they don't open up, that's not going to tell us if he's around, now is it?'

Ryona sighs. 'But I'm thinking it's worth a go baby, we've nothing to lose.' Roberto smiles patting her hand. 'Ok, Like you say, nothing to lose, but let's not leave it too late, if our boy is home then it'll be now, I'm thinking when Norbert gave us the Blow Hole as his haunt, he was going by late night appearances.'

Ryona. 'Yes, remember that bouncer saying nothing got going till after ten?' Roberto nods.'Let's have a good look around before the argument act. We may not need to do it.'

It was a good half hour later that they arrived at the apartment building and Roberto directed Ryona down a flight of stairs into the building's underground car park, where a series of numbers had been put into bays depicting who the spaces were allotted too, In space marked Apt. 7 was sitting a dark blue 4x4 BMW. While 4 spaces to the left was Apt.11. The space was void of any vehicle.

Ryona smiles. 'Seems we could well have Thomas at home with his family.'

Roberto gives a thumbs up. 'Let's hope.'

Moments after the pair are in the elevator n their way up to the first floor. The doors open and surprise, surprise, Thomas Kline his standing ready to enter.

He looks with suspicion at the pair and asks. 'Sure you have the right floor?'

Ryona answers with. 'This is the first floor isn't it?'

Kline nods. 'Sorry but we don't seem to have met, might I ask what apartment you're looking for? ...It's just that we've had quite a few burglaries in our vicinity lately, not that I'm implying that you have that look.'

He steps aside allowing Ryona and Roberto to exit. With Roberto holding a hand to the entry not allowing the door to close.

Kline goes on to add. 'But one can never be sure when it comes to really knowing who's robbing who these days.'

Roberto tells him that they're here to insect apartment 11 and have an appointment with the sales agent Theo Hass.

Kline looking a little confused asks. 'Hass don't know him, is he with Muller and Wagner? ..must be new.'

He points to his left. 'Eleven it's four doors down. Von Stein's, he passed away last month.'

He smiles. 'Not at home, he died in hospital, heart attack, nice old guy.'

He holds out a hand to shake. ..'Names Thomas Kline I'm in seven.'

He steps past Roberto going into the elevator. Saying. 'Good luck.'

It's at that moment Kline blacks out after receiving a blow and a neck grip from Ryona's expertise in the Israeli art of Krav Maga.

Roberto. 'Quickly girl, down to the car park, get the keys for his BM they'll be in his pocket. We tie and gag him then take him back to base.'

Ryona said. 'I think we ought to drive out of Berlin, let Joe come and collect.'

Roberto nods. 'We can do that, no witnesses, get rid of the car at some sex den's park.'

He smiles, nudges her. 'Cool baby, let's hope there's no one waiting in the downstairs parking bays..Last thing we need is a witness here. We have something like twenty metres carrying our friend ...it's gotta be a fireman's lift.'

Ryona. 'Ok, get him ready, I'll see that the close is clear... Let's be lucky.'

Ryona was first out of the basement landing leaving Roberto holding the stunned Kline, in a fireman's lift over his shoulder. She quickly returned saying the coast was clear and the BM boot opened. Kline had been bound with electrical tie wrap, with his hands behind his back. Gaffe tape was across his mouth. His legs bound at the ankles with the tape.

Roberto, on reaching the vehicle, unceremoniously dumped the body into the boot, Ryona was already behind the wheel ready to go. Roberto slammed the boot shut before sprinting into the front passenger seat and waved her to go. Reminding her to keep to the speed limits and head out east Berlin, destination a large remote forest area.

It was then he put in a call to Joe and gave him the news.

Joe replied saying the team were on their way and would meet up at Wassily Point, a place rarely visited by tourists, mainly because of a series of murders that had taken place in the last few years, a count of nine in three years.

Kline's interrogation would take place at one of the isolated cabins that ran alongside the river Spree. The cabin had been acquired, last minute by General Porter, who assured Joe that all facilities would be taken care of, such as food and a 24 hour around the clock area patrol, Thus ensuring no interruptions. The BM would be taken back to a notorious sex den, 'House of Sin' in central Berlin, then left unattended in its car park.

Ryona asked Roberto if he'd set-up the BM's sat-nav for their given rendezvous with Joe, the cabins name being'Riverside Rest' situated three kilometres east, down Old Log Hauling Road.

Roberto smiled saying he didn't need any sat-nav. He was well familiarised with the area, having searched the forest, seeking body parts in past CIA operations. An area not recommended for nature walks after sundown.

Joe had been totally taken off guard, suprised by the call from Roberto that the fish had been hooked, Roberto's way of telling him that they had Kline and were on a heading east out of Berlin in the Zeta's BMW. Roberto had explained, leaving nothing out. Telling Joe that sometimes, but not often enough, you need a little luck with opportunity, to good to miss falling your way.

The brought a smile from Joe , thinking who come to think of it, would have thought that; Kline appearing about to take the elevator and walking into the open arms of Ryona and Roberto. That could only be put down as one incredibly piece of luck. He repeated their Luck to the head shaking Norman and Frazier as they too sat in a Ford people carrier heading out east from Berlin.

Norman said, 'Now we have the sprat to catch the mac, Joe…Let's hope our luck continues.

Joe nods 'What I thought was going to be difficult has become easy…But I'm confident we can break our Zeta, and make the Alpha.

He smiles, turning to them. 'Oh, one more thing, Anton has asked me to take in Lenny Jameson.'

He winks, 'Of course I agreed..Seems he's hit a problem whilst working the Irish…his undercover must have blown.'

He gives a shrug. 'Besides he knows us all ..After that Highgate cemetery fiasco. I think we owe him one.'

Norman with a surprised look. 'Lenny, Joe?…but he's always worked undercover.'

Gives his head a shake. 'Wonder what's brought Lenny in from the cold…He's a top A, Joe…Be a good inclusion to the team..But I'm thinking you're right …he's had his cover blown..I know Lenny and he's a loner.'

Frazier shrugs, saying. 'Do I know him?'

Joe shakes his head. 'No, you don't know him Dave..Not many do, he goes way back working for the firm. He's what you call in our business a Ghost..That right Norm?'

Norman nodding. 'Lenny's a spectre alright ..I remember, I'm sure you do too Joe, the Marseilles gun runners. We had Lenny working for us, he was a fucking diamond..That warehouse Joe, he saved our lives.'

Joe nods. 'That was a close call Dave…Theywere running the arm up through Morocco…We had a distribution warehouse given, our orders were to storm and take down all.'

He shakes his head. 'Lenny told us of an ambush being set up, that we'd be heading into a graveyard....He was right.'

Norman goes on to say, that Lenny had gone so close to losing his own life in getting the information back to them.

Joes final words on Lenny Jameson being. 'A ghost, a loner.'

He nods, sighs.'Guess that's Lenny all over...But when it comes to going beyond the call of duty.'

Joe waves a hand. 'He's top of the tree..How he's survived all these years God only knows.'

Norman laughs. 'He's going to be one hell of an assist to us, I can guarantee.'

Joe. 'He's due at SIS headquarters Berlin sometime tomorrow. Anton will probably be along with him, for initial introductions.'

He smiles, shrugs. 'What am I saying, Lenny, he will know the score, would have gone through the team sheet.'

It was Dave who was driving, pointing to the sat-nav it was indicating that they had arrived at their turn off. A road sign was displaying Wassily point was 2 kilometres, a slip road off to the right.

With Joe asking. 'The sat-nav, Dave?...With this light out there fast fading, I'm hoping that we haven't far to drive ... having to use headlights is a good way of blowing a fanfare that we've arrived.'

Norman smiles. 'If you ask me Joe, with pine knitted timber, black so dense, I'd say that there was little chance of anyone creeping about.'

He shrugs. 'If there is, then they'll be shit scared of who's driving these woods after sundown...What with the murder rate in this location.'

Joe, nods. 'Could be you're right Norm...But there's an old saying I'm sure you've heard; every village has an idiot, every town two or three, every city hundreds.'

Frazier smiles. 'So, what you're saying, Joe is there could be a few idiots in Wassily Point?'

Joe laughs. 'Well let's look at it this way Dave, whoever'screeping about this dense Black Forest after dark... They're not a full shilling.'

Norman laughs. 'That must include us, Joe.'

After a two kilometres drive, on uneven ground, Frazier comes to what looks to be an old unused timber track that snakes to the left. Nailed to its first towering pine, an arrow sign points, saying. Riverside Rest.

He shrugs. 'Looks like we're about to enter the driveway, guys.'

Turns to Joe. 'Think they'll be here, already Joe?'

Joe nods. 'They had an good hour start on us.' He looks to his watch. 'If they haven't arrive they've hit trouble or got a flat.'

Norman, says. 'Knowing the two R's , they'll be here, just hope Ryonas got that coffee pot on.'

5
RIVERSIDE REST

Back in apartment seven Turid Kline is getting hot and bothered at her husband for not replying to her phone calls. He had told her he'd be no longer than a hour after visiting Hans Ottermanze for his forthcoming North American adventure. His visiting visa having been forged to give him the alias, a new identity in the name of Bulgarian engineer Fredrik Zenakoff. Hans had all the papers he would need to get him safely into the United States.

Turids cell phone began bleeping, she gives a deep sigh of relief and takes the call, saying. 'Oh, at last, where the hell are you?...you said you'd be just an hour...that, Thomas Kline, was three hours ago.'

A man's voice, not her husband's ; 'Turid ...Turid Kline?'

Turid gasps. 'Who is this?'

Voice. 'Am I speaking to Turid Kline ...wife of Thomas?'

Turid. 'Yes, yes...I'm Thomas Klien's wife, Turid...what, who.'

Voice. 'I take it Thomas is not with you?'

Turid, her voice barely a whisper. 'Who...who is this ... who, where's Thomas?'

Voice. 'My name is Hans...Hans Ottermanze, Thomas, your husband, we had an arrangement to meet, as you were saying, 3 hours ago.'

Turid. 'Yes that's where he said he was going...To meet a Hans Ottermanze...You.'

Her voice regains its strength. 'Are you saying he's not with you?'

Hans replies. 'He's not here, nor has he been, he's in trouble if he doesn't show.'

His voice turns into one angry snarl, it's vibration Turid can sense, sends a shiver down her spine. He finishes the call by saying.

'He's got till ten....If he doesn't show at mine by then.'

She hears the snarl. The call ends.

Turid in desperation. 'What if he doesn't show, what? something's happened...an accident, the hospitals.'

She's finding it hard to concentrate. Screams out in despair.

'Where the fuck are you Thomas Kline? ...Pick up your phone and talk to me, Ottermanze, he's given you till ten... Oh sweet Jesus, talk to me baby.'

Her son Thor enters the room, playing with a model toy racing car, she goes to him and hugs and kisses him, saying.

'It's OK, baby, daddy will be home soon.'

With headlights on dipped beam the Ford people carrier finally picks out the final gateway to Riverside Rest. Sitting back and surrounded by a circle of towering pines, the cabin is showing light coming through closed curtained windows, presumably from a storm lantern.

Joe puts out a hand and tugs Frazier's sleeve. 'Can't see any BM, can you?' Frazier shrugs. 'Your call Joe, what are your thoughts?....You wanna look see? with that light I'd say someone's home.'

Norman. 'Could be the BM's around the back, I'll go take a peek.'

Norman, with care opens a door and slides out. Crouching low, he begins to move towards the window. He goes forward barely two metres when an area is suddenly ablaze from a overhead spotlight. Norman freezes then drops to the ground. In his hand he now holds his pistol.

The cabin door opens and a voice calls out. 'You coming in or are you going to lay there all night Norm.?'

With his unmistakable American accent, a call coming from Roberto. Norman jumps to his feet, smiles, shaking his head, saying.

'Fuck me, Roberto,' He shades his eyes and points up to the spotlight.

'Missed your Beamer...caught me cold.'

Roberto steps out to greet him as Joe and Frazier exit the Ford. Joe, shouts.'Where's the BMW?' ...We couldn't see it and it brought on suspicion....Hope you've got coffee on the go.'

Roberto. 'Why don't you get Frazier to park the Ford around the back, the BM's gone.'

Giving a long arm wave, indicating distance. 'General Porter's had two guys take it back into Berlin Central... Notorious sex den, House of Sin'

Joe nods ' Yeah, Norbert, he did mention it, good that it's away out of sight, out of mind.'

Joe then asks. 'So you have Klien in the cabin, I'm hoping to start on him as soon as possible.'

Roberto sighs, 'Sorry to disappoint Joe, but the Zeta's not in the cabin ...much too good for him in there....We have him in a dug out earth pit...Looks like the owners are about to install some sewage tank...We put Kline in there, he's bound and gagged, ain't going nowhere …Keeps up the pressure, his brains all of a scramble right now….He hasn't a clue what we're about…He's not had food or water…He's in one hell of a weak mess Joe.'

Roberto smiles. 'Thought you'd get to him more easily by slowly turning the screw.'

Norman, nodding his agreement says. 'After what they did to the CIA guys…I'd have the bastard eating his own shit and drinking piss.'

Joe. 'What you have given us, is extra play time, by taking him down, great job Roberto, not forgetting Ryona too.'

Roberto gives a backwards glance. 'Why don't we go in and get some of that coffee you've been crying for Joe, …The lady, she's in there with coffee and cookies..You can tell her yourself, Joe.'

Frazier, having parked the Ford, entered the cabin and was handed a steaming mug of fresh ground coffee with several cookies. He sits, joining the team who have gathered around a large pine table.

Joe looks at his watch; it's showing ten-forty-five. He winks.

'We leave him till eleven ..then we hit him.'

Meanwhile back in Vauxhall, London, Anton Spicer was going through a brief with Lenny Jameson. Anton had received a full report on the ongoing situation in regard to The Wolves Bravarian festival. Now it was a matter of Lenny getting out of the London Irish undercover work, out of the mire and to be adopted, accepted into the team run by Colonel Joe Delph. His position had become unsafe after a slip up by MI5 agent Keith Branson. Branson's error had thrown the Irish operation into complete turmoil…causing Lenny to be put on the New IRA's wanted list.

Anton was well aware of Lenny's value to SIS having done eighteen years military service from a young twenty year old Paratrooper to a Pathfinder all area operator, finally getting snatched by MI5's Special Anti-terrorist section, United Kingdom. Now in his ninth year. Gaining a highly rated top A, and a rank of Major. Nicknamed, Spook. He'd always had a long ongoing friendship with Joe and Norman, having worked together in Able Squad, a forty man Pathfinder unit that was based in Afghanistan but mainly at everyone's call. The Marseilles-Moroccan gunrunners being just one that could be brought to mind. One thing for sure, Lenny could and would, strengthen Joe's team.

Anton was hoping that Ryona and Roberto would come back into the fold, They had started a prosperous business as Private Investigators working in companies insurance fraud with officers in both North America and the UK.

At the moment they have had to sub-let their business out to other similar firms whilst operation Wolf was on the go. Anton carried the thought, that if the truth be known, they missed the excitement. Most of the time chasing insurance fraud was dull and boring.

If they did decide to go back to their dull and boring way of life then Lenny would help fill the large hole they would leave. But that, for the moment was all up in the air.

As for Lenny, he couldn't wait to join up with old friends. It was for him a dream move, working once more with people he'd trust with his life.

A very worried Turid Kline was sitting watching the hands of the clock climbing towards 10pm. With no call from Thomas and countless phone enquiries to Berlin Hospitals and police stations she had, unsurprisingly, come to the end of her tether. She walked into Thor's bedroom and gazed down at her sleeping son.

Tears began to flow. She being an atheist, was now asking for God to help her. Any God, asking them to look for Thomas and get him to phone, call, anything, just let him be OK, safe and on his way home. Her cell phone starts buzzing. She looks up to the ceiling, whispers. 'Thank you..Lord.' Then gasps, sighs..saying 'Oh, no.'

The face of Hans Ottermanze shows on her display screen, he's saying, 'He's not called …. his time has finally run out…. his position will be given to a more loyal soldier… a new Zeta…Your ungrateful husband will become as lifeless as the Dead Sea…one last word of warning…'Silence is Golden…You talk of this, we take your son Thor.'

Ottermanze deletes the call.

Turid screams out..'Don't you go fucking threatening me…You take my baby and I'll see you in hell, Ottermanze… You and your leather clad two wheeled pirate-cowboys… Something's happened to my Thomas…Go find out what….you stupid man.'

Turid's cries all falling on deaf ears, cries that Hans Ottermanze doesn't get to hear.

Ryona cleared away the last of the empty plates, A fresh brew had been called for, the Blue Mountain fresh ground being that little bit special, a silky smooth taste that Joe had not sampled before. So good he'd taken down the name of its distributor for some future purchase.

Joe pointing to the Black Forest cuckoo clock that was hanging down from its wall fixings and about to announce that the time was coming up to eleven fifteen.

Joe smiles. 'I'm thinking it's Thomas Kline time, guys..Shall we bring the Zeta Wolf into the arena?'

Norman stretches. 'Time's about right, Joe.' He stands, nods to Frazier. 'Let's go get the Wolf, Dave.' He turns to Joe and asks him where he'd like him.

Joe smiles, opening his arms wide. 'Why not in here? make sure he's clean and blindfolded.'

Ryona rises and walks to a side table, on it a bowl that's contains various fruits; apples pears, oranges and peaches. She brings it to the table and sets it in front of Joe.

Joe, nodding, says 'What about a cafeteria of Blue Mountain, Ryona?...Let's really tempt the man.'

Ryona puts up a thumb, walks to the percolating unit, shouts back. 'On its way chief.'

Roberto stands. 'I'll give Norm and Dave a hand,' He walks to the cabin's rear door saying. 'I'm hoping Klien's not shit himself, that could be a bit of a scrub down.'

Ryona smiles. 'There's a hose connected to the back gable wall, you could give him a full wash down.'

Norman shake, of the head, smiles. 'Let's give him the shower anyway...while he's down in that hole.'

Joe. 'OK, let's do that, but only if he stinks. .I don't want him drip drying in this cabin.'

Roberto adds. 'We've his wallet and a small note book, loads of phone numbers ....They've got to be important I'd have thought.'

Ryona goes into her purse and takes them out, placing them down for Joe to view. 'There's his wife's cell in there, one Turid Kline.'

As the three approach the earth pit, a ten foot square, eight feet deep. A large sewerage tank stood close by ready to be inserted into the hole.

Still gagged they could hear Klien moaning and sobbing. The sobbing stopped. Norman, holding a torch, shone its beam down into the hole. Klien was sitting in a corner hog tied, and hooded.

Roberto meanwhile had brought a 12 foot ladder and lowered it down into the hole. Norman turning to Frazier, saying.

'Get him out of there Dave, our boy is ready.'

Frazier descends the ladder going the few steps down into the hole. He produces a Swiss Army knife and cut's the ties off Kliens ankles, then undoes his wrists, bringing them from his back and putting them onto the ruck of the ladder. He then prods the back of the Zeta, an indication to climb.

Maybe it's his eagerness to exit the hole but Klien seems to find an extra strength in ascending the ladder. Dave, who's behind and following, can smell nothing coming from Kline's jeans, thankfully there's no smell of excrement. On his leaving the pit, the wrists of the Zeta are again cable tied, by Norman, around his back. Still hooded he's prodded to walk in the direction of the cabin.

Klien begins to protest but a strong hand from Frazier goes over his face forcefully pressing the hood into his mouth, silencing him.

Norman says. 'Let's get him inside, the hood remains.'

Frazier prods the blind Klien forward and takes him into the cabin. Joe points to a chair and tells Frazier to sit him in it. Norman sits along-sides Klien and pours himself a coffee, waves it under the Zetas nose.

Ryona meanwhile had taken the time to fry up some sausages and bacon. This she had put down on the table. They watched Kliens reaction to the aroma. Knowing there was nothing that could be compared to the smell of hot bacon, his nose began to sniff, his tongue licking his lips in some kind of expectation.

Klien's muffled voice comes out from under the hood. 'I don't know what this abducting me is all about.' His voice gets louder. 'But you're in serious trouble. My people. You just don't know who you're dealing with.' He snarls.'Man, you have problems.'

Joe. 'Why don't you tell us about them Thomas, that pretty little wife of yours...Turid... your son Thor, bet they're missing daddy,'

He sighs. 'It's not us with the problems Thomas, it's you.'

Norman whispers in German into Kliens ear. 'Your Alpha, what's his name now...Err is it Corneille?'

Klien, laughs. 'My Alpha ...Corneille Dewer...You fucking serious ...He isn't good enough, to polish my boots.'

Norman continue:. 'I'll remind him that you said that.'....Klien is under the hood,thinking, who the fuck are these guys...Do they realise just who they're taking on...The Bratva, the Black Angels, the Pakham.

Joe, deep sigh, winks, addresses the team. 'It's looking like we have to go pay Turid Klien a visit ...Bring her here, give her a day or two in the pit.' He begins whistling...We could well get more out of her than this piece of shite.' He gives Klien a pat on the cheek.

Klien, snarls. 'What is it you fuckers want?...My wife and son, You bastards are hitting below the belt..what the fuck is it you want?'

Joe. 'Oh, now we're getting somewhere.'

Joe, laughs. 'The man here suddenly realises that we're wanting something from him.'

Roberto, tugging Kliens hair, saying. 'I'm one bastard who's witnessed the murders of three good men...and therefore I'm prepared to go the whole fucking distance with torturous methods to get us want we want.'

He gives a few more tugs, whispers in Kliens ear. 'That includes your family...The full torturous distance.'

The head under the hood drops, he speaks. 'My wife, my son, they are OK,yes?'

Joe. 'For the moment.' Kline shaking his head. 'You have my phone...can I speak to her? she'll be worried...I need to know she's OK, then I will answer your questions.'

Joe nods to Roberto who brings out Kliens cell-phone. He hands it over to Joe along with a small address book. He checks on the number, prods Klien, saying. 'You have one minute...don't fuck it up.'

Moments later, in apartment seven, Turid Klien's phone begins to buzz. She races to it and sees the name Thomas on its display screen. She looks up to the heavens, to herself she utters. 'Thank God.' Before answering.

'Thomas...Where are you? ..I'm so worried...Get yourself home...are you OK,...not been in an accident? ..Why aren't you here?' Words keep coming out at a non stop pace ending with Kliens having to shout, telling her to stop and listen. He goes on to ask if she and Thor are ok, and that there's no one in the apartment, strange men or if any have called. He then tells her to lock up tight and see that the Glock pistol is easy to access, that he won't be home for a while and that tomorrow she should take Thor and go and visit her mother in Denmark for a few days, adding that he will be in touch, and not to worry.

It's then Turid tells him of the phone calls that Ottermanze had made. Saying he had til ten to appear. If he didn't , then he was finished, Like the Dead Sea were his very words. Also that if she mentioned their conversation to anyone, he would come for Thor.

It's then Joe nudges him to end the conversation. Klien pleads with his wife, begging her to do as he asks, then ends by telling her how much he loves them both.

Joe takes the phone away from the hood and slides it off. Klien can be heard to say a thank you.

Joe, 'OK, you give us what we want and you'll eat...you may just get to see your family again...depending on the information you give will decide your fate.' Joe, tapping the top of his head, adds. 'You're not out of the woods yet...You understand what I'm saying?'

Klien nods and replies. 'Let's hear your questions..I'm hungry.'

Joe. 'Let's see if you'll be eating tonight. Give me the name of the Alpha, who's giving out the orders...the one who knows what's going down?'

Kline doesn't even hesitate for a second in telling Joe of Alpha Hans Ottermanze. The threats given to Kline's family with his death sentence. He was more than happy to give Ottermanze up.

Joe, 'This Ottermanze, where does he reside, Where will we find find him?'

Thomas again with no hesitation. 'He owns a sex den called the Blow Hole...He lives above it with a fourteen year old Romanian girl.'

Joe hears a sigh coming from under the hood. 'He wants my wife...my son..and me dead. He is overseeing an operation for the Pakham.'

Again a sigh. 'I was to report to him this evening, 4pm. ... Your two agents caused me to miss that meet...I'm now on his most wanted list'

Joe asks 'Your meeting with this Alpha, Ottermanze... what was it for?'

Kline. 'He had papers made out for me.'

Norman, nudges him. 'Papers...What papers?'

'Fake passport and new identification papers. Dresden engineering company representative.' Joe asks. 'What was the passport for?'

Kline. 'For me to gain a safe passage into North America...Chicago's O'Hare...I, being just one of ten Zetas.' Roberto looks to Joe and shrugs.

Joe continues 'Why Chicago...What's going down there... Why ten Zetas?'

Kline shrugs. 'Only Ottermanze can answer you that..Zetas we know nothing until deadline time...Then we're told very little.'

Joe. 'OK, Thomas you've just bought yourself a Currywurst with fries....Now I'm wanting to know this Ottermanze, his weakness..Who does he love, tell us about his family...Tell me who he'd give his life up for?'

Kline is silent. Joe taps the Zeta's shoulder. 'Did you hear me Thomas?'

Kline nods, tells Joe he's thinking. He asks if he could have a drink of water. Ryona walks up, gives Joe the glass of water, Joe indicates to Norman to give him the drink. Again Joe hears a whispered thank you coming from under the hood.

Kline coughs on taking the liquid that's being given to him. Norman lifting the head cover to lips level.

'All I can tell you, he has a mother that lives in Essen, a sister in Hamburg...They are very close as a family...But that's all I can give you....On his love, he loves only himself. You must understand he's a killer, applying pain. Hitler would have loved to have had an army of Ottermanzes. He would have ruled the world...Believe me, he will be hard for you to capture and break.'

Joe, nodding deep in thought, turns to the team. 'Seems it's Hans Ottermanze who's our target...I think our Zeta here's earned himself a meal and a coffee.'

Nodding to Ryona. 'Lets sample another Blue Mountain brew, I don't think Mister Klien has anything more.'

Klien utters. 'You better get your skates on if you're aiming to catch Ottermanze.' Norman, asks. 'Why's that?'

Klien. 'He's due to leave for Chicago sometime tonight... I'm supposed to be on the flight with him...Think you can take him, along with ten Zetas?...I don't think so.'

Joe, nods at Klien, looks to Frazier. 'Take our friend here, away...He gets coffee and a bite of the sausages...I've got calls to make.'

Frazier asks. 'You wanting I should pop him back in the pit?'

Klien can be seen to stiffen. Joe shakes his head. Roberto suggest that they keep him securely tied, baby feed him, in the cabins outhouse. A small shed where game is hung.

Joe, nodding. 'Sounds good...Lock him in there, gag and hog-tie him.'

He puts up a finger and wags it. 'I don't want him doing a sleepwalk on us...Keep a check on him.'

Joe, as an afterthought, says to let him have a couple of blankets. Roberto tells Joe that in the outhouse there's a pile of large empty sacks. Klien could be put in a couple, a make do sleeping bag.

Joe puts up a thumb, saying. 'Ok, see to it.'

On that Roberto and Dave take Klien out of the cabin.

Ryona asks Joe if he's sure that there's nothing more going to come out of Klien. Surely he's some idea on the Alpha Ottermanze plan.

Joe. 'There's nothing more, fact is, he hates this Alpha...A man who's threatened his wife with abduction of his son.'

Smiles. 'Why, give Klien a gun and he'd shoot the bastard...Let's just get our heads together on how we're going to get this Alpha.'

Norman shrugs. 'We have to go to Chicago and take it on from there...I think we've missed the boat here.'

Joe nods. 'Your probably right Norm...Let's just see what Norbert and Anton want us to do.'

Ryona. 'No prizes for guessing that Joe, it's going to be Chicago, Chicago that wonderful town.'

Joe and Norman smile. Ryona arms spread asks. 'Well isn't that how that Sinatra song goes?'

Roberto and Frazier re-enter the cabin with Roberto asking 'What Sinatra song is that, dearest?'

Ryona. 'Joe, was wondering what Norbert and Anton would want from us next.' She holds out a hand. 'I was thinking Chicago...Sinatra's wonderful town.' Roberto shrugs, winks to Joe, 'Sinatra?'

Ryona gives him a what school did you go to look before giving him a push and saying. 'The song?'....Then,what can I expect from someone who thought Ken Dodd was a London Mobster.' They all laugh, with Norman saying, 'He never?'

Ryona gives a serious nod then laughs. 'He bloody well did...we were in Blackpool and I asked him if he'd like to go see Ken Dodd...He asked what prison he was in.'

Joe. 'Well he nearly was, doing porridge, that is...couple of years ago ..wasn't he up, if I remember right, for tax evasion?'

Roberto pulls his tongue out at her . 'See, I must have thought he'd been given a prison term.'

Joe. 'Nice try Roberto, but I'm remembering Ken as a brilliant Liverpool comedian, never a London Mobster...Bit of your Bob Hope...Then again, Bob was born in London Town.'

Roberto, looks to the heavens, says. 'Sorry Ken.'

Norman asks Frazier if Klien has been made comfortable?...Dave nods and replies. 'He's going nowhere, not without someone's help, he's all wrapped up, hog-tied in his sack bed...Like a bug in a rug.'

Joe, smiles. 'Good man....Let's discuss just how to approach the situation now that the Alpha's on his way to Chicago...I'm going with Ryona, her thinking that Norbert's going to ask us to follow the paper trail.'

Roberto nods his agreement telling them to remember that the operation of abducting Ottermanze has got more difficult, that they'd have to include the Alphas entourage, the ten Zetas that would now be with him.'

Norman sighs. 'Let's be honest about this, the whole initial plan of snatch Ottermanze is binned. ...We now have to take all...That's eleven soldiers, trained killing machines.'

He gives a deep sigh. 'It's not going to be easy.'

He turns to Joe. 'Whatever we decide.'

Joe .'First things first, Let me give Norbert and Anton a call, get their thoughts....Then we can get the green light.'

Joe had already decided on calling Anton, after all he was his chief...He'd leave Roberto to inform Norbert of the situation, Norman as always was deep in thought. Dave Frazier entered the cabin he approached Joe with the question of what, if anything, had been planned for Thomas Kline.

Joe, 'Kline...he will become Norbert's property...as will his wife and son...No longer our problem Dave, we've got to get our heads together on Chicago...Ottermanze and his entourage.'

Norman, nods says. 'It's not going to be easy...we take the Alpha...from what I can gather, a tough cookie...he will be missed...ten Zeta's are then without a leader. Alarm bells will ring...Then of course there's the question..will he give us the Pakhams plan?..best remember it's his life, his death sentence, on revealing it.'

Roberto sighs. 'Norman's right Joe, we can't allow them to shut up shop, taking the Alpha and his crew will not fall favourably with us.'

Joe to Dave. 'You got any thoughts on this Dave... anything at all, every little helps.'

Dave taps the table, saying, There's one thing for sure, Joe. The way I see it, we have to take this Ottermanze, there's no doubt about that, maybe along with the

Zetas....Only way to keep us out, put the job onto some other party.'

Joe adds. 'Thing about that, it still leaves us with a problem ...If we don't break the Alpha...and there is always the possibility...then I can't see us getting another go...Our task then becomes harder than ever.'

Ryona, on bringing another cafeteria of coffee to the table, shrugs. 'Put your Glock to his mother's and sister's head...you'll bust him, Joe.'

Joe nods to them all. 'The lady could well be right...If Ottermanze knows anything at all on the Pakham's operation then he's not stupid ...he's going to make changes to his plan.'

Norman raising his hand. 'Could only be the Chicago part ...There's a lot of bread been spent on this operation ...it's big, he's not going to call it a day for one missing Alpha... He's just going to adopt a new plan.'

Ryona. 'Maybe so Norm...but he's got to be thinking about how much we know...did we break Ottermanze?...he's put down Fort Knox on this, he's got to continue.'

Joe. 'Whatever he had in mind I feel in some way involved Chicago.' He sighs. 'But then Chicago could be his landing point...Ottermanze has flown into O'Hare...not New York, Washington, or LA...why Chicago?'

Roberto smiles. 'I'm hoping General Porter can enlighten us on why, Joe...I've given him what Klien has told us. He's got agents at O'Hare waiting the Wolves arrival. The flight Ottermanze had taken is scheduled to arrive around 6am tomorrow...he's arranged for us to take a chopper back into Berlin, he just needs us to say we're ready to go.'

Joe turns to Norman. 'Best we give Norbert's babes in the wood out there the nod, that we're ready to leave, tell them to go easy on Kline. He's got problems too...Main one is keeping his family alive.'

6
HANS 'THE ALPHA' OTTERMANZE

It took Joe and the team a couple more hours to finally get back to the office of Norbert Porter. The Zeta Kline had been taken away by the forest patrol squad. Thomas Kline was now Norbert's baby.

Joe was looking forward to meeting Anton, along with his old friend and associate, Lenny Jameson.

Joe was somewhat puzzled as to what had gone wrong, to bring Lenny in from the cold. He couldn't figure out why Lenny, a lone undercover agent, had been doubled up with a new face. Lenny had always worked solo. That fact alone being why he'd been active, undiscovered, on countless operations.

Joe was more than pleased to welcome Lenny aboard. The forty- year-old, lightning fast, ex Pathfinder was the Lon Chaney, master of disguise. A man who could tell you a lie and convince you he's telling the truth. At five-eleven and weighing in at 150 lbs he was a classified A1. operator. Furthermore both Joe and Norman knew his qualities, having worked with him in their Pathfinder days.

After initial introductions they'd all positioned themselves sitting around the large table in CIA's Operations Room.

Coffee was on the go along with biscuits not unlike the Hob-Nob. With General Porter left to open the meeting with a spirited. 'Welcome all..especially to the two new faces around my table, Dave and Lenny.' He gives the table top a tap.

'Tonight you fly out to Chicago where my colleagues have surveillance on the hotel that our friend Hans Ottermanze and his cronies have booked into. It's pretty central, overlooking the East River close to the Trump building. Rather expensive for a soccer team of prowling Wolves.' He shrugs. 'Five star digs...seems our Russian Pakham is throwing a lot of dollars at this heist.'

Roberto. 'Heist General?'

Norbert nods, continues. 'Heist, yes Roberto...What else could it be? ...bloody Bavarian festival, with a Black Angel in attendance, coming into the States with fake passports.'

Norman says. 'It's not like America to let them in Sir.'

Norbert sighs. 'Yes, that had taken some secret negotiations with Custom Control....We had to let them through the gate because we need to know what the bastards are up to.' He puts a hand up in the air. 'Let's not sway on this point...we all know they'd have got into the U.S. anyway found a hole, illegally, if need be.'

Joe 'So what's the plan General? ...we take these cronies out, over in Chicago ...Putting the screws on Ottermanze? ..Surely that's going to cause an immediate blockage.. causing a tightening of their net...what's worth a billion dollars over there in Chicago, Sir?'

Norbert smiles. 'That's for you to find out Joe by hitting that Alpha hard. ..What he knows, squeezing it out by any means.'

He winks to them all. 'By the way this meeting is unrecorded, and 'squeezing it out by any means', You didn't hear me say that.'

He shakes his head, saying. 'What I need is a vacation... this job is enough to drive a man insane.'

Anton under his breath,sighs.'Don't we all.'

Joe, stresses 'We've got to take a good look into this...let's try to think on how we can successfully achieve our goal.' He wags a finger, 'We know the taking of Ottermanze is priority...we now need to know the best way, the most suitable strategy.'

Norman. 'We're like Salmon returning to spawn, swimming up a rushing hazardous stream...It's not going to be easy.'

Ryona, sighs, saying 'Keeping such an action in house... no leaks...It's Chicago guys.' She shakes her head. 'It's going to be difficult.'

Lenny, who had been previously told by Anton of the situation, cuts in with.'There's only one way to go on this problem.'

Joe. 'Go on Lenny, let's hear it.' Lenny shrugs. 'There's got to be an accident...with one survivor, the Alpha, but we add a John Doe to the ten, like there's been eleven. We have to take them out, something like a burnt out vehicle, bodies unrecognisable...a staged accident.'

Lenny's thoughts had brought a moment's silence to the table. Joe, looks at him, smiles, shake of his head, asking the team's thoughts on what Lenny had said.

Norbert looks to Anton, saying. 'The man's a genius.'

Joe, 'We take the Zetas out...Doesn't matter where...then stage the accident. ..good thinking Lenny.'

Lenny. 'It's just a suggestion Joe, you have to get them all together.'

He makes like throwing a spear. 'One strike...a do or die situation, that of course is always surmising that you want a complete extermination?' Norbert, laughs. 'You're forgetting what these bastards did to three of my top agents, Lenny....fucking cut out their hearts, then fed them to a Black Angels pet Wolf.'

Norbert looks to Anton. 'Jesus Christ, Anton, they're sadistic killers.'

Anton nods. 'You don't need to ask me what I'd do, old friend.'

He puts up a finger. 'Once a killer always a killer.' He addresses Joe. 'You know what I'm saying, Joe?'

Joe nods. 'You have me on the main line Anton, but if this Ottermanze is a soldier of silence, then I'm thinking the shutters may be drawn and we're left on a road to nowhere.'

Roberto nods, saying. 'Joe's correct to give this action some serious thought.'

He wags a finger. 'Let's look a little deeper into this wolverine venture. ..These plans have been put in place with supreme care. For such a large operation being assembled takes a whole lot of dough so whatever it is being aimed at is big...big with a hefty return on its success.' He continues. 'This operation has been given the green light from the Capo Di Tutti Capi' ...He smiles. 'For those not familiar with the Italian lingo, its English translation ....'The Boss of Bosses.'

Norman asks who that might be to Roberto...Roberto shrugs. 'Let's first say who it's likely to be...The Pakham, he's powerful enough to bring in the Black Angels...in return the Angels would need to sign a special pact to join up with the Pakham, an agreement issued by the Boss, the Pakham.'

Ryona. 'But this Capo, Roberto...are we talking Mafia... Cosa Nostra, after all we are in America and nothing moves without their approval....surely they've got a foot in the door in all of this.'

Lenny adds. 'Then we have the American Hells Angels... would they be letting a bunch of European Wolves prowl their domain? I don't think so.'

Roberto . 'Going back to what Joe has just uttered.. this Alpha Ottermanze will be under the oath of death if he reveals ...even the slightest conversation with us...To quote an old Sicilian brotherhood oath...'Speak and die, stay silent and live.'

Joe looks to Dave Frazier who seems to be pondering something on his mind. Joe was having thoughts that Dave, with a NCO sergeants rank, was wanting the opportunity to enter into the conversation, but was holding back by letting the officers take centre stage.

Joe nods to him, saying. 'You got anything to add Dave?' He winks. 'You're a fully fledged member of this team now.' Joe waves an outstretched hand over the assembly before continuing. 'You're on equal status and a most valued member...we have no rankings Dave so please let's hear what's on that fine Scottish brain of yours.'

Dave nods, smiles. 'Its not that Joe, I was just giving thought to our old enemy the Fly...wondering if he could be in some way involved...could he possibly be a part of what's going down?'

Norman seated next to Dave, gives him a wink and a pat saying.'Good thinking brother.'

Norm to Joe 'Dave could have something there Joe, the Fly, his inclusion...We sure enough hurt the bastard and you can be sure he's not forgotten what cost we caused him..think he could be looking for a return?'

Ryona shrugs. 'Not with the Pakham involved, Norm ... I'm thinking of the Sicilian murders that the Fly did to crush the Russians organisation. They were a heavy stab to the Baltic heart ...If the Fly's involved then he's got to have a new team ...he's lost all respect as far as the Albanians,

Romanian, Serbs and the rest of the Baltic entourage are concerned...so what remains is to pursue whatever lies at the end of this rainbow with a completely new outfit...I'm thinking if, and it's a big if, he dares take on the Pakham and the Black Angels.'

She smiles. 'Don't underestimate this Fly...he's a multi billionaire, a man of power,'

Joe sighs, turns to Lenny Jameson. 'Lenny you got any thoughts on what's just been discussed?' Lenny turns to the team. 'There's a number of new kids on the block that this Fly could recruit. But he'd want the best and would have to go and negotiate with the new, top of the tree, terrorist killing machines and that would be the most feared outfit on the planet...the IS...Islamic State.'

Norbert interrupts 'But I don't think they're in the US, Lenny...I'd have heard from my people if they'd penetrated.'

Lenny. 'Sorry to disappoint you General...but the Americas, Europe, just happens to be were the gold is ...With the Taliban...now sitting at number two...There's a race on and if the Fly has joined up with either, then America has a huge headache coming on.'

Joe. 'So let's take it one step at a time...we go for Ottermanze...we need to start with the Alpha.'

Lenny shrugs. 'Let's hope he talks, Joe.' Joe, smiles. 'Believe me Lenny he's going to talk.'

Roberto. 'Seems we're on the starting block of one baffling unknown quest. Looks like the Windy City, Chicago, is were we need to find some answers.'

Norbert holds out a hand, palm up, 'Flight s are already booked guys...Joe, on your call...courtesy of one Uncle Sam, airforce transporter...I thought it best kept in house...It's scheduled to land in Minnesota... where you'll take your own vehicle into Chicago....I have it on good authority that Ottermanze and his Wolves have booked themselves into

'The Templeman.' The hotel overlooks the Trump Tower that sits opposite, over the East River.'

Joe asks Norbert for a safe house that could give the team complete cover, no outside interference, preferably a remote private hideaway.

The General nods. 'Let's get in touch with my man Colin Stone...he's stationed in Gary Indiana ...but what Colin doesn't know just ain't worth knowing. ..You'll have that hole in the wall given on your arrival, Joe.'

Joe gives a nod of thanks, asking. 'What times our flight General? ..We need to keep up to the arses of Ottermanze and his pack.'

Norbert. 'Whenever you've ready, Joe...Captain Peter Sassinger is holding his flight for ten hours, awaiting your green light.'

Joe looks to his team . 'We go inside the next two hours General.' He checks his watch. It's showing 7.46 pm. 'Tell Captain Peter we're ready.'

7
ENTER THE SCARAB

Over on the French German border town of Colmar the five sat down to a fine three course dinner of a Soupe a l'oignon starter, a Confit de Canard main and to finish, Tarte Tatin with ice cream. The drink on display was an absinthe Green Fairy.

Conrad Wolff sat at the tables head, to his right hand Ferdinand Cortez and to his left sat the Pakham betrayer Sergio Romano. All three were eyeing their guests with an air of suspicion. But who could blame them for that. The two infamous terrorist killers and leaders of the breakaway group from the IS, sat, somewhat out of place, in their Middle Eastern robes looking like pirates out of ..Frisco Bay.

They ate, disregarding the silver knife and forks, using their fingers, and occasionally, the spoon. Tearing like hyenas at the duck main course.

At the young age of thirty five years Jahaad Shadeer was known to be the youngest ever leader of the new terrorist organisation the Scarabs. Coming out of the Afghanistan mountains he had been brought up on a born-to-kill all westerners program. He sat with an Islamic bandana wrapt around his long black hair, his face half covered with a heavy bushy black beard.

He grunted as he ate in a purple full gown that was belted with a colourful throng that showed the carved bone knife handle on display. He wore boots of camel skin leather his fingers held many rings. His body was brown skinned going into black. Overall he gave off an image of a man to be feared. He was known as The Impaler and was said to have beheaded several hundred men and then spiked them on a high pole scaffold as a warning to all who fell short of his expectations. Sitting to his left was his shared command, Koo Kourijarri, dressed similar attire in a robe of a dull orange colour, around his waist a thick leather belt with holster. It's contents covered by an over flap. He sat in sandals. Looking like he was well into his forties, and a large six foot hulk of a man. he too wore a full beard. They both had hung around their necks, a gold chain with a gold Scarab attached. Hence their organisation name of 'Scarab'.

The dinner ended and little had been discussed between the two parties.Now was the time. The Scarabs took coffee, declining the Green Fairy that was offered. It was Jahaad who opened the conversation by saying what a wonderful dinner their host Conrad had served them. He hoped the host wasn't offended by their refusal of the Green Fairy.

Conrad replied 'Not at all, it's each to his own.'

Jahaad goes on. 'First let me say, and I speak for my partner Koo here, that we were somewhat surprised by your calling card that your servant Sergio presented...Surprised to say, and you must understand us, with no disrespect to your status.'

He holds up a palm.'The Russian Bratva, why did you pull out and so left the door open for them to negotiate with the Pakham, bringing in the BlackAngels? You must tell us this Conrad, I will then translate to Koo who knows no languages but that of his ancestry tribal tongue.'

Conrad smiles, nods. 'What you ask Jahaad is what I would ask if our positions were reversed.'

Conrad turns to Ferdinand, he waves a hand to him.

'My aid Ferdinand, through his many contacts with the underworld, heard that the Bratva had approached the Pakham with their intention of seeking revenge for the Sicilian murders I instigated. Also that they would receive a guaranteed quarter part for revealing to them my original plan. The Pakham, as suspected, agreed, saying he would pursue, with his strongest team, an entourage that would bring in the Black Angels.

Conrad laughs. 'He yearns for revenge to see my body bound and chained on the mast head of 'The Constellation' his personal sailing vessel.'

He rubs the shoulder of Ferdinand. 'My closest friend Ferdinand informed me of your existence...your ever growing power...you and your Scarab organisation were enough to convince me to ask for your involvement...A partnership.'

He sighs, 'But I'm a man of his word Jahaad...by giving you half of the spoils..my half will go, equal shares, to be split between the German based biker group the Bandido's a strong group of South American Grouchos , Iraqi Al Salam 313 and the Arab Hezbolla.'

He bows before going on. 'Of course they will act as your soldiers for Koo and yourself will be in command...Our opponents, the fucking Rakham and his army, will find themselves facing a gale force wind in trying to outsmart the Scarabs...one could say a hurricane will hit them.'

He smiles and touches Jahaad gently on the arm. 'You should remember my friend that you are exterminating the westerners that you so rightly hate.'

He holds out a hand palm-up and looks into the Scarab leader's eyes showing fire. 'Your soldiers Bandidos 313 and Hezbolla are all IS in some small way. They are eager to follow your lead.'

Jahaad turns to Koo and translates Conrad's words. Koo begins to nod whilst staring at the three Frenchmen. He smiles, showing a mouth with several gold fillings, before replying to Jahaad.

Jahaad shrugs. 'We will go with you on this journey my French friend. But we feel the need to go through your plan with care, we are not in the habit of loosing soldiers, be they true blooded beetles or biker mercenaries.'

He winks to Conrad.'Your fruit has fallen, in your most recent ventures, uneaten and rotting ,while ours continues to ripen to its full maturity.'

Again he shrugs. 'You have been hurt and have lost much respect.'

He gives Conrad a gentle nudge fist to fist....'So let's get your orchard back to what it was...out of the fog and into the sunshine...what say you friend?'

Conrad nods, smiles. 'It's true, your words Jahaad, yes, I'm needing a little sunshine ...No, not a little, a lot. We must do this in full agreement, satisfaction for all parties.'

He sighs 'If God is good,my friend.'

Jahaad laughs, saying. 'Your God, Our God is that great yellow ball of fire in the sky, the Sun....he is the power, with out his shining light we all die.' He slowly puts his hands together in prayer and looks up. 'Gold melts, iron rusts, brass will tarnish as steel will bend...That's a known truth..if that ball explodes there will follow a nothingness, a black hole ...that also a known truth...The Sun he is the power..He and only he is my God mon ami.'

It was a somewhat bitter cold late afternoon when the US air cargo transporter landed in Minnesota at the Camp Ripley National Guard Base...A Strip that was near to St. Cloud.

Joe Delph and his team bade farewell to Captain Peter Sassinger and his Loadmaster crew to find, as promised, on arrival their escort Colin Stone ready to move them. As far as Joe could make out, to a safe house that was once an iron ore office block that stood in a heavily wired off compound.

Colin was saying it was to keep the kids out as some of the abandoned pits could become death traps. He also said it was known to be used by a few FBI agents to keep a prized prosecution witness, safely tucked away, before certain trials of known mobsters.

Colin added. 'The airs not too good but the office itself is large and comfortable, with sleeping quarters for eight persons. It's got all the facilities; water closet, kitchen with fridge and microwave. On General Porters orders it's stocked to capacity.'

He winks. 'There's a separate fridge of nice cold beer, multi channel TV, along with wi-fi. All the comforts of homes. So good I'd often thought of moving in myself... probably would if it wasn't for the bleak winters. Sometimes nothing can move, with snow drifts some ten feet high. Then of course I'd have to move George Parker out...He's the caretaker...Don't worry, he's been given a month's holiday he's off visiting his daughter in sunny San Francisco. He thinks there's a witness. a trial on the go.'

Joe enquires. 'The General said something about transport, we have that I hope?'

Colin smiles and says. 'That's right Joe, you're in it...It's not a Ferrari but it'll take you over any road, dirt, and up a mountain those winter days.'

He pats the dash. 'With this baby you have a chance, with a Ferrari you got a lockdown...four wheel drive, you'll need the road suspension she's got rubber on her wheels like a wrestlers jockstrap.'

Joe laughs. 'Ok, Colin you've convinced me, I'll take your word....Norbert said there was nothing you wouldn't know... our needs, we'd only to ask. But an auto expert..now that's one prized extra on your ticket...What more can I say but thank you for that...It's nice to know that your horse can jump.'

Roberto queries. 'Seems a little ways off Chicago, Colin, I'd have thought a safe house a little closer.'

Norman agreed saying. 'Theres got to be some reason. Like Roberto says, it's a long way to take the shopping home.'

Ryona adds.'Maybe we should take a closer look at the reason why Ottermanze is billeted in Chicago, not Washington DC, This action isn't going down on the West Coast ..San Francisco, Portland or Seattle. To me, it's due to break in the land of the Bears.' She sighs. 'Then again it's just a woman's opinion.'

Lenny and Frazier look at each other and nod towards Ryona. Lenny puts up a finger, saying. 'I'll go along with the woman's thinking.'

With Frazier commenting. 'Sounds as good as any we're likely to hear, especially coming from a woman with a brain.'

Ryona smiles puts up a thumb. 'Well thank you guys, nice to be appreciated.'

Joe, nudges Colin. 'See what a team of togetherness I have.' He winks. 'Really they could do this job without me.'

Colin replies. 'You cannot substitute strength in numbers, Joe..it's good that you know who's walking alongside when the kettle's boiling.'

Norman. 'Speaking of Kettles boiling..How about we pull in somewhere for a brew?'

Colin. 'Just say the word guys, there's a truck stop coming up...I'll take a break, could go for a leak anyway.'

Joe. 'OK but no more than half an hour....how long to our destination Colin?'

We have another hour, Joe, One and half with the truck stop.'

Joe looks down at his watch. 'So we're expecting a late night arrival...What's this site called?'

Colin answering to all, 'The mine was named The Penabscot Hollow...it's been dead these last twenty five years...It's situated north west of Hibbing. They opened up late, ended early. A shaft collapse with sixteen men lost. Tunnelling was said to be unsafe, after a period of what the miners call weight bumps. Of its thirty year life it took a good many souls to their graves. Some are still down that hole....Our watchman George once told me that he can, on some nights, still hear their cries coming up through the shaft.'

Ryona shrugs 'I thought you said it had all the comforts of home, Colin...Cries from mouths of the dead...I don't think so.'

Lenny. 'So this ideal home Colin, what's the distance in mileage from Chicago?'

Colin replies. 'It's some Five and a half hundred miles, it would take you around nine hours to move taking the main routes.53 south and 1-94 east.'

He gives a big smile and a wink to Joe. 'May seem a bit of a journey to you Brits. ..but a drive in the park for us Yanks.'

Norman, with the shake of his head, says. 'So whenever we take this Alpha..we have to carry him a nine hour journey back to base?'..somehow don't seem right to me, Joe.' He shrugs. 'Just has to be another way.'

Joe , 'If anyone has a better idea then let's hear it, we're all ears on this.'

Ryona speaks with much certainty. 'Haven't we got our friend in Delta Force, Colonel Scott.' Bet he could move the Alpha quicker than a hound out of trap.'

Joe claps a hand and smiles,saying. 'Now you see, Colin Stone, just why.' He points at Ryona, that fine little missy's in my team...she's an all action woman that carries a fine brain in that pretty looking head.'

Joe, addressing the team, 'What Ryona has suggested is the perfect answer to Norman's feeling of uncertainty on how we handle Ottermanze...I will give Scott a crimson call... or maybe it's better to go through Norbert.'

Roberto adds. 'Going through General Porter would be best Joe, he'd appreciate your trust in him, that I can be pretty sure of.'

Joe nods. 'OK, that's how we carry the shopping home, Colonel Scott...that, of course, is always assuming he's available.'

Roberto, 'I'm sure the General will more than see that he is, Joe.'

Frazier mumbles, 'We've got to take this Alpha down first.'

Lenny adds, 'We're still nine hours and a day away from that, Dave...That's by road, If we fly, then we'll be there inside an hour, I'd have thought.'

8
PENABSCOT HOLLOW

The team took their intended break in the Honks 17 Truck Stop. getting strange looks from the restaurant tables that were occupied with what looked to be an all nations tug-of-war team; drivers of the large ion-ore carriers that filled the joint's parking space. Neatly lined in rows of four abreast. Some filled to a state of overload.

Colin had said these had come down from Hibbing, destination anyone's guess. The empties would be driven to the pits to be filled and would be back in this very park tomorrow. Sadly, none would fill at the abandoned Penabscot Hollow, known by all the red iron ore digging miners as The Cemetery.

The team stuck to the half hour that Joe had given them with little discussion of Chicago, the next stage of the mission. Colin had returned to the table after insisting on paying the tab. He smiled as he approached and whispered.

'Old Honk over there behind the service bar was asking me who you were...I told him that you were time and motion staff. keeping an eye out for the ore companies on any quicker delivery service to their customers.'

Joe grimaces. 'For fucks sake Colin, tell me your joking.'

He looks over at the tables the men that were quickly vacating Truck 17 becoming empty as the drivers made for their vehicles.

Joe turns to the team, 'I Think we'd better make our exit too, we've just cost old Honk a lot of business. As they left Honk shouted out,

'Company cockroaches...go take your stop watches somewhere else to do your calculations...I don't need your tick tocks to tell you to get the fuck off my park.'

Colin, putting a finger to his lips hushes Honk, telling him.

'There's a lady present mouth, so just shut it, keep it closed or we will hit you everyday and night for a month, see how your business thrives then.'

With that Honk seems to panic somewhat mumbling a sorry, apologises in Ryonas direction. They all leave grinning like Cheshire cats.

The rest of the drive was spent discussing the Chicago hit. Joe had already gone for letting Ryona and Roberto book into the Templeman to give a twenty four seven watch on the Alpha and his Killing crew...Joe stressed to them. 'Find his, the Ottermanze's weaknesses. On their leaving, then be prepared to follow...Lenny and myself will give back up. In regard to first changeover...Norman and Frazier will be in the vehicle with Colin driving, Colin will, on the changeover, pick up Ryona and Roberto.'

Joe can see the teams attentiveness, their eagerness. 'Should there be need for a second interchange then Norman and Dave will leave the vehicle and follow the Wolf droppings. Lenny and I meantime will take their place in the vehicle.'

He began to jab with a finger raised. 'On no account lose them...If you need to, use any means to keep them in view, ask for assistance and we're right behind you.'

Joe pulls out a small box from his pocket and passes it to Roberto.

'In the box is a bug, a stick on little gadget that once fixed gives a beep to a little monitor that will be with Colin in the bus. Somehow Roberto you have to get that bug attached to a Wolf ...Ottermanze would be the best target...You will see it's so tiny no bigger than a watch battery get that attached and our job becomes a lot easier.'

Roberto smiles, 'I may have to hug and kiss him like some lost brother, Joe, but not to worry we'll think of something.'

Joe.sighs, 'Let's hope, but listen to me carefully now, don't take risks.' He tells his team, 'That goes for each and every one of you...we will probably have only one opportunity to take Ottermanze...we cannot afford to miss it...so let's do this like the professionals we are...Ok, thats enough said for now, let's get to base and a good night's kip, we fire off to the Windy City come the morrow.'

It was late when Joe and the team finally arrived at Penabscot Hollow...they had each given the nod to Joe's plan of waiting for the right opportunity to take the Alpha, with Lenny also adding that they would need to include the extermination of Ottermanze's soldiers for the operation to be a complete success. Joe asked them all to give it some thought, but saying enough for one day, who knows what Chicago will bring.

Penabscot looked like it could never again begin to produce the red ore from its abandonment, rust and decay were scattered all up to the mineshaft head, with its broken windows on every outbuilding and electric cabling hanging like a lion tamer's whip. First impressions of just like home sweet home, it was not. But then Colin pulled up alongside of what looked in complete contrast to its surroundings. With windows all intact and clean, electricity at the flick of a switch, fresh water in its pipes, seemed the caretaker George had not let his residency run down. For a watchman he lived in style.

Joe nudged Colin, saying. 'What a nice surprise...I was beginning to feel...well, ugh to this place.'Colin. 'Thought you'd like it.' He winks, 'Just don't let the miners down the hole keep you awake.'

Joe winks back at him. 'They won't.'

Strange as it was a few of the team would find it difficult to sleep, those doomed men of so many years past, would keep them up and awake most of the night.

Meanwhile it had been party night at the Templeman in Chicago. Ottermanze and his Wolves had taken time out to celebrate their entry into America. All the false passports and identification papers had caused no reaction from Custom and Excise. That left the Pack feeling good...the forger Zeztak had obviously done a brilliant job.

Ottermanze had told his Zetas of a call he was expecting. One very important call that would be giving them their next instruction. Stay out of trouble. The party they'd just had would be their last till the action was over. That the Templeman was only a temporary base...the part they would play was destined for elsewhere. Arrangements were being done to finalise this. Once completed then he would know. He finished with a grin saying.

'Is it too much to ask for you fucks to stay sober with no Vixen to shag for a while?'

Stravac the Red answers. 'Only if you happen to be a tea totalling puff my Alpha.'

This brings roars of laughter from the pack with Hans himself having to join in with a clap.

Hans smiles. 'I don't think, Red, that we have any gays in our pack..do we?..Speak up now or forever keep your leather zipper up.'

They again laugh. Ottermanze holds up a hand then warns them.

'You must have your joke but I'm fucking serious when I say to you. No women, no heavy drinking.'

He sighs, 'If you break these rules, then I will come down on you.'

He shakes an angry fist at them before softening with,

'But tonight you enjoy yourselves my rules begin to take effect from tomorrow.'

O'Hare International Airport, and into the arrivals walked the three journeymen from the Air France Jumbo They'd intentionally split into two parties, with Rahaad and Koo in long white robes each carrying a man's shoulder bag. As they lined up at their designated passport checkout Rahaad looked back at the figure of Sergio Romano who was a short distance away and following an elderly couple.

A feeling of suspicion came from the female officer on taking a look at Koos details. She asked. 'You are a tea salesman, how long do you intend to stay in the United States..Mister Goresha?'

It was Jahaad that answered for him, saying that Mister Goresha knew little English and that he, as she would see, belonged to the same Pakistan company 'Greenleaf' that Mister Goresha was the company's main tester and he being his translator would answer any queries on their sample products, which were in baggage control, and that they would be staying for no longer than one month.

The woman seemed satisfied and asked Rahaad for his passport, seeing his title of translator indicated, she stamped both and handed them over, saying.

'You'll find we're coffee drinkers here in the US..Mister Lassaram.' She shrugs. But best of luck, enjoy your stay.'

When it came to Sergio Romano, he was just a tourist in Chicago to take in the sights and sounds being a huge jazz and blues fan. But he'd come mainly to watch the Chicago Bears who were right on the edge of making the Super Bowl final. He was hoping she didn't ask him any questions on the current team, it's line up, it's stars, because he wouldn't be able to give her an answer. But thankfully, she wasn't a football fan..more baseball and a White Sox.

She looked through his passport and stamped it. 'Have a nice holiday Mister Cohen.' She smiled and waved him through.

He sailed through Custom Control his baggage being a small designer Louis Vuitton. He could see that Koo was having a problem; with customs opening and going through every sample of tea he was bringing in. Jahaad gave him a shrug and he continued to exit and find where their vehicle and its driver was parked. He glanced at one hulk of a man in a short sleeved shirt and black waistcoat with a Bears cap. He was holding up a card with the name Sebastian Cohen written on it. He waved and made towards the man.

It was some half an hour later that Jahaad and Koo finally came out of the terminal. Jahaad snarling and shaking his head. He spoke to Sergio. 'Thought we'd never get out....anybody would have taken us for some kind of terrorists.' He laughed slapping Sergio on the shoulder. He looked at the driver. 'And you are?'

The driver answered giving his name as Andreas, offering his hand. Jahaad declined to take it saying. 'Get us out of here, you know where we're going. Is it far because I am tired?'

He gives a deep sigh. 'I need to rest.'

Andreas tells them it's a mountain retreat that's about seventeen hours away, some 1250 miles crossing America north to west. The other members have been arriving in small numbers. That he feels there's no more to come. He's calculated that about a hundred or so have gathered, awaiting their arrival.

Sergio asks. 'This retreat, it's secure and guards have been posted to ensure the utmost privacy?'

Andreas assures him that this has been done. That the lodge was situated on a plateau that overlooked a dense forest. It has remained a private residence of one Sadat Malik the oil billionaire.

Sergio winks to Jahaad saying. 'I know of this man, he's a close friend of Conrad. His wealth he owes to my boss.'

Jahaad nods saying ' A man who owes is not always a friend Sergio.'

He smiles. 'Didn't you yourself betray a lifetime friend for money? ..That action alone would make all who came in contact with you guard their interests.'

Sergio shrugs taking his eyes off Rahaad, but in doing so, can feel the doubt that is being emitted from the Scarab leader.

9
THE OVERSEER

Nadia Metzikova and her father Boris had arrived from St Petersburg for the American Tennis Championships that were to be held in the forthcoming week at New York's Flushing Meadow...Nadia had a world ranking of seven and had been training exceptionally hard, hoping to take back to Russia her first championship trophy. It had come to them both as a great surprise to be offered the private jet of Ivor Stenenski the Pakham. His kindness making her more determined than ever to return triumphant.

Little did they know that, hidden safely away in the jets fuselage, was Bratski Onasskikoff, a 50-year-old Black Angel. This son of Satan was feared, coming straight out of the Gates of Hell. Known as the Overseer he had arrived to control the Wolverine operation.

It was hard to imagine that the Black Angel brotherhood had existed at the time of Christ and the Devil's servant Judas who had taken the pieces of silver and betrayed the son of God. The brotherhood could be attributed to many evil acts in their long history. Though few people know the Sicilian Mafioso word of honour, 'Omertà' had originally been a Black Angel origination long before the earliest born Mafia adopted it.

Sitting somewhere in a secret location, believed to be a cave in the French Alps mountain range, it was said by a Middle Eastern seller of antiquities, that they'd bought from him a piece of rock from the Garden of Gethsemanie and mounted in it were pieces of silver and a cross, bearing Christ, that hung upside down. It has never been confirmed but it's said that the Black Angels have had, for centuries, the much sort after chalice, The Holy Grail. And so the stories continue with only the Brotherhood knowing the truthfulness of it all.

A tiring day for the three, and Jahaad had no intention of facing the gathered multi-racial bikers. He informed Andreas to leave any such ideas that the faithful might have till the morrow. He just hoped that the gangs had taken to his Scarab army of fifty assassins. Andreas nodding and saying. 'You will not be disturbed Excellency.'

Jahaad went on to add that Andreas could wake him the minute the sun rose though he doubted it's godly appearance would show before 6am.

Jahaad lay in his bed knowing only too well what the bikers gangs were likely to do. Conrad having already gone through each stage of his original plan, had gone on to say that his plan would only work if, like some giant jigsaw, you had all the pieces, with no parts missing. With both Koo and Sergio in agreement on how he would play it he could see nothing that could go wrong. Yes, it would all knit together nicely.

So a after a good few hours sleep, come tomorrow, he would address those gathered on the mission he'd named 'The Take.' His last thoughts before his body gave way to exhaustion was that he had the very best team of assassins that money could buy, money always being the main issue in any, known mercenaries operation, especially when it comes to putting your life on the line. He smiled, these Wolverines being mere amateurs in comparison to his Scarabs, a name most sacred and revered by the ancient Egyptians. He had the professionals.

So trusting Conrad on his word that the support he'd contracted out would not disappoint, the Bandido's, 313's, and the Hezbolla, would have to perform has he would not put his Scarabs in first line action, His beloved Scarabs would remain in reserve, should things go wrong.

Although he'd thought the Wolverines amateur status, he'd always been taught by the best terrorist organiser, Bin Laden never ever to underestimate your opponent. That It doesn't take a pro to pull a trigger, that everyone has his weak point as well as his strong. He had stressed to Conrad that it wasn't easy to find an opponent's weaknesses.

Conrad had smiled asking him. 'Are you telling me that you, Rahaad have a spot, a weakness?'

He'd laughed and answered. 'Now that would be some admittance Mister Wolff...Why, I have had many enemies trying to find that out.'

He had shrugged before saying. 'But that day will surely come...maybe when my last Sun is going down, with all of my body functions fading...Only a very wise man will find my secret and what he must do to take my crown.'

Conrad had nodded. 'I only know in my wisdom that a man's weakness is always a deep love of his family...I only say this from experience, for I have been betrayed, due to this truth and love of their family they have broken their Omertà...I tell you no lies when I say, to their heavy cost.'

He laughed. 'But see I'm still in control, Jahaad..,There's an old ancient saying 'Out of the fire will fly the new born Phoenix.' Jahaad had smiled at that and told him.

'We are of similar make, Conrad, like brothers. Your weakness along with mine lies deep in the soul. We will always be strong, my brother, unstoppable like the earths great oceans You have my respect.'

Conrad had shaken his hand with a firm grip.

'Your respect, Jahaad, and mine yours my brother.'

Awash with these thoughts the Scarab leader drifted into a restful sleep.

It was 6.30 am and Joe was being woke by Norman It's 6.30, Joe , you said for me I to get you out of the feather....You slept good I hope ...Ryona and Roberto's got breakfast on the go.'

Joe stretches . 'That's good Norm, tell you the truth, it's coffee I'm after.' He yawns. 'Everybody up Norm?'

Norman smiles. 'You're the last to rise, Joe, nobody had the heart to wake you, you sure was driving the sheep home.'

Joe nods. 'That's the best night's kip I've had for a long time....If those poor buried miners were crying out I wouldn't have heard them.'

Norman. 'They must have had a good night too, Joe, not a peep from them although Dave and Lenny swore they could hear them.'

It was Ryona who shouted into the room.

'You got Rip Van up yet Norm?'

Norman answers. 'He's up on his feet girl ready for a full english...best serve the coffee.'

Joe shouts out to her. 'Thank you Ryona...give me two and I'll be with you.'

He turns back to Norman. 'Is Colin about Norm?'

Norman nods. 'Yes ,he's just given our ride it's oil and water check, tank full of fuel.'

Joe. 'Good, it's just that I got a request from Norbert last night asking if I'd like to keep Colin aboard.'

He shrugs. 'I told him yes we could fit him in...So Colin's our new team member. According to Norbert he's highly thought of and has seen a lot of action.'

Norman nods. 'I like the guy, Joe, he told me in conversation he was ex Delta Force, so can't be bad.'

Joe. 'Oh that reminds me, I also received a call from our good friend Colonel Scott Brady Jones saying he's got the bacon on...That he'd be bringing a ten man squad of top A's ...He was saying that it's time we finished what we started back in Texas with these terrorising bastards, put them all six feet under for once and for all.'

It's whilst sitting at breakfast that Joe tells of the new addition to his team. He could see his announcement had even suprised Colin, apparently Norbert hadn't told him, leaving it for Joe to give him the good news. Colin turned to them all and thanked them for accepting him. Adding that the people carrier was all fuelled up and ready to roll. Roberto said he would share the drive as nine hours was too much to ask of one man. Colin estimated they would reach Chicago around 5 pm. that's if Joe decides to move in the next hour.

Joe stands and gives Colin a pat on his shoulder saying. 'Let's rock and roll Colin... We have nice accommodation in a remote guest house... Ryona and Roberto have a room in the Templeman.

It had taken a little over the nine hours to finally arrive on Chicago's outskirts. This was mainly due to a pit stop, but not at the infamous Honks Truck Sop 17, but a restaurant some hundred miles south-east of it where a funny event happened. On the teams entry, a group of Truckers rose from their tables and made for the exit.

Colin smiled, saying.'Seems us being time and motion is moving through the state. One of the drivers I'd seen previously in Honks joint.'

They'd arrived at Sandra Peterson's guest house which was situated about three miles from the famous Wrigley Field, home of the Chicago Cubs baseball team. With Joe saying, 'If we get finished I'd like to watch the Cubs.'

Sandra's place was an exclusive lodging house for CIA agents who entered Chicago from all over the USA...The widowed forty two year old was a pretty good looking lady. Colin went on to explain that her husband Bill was ex CIA who had sadly lost his life in action when a Cartel gangs shoot out had resulted in three CIA agents dead, Bill being one of them. Mexico City streets still continue to gutter the dead of these gang held interchanges. Sometimes fifty bodies can be found each morning after a night's tit for tat war.

Now Sandra opened the house to the CIA's agents. Many having passed through on their way to various missions. There was nothing Sandra missed on the gossip that flowed safely through her home. She even knew of the three executed agents murdered by the Black Angel in Bavaria.

She did go on to say that Joe and his team were the first Brits to stay at 'Peterson Lodge'. Finding that Dave Frazier was Scottish made her look out for him all the more as she herself just happened to be of the same bloodline with her maiden name being McFee. She gave big Dave Frazier that little bit of extra attention, especially when finding out that Dave was unmarried.

Furthermore, she'd given him and Norman the best room in the house, not that the other nine weren't first class. Norman had observed that she'd gone so far as to have taken down all of Bills photographs. He'd given Dave the nod and a wink, saying. 'Sandras sure got an eye on you Davie boy, and I tell you no lie in saying she's a very pretty woman.' He winks. 'You know my fine friend you could do no wrong in taking on such a class lassie as Sandra.'

Dave smiled, saying 'I'm giving it some thought Norm but remember she lost her first husband whilst he was with the CIA, hate for it to happen to her again. But one thing she's got going for her that's a definite plus.'

Norm asking. 'What's that Dave..this plus?'

Dave smiles and winks. 'Why she's a Jock, Norm...a McFee.'

With Ryona and Roberto firmly settled in the Templeman, what it now all boiled down to was for the Alpha to make his move. Ryona thought it a good time to move first. This was on learning that Hans Ottermanze was a man who enjoyed any spa facilities that happened to be going, had to be free of charge, with no sudden surprise come the time for the check-out.

So it came as expected that the man would partake in an early morning sauna. Roberto finding him standing outside the steam room in his Bermuda shorts and towel ready for its 6-30am opening. Roberto had immediately informed Joe of the chance of a possible take. Ottermanze was a private person when it came down to his toilet. He was not one for company and hoped that the sauna was his for the first hour. He needed to sweat off a few pounds and found the steam room the best place to achieve it. Hans certainly wasn't one for jogging around the park.

Joe gave Roberto the thumbs-up saying, 'Let's go for it, you needle him and we will get him to Minnesota with Scott Brady's little bird.'

Ryona asks about the other ten Zetas? 'Surelythey must vanish along with him.'

Joe, so certain that the play's going to work replies. 'Don't you worry about the wolverine support They'll be cuffed and taken to a Delta holding cell. Lenny and Frazier will accompany Delta with that, just you see to Ottermanze. Remember he's a born killing machine. Get him to the Templeman kitchen where Norman and myself will be waiting with a gurney. Ok.?'

Roberto asks, 'What about the kitchen staff, won't they be enquiring, asking what's going on?'

Joe. 'Oh, they'll be told that Ottermanze has suffered a heart attack in the steam room....As long it's not their food that's caused it, they won't give a fuck...Look you two, this is how we're going to make this play.

Roberto I'll drop you off an instant sleeper, a loaded hypodermic. Give him five minutes to settle. ..Ryona make a sign saying 'Steam room out of order....Roberto follows him in. Under his towel he's carrying the hypodermic. Plunges it into into his neck and in less than a minute he's down.'

Ryona tells Joe to consider it done.

So it's 6.25am. on the following morning agent Roberto Vincento watches a whistling Ottermanze making his way to the Steam Room. Joe gives him a call to say the Zetas are all been cuffed and removed from the building. At exactly 6. 30 am Hans enters the stream room and sits over in a far corner. 10 minutes later and Roberto follows him in. He feels his way over and sits to the left of Ottermanze.

Roberto trying to be friendly says a 'Good morning:' to the Alpha who doesn't really reply but gives a grunt.

Roberto goes on, 'I was thinking that being early I would be alone..But then sometimes it's nice to have company, don't you think?'

There's still nothing coming from Ottermanze.

Roberto tries again. 'You must be new to the Templeman, I'm a resident here..Must say I haven't come across you before, what did you say your name was?'

Ottermanze finally gives in snarling. 'I didn't give you my name, it's my second day here and I'm a man who likes his privacy.' He snorts, 'So why don't you be a nice guy and fuck off out of my space Ok?'

Roberto rises saying. 'Sure, say no more.'

Then as quick as lightning he plunges the needle into the Alpha's neck. Ottermanze tries to rise but his knees buckles and he falls headlong down onto his face, spark out. Roberto presses down on his phone and moments later Joe and Norman appear in white coats, they're pushing a gurney with Joe asking.'So where is this heart attack victim?'

Roberto smiles. 'He's over here, he's fast on. Are we ready to go, Joe?'

Joe 'You bet, good work Roberto. I've got Scott waiting to whisk him of to the Hollow...I'm away with him, I'll take Norman with me. You and Ryona join Colin along with Lenny and Frazier.' He laughs. 'That's if you can pull Dave away from Sandra, the Merry Widow...So let's, how they say in a America, high tail it out of here, because we're all done.'

It was early afternoon when Ottermanze, after being airlifted by Colonel Scott Brady, along with Joe and Norman, a little dizzy still, came out of the drugged sleep that Roberto had administered. He found himself bound at the wrist, ankles and torso to a heavy chair. The chair had been secured to a flat bogey on an iron rail track. He began to gain a little more vision and could make out that he was in a twenty foot square corrugated hut of some kind. He looked, slightly confused, at a hanging steel rope. The rope was six inch diameter heavy gauge, It was coming through the ceiling and going down through a great black hole in the floor. That was directly in front, some ten meters away. He then gazed up through a break in the huts corrugated roofing at a giant spoked wheel where the rope was going around its rim. He struggled against his bondage, shouting out loudly in German.

'What the fuck's going down here?....Where are you … You…you Italian piece of horse shit….You fucking bastard?'…He snarls. 'You dare to fuck with me?'

It was at that moment Joe, calm as you like walked in through a clattering door which had one hinge missing.

The Alpha stared at the athletic looking Joe Delph before asking.

'Who the fuck are you?...Another piece of Italian horse shit.'

Joe smiles, going face to face with the Alpha, he prods him in the chest, saying in English.

'You seem to like using your mouth and the foul words that come out of it Mister Hans Ottermanze the sauna's lover.'

Hans in English with eyes blazing 'I asked you who the fuck am I talking to?'

Joe taps him lightly on the shoulder and says. 'I'm the man, Alpha Hans…The man who decides wether you live or die…A man who, if he doesn't get what he wants will push you in your chair.'

Joe points at the black hole and pushes the chair nearer to it.

'Push you down that shaft ..that's nearly a quarter of a mile deep..Also I will be leaving you with the knowledge that your beloved mother, Gretna, and her house in Essen, will be burnt to the ground

Hans again struggles but to no avail, he snarks, saying .

'You wouldn't dare…Your bluff is weak and holds no threat.'

Joe laughs. 'You think I'm bluffing, after you and your cult of sickos murdered three of my friends, cutting out their hearts and feeding them to a fucking pet wolf..You think I'm bluffing? ..think again you evil bastard.'

With that Joe pushes the chair to within a meter from the great abyss.

Ottermanze begins to sweat profusely, he stammers;

'OK, Englishman..what is it I have that you so desperately seek?'

Joe smiles,winks at him, 'Now we're talking Alpha...but bear this in mind when you answer my question.'

He prods the Alpha again, harder this time.

' If I don't get what I want from you, he winks. 'Then I go elsewhere. But for you Hans Ottermanze your life will end here, your dear mother's, in Essen.'

Hans, showing fear, 'So let's get the fuck on with it. What's your question?'

Joe smiles. 'What are you and your pack doing in America, carrying false passports?'

Joe stabs a finger at him,saying. 'I warn you now, Alpha, give me the wrong answer and you go into the abyss.'

Hans replies. 'Let's get this out English ..You know my name and more...what is yours?'

Joe. 'My name is life or death and that's all you need to know Alpha.'

Hans asks. 'How do I know you will not push me anyway...What guarantee do I have?'

Joe shrugs. 'Only my word...That's if your answer pleases me.'

Ottermanze seems to be in two minds wether he can trust this Englishman's word...Joe interrupting him, saying, ' Well, Mister Ottermanze I'm waiting, which is not a good start on your part.'

Hans bites his lip then answers.'OK,..If this gets about that I've told you ,then I'm a dead man. To live I would need your protection.'

Joe . 'Let's hear if it warrants such an act on my part.'

Hans nods. 'Of course you want to know why my men and I are here.'

He shakes his head, still unsure wether to spill the beans, wondering how much this Englander know. If he slips up then it's into the black hole. He decides to go as far as he dare.

'We have been chosen to take part in a billion dollar heist. A convoy is soon to leave its base manufacturing plant Pantex,Texas. It's destination, the US.submarine base located in Washington west coast. Four, maybe six tractor trailers carrying nuclear warheads. We, being just part of over two, maybe I don't know, three hundred Wolves that will ambush and take over the convoy. We will escort it using our drivers up into Alaska, destination Anchorage. Where the cargo will be airlifted into Russia.'

Joe. 'You say we, who is this we?' Hans laughs. 'You say you know of your friends execution, of their hearts torn from their bodies. Then you must know it's the Black Angels that are masterminding the play.' He grins, 'With the Pakham and the Bratva involved there will be no room for making mistakes, English...All are expert killers with no fear. It will be like world war three has started.'

Joe laughs. 'So you think three hundred Wolves can take on America's most guarded cargo? nuclear warheads to take them out of the country....A convoy that which will be shadowed by the FBI and escorted through every State by local police departments...Little birds will be flying overhead, covering every mile, reporting in on any violation of that cargo, giving warning of any attack befalling the convoy.' He stabs his finger into the Alpha's neck.

'The USA has not forgotten nine-eleven and will in no way let this terrorist action take place....once bitten twice shy Mister Hans Ottermanze. But you won't have to worry about it because you won't be around to find out.'

Hans snarls. 'You gave your word..haven't I told you all I know?'

Joe shrugs, 'I suppose you did and I believe you. Speaking of my word...it's a pity you didn't know me better... Then you'd find me such a liar.'

With that Joe pushes the bogey over the edge and into the abyss. There's a series of screams, bellowing, echoing, then silence.

Moments later the old corrugated door creaks and Colonel Scott and Norman enter. Scott shakes his head wagging a finger at Joe, saying. 'I didn't think you'd push.'

Joe. 'I take it you both heard everything, it's good he gave in, they'll be no surprises for our people,'

Scott nods, 'My people will be warned and so there could well be a last minute change to the Minot Base.'

Norman adds, 'You know Scott, Joe didn't push that bastard hard enough'

Scott winks at them both, saying. 'I wonder what made him throw himself down that hole.'

Joe pats Scott on the shoulder,whispers.

'Thanks for your observation, Colonel, I think we really are done here don't you?'

10

THE WEST COAST

Over in New York Bratski Onasskikoff was secretly leaving the airport in a most elegant dark blue, Italian cut, suit with an Air Force blue shirt and black tie. Four men in their early thirties were taking him out through the staff gates in a black Mercedes with tinted one way windows. Their man aside him offered his hand, saying, 'I'm Ricardo Alfredo....Your host till your business is over, we are taking you on quite a long journey.' He shrugs. 'This is what my instructions are, pick up, NewYork then over to the west coast. You will be staying as arranged by your peers.'

Bratski nodded. 'How far, because I'm ready to rest, I've been trussed up like a fucking sardine for over sixteen hours.'

Ricardo smiles. 'You will rest, sleep all through the night, I'm taking you to catch the Amtrack express that will be going coast to coast, east to west finally arriving in Portland Oregon and my fathers ranch, a breeding farm for the thoroughbred race horse, it's my retired father's speciality.

His dream is to have bred a triple crown winner. Like American Pharaoh, who's giving the mare's his all, down in Kentucky.'

Bratski smiles asking. 'You want I should steal this Pharaoh for you? Say yes and he's yours, but at a cost of one million American dollars.'

Ricardo laughs. 'That would be fine by me ...but my father Don Carlotto he's a man of honour and he would not wish to gain his dream by such an act. I'm afraid my answer would be yes, his no.'

Ricardo had already gone against his father's wishes by bringing, what his father had warned, troubled times. But he was now retired and it was his decision as the new Don to say what goes and what doesn't.

He had upset the old Don Carlotto by shouting at him, something that he'd never done before. He'd soon have a change of mind when seeing the five million dollars that the family would receive when the job was over. He'd given his word that the family were taking no part in its mission.The money was being paid for the housing of the terrorist army.

He told him that he would buy a date of seduction for his favourite mare 'Zara's Sister, a past winner of a group one at a mile. A colt off her from the loins of American Pharaoh. Couldn't that bring him closer to his dream of a Tripple Crown, His father could not be moved from his thoughts of a rocky road ahead, he'd warned him against such a venture but to no avail.

Entering a world of the terrorists was not the way of the family...Seeing black crows his fields was a sign, a bad omen.

Ricardo, on their journey west, could feel that Bratski the Black Angel was worried. After endless phone calls there'd been no word from Chicago. He had gone so far as to toss his phone hard against the train compartment's door.

He had finally asked,of Ricardo, a favour, wanting him to contact a family member in Chicago asking that he go visit the Templeman Hotel an discretely enquire if his people were about. That's all he was asking, that Ricardo do this for him. He needed to know this most urgently and it must be done under top security.

Ricardo could hear him tossing and turning all through the night. Yes the Angel was a very worried man, more so on hearing, two hours later, that Ottermanze and his pack were no longer at the Templeman. Ricardo's contact a member of the Bengamino family, went further, to say that the whole team had left yesterday morning. Their hotel tab paid, leaving no further forwarding address. The now, bad tempered Bratski demanded, no ordered Ricargo to find them.

This ordering wasn't to Ricardo's liking and he said so in not too many words, telling the Black Angel that he wasn't a bounty hunter, his contract was for the housing of the Wolverines.

It was only when Bratski offered a further half million dollars that Ricardo said ok, that he'd find them.

Bratski said he'd only pay if Ottermanze was found within the next 24 hours. That was the deal. Ricardo accepted and so, through the Alfredo family, the search began.

Meanwhile over in Minnesota. Scott was asking. 'Something wrong, Joe...like that Alpha not telling you the truth?'

Joe, nodding his head. 'That's exactly what I'm thinking Scott...Ottermanze knew I was going to kill him. I went a little too far, showing my anger at the murders of the three CIA agents...Oh, he knew he was going to die.'

Norman shrugs. 'So, why tell you of the cargo, the warheads, Texas to Washington, If he knew he was going to die, then better to have kept his mouth shut.'

Scott agrees, saying. 'Norman's right about that, Joe. Why go to such a length to lie?'

Joe replies. 'He's thinking he's a very smart guy, does the Alpha, or thinks he is.'

Joe smiles. 'What he told me was believable..and he's gone down the hole thinking he's served his Omertà to the Black Angels.'

Joe puts up a fist and goes on to say. 'Don't you see, it's a bluff.' He looks to Scott. 'Scott I'm asking you ..because I know you'll have the answer to my question.'

Scott. 'Which is?'

Joe. 'Where would a cargo of Nuclear Warheads be coming from? Who puts these deadly's together?'

Scott smiles. 'Being in the military, I just happen to know this. They'd bet dispatched under the most heaviest of security, loaded on tractor trailers out through the gates of the Pantex Plant. An industry close to Amarillo, Texas.'

Joe, scratching his chin, 'How would we get to know of its next large shipment that would be leaving the plant and its heading?'

He looks at Scott who's giving a low whistle on Joe's question, who goes on to say.

'We need that information Scott..I know that would come under a top secret dossier and they'd want to know who's asking and why.'

Scott gives Joe a weak smile, saying. 'You'd need to leave that with me, Joe...That would be a going down a channel and opening a few doors to our mission.' He shrugs. 'Now would that be wise?'

Joe. 'Think Scott, is there one man who we could approach and boycott these doors?'

Scott taps his brain. 'I'm thinking, Joe...I'm thinking of an old friend of my fathers...A man who's climbed the ladder into the White House....He's Tom Ryland Hawks. He's first agent to the President...He's like Robert Kennedy was to his brother JFK.'

Norm laughs, staying. 'No disrespect Scott, but looked what happened to them...Wasn't it thought to be Mafia hits?'

Joe jumps in with, 'You think the Mob will be involved in the heist, Scott ?'

Scott gives them a wink, 'Better you ask your man Roberto on that one Joe, he's quite the authority on the crime syndicate families.'

Joe takes out his phone. Norman puts up a hand.

Joe asks, 'What is it Norm?'

Norman. 'It's just that I was thinking, shouldn't we be informing General Porter and Anton Spicer...They should be told of what's going down. But your the boss, if you thinking otherwise.'

Joe nods. 'You're right of course Norm ..but let's get this important issue over with and I'll give them both an update.'

Joe puts in a crimson call to Roberto.

Roberto answers. 'Yes, Joe?'

Joe. 'Where are you?'

Roberto tells him; along with Ryona they've just picked up Lenny and Dave from a Delta base in Wisconsin. That being where the Wolverine's were being housed in the holding cells.

Joe. 'OK, I want the team back together, Saint Cloud, Camp Ripley.'

He looks at Scott. 'Camp Ripley, they know us there.'

Joe. 'Roberto you hear that?'

Roberto shouts. 'We're on our way.'

It was several hours later that the team had finally managed to assemble at the Camp Ripley National Guard base, St. Cloud, with Joe having explained that Alpha Hans

Ottermanze was now deceased. He went on to ask Roberto of a possible Mafia link. What his thoughts might be?.

Roberto replied that if anything heavy duty was going down in the world of International Crime and Terrorism, especially in America, then the Mob would be somehow involved. Nothing moves without their knowing. The situation being as it seemed having multiple parties, each wanting a fair slice of the cake.

Yes, Roberto thought they'd be involved...The one thing that would be in the team's favour was a family that was against any hurt being brought to America..the thought of using these Nuclear Warheads, like some attack on Its cities, would bring an about turn reaction.

Roberto saying that even the crime families would not want to see another 'Ground Zero'.

Joe, 'Thanks Roberto, I think we're all getting a clearer picture of what's got to be done...Remember these invaders are all killers. They'll stop at nothing to have the cargo back in Soviet Russia...So, for us, it's a shoot to kill...defending those Warheads...Colonel Scott will be secretly giving his all along with Delta Force to ensure a victory by hitting these killers like never been hit before.'

He went on to say that at the moment we are just guessing on the cargo. If it's the Warheads, how many?... Their destination, we don't know, but in saying that, it's coming out of the Pantex Plant in Texas and likely to be heading for.'....He looks to Scott.

Scott. 'I'm on to this, a guess, but I'm thinking about destination being the Kitsap Naval Base in Washington. It's located on the Hood Canal some twenty miles West of Seattle. It's the home of America's Nuclear submarines, the Seawolves.'

Joe. 'So let's put together our progress so far. First thing first, we have an idea what the killers are here in America for.'

He looks down the table at their grim faces. 'We now know it's not for peanuts, depending on the size of the convoy it could be billions of dollars.'

He opens his arms to them. 'Ottermanze, he throws 300 Wolverine killers at me, but I'm thinking 150 to 200 is nearer to the truth..'

Ryona interrupts saying. 'That's still high, Joe. I don't know what Colonel Scott will get as support against their intrusion into America.' She sighs, but at this moment in time, we are seven. Odds you'd say, in their favour.'

Norman, to Ryona smiles, 'You have to remember Ryona, the convoy's guards...They won't be light handed in the protection of billion dollar Nuclear spears.'

Lenny nods, 'Not forgetting the FBI and all the various State Police Departments, so I'd say those odds are ever shortening.'

Joe, tapping the table. 'Ok, there's also Colonel Scott with a very important gentleman to see. On his meeting, it's then we will know our true strength...Scott.'

Scott smiles, 'I may be talking out of shop, but I'm thinking they'll be a fair squadron of Delta supreme, some forty men at my request..That goes without saying...They'd be hand picked by me, 40 specials with the experience of fighting the terrorist. With a knowledge of what to expect. Islamic State, The Taliban...Also you can add.'

He waves his hand across the room, 'Where we are today...The National Guard....So, you see my friends that we have many options open to us, surely that rolls the dice back in our favour.'

Joe shakes his head. 'The only thing that I'm against, with a too many cooks situation is, It's likely to have at least one infiltration working for the enemy, and that wouldn't be good. Wouldn't we lose the chance of surprise?'

Roberto, nods 'Joe's right, take the Mob, the Mafia would have eyes and ears on everything, they'd have someone breaking their neck to give them such news of any plan we may have decided on.'

He smiles at the team, winks. 'That's always assuming they know.'

It's Ryona who puts up a finger to Roberto.

She smiles. ' That would be a hard thing to keep under cover. But there's another option. We could give out a falsehood, saying the mission is to protect the President, that the CIA have heard that an attempt will be made on the President's life.'

Joe nods. 'What Ryona has suggested isn't a bad idea, in fact it's a bloody good one, definitely worth thinking about.'

Scott adds. 'That's a pitcher's dream ball Ryona has just thrown, I'm all for that, Joe.'

Norman shrugs, 'What about the media's reaction, they're sure to find out if the press and television are anything like in the UK. ..It's good, Ryona's idea, but only if it's acted out in a convincing manner...without flaws .'

Scott laughs, ' I'm just thinking about an attempt on the President getting to the press...We have a bunch of Hilly Billy mercenaries with crazy training camps all over the US....Their racist hands hate anyone who hasn't got a white skin, or come to that any foreign invaders. They'd have a field day exercising their loyalty to America by hunting out these terrorists...Better the press are silenced. These nutters read papers, watch television and look for anything that would start a war.'

Joe holds up a hand, saying, 'Enough, we don't know half of what we need to know. Somewhere, right at this very minute, those terrorists are here in America.'

He shakes his head, 'They're waiting, just as we are, for those plant gates to open. Furthermore, this I can assure you, they know
where that convoy is heading.'

He looks at every attentiveness showing in his team's faces. He bangs a fist down hard on the table.

'We have to stop these bastards ..But first we have to find them…We check every state police department that runs a route from Texas to Seattle, Washington…asking for any unusual activity that's recently occurred within their boundaries…Any damned thing.'

Dave gives a shrug. 'Ain't we telling them we're active, Joe?'

Joe, sighs, nods .'More than likely Dave, but we go with caution, with each team member taking a city on those assumed routes.'

Lenny adds, 'We have to look where they'd not be noticed…An army of 200 men, they'd be foolish to be camping in the vicinity of a city.' He scratches his head in thought. 'I'm thinking a small town, a farm, some rural area.'

Joe can see, just by looking at his teams faces, their nods, that Lenny's point has been taken in.

Scott tells them that whatever route is chosen it will not be taken without full surveillance of every mile.' He puts up a finger. 'The haul will not be done in a day, they'll come up the Texas Panhandle, sweeping past Denver Colorado avoiding, Salt Lake City…These infiltrates will have already picked the ambush spot.'

He turns to Joe, ' I'm thinking they'd be maybe some twenty miles from that takeover area, Joe.'

Joe nods saying.'You could be right on that, Scott, but what I'm thinking is, how the fuck are they going to move it through the Canadian border…Surely that can't be done if it's destination is Anchorage, there's just no way.'

Roberto throws up a hand. 'This is a very expensive cargo and like Joe says, would not be given the time to haul it up into Alaska even if the Canadian border post was attacked, because that's what they would need to do.'

He taps a finger down onto the table and goes on.'They would have to have planned another way..air or sea.'

Lenny, 'They could hide it in some isolated cave in the mountains...Then it would have to be a huge den. Bet there's a few of them old gold or silver mines, holes that have long since been abandoned.'

He waits for a response from Colin, who up to now has just listened to the various thoughts coming out from the team, which Colin does after seeing Lenny giving him the nod.

'When you talk of these abandoned mines, these ghost towns, they're littered all over the place. You'd have to be looking at company developments, these having large entrances that you could drive a freight train through. This is what you'd need, it's all about time. How long can they hold them? They know there'd be a country wide search to locate them.'

Ryona smiles, saying, 'Come on now guys, your all talking of these killers successfully getting these warheads, put those thoughts out of your heads because there's no way they're going to win....Well is there?'

Joe claps, saying, 'You know, Ryonas taken us all into reality...She's hit the nail on the head by saying it's up to us, to see that we don't fucking lose.'

11
THE ALFREDO RANCH

It's early morning and the suns already on the rise at the horse breeding farm situated some thirty miles south of Portland, Oregon.

The old Don was sitting on his porch with contempt of his son's idea of making money by betraying a country he had come to love. Wasn't it his father before him that had said, on their arrival from Sicily, 'If you plant the seed, water and tend to it, the olive tree will grow and live a thousand years.'

He looked about, past his olive tree, a two thousand acreage of fertile land as green as the baize on a pool table. His white wicker fenced compounds that held his thoroughbred horses, a mix of six proven Stallions and some ten Fillies.

It hurt him to see these known killers parading around his ranch like they owned the place. It brought a nasty taste to his mouth. He'd asked his son Ricardo how they'd all managed to enter America, 200 evil men having committed known atrocities. Ricardo had told him they'd entered on various tickets, some for the Tennis at Flushing Meadows.

Some for a motorcycle gathering on Daytona Beach. Others for Hollywood and a chance to see the Stars, The famous Chinese Theatre and the Oscars ceremony, everything planned down to the last detail.

Don Carlotto replied to that, saying. The Tennis, Flushing Meadows, it's in New York, Daytonas in Florida, Hollywood's in California. His son's reply to that was,

'I just take their money for the lodge...It's easy pickings... 4 fucking million for a week or two...Ask any other family if they'd refuse.'

That's exactly what Don Carlotto did. He contacted a few of his old and trusted friends asking for their thoughts on the infiltration of the killers and their planned heist. Asking, why in Gods name were the Mafia involved in this?

He said. 'Don't we love America and hate the fucking Russians and their constant breaking of agreements? Why they're building a fucking Arsenal of nuclear missiles that could on any given day, destroy the United States.'

Don Carlotto told them of his fear of what the Russians could obtain from this heist. Saying, 'I've spoken with Don Antonio Balimissio who, as you know, is up on this kind of knowledge.'

He sighs, 'Antonio tells me that the Soviets have around 3000 Nuclear Missiles, some heavy ballistic babies that can be fired and arrive in the United States 30 minutes later. They're known as Saturn 2's...That's not all. They also have RDS-220's plus Tzar 100 megaton bombs...When you think that weapons grade plutonium would cost 100 dollars a gram, thousands of dollars a kilogram.....A pound of plutonium 238 would cost 4 million dollars to make. ..Plutonium 239 in a critical mass of 6 kilograms would cost 31 million dollars.'

Carlotto asks them, 'Surely we don't want these Warheads...America's defence being taken by the Russians,

Have we gone mad, out of our fucking minds, has madness crept into our organisation?'

Their reply to that was that Don Carlotto must look over his shoulder into his own back yard. Was it his son who was getting a slice of any profits that came from a successful heist...Not all the families were happy with his greed, in having a 4 million dollar thank you coming from Russia. They thought that Ricardo Alfredo had no consideration on what could become a most disastrous time for America. He'd shown nothing but a total disregard for the safety and security of his country. They told Don Carlotto that it was he who must tend to his son's actions, in anyway he thinks fit. Carlotto thanked his friends for their honest reply to his dilemma. Yes, the ball was in his court, he must think carefully on how to play it. His main worry was the life of his son...and his fine stock of horse flesh standing out in the pasture. At all cost harm to either must be avoided. He would sleep on it, that's always assuming he would get any sleep with his brain slowly getting overloaded.

The old wise Don knew what was to come, a mighty showdown. God forbid it happening on his land, near his horses.

In the meantime Jahaad , Koo, and Sergio were leaving Chicago to rendezvous with their Middle Eastern assassins the 313's along with the Hezballo. The Mexican Bandido's having arrived as visiting soccer fans for a forthcoming World Cup qualifier against the USA. The match was scheduled to take place in two weeks time at the L.A. ground of the Galaxy.

The meet was pre-arranged to take place at some luxurious forest lodge that was owned by an Arabian oil Barron, a billionaire who had strong ties with Iran. He'd offered all the lodge facilities for free knowing the power of the Scarabs leader. He'd opened his oasis knowing it was foolish to refuse.

If truth be known he'd supplied all the AK's and ammunition for the mission. But unbeknown to him a leak of his weird activities was being brought to the Mobs attention.. The supplier having business connections with the Mafioso families had leaked out information that asked what the oil man needed 100 Kalashnikov's for.

The Mob already knew of the young Don Ricardo Alfredo's involvement in contract making, but this was to Europeans, the oil Barron, Sadat Malik, was an Arab. This got the Mob into thinking what the fuck was going on, and that they had to be careful of not getting too involved in any future bloodbaths. They knew of Sadat's lodge in the Colorado mountains and so decided to take a special interest in its comings and goings.

The New York boss of all bosses, Don Vito Massarella, said to his Colorado associate Don Sandro Barratello.

'We must not get caught with our pants down, keep me informed Sandro my friend, this young Ricardo and his house of shit worries me.'

Sandro replied. 'It shall be done my Godfather...please do not worry.'

Over in Oregon the Black Angel Bratski was doing cartwheels over not receiving information about Hans Ottermanze and his crew. Ricardo had urgently urged his seekers to find these idiots. There had been no reports of accidents after full hospital checks or of police involvement. How can eleven men suddenly disappear of the face off the earth? Their hotel tab had been paid, then nothing, not a single sighting. Bratski had reported back to his peers of the situation, asking,

'Are we still green to go?'

It was answered by the Pakham himself saying. 'We have millions tied up in this operation, you find this Imbecile Ottermanze and you fucking shoot him. Give the orders to one of your most trusted Alphas , this operation must go through whatever the cost, we are too far into the play. Many are already armed and eager for the heist...You have all before you, the take, The Angels tell me that your the best, Bratski...Well go on and prove it to me....We are still green.'

Scott had suggested that Joe came along to accompany him on his meeting with Tom Ryland Hawk. He'd told Joe that the President was likely to be with Tom to hear about an attack on the United States. Scott had already gone so far as to say that what they had to bring to this meeting was news of an important security leak that involved an attack on America's Nuclear Arsenal. These terrorists were already on American soil, some 200 plus known killers out of Europe and Soviet Russia. Thought to be in hiding, waiting on a given signal, ready to strike.

Joe had thought their hole in the wall was somewhere along the Western coastline. San Francisco to Seattle. These highly trained killing machines had been recruited; the very best shooters that the Russian Pakham could find from the biker gang of German Wolverines, a deadly force in their own right, was a contracted partnership that involved the Russian Mafia, the Bratva, and all to be led by the infamous Black Angels, a secret cult of Satan lovers, Medieval torturous high priests. These sons of Satan were to be feared for they gave no quarter.

What Joe and his team required was Scott and a squad of his finest men out of Delta Force. A complete silence of the press and TV plus authority to go out on a shoot-to-kill if and when necessary. Scott had already done his bit in alerting Tom Hawks of the severity of the terrorist's operation, that the time had come for America to be prepared.

12
THE PRESIDENT OF THE UNITED STATES OF AMERICA

Tom had responded inside the hour saying the meet would take place the following morning at 11 am. They would go through everything in the White House, the Oval Office. A sky bird would be made available for the two to visit, landing on the lawn of the White House. They had been allotted one hour; an extension would be added if called for. Tom had given that the President himself would be present and it will be he and he alone who would have the final say on what's to be done. Always taking in what Joe and Scott had brought to the table Joe could not belive he was to meet up with the President of the United States and all its outer colonies. The President was now in his second period of office and was already regarded as one of the best ever Presidents. Getting to grips with the unemployment issues he had been heavily involved in building new plants and bringing back the shipbuilding yards.

He was helping the car manufacturers by trying to cut the foreign imports saying to congress that America once upon a time, had the finest motor industry in the world. He had promised to bring it all back. He was into health care in a big way, giving the poor man a hospital bed without conflicting insurance issues. John S MacArthur was definitely the people's president.

Knowing this gave Joe good feelings that this man would bow to their needs, giving them full backing on any decisions the team may have to make in regard to a full blown battle.

So after a brief moment with the Presidential bodyguards they entered the outer hall that led to the famous Oval Office of the White House, where there to greet them stood Tom Ryland Hawks. The man Joe noted was in his early sixties. He stood over six feet tall in his high glossed shoes, wearing a dark blue suit and while shirt unbuttoned slightly at the collar. Around his bull neck hung a tie of the Washington Redskins. He still had a good, strong looking, head of hair, black but with touches of grey around his temples. For a sixty plus man he had kept himself in good shape..His body looked like it could do a marathon. He walked up to Scott and hugged him like a lost son.

Saying 'Long time Scott, I was thinking only last week of your father. What with the Dallas Cowboys, Redskin game, sort of brought back all the memories of the days when we used to bet on the game. He still watching the Cowboys, Scott?'

Scott, smiled, saying . 'He's well, Sir, but doesn't like his retirement...He's still a cowboy.'

Tom laughs,'Now that doesn't surprise me at all...I can picture him now sitting in front of the TV. He'll be tuned into CNN.. questioning those political talk shows, throwing his valid opinions at them. Then it's big game time, the

Dallas Cowboys, I've lost many a dollar to him betting against that team...Why one time when the Redskins whopped them good, he didn't speak to me for two weeks.'

Tom laughs. 'You should have brought him with you ...it would have been like old times.'

He turns to, Joe. 'So this is Joe Delph, MI6 from across the pond.'

Tom holds out his hand, Joe takes it. He looks at Scott, saying. 'I already know quite a lot about, Joe.'

He smiles at Joe. 'That's because I looked you up, Joe... When Scott told me your name and that he was bringing you along. I thought.' Tom puts a finger to his brow.

'I've heard that name before, it rings a bell. Then it came to me. The Dallas court killings..That was sure bad medicine...But you poisoned the bastards, fitting end to a sad day for the FBI after losing agents and one up and coming young defence attorney.'

Joe nods, saying. 'I lost one of ours, indeed a sad day Sir.'
...
There's a moments silence before Tom claps a hand and says.

'Let's go in to the Oval and meet John S MacArthur our President, shall we? ...I know he's wanting to meet up with you.'

On the outside of the Oval an agent was sitting reading some sport magazine which he quickly put down and stood up as the trio approached. Tom smiled and gave a quick as you were to the man, who was named Bill. Then went on to ask Bill if the President was in his office. Bill nodded saying that John S had been in there for only a few minutes. Tom pointed to a ledger that was lying on a nearby side table.

'Put us down at entering eleven o five, Bill. ...Scott, Joe, and myself. It's all there in the appointment listings for 1100 hours.' Bill nodded, replying. 'Count it as done, Tom.'

Tom gave a quick rap on the Oval Office doors.

A cry of 'Enter' came out from within.

The President, standing, gave a smile and a nod to Tom. John S. MacArthur was a tall lean man who Joe thought, someway, had a look of the actor Gary Cooper about him. With his hair short cropped and already into the grey, with ice blue eyes, a man who had fought for justice all of his life. He'd been born in Paris, Kentucky and brought up to appreciate both sides of the rail track, having fought proudly for the rights of all men, black, yellow, red or white. His father, like his father before him, taught him to respect and give ear to any man that nursed a problem. Give advice, but only if it would come as a way to solve that problem.

He, like the late Martin Luther King, had a dream. That America could and would, lead all peoples of the world to live in that paradise. Walk the road that would bring peace and no more wars. That the bomb maker and the dogs of war would one day be buried deep, in no marked graves.

And so he stood today with two men, who sadly, had come to him with a problem. Telling him that his America had a problem. A problem that must be solved by any means in a do or die situation. A terrorist infiltration onto American soil, with a far bigger threat than Nine-Eleven ever was. As if that for God's sake wasn't enough. But solve it they would, and they'd work out a plan before leaving his office.

John S turned to his audience, asking. 'So how do we stand at the moment on this. We got anything on these invaders?'

Scott looks to Joe to answer, Joe shrugs. 'We have a good idea Mr. President...We're looking at the West coast, Sir... Somewhere between San Francisco and Seattle.'

The President nods, saying. 'Please, before we get into this discussion, let's get down to using first names; I'm

John...it's much easier when you take away the rankings don't you think?'

Tom puts up a hand, saying. 'I think John has always, through his life, thought all men equal.'

Joe, nodding. 'I have the same rapport with my team, John.'

He shrugs.'Suddenly talking to you man to man makes, for me, a more relaxed atmosphere ...So thank you for that.'

John nods, holding up a hand. 'That's just the way I've been brought up, Joe...My father always said that life was so precious, a beautiful gift handed out to so few...He sort of put everything in pairs...Like from cradle to grave...good to evil, best to worst, Christ and Satan.'

He shakes his head. 'Peace or War...We and so many decent law abiding countries in this world of ours, formed, worked out pacts...These documents were to bring all nations together, to work for this peace.'

He sighs. 'Like I was saying. 'Pairs', they had to be in these worked out agreements somewhere, and they were. Good and Bad, For and Against, Givers and Takers, so it goes on and on. It brought to America Nine -Eleven, a terrorist action that ricocheted around the world and sadly is still with us with no sign of an end.'

Again he shakes his head. 'We have these nuclear ballistic weapons simply because they have them and we need to defend our country...These brain dead zombies, who call themselves servants of Allah, must and will be destroyed.'

He looks to the two of them, then Tom. 'See that Joe and Scott have everything that they need, Tom, but we must keep it secure and safely blocked away from the press, get Frank Osborne to throw a few of his threats at them.' He looks back Joe. Asking. 'You say this heist is a planned Russian ploy, Joe?...If so we have deadly opponents, but to hell with it, we're in a live or die situation ...Which I promise you now, they won't win....Thank God you've come to me with this.'

Joe nods, 'I'm hoping we can overpower these killers and so avoid a massive bloodbath, John...We really don't want that, but I fear it's likely that it will happen...These Black Angels don't bring flowers.'

Joe then went through all that had been established so far, the terrible suicidal leap down the mine shaft of one Alpha Hans Ottermanze, Scott's Delta Force rescue unit having to descend the shaft and recover the body that's now buried in a pauper's grave with no markings.

John S listened intently to Joe telling how they first came to first find out about the heist. The horrible satanic deaths of the three CIA agents, the festival in Bavaria along with the abduction of a Zeta one Thomas Kline, and breaking him into telling of his part in the mission; that he was to travel with Ottermanze to Chicago along with nine other Zetas.

Joe went on to tell of Ottermanze's love of an early morning sauna, which brought about his downfall. Scott and his men took over the Templeman Hotel and arrested the Zetas on charges of entering the United States carrying false identification passports. Overall Joe and his team were slightly ahead with their knowledge of the heist. With Colonel Scott giving his fully appreciated support they'd moved closer to getting nearer to some kind of location of these 200 killers.

Joe shrugs. 'And so you have it, John...I'm hoping we'll be allowed to keep Scott working alongside us. It's all down to finding these 200 assassins before it comes to one hell of a bloodbath. They could have already split into groups, ready to act on the Black Angel's call.'

John S nods, 'Scott will of course remain with you. We must take this Angel from hell down, including his close associates the Alpha...Without the foundation then their building crumbles, with no commandant, they become statically dead.'

He smiles. 'Do you know what Martin Luther King said, Joe?'

Joe smiles, replying. 'I know he spoke some fine words, John...Like the ones your going to tell me.'

John S, laughs nods. 'He said. 'Wars are poor chisels for carving out peaceful tomorrows'....He was a good man, Joe. We could have done with a lot more like him... One day peace will come, that'll be when we have that Super Nova.'

He looks over at Tom and says. 'Give Joe, Scott and their men all the backing they need on this, Tom.'

He turns back to Joe and Scott. 'Now you two get your backsides out of here...You have a very tricky mission on your hands. Go with God and have good fortune.'

13
THE WAY TO AMARILLO

In the luxurious lodge of the billionaire oil Barron Sardat Malik. Jahaad sat with Koo and Sergio discussing their plan for the eventual takeover of the warheads. Rahaad was having to speak in two languages; an Arabic nomadic tribal for Koo then Italian for Sergio which he preferred.Jahaad had offered him a choice of three; Italian, French or English, the Scarab leader being fluent in many languages. He'd had the schooling, having been taught by a great Afghanistan scholar. He held a memory like no other.

He had just completed a fairly long discussion with Koo, with Sergio looking on, wearing a blank expression, trying his hardest to pick up any of the words but they were all alien to him. Koo had listened, giving nods to every word that Rahaad had uttered.

Jahaad turned to him and smiled. Sergio was stunned at the fluent English and Italian that Jahaad was speaking. His Italian was perfect, so good you'd have to think Jahaad hand been born in the land of spaghetti.

Jahaad tells him that having spoken with Koo on his thoughts of his plan, he wanted to make sure that Sergio understood this was his plan, and to entrench it firmly into the Italian's brain.

This wasn't the plan that had been first presented by Conrad Wolff and Ferdinand Cortez. This was the plan devised by Jahaad that had already been discussed with Koo and given his backing.

Sergio shrugs, 'Am I to take it that the plan devised by Conrad will not be implemented...Have you informed him of these new changes?'

Jahaad smiles, 'It's obvious you don't understand why these changes have been made, Sergio.'

He holds out a stabbing finger to the startled Italian.

'How these Wolverines are going to play this heist. I, for one, can imagine...Oh yes, they'll most likely be ambushing the convoy.'

Sill jabbing his finger, 'It will be at night, in the period between midnight and 3am.'

Sergio interrupts. 'But didn't Conrad say that; A night hit, Jahaad?'

Jahaad, shaking his head. 'No he did not, he never did mention anything that indicated a time...What he actually said, I quote his very words, was, when the Wolves have the cargo of warheads securely in their hands we do our play and bring them out of America...But, and I stress this. that time has got to be right. The Pakham is no fool, Sergio, he knows a daylight hit is out of the question, he would have planned for a night ambush. He will surround the attack site, Cutting off any means of the convoy getting out a distress call.' He shrugs. 'Then he has perhaps a little over three hours to clean up and get those warheads hidden.'

He slowly nods his head, thinking, before continuing.

'The Pakham, he would have calculated exactly on where this heist could take place and bring off a successful campaign for the Wolverines.'

Sergio smiles, nodding. 'Then we must find the area Jahaad, just where that ambush is most likely to be, we cannot have that much of a timeframe to position our assault teams.'

Jahaad smiles, winks. 'So you see, Sergio, we cannot always work out successful plans whilst sitting in a cosy armchair drinking Green Fairy...Your Conrads and Ferdinands of this world must overlook the playground and cast out any doubts and replace them with fresh, on the spot, ideas.'

He shrugs, 'But they are not here, Sergio. So all these decisions are left for me to decide.'

Sergio holds up a hand to Jahaad saying, 'But isn't that what you're being paid for?'

Jahaad nods. 'I suppose you could say that my Italian ravioli...Yes, of course you are right to think of it in that way.'

He walked over and patted Sergio on the shoulder, thinking that he didn't like this Italian, he would need to keep a close eye on Conrad's representative, after all the man was a born snake in the grass. Didn't he betray his childhood friend and the Pakham by poisoning all of his Dons. This Conrad must be one hell of a man to persuade the Italian to do this. Many dollars would have to have fallen Sergio's way. This left Jahaad with a bitter taste in his mouth and with the thought, Once a thief always a thief, once a betrayer always a betrayer....Yes, this Sergio would need to be kept under scrutiny. With this he immediately told Koo, who gave the Italian a good once over look.

A look that made Sergio shudder, like someone had walked over his grave. It had him wishing that they could all converse in one language. English would be good, but in his heart he knew that Koo would never have the ability to know anything more than this jabbing Nomadic Arabic. One murdering son of a camel walker his sole attribute being his knowledge of torture and using the meter long curved sabre that he was always sharpening, going as far as caressing this instrument of decapitation.

Jahaad gave a sharp clap of his hands.

'OK, Sergio, I'm thinking it's time to get our act into some order, don't you think?' Sergio nods. 'I'm listening, Jahaad.'

Jahaad continues saying that he will converse with Koo later about their talk.

'We agree that this heist will be done in the late night time hours. Let's say that we go by…Midnight to 3am.' Sergio gives a nod.

Jahaad goes on. 'This hit must be to take out all of the convoy. Just how many tractor trailers we don't know, but the hit has to take out all means of communication rendering the convoy with no means of raising an alarm.' Again Sergio nods.

Jahaad gives a shake of the head. 'It's not going to be easy this I'm absolutely sure about. I'm thinking of one great almighty bloodbath…Many will die, all of the convoys drivers and guards. This must happen to ensure a Pakham success.'

Sergio interrupts.' OK Jahaad… So let's pack it all in and go home…Why not?'

Jahaad smiles. 'Because the reason we stay, my Italian ravioli, is that on this opening play we are in no way involved…The successful heist executed by the Wolves will leave them weakened. Unaware of any further attack coming from our soldiers we will hit them hard, taking them down to their last man.'

He sighs. 'But it's the aftermath that concerns me, we must have that ticket for taking those warheads out of

America, a place to hide, that's got to be the only answer. Then to take them out at some future date. I'm thinking shipping. We would need internal help, this can only come from our Billionaire friend Sadat Malik.' He smiles. 'Yes, the oil man must know people at the right price, that are willing, able, to shift the cargo into a Middle Eastern port...Into calm waters...waters that are a closed door to the West.'

Sergio nods. 'Yes, Jahaad, your thoughts, I must agree, are good and well founded. I can see no faults within your play.'

Jahaad, 'I thought I would please your Siciliano brain but first we must find out where the Wolves have their den. We must be on top, know of their plans right down to the last detail...Because we may have to take them down at their hole in the wall, their storage bays.'

He nods over at the polishing Koo.

'I will leave Koo here, he'd be a risk with any authority check, you and I will do the tea selling.'

Sergio laughs. 'You're not serious about us going out selling tea?'

He looks at the smiling expressions coming from the Scarab, asking. 'Jahaad ?'

The Scarab, nodding. 'Oh yes, isn't that why we're here in America?'

Sergio gives a shrug saying, 'Sometimes you never fail to amaze me.'

Jahaad put up a hand saying, 'So let's go sell some tea.'

Joe and Scott had returned from their meeting with Tom Hawks and the President, John S. MacArthur. Back at Camp Ripley they were going through all that eventful morning with the team of just being in the famed Oval Office and their never to be forgotten talk with the President of the United States.

What was good to hear was that the team, with Ryonas organisation, had worked out pairings for a proposed search, looking for the locality of the Wolves.

Joe gives a smile. 'Ok, let's hear it.'

The team look to Ryona to explain, which she does, giving a wink. 'Why our two Colonels were busy taking in, what I imagine to be a wonderful morning in the White House, the guys and myself were working on what we assume would be the areas to search for this Pakham army. We went by what you'd already said, Joe, that they would be holed out somewhere on a stretch of the West Coast. We decided on pairing up, three pairs, each given a different area to cover.' She looks at Joe for any reaction.

Joe smiles.'Go on Ryona, I'm listening.'

She nods. 'Well, Norman was paired up with Dave, they would cover San Francisco, taking a look-see into the Great Basin, Utah, before heading north from Salt Lake City to Boise, Idaho. Then meeting up in Portland, Oregon'

She then says. 'Roberto and myself would take the area coming out of the Texas Panhandle, making Denver, Colorado on a route up to Wyoming taking in the Bighorn basin then West to Portland, Oregon...That left Lenny and your good self to muster down South from Seattle, Washington...But taking a look around Spokane, a peek into Montana, Missouri River areas. Then west into Portland.'

She looked to Scott with a shrug, saying, 'We thought Colonel Scott would be pre occupied setting up his Delta Force squad...All the pairings, Scott included, would remain on crimson contact throughout this venture and give out any suspected sighting for future consideration. This, we all agreed, would need a period of surveillance on any such interest.'

She shrugs. 'So you have it, Joe...Oh, any such definite sightings of a Wolf should be reported back without contact.'

Joe claps his hands, 'Sounds good, Ryona. May I add, all personal must carry small arms, tucked away out of sight.'

He puts up a finger. 'Never forget who we are dealing with here...These people are killers,you must protect yourselves by shooting to kill first.' He looks to Scott.

'I'm thinking Scott can secure the pistols from here on this Camp....General Barnaby Walsh it's commanding officer, I'm sure will supply us with the necessary arms.'

Scott replies, 'Consider it done, Joe, I'll get on with it.'

Joe gives a pleasing look to Ryona, then to his team, saying

'Fine job guys...We go with it first light. It's been one hell of a busy day but we're getting there. So let's eat and get a good night's sleep because we have another busy day tomorrow. Who knows, maybe two or three more to follow.'

It was after a good nights sleep, at 6. 30am. breakfast call, that the pre-selected pairs took to their assigned vehicles, a selection of various makes of everyday cars, that would travel without suspicion.

Roberto took the wheel of a Buick 4x4 and set out for a likely route that the convoy could take out of Amarillo on to Denver. Swinging around the city and taking in Cheyenne before heading on to Casper, Wyoming. Their interest was in the Rocky Mountains around Butte, a likely hideaway spot.

Somehow Ryona was particularly drawn to that area. Besides they could probably call into Billings which had, supposedly, one fine Italian restaurant. But that was more than likely a day later or maybe two, who knows .

They certainly weren't in any rush to miss the wonders of the Rockies although they knew, somewhere in this neck of America, an explosive clock was ticking.

Amarillo to Butte Roberto reckoned was around 1000 miles. Then they had their overland drive from Saint Cloud, a distance of somewhere near another 1000 miles to Amarillo.

Ryona asks, 'So why not start at Butte and drive down south to Amarillo?'

Roberto,tapping his brow, answers. 'Because whatever way we look at it there's really nothing in it, distances measures about the same...I did think of that my heart.'

Ryona pouts her lips. 'OK, So it's Amarillo, do you think we'll see sweet Marie there?'

Roberto coughs. 'Marie?...I'm not with you sweetheart.'

She laughs, nudging him. 'The song.'

She starts to sing the massive Tony Christy hit. 'Is this the way to Amarillo...'

She winks.'That was so big in the UK Roberto.'

Roberto nods. 'I think here in the states too...especially in Amarillo...great driving music.'

Ryona nods. 'So let's go see our sweet Marie...Hey, don't we ride the old Route 66?'

Roberto gives a smile and a nod. 'Now who's becoming oh so nostalgic in her old age...But yes, we'll go Kansas, Oklahoma City then it'll be 66 right to Amarillo. Although they've cut off the old route, with these super new highways, killing the American Dream...66, a tourist must-drive-before- I-die road. Many of the old places are gone, leaving so little of the great highway left to see...It's a crying shame, needs to be revitalised, bring back the old days...The 1960's, because when it's gone it's gone.'

Ryona smiles and punches his shoulder. 'Now who's being a little nostalgic in their very old age.'

Roberto laughs. 'I deserved that.'

He looks through the Buick's internal mirror then gazes across at her. 'We're not looking that old....Are we?'

She smiles, gives him a wink. 'Only you sweetheart..Now have I got you well insured?..Let's see now.' She pretends to look through her shoulder bag.

Roberto, nods, 'OK, you win, let's just get you down that old glory road to Amarillo.'

A smile, a wave to the other pairs, followed by a shout of 'Good hunting' and Roberto rolled the Buick out of Camp Ripley. It was to take them nearly a week to hit Butte, without a sighting of the Wolf pack. A regular contact on crimson to the others found that neither, Joe and Lenny, Norm and Dave were having disimilar results.

Ryona, slaps a hand hard down on the vehicle dash, shaking her head and asking.

'Where are these guys? ...I felt sure it'd be the Rockies, they've got to be around here somewhere.'

Roberto shrugs. 'Let's go over to Billing, that fine Italian restaurant, the Colosseum. Dinner with a nice bottle of Chianti.' He puts up a hand. 'We need to relax a little, then later we can get our heads around a local map, there could be something showing that we've missed.'

Jahaad felt refreshed after a good 8 hours undisturbed sleep. A breakfast of fruit and nuts covered with an Arab date sauce and black Turkish coffee was served to him in his room. A room giving panoramic views of the Montana Rocky Mountains. The morning August sun was slowly showing its face, rising above the peaks. The mountain air was divine, giving a fresh pine forest delight to the Scarab leader. His billionaire host had planned a dinner for his guests at the five star Italian restaurant. 'The Colosseum some 15 miles away in Billing. Sadat Malik wanted to please Jahaad by opening a new oil flow into Afghanistan. He'd even gone so far as to import two 18 year old Iranian virgin girl belly dancers for entertainment, if required.

Jahaad had smiled, knowing that this would excite Koo who was known for being a man for the ladies. This billionaire Sadat was a worker, a man who sought to please.

So far his arrangements could not be faulted.

Jahaad was against all such forms of sexual entertainment, even though belly dancing had been around Turkey and some Middle Eastern countries for centuries. It was thought the western form of strip-tease had developed from the belly dance. Still Sadat had only shown good intentions to the Scarab leaders and their Italian sidekick. Jahaad caught the sun's rays, glistening with flashes of silver, reflecting off the mountain peaks. The oilman had chosen well in finding and securing a setting fit for a king. A truly beautiful spot that must have cost him a few million dollars, so isolated, sitting amongst the pine woods that seemed to stretch for miles.

He had the very best as far as security went. Guards from a native Iranian province, ex mercenaries who carried AK's, each walking with an African hunting dog, so fierce they would fight to kill. With warning posters every fifty meters or so. 'Private Property No Admittance.' ...'Trespassers will be shot.' All this plus electrified fencing. One really secure fortress. Ideal for the Scarab army's hideaway.

Jahaad looked at his watch, a gold Omega that the Syrian President had given him for a service well rendered. One loud mouthed opposition opponent who was to be silenced, buried in some unknown desert grave, with no comeback to the Presidential office.

Sadat's dinner was scheduled for 7pm. His watch showed 10am. Some nine hours away. He was due to address his army at two. Just an introduction of Omertà to the cause, a serious act that must abide by the code of the Scarabs. An act that the bikers would need to follow. No one would be allowed to leave the encampment. Any breaking of the silence rule would mean instant death. No mobile phones or other means of communication would be allowed. If caught the same would apply, instant death.

Jahaad decided he would take more coffee on the main house veranda. He would ask Koo and Sergio to join him. He would like to know more about the life of Sergio Romano, for the Scarab leader wasn't a man to have too close a relationship with people outside of the Scarab family. This man Sergio worried him a little and most certainly needed to be watched.

Ryona and Roberto had decided to call it a day. Their search taking in Butte and the off trails had once again drawn a blank so a nothing to report call to Joe on crimson. Joe too had nothing, telling them Scott had the little birds flying down the suspected routes that the Warhead convoy might possibly take. But news from Tom Hawk that the convoy was likely to be on the move inside the next few days. He had received information from good authority that this coming Saturday evening was the likely day. Ryona noted that today being the Seventeenth of August, a Wednesday, they had barely less than three days to find these infiltrators. Her watch showed 6.39pm. She turns to Roberto asking.

'What time did you book the Italian, sweetheart?'

Roberto answers with 'They gave me 7.45.'

'She nods. 'Best we make a move, I think our vacation time's just about to end baby...Somebody's got to come up with a sighting soon. ..We should be getting into some positioning by now...Last minute plans usually cause problems...We need to really scrutinise that map Roberto, it's getting like sticking a pin and hoping for the best...A needle in the haystack.'

Roberto. 'I'm truly surprised how these terrorists have managed to keep in hiding ..with no apparent sightings...200

men, there must be a blot on the landscape. But let's take that dinner date. Then it's an early starter come tomorrow.'

14
A SURPRISE PARTY AT THE COLOSSEUM

It was 7.35 when Roberto pulled onto the driveway of the Colosseum Restaurant, a wonderful looking white marble building who's entrance was donned by two bronze Roman soldiers, each a spear in one hand, whilst the other held reins of a roaring lion.

Ryona gave a low whistle before saying. 'Wow, Hope the food's as good as the building.'

They walked into reception and were met by a smiling blonde-haired young man who was dressed in a white toga and sandals. He smiled, asking if they'd booked.

Roberto answered. 'We're bang on the minute, we have booked for 7.45.' He points to the ledger that the young man's holding. 'Under Mr. and Mrs.Vincato.'

The young man looks, smiles. 'Ah...Yes Sir...We have you a table for two on our terrace...If you'd kindly follow me.'

Ryona shrugs. ' Are you saying your main room....'

She points to a sign that's saying 'The Arena'...That your Arena is full booked?'

The man nods his head, 'Unfortunately yes madam the Arena has been fully booked by Mr. Sadat Malik the Oil Barron, only his guests will be allowed to dine in there this evening.'

Roberto, shake of the head. 'There must be at least 20 tables in there, and he's taken them all?'

The young man smiles. 'No, not all Sir just the two at centre stage...if you were to visit us tomorrow then the Arena could have a table free.'

He asks. 'Would you like me to look for you? ..we don't have many vacancies, nights that are not packed to the rafters are few, take last year, we were booked solid for 6 months in advance.'

Ryona smiles. 'Food must be Michelin class. So show us this terrace seating.' The man nods and takes them through a door that leads down the 4 steps to the terrace. A complete delight, the mosaic Roman tiles, the sweet smells of Jasmin and honeysuckle, the fountain with its pool full of Japanese Carp.

Roberto nods. 'I think we've come out best with the terrace baby, they can keep their indoor arena ,with its 15 feet in diameter chandeliers. They looked about at the other guests. The tables were nearly all occupied. Those that were vacant displayed a Reserved sign.

The diners, quite a selection of who seemed to be tourists, mostly elderly.

Ryona wanted the rest room to freshen up. She asked Roberto to order, something divine, expensive. Winking and saying. 'Surprise me.'

Robert, being Italian found looking through the menu and coming across his mother's all time favourite dish quite a surprise. Not many restaurants carried a pasta in white. A

Siciliano special with herbs and spices from the volcanic lava beds that once destroyed Pompeii. The wine, a white grape that exploded and swirled in the mouth like a fortified fruit orchard. A wine that rivalled the best aged Champagne, a wine that would cost Roberto 120 dollars a bottle.

He smiled, knowing that his mama concocted a dish of such finesse for a few lira. A dish passed down through family generations, his mama taught by his grandmother. The dish on the menu was priced at a cool 180 dollars.

He nodded thinking, so the lady wants a divine expensive plate of food, so let's serve her with the best. He looked at the waiter who was standing by to take his order.

'We'll have the Pasta White...and I know this dish...It better be right...Sicilian standard and more. This dish with the wine, The Sicilian White 61?'

The waiter smiles. 'The 61, yes Sir, we have a beautiful tomato and basil soup for a starter that I highly recommend, then to finish, the finest trifle that ever was dished.'

Roberto on seeing Ryona returning, says. 'OK, let's have the soup and the desert....Tell the chef it's our anniversary so it's got to be Michelin class.'

With that the waiter departs, but not before ensuring Roberto that he won't be disappointed.

Ryona comes back and sits down pulling, Roberto closer, and whispers,

'My heart, you're not going to believe who I've just seen. A face from my past, when I was known as Mari Bambella.'

Roberto, 'What here in this restaurant?, what table, male or female?'

She, still whispering, 'It's a male and he's not here on the terrace, he's in the Arena....He's an Afghanistan chieftain's son who was at Cambridge the same time as myself...his name is Jahaad Shadeer....What's he doing here Roberto?'

Roberto shrugs, 'So, you tell me my love, should we be worried?'

Ryona sighs. 'I don't know..his language skills brilliant in so many, fluent. His memory ace. Degrees in engineering, business management, language and technology. He was what you might call top of the tree.'

She gives her head a shake, ..We used to sit in the library picking each other's brain on certain educational stuff...He's here, he's given me several glances, I'm sure he's recognised me...You'd think he'd want to talk, but he's showing no inclination to come over to say hello...like he doesn't want to have a natter over old times, I felt sure he'd come over and ask me what I was doing here in Montana....But he doesn't seem to want to know...But why?'

Roberto squeezes her hand, 'With a CV like that man's got to be taking into consideration why we are here...Then I'm thinking. Yes....We should get Joe on crimson and tell him, like you've told me about this Jahaad Shadeer....He's in the wrong place at the wrong time...This guy...Yes, he worries me, baby.'

Ryona nods. 'Let's enjoy my surprise plate of divine expensive food...Shadeer's going nowhere at the moment so how about you remembering that little bug that's in my purse? ' ...She goes into her purse and brings out a magnetic button bug.. 'Just attach this to that dark windowed Lincoln that's out there, Then when they leave, we'll know where they're heading.'

Roberto taps her hand. 'You know my love, you never fail to surprise me, you're too good for this game.'

Ryona laughs, suddenly realising the loudness of it she goes back to whispering. 'I'm hoping you're learning a little from me, my sweet.'

Roberto smiles, 'But first we eat this divine expensive plate of Italian.' He holds up a hand. 'What am I saying?

Mama would kill me...Italian, no, no, Siciliano dish....Sicily, because that's the only place you would ever get served it. To have it here in Montana of all places, Then the Chef here must be a Sicilian, ten times out of ten...it's a woman.'

Over in the restaurant's Arena there is merrymaking all round with Jahaad saying nothing about the inclusion of the belly dancers. His thoughts had somehow wandered a little on his noticing the beautiful athletic looking figure of Mari Bambella walking along the outer corridor and entering the rest room. His mind racing with thoughts of what was an ex Cambridge University college student, a woman of great sporting achievements and in Marshall Arts, a fine knowledge of many languages, a woman with countless degree's be doing here in Montana.

He must not jump the gun on this, it could be just a coincidence. Maybe the owner of this fabulous restaurant, Giovanni, knows her. She could of course live in the State. Now that would would be most unusual.

Then she could be on vacation. The Rocky Mountains and their beauty would give her every reason, being a top tourist attraction. He would find out. He waved Giovanni over and whispered to him.

'There's a lady sitting, I presume, outside on the terrace. A most beautiful lady..She's dressed in a black trouser suit and white silk blouse...You know of her Giovanni?'

This man shrugs. 'Her first time here, Jahaad . She and her husband...let me see now...They booked in as Mr. And Mrs. Veneto...I'm guessing, tourists.'

Jahaad nodding. 'So, she's with her husband.'

He puts up a finger, 'Tell Pascal, your bodyguard to see if he can find out more for me.'

Wags the finger at Giovanni. 'But discreetly Giovanni, and I do mean discreetly. Ok?'

Giovanni smiles. 'It shall be done as you wish Jahaad .' He winks.'Discreetly.'

Jahaad waves him away, saying 'Good man.'

It was 9pm Ryona congratulates Roberto on his divine expensive dish, saying that it was undoubtedly the very best pasta dish she had ever eaten. The dish, coupled with wine from the orchards of Sicily, the Sicilian White was more than she'd ever bargained for, the soup was a Royal Red Tomato, the desert a superb trifle.

Roberto had even gone so far as to order coffee, with cheese board, and biscuits, to end a feast of all feasts.

He turned to her whispering. 'Must visit the rest room and take a little of the cool night air.' He winks. She looks at him, then takes in the terrace only to notice a rather large man, in a black suit and bow-tie, trying his hardest to keep from glancing across at her. She whispers to Roberto.

'I think we have a watcher. Dose he think we're about to do a runner? Roberto please be careful he's showing a shoulder arm under that jacket.'

Roberto nods. 'He's here for you my love ...I think you've got this Shadeer son of a tribal chief worried. He's hoping we're in Montana to take in the Rockies, Whatever he's here for, he's not saying, but I'll tell you this my love, it's nothing to do with oil.'

Ryona. 'Do be careful, if it's a risk, then don't you dare take it. I'm sure this oil Barron lives in and around Billing. Shouldn't be too hard to find his place.' She sighs. 'I'd sooner for us to be safe and wait for Joe than be caught in a spiders web.'

Roberto gives her cheek a peck. 'I'm not about to do anything stupid...If it's a problem getting the bug home then I'm for leaving ...Look it's getting dark and there could well be an opportunity to get this bug attached.'

Ryona sternly. 'No, let's get Joe here. Well not here but some nice little hotel....Get his thoughts on Jahaad Shadeer.' Roberto shrugs, 'You sure girl...it's your call?' She nods, 'I'm sure.'

Assuming Scott had been right giving them the submarine base as the delivery. Joe was convinced that Scott was on the ball with his assumptions. That the Kitsap Naval Base in Washington was where the Warheads where finally to end up. They were for the nuclear capable submarines the Seawolves .

It was almost 9.25pm when the crimson call came in from Ryona. At precisely 9 40   Joe and Lenny found themselves heading east to Billing where Ryona and Roberto were waiting for them to arrive at a rural guesthouse just a 2 mile stride from the Billing outskirts.

Joe could feel the adrenaline pumping, he felt sure, after what Ryona had told him, that she'd hit on something. He'd gone so far as to crimson Anton Spicer to see if he could give them a note on who this Jahaad Shadeer was. Some Afghan son of a chieftain, Cambridge man of letters, what was this man doing in the search zone dining with a notorious oil billionaire?

Lenny gave a thumbs up to Ryonas call, saying. 'This could be the break we've been searching for Joe, shouldn't we call Norm and Dave in?'

Joe smiles. 'Let's take a look around first, Lenny my son, remember what Ryona has given us does not include any Wolverines, this Shadeer could be a go between, the middle man, the buyer.'

Lenny nods in agreement. Joe goes on to say. 'Let's hear what Anton comes up with on our Son of an Afghan Chief. The Cambridge man of letters Jahaad Shadeer.'

Joe and Lenny had been surveying an area around Moses Lake south west of Spokane. Billings, Joe estimated, was around 600 miles east of them and a good days journey in their Chevrolet.

Meanwhile, Norman and Dave had drawn a blank in getting any sightings. They were searching Twin Falls on the Snake River and were looking to pay a visit up to Shoshone when Joe's crimson call hit Norman's receiver. Joe went through what Ryona had called in with. He then added that Dave and himself may be required in Billing.

Norman replied that the two of them were not that far away..being in Idaho, they'd travel up through Yellowstone Wyoming to Montana. He added that so far their search was bringing no favourable results. There'd been movement coming over from the east to Reno, only to find it was a young people's rock festival, with Bob Segar and the Silver Bullet band headlining.

A crowd of 200,000 people were expected over its three day event. Norman added, 'Now if it had been Ozzy Osbourne headlining then maybe the Wolves would be in that 200,000.'

Joe, on hearing Norman's joke, smiled. 'Now that wouldn't surprise me at all, Norm...But leave it for us to take a look-see, then if your needed I'll give you a buzz, OK?'

Norman, ended with. 'We have you, Joe...Good hunting.' Joe, turns to Lenny, shrugs. 'It's just a thought, but maybe Norm and Dave are closer to our Wolves than the man in Billing.'

Lenny laughs. 'We've known that happen a few times before, Joe.' He smiles saying. 'Remember that time in Nantes,France...When we brought up reinforcements from Bordeaux ...The house in Saint Nazaire which we thought contained the arms and ammunition destined for the IRA?'

Joe nods. 'I remember, Lenny, that was a right fuck-up those gunrunners got them out of Pointe de la Courbet up through the Bay of Biscay, We had that covered until one last minute order that came from our, later to be found traitor, Colonel Harry Windrush. We surveyed that house for three days. Whilst the arms shipment was being unloaded in Bantry Bay. Ireland.'

Joe shakes his head. 'Didn't that shipment come out of Boston USA?' Lenny nods. 'We could have stopped that run at sauce, but we let it sail, in the hope of nailing the receivers...Like you said Joe, what a fuck-up.'

Ryona and Roberto had already left the Colosseum and headed out for the guest house lodge. Roberto had remained seated awaiting his bill, While Ryona had taken the terrace garden route to the car not wanting dicky bow, the watcher, to see her leave.

Pascal Giovanni's bodyguard began to look over the garden area for a sighting of Ryona. And whilst this was taking place Roberto had paid the bill and made for the motor taking the restaurants main exit and quickly made for the car.

Pascal returned to the terrace and stared at the empty table. He raced to the car park only to find the Buick gone. He nervously walked back to the restaurant. Giovanni met up with him at reception.

He took Pascal by the arm and pulled him into an alcove, away from any unwanted ears, then asked, 'So what gives with the lady...Jahaad is eager for news...What can I tell him?'

Pascal looking a little uneasy at Giovanni, gulps, replies with a lie, 'No one knows of her boss, she's a lady of mystery, I was told by another tourist that they were staying in Butte, but they didn't know where.'

Giovanni looks at him and can see he's lying, so he goes on and ask who gave him this information; to take him to this person.

Pascal begins to stutter saying the woman who told him had already left the Coliseum. She was a tourist on her way to San Francisco.

Giovanni punches Pascals chest, saying. 'Bullshit..You're giving me bullshit, Pascal...I don't have a liar working for me, you want to go tell Jahaad you have nothing to for him? ..Well do you?' He goes on tapping Pascals chest.

'These people dining in the Arena are very important clients, and they expect excellent service from the Colosseum. That we try our best to give....Sadat Malik has paid many dollars to secure the Arena, now I'm at a loss what to say to him.'

He jabs his finger harder into his aids chest, 'I'm betting that you didn't take the Buick's registration? what State it was from, was there a Hertze sticker to indicate whether it was hired, Fucking no? ...Do I have to boot out of my restaurant? ...get out of my sight, while I think about it.'

With that being his final word he selects a bottle of Dom Perignon before walking over to explain to Jahaad that Pascal has failed to get the information he had asked of him.

He tells Jahaad, who simply shrugs and says. 'I think we sent a boy to do a man's job Giovanni, but not to worry, I will make enquiries about the lady.'

Giovanni can't stop from apologising, with Jahaad assuring him that it's OK. 'If she's new to the area, then I wasn't expecting you to know.'

Giovanni can only say that the lady has never visited his establishment before this evening. With that he presents Jahaad with the champagne, asking him to enjoy the rest of his evening.

Joe and Lenny had driven on through the night, stopping only once at roadside diner to take in breakfast and top up the fuel tank. Sharing the drive had allowed them to make good time on the drive to Billing and the meet up with Ryona and Roberto at the 'Warm Welcome' guest house.

Ryona began to go through the last evening's visit to the Restaurant, and how the billionaire oil baron had booked the Arena, the restaurant's premiere dining area of some maybe thirty tables to use only two.

She went on to give a full portrayal of the Cambridge champion Jahaad Sadeer. His achievements in gaining degrees in languages, business studies, science technology and engineering, The son of an Afghan Chieftain was a very powerful, knowledgeable guy. She finished by asking what this guy was doing in their search area?.

Joe asks. 'So you think this Afghan recognised you, but after a three year stint at Cambridge, where you and he used to iron out educational issues together I'd think that strange that the man didn't attempt to come over to say hello?...In fact, put a watch on you. That's most unusual.'

Ryona, nods. 'You're right on the button with that Joe.'

Joe looks to Roberto. 'You didn't bug the Lincoln, that's good. If we have an extra face coming into the heist, then best you keep a low profile. Just be what they'll be assuming that you're tourists.'

Roberto shrugs. 'We know where he's staying ...He's with the billionaire Sadat Malik...We didn't nosey too much but I managed to casually get the info on the oil baron from a filling station attendant. Seems he's got a few hundred acres of prime grass and forestry which, ...going on what the guy at the gas station told us is fenced off, electrified with full security cameras ...He has guards carrying automatic rifles patrolling. The guy called them Tommy guns. But I assumed he'd been watching to many Jimmy Cagney movies, his Sten gun ...They'd be AK's or something similar. Seems he's a shut-up shop, Joe.'

Joe tells them he's awaiting a reply on the business side to this, Jahaad Shadeer...That he's crimsoned Anton. If the SIS have anything on him then we'll soon know.'

Lenny nods. 'He's got to be big time, but I'm thinking not European or the USA for that matter. The oil billionaire putting out the red carpet for this man, he's got to be Middle East. Could have IS connections or the Taliban...Mark my words, Shadeer is a player, with his foot planted in the heist.'

Joe smiles. 'Let's hear what Anton comes up with before jumping to conclusions. If he's like Lenny thinks, a player, then he's got to be involved, with an army behind him. If he's a loner on this ... Then it's best not to forget oil is big dollar profits too.' Ryona, nodding says. 'I think what we haven't mentioned is the man at the filling station saying that this oil baron has been in his forest domain for at least 4 years, maybe longer. That he was there when he took up his contract of employment with the stations owners, the Red Line Oil Company.'

Joe sighs, 'Knowing that little bit of information makes one hell of a difference.'

He shrugs, 'Could be he's just here doing an oil deal like Ryonas said, he had degrees in business...This oilman comes from the same neck of the woods as Shadeer ...I've got him down on the web as an Iraqi and that's next door to Afghanistan.'

Lenny asks Joe. 'So what's this Afghan all about Joe, you get anything on him through the internet?'

Joe. 'It's quite possible that he was involved with an underground movement that fought off the Russians, driving them out of his mountainous home land. It's believed, but not confirmed he joined the Islamic State...and I don't need to tell you of their power. The IS, a terrorist group that's overtaken the Taliban in killing all things Western.'

He shrugs saying. 'That's about it other than he's no longer there. That's if he ever was in the first place.'

He puts up a finger adding 'I'm hoping Anton has the answer for us on that.'

15
WAR BONNET

Over in the Ranch house of Don Carlotto Alfredo, the horse breeding ex head of the Oregon mob, a full heated argument was taking place between the old Don and the new. His son Ricardo. ....Carlotto had been worried about his prime stock of Stallions and receiving mares becoming unsettled. The reason being argued was the vast army of terrorist mercenaries that were striding his barns and paddocks. The Mares were breaking down. This, the old Don told Ricardo was not good and went so far as to tell his son to get these killers of his ranch. If he didn't then he'd have to do something about this uneasy situation. Ricardo fired at his father,

'Do you want all your horses slaughtered, Yourself and me included? ...You better keep that mouth of yours shut father, I'm in too far in with these people they are in control, thousands, no millions of dollars are involved...If we end this they'll fuck us good and proper.'

Carlotto snarls. 'I didn't know, that out of my loins would be born a fucking idiot of a son. Your dear mother, God bless her, will be turning in her grave if she knew that her son was selling America to the hated Russians.'

He gives a deep sigh, before continuing, 'I have spoken to some of our families...Nero of the Leons Piero of the Cosavenellos They are angry at your actions ...They feel you should send these Baltic Reds down the river by putting a call in to the FBI.'

Ricardo slams a fist hard against the wall. Shouts, screams.

'Have you completely lost it? giving information out to West Coastal families? That alone could well cost us our lives, I'm hoping to fuck that I'm the only one who knows of your stupidity.'

He shakes his head and begins to pace the room. 'You don't know what will happen if this gets out...Bratski the Black Angel, he will withdraw from his mission, and you my dear stupid father will suffer like no man has ever suffered before torturous methods resulting in a slow and painful death.'

Carlotto growls,'Not if I get to him first...I may be old but I've been through lots of killing fields and I'm not one who falls easily to my enemies...In the old takeover mob wars...To be still alive after thirty years of tit for tat assassinations, makes your father one to be feared.'

Ricardo laughs.'Your one man army against the two to three hundred he's got parading your paddocks...Come on now old man, you've got to be fucking dreaming.'

He shrugs. 'Look father, why don't you disappear for a few days...take in the Kentucky horse sales?..I'll have a word with Bratski, you need to take a break from all that's going down here.'

Carlotto shakes his head gives a fierce reaction to his son's suggestion.

'Oh, so I've got to ask some piece of shite of a terrorist, permission to leave my own fucking ranch. He's already got my stable staff confirmed to barracks Everyone kept from leaving, all phones and communication items have been taken away from them...Things have got to change boy ,..This ain't going to work...That drawbridge he's erected has got to come down ....I for one can't take much more of this ...My business is going downhill...only this morning I've had to cancel Robin Tyler's request for the siring of four of his mares. That I'd assigned to my top earning stallion.'War Bonnet ' and that is quite a few dollars gone down the drain.'

Ricardo walks over and pats his fathers shoulder.

'War Bonnet'? you mean to tell me they're still putting up the dollars for a foal from that old hack?'

Carlotto shouts, 'You know nothing of bloodlines Sonny Jim, that horse your calling an old hack happens to be on a line going back to the great 'Northern Dancer' who sired more English Derby winners than any stallion I know.'

Ricardo holds up a hand. 'Ok, ok, ..But I'm begging you father, keep that mouth of yours shut, and take the holiday if it's offered.'

Carlotto gives a head shake saying, 'I'm not leaving my ranch while your terrorist friends have cleared the fuck off and that's final.'

It took only minutes after the father and sons heated discussion had ended that unbeknown to them Bratski had a Wolf listening, recording their argument.

Alex Grobnoff was a Top Alpha, One of four personal aids to the Black Angel. Bratski had given him the job of keeping an eye on the old Don For Bratski knew if ever there was doubt, a weak link in the American accommodation set-up then Carlotto would carry that mark.

Grobnoff entered the house of the head boy Jack Staines who had been given the order to find fresh accommodation in the ranch staff dormitory. This allowed Bratski to move in.

Bratski. 'Ok, Alex, what have you got for me?'

Alex pulls out a hand held mini dictation recorder and presents it to Bratski. 'You have to listen to this farmer and son conversation, or should I say argument…It's not good my master…You were right to doubt the old Don …But listen and tell me your wish master, I'll see that it's taken care of.'

Bratski indicates with a quick finger movement for Alex to play the machine, he points to a seat, asking: 'This recording will it take long?'

Alex shrugs, 'A good half hour master.' Bratski nods. 'Then let's hear this argument between the two Alfredos I'm eagerly awaiting its content.'

The recording ends with a deep sigh coming from the Black Angel. He looks at Alex and smiles. 'It seems to me that this Carlotto Alfredo needs to be taught a lesson …the idiot son Ricardo was right about one thing Alex.'

Alex mumbles. 'Master?'

'He did warn his father that opening his mouth would be a sad idea…It would involve a whole lot of pain for the old Don.'

He claps his hands, 'So what, are we going to do that would cause so much pain for a horse breeding ranch?…Pain that would make that crazy old fucker keep that arsehole of a mouth shut…knowing that one more slip of the tongue, would mean greater torturous pain.'

He looks at Alex requiring his aid to answer. Bratski can see that Alex is searching for a most suitable answer.

He laughs. 'Can you not see, Alex? …Its in the recording …The one thing that Carlotto loves more than his idiot son.'

Alex clicks a finger, smiling. 'The stallion, his pride and joy…The horse War Bonnet.'

Bratski nods, 'I can see why they made you one of my aids...Yes, that fucking horse...War Bonnet.'

Alex, nodding enthusiastically. 'We kill it, Master?'

Bratski shakes his head. 'Oh no my fine friend....Not kill...We castrate it and put its balls under a silver serving dish on Carlotto's door-step...That I know would give Carlotto so much pain.'

Alex smiles then goes into thoughts of what could result in such an action. Bratski can see the troubled face of Alex and so asks.

'Alex, your thoughts, let me hear what's in that super brain of yours?'

Alex holds up a hand.

'I'm sorry Master but couldn't this make Carlotto so angry that he'd go to the Feds?'

Bratski winks, 'Not if we add a note saying the next serving dish will contain his son's heart.'

With that the Angel points to the door.

'So go, Alex. You have urgent work to do...Clear that stallion's box of any attendants...Then bring to me War Bonnets pair of money earners...In the meantime I will have prepared for you the note...I want that old Don to wake come the morrow with pain in his heart and a ticket to those Kentucky horse sales....Yes, I will allow him to leave but accompanied by you my trusted aid.'

He grips Alex on the shoulder. 'You will end his life if he makes any move that could jeopardise our plans.'

It was just after 7.30 am when Joe was woken by his phone flashing 'Anton Crimson.' Joe swipes to receive. Anton's voice comes through to him crystal clear.

'Hi Joe, I've got you the run down on that Jahaad Shadeer, and boy have you got a bomb in your suitcase....You hearing me OK?'

Joe, Crystal Ant...Let's have it on this Afghan time bomb...You saying he's high explosive?'

Anton at his most serious. 'Remember Bin Laden...he's a replica clone of that weird bastard...He has instigated many murderous actions when riding with Islamic State...Now he's heading a new terrorist organisation called the Scarabs... They're becoming some of the most feared evil butchers in the Middle East ...They've not infiltrated Europe as far as we know...But with America, it looks like they are flexing their claws into this heist...Forget the oil, Joe, he's not in the USA to talk oil, he's after a slice of a multi billion dollar cake.' Anton paused,

'Joe. He's there for the nuclear warheads, we know so little about him...Our Middle East operators say he's called the Impaler...You must go easy on this man ...I'm not wanting to hear of Joe Delph or any of the team with their decapitated heads stuck on a pole alongside some American freeway...Joe, you hearing me? This fucker Shadeer is heavy duty.'

Joe answers. 'You know Ant, we have to eliminate him from this future heist...I'm not wanting to lose any of my team, or any other member of Scott's Delta Force to this tyrant...But hit him we will, and I tell you this now, he'll not know what's coming.'

Anton says. 'OK, it's your baby, but I'm inclined to let Norbert Porter in on this change of situation...We need to tighten the power blocker on this operation ...Seems to me there's a lot of chefs in the kitchen...Personally I don't think they're cooking for one big party.'

Joe interrupts. 'I have the same feeling Ant, there's something not right about this heist...We've got Wolves, Scarabs, and God only knows how many more involved... Someone's wanting this play to go the full distance...Russia, Iraq, Iran, North Korea ...all opening their bank vaults. The

Pakham, his Bratva, steering the catch towards mother Russia putting extra pressure on the Baltic States. Iran, Iraq, putting fear into the Saudis, North Korea threatening the South and all who interfere.'

Anton ends the call with. 'Joe, just be careful...You're up against a hurricane, with little more than an umbrella...Let's strengthen our defence, I need you to get back to me on this.'

Joe, 'When I know more, then so will you Ant, let my team and I get our heads around this....Anton, thanks for the information...Talk again soon.'

With that, Joe switched off the call.

It's 8.15am on the Carlotto ranch and the old Don is awakened by frantic knocking on the main house door. Ricardo comes in from the bedroom across the way shouting, 'What the fuck's going on?'

Carlotto hushes his son, 'That's Toby's voice, something must be going on for him to disturb me.'

Ricardo grunts. 'Disturb you ...He's waking every fucker up on the ranch.'

Putting on his gown, heading for the door, mumbling angrily;

'This better be good or he's dismissed....What am I saying...He won't be able to fucking leave.'

Carlotto laughs, 'Oh now it's getting to sink into that thick brain of yours is it? that we're all in fucking lockdown, thanks to your wheeler dealing with crazy no good Russian terrorists.'

Ricardo shouts back at him, 'Go stick one of your mares, then shouts at the door. 'If that's you Toby...this will have to be good...You hear me?'

A terrified voice answers. 'It's War Bonnet, Sir...He's been got at...it's not good.'

That very answer brings Carlotto tearing past Ricardo and unlocking the door. He sees the terrified image of Toby, War Bonnets stable lad, who's shaking, holding out a silver serving dish to his Don.

Carlotto angrily. 'What's in the dish, man?"

Toby places the dish at the feet of Carlotto and turns running away, back towards the stables. Crying out and not turning to look at the two Dons. With Carlotto shouting after him, 'Toby....Toby..? You get that arse of yours back here now.'

Ricardo putting a hand on his fathers shoulder asks.

'What the fucks going on here as everyone gone completely mad?'

He points at the dish,. 'What the fuck's that all about?'

Carlotto bends and lifts the lid only to see the balls of a horse with a roll of blood stained paper neatly tied in a red ribbon.

Carlotto turns to his son. 'What's all this shit, you know anything about this?'

Ricardo crosses himself, saying. 'I swear on my mother's grave, father, I know nothing of this joke.' He pIcks up the scroll rips away the ribbon and reads,

Carlotto snarls. 'We'll what's it say?'

Ricardo shakes his head and gives the paper to his father.

'Now see what you've done...You and your threats...That big mouth of yours...I fucking told you what would happen if you upset these people... For fucks sake fathers they're terrorists killers....Oh my God, what have you Done?'

Carlotto stands his hands shaking has he goes through Bratski's letter. He lets the paper fall to the ground. He turns from his son and enters the house. With an Anxious Ricardo shouting after him, following him.

'What are you doing ...He says you can go visit the Kentucky sales...Come home when it's all over and they've departed.' He shakes his head, balling a fist. 'You're not going to do anything foolish are you?'

He points, shaking his finger at the old Don and then to the outside.

'Father there's 2 to 300 killers out there. They'd cut you down and ……' He trembles at the thought.

'Fuck me too...the horses, the ranch they'll burn to the ground, You do not mess with this man.'

He screams, 'Father you hearing me?'

Carlotto just ignores his son, his brain has gone past caring. He takes from under a window box seat a silver walking cane. that Ricardo knows holds live ammunition, a trigger cane. He turns to his son.

'I hoped for a son...I got a whelp....Get out of my way, whelp.'

Ricardo grabs his father giving him a firm bear hug, he kisses the top of Carlotto's head and gently whispers in his ear.

'Don't do this father...I'm begging you...Please take the Kentucky vacation that's been offered.'

Again he kisses his father an gives a pressure hug before releasing him.

Carlotto stands vigorously shaking his head and cries out. 'The bastard...he's castrated War Bonnet, boy, For that reason alone he has to pay with his life...He jabs a finger at Ricardo.

'He better get his calculations right ...and you to. This is my home, my ranch and they entered without an invitation from me...He can keep his millions, I have no interest..I have money..You tell your Russian fucking Angel he's got 24 hours to get his arse and his killers off my estate. I've a phone...I'll call the families telling them, he's here to destroy America.'

Ricardo nods, laughs, shaking his head replies.

'I don't have to tell him anything…he'll know already… How do you think he got the information on War Bonnet?… He's got the ranch bugged.' He jabs a finger back at his father. 'So you think he's going to let you get anywhere near him with that fucking pop gun….You're sure hoping for a miracle for that to happen.'

He shrugs, points to the door and continues,

'So go out there and die along with everything you've ever worked for.'

He puts his hands together praying, looks up to the heavens.

'Won't somebody up there shine a light of common sense into my fathers scrambled brain?'

16
AN EYE FOR AN EYE

Joe had finished telling Ryona, Roberto and Lenny about his crimson conversation with Anton. He looked over at Ryona who's slowly shaking her head on hearing the information about Rahaad Shadeed with her mouth agape and muttering.

'I can't believe what I'm hearing...Never...He sure fooled me, I'd never had labelled him a terrorist.'

Joe shrugs. 'Guess that's what you'd now call your old Cambridge college friend.'

Joe shakes his head at her, 'Your, Jahaad Shadeer is, I'm afraid to say, an Afghan killer. With a long reputation of decapitating his enemies.' He looks to the team and puts up a finger.

'His ambition, and I go with Anton's report that came from one of our agents in Kabul, is to carry on the work of his mentor and hero, Bin Laden...To gain the status that he had held with the Taliban...which is to take over were he left off.'

Lenny, rubbing his chin and asking. 'So what's the plan, Joe...Do we take him out? ...Like...no more Shadeer?'

Roberto, before Joe can answer.

'That Lenny, is a must..I had a feeling about this bastard, when he failed to acknowledge my wife, then went further by putting a man to watch us....This guy is no idiot, Joe. But one dangerous snake whose venom will poison us all if we're not careful.'

Joe nods, saying.'Hold on guys there's a couple of things that this genius has no knowledge of...One, he's no idea about Lenny and I being here, that could be a good thing, but then again, we don't know this for sure...with Ryona telling us he's part genius; that's if you were to look through his academic schooling.'

Ryona adds. 'He would not be afraid to throw a gauntlet at the IS, now that for me says he's got power.'

She shrugs. 'He's not here on his lonesome, he's more than likely to have an army of Scarabs in support, and the oil barons fortress a private secluded spot to prepare for a war. ...I say war because that's what it'll be when green turns to red.'

Lenny nods, 'The lady makes sense with her thoughts....This guy ain't going to go in without a full team to attack and win ...Winning because he's not going to be a loser...Defend, no way, these sort of thoughts don't come into this guy's mind.'

Joe, 'Ok, So how do we break down his door and find out his strength?...He's in that billionaire's compound with an unbreakable security set-up, 24 hour around the clock guards with AK's and African Hunting dogs, That, according to the filling station guy.'

He scratches his head. ..'Seems we have a problem, wouldn't you say?'

Roberto points out what they already know, by saying.

'We know that the Wolves have brought in, according to the Alpha Ottermanze, some 200 soldiers.'

He shrugs, 'Of course we haven't got any verification of that, just the word of a now dead Wolf...But let's take it as a possible fact.....Then I'm inclined to think that this Afghan has his match.'

Again, sighs, 'I don't know if it's a good idea but we could go through customs and get a check out on recent arrivals into the States from the Middle East.'

He looks to Joe. 'Probably Norbert would get that sort of info to us.'

Joe sort of smirks, 'Sorry Roberto but wouldn't that bring a few questions of why?....Why were we seeking this information and giving a few unwanted listener's ears a wagging...We can't afford for this heist to become open for discussion. It goes without saying that there's sure to be a few infiltrators, even in the officers of the FBI. ..Especially with mob connections, their noses sniffing into areas that could make our job a hell of a lot harder.'

Lenny nods, 'Joe's just about right with that assumption.'

He laughs, 'Maybe if they cancel the convoy...Then everybody could just pack it in and go home.'

Ryona shakes her head, 'Then these billions of dollar warheads would go into storage, with America weaker as far as their defence program would look...They, we, need those warheads in the bodies of the Seawolves shifting through the oceans of our planet. Isn't that what they were commissioned for? Part of America's great deterrent....in a unstable world.'

Joe smiles and begins to clap Ryona.

'The lady's right on the ball...There's nothing more to be said on this...Let's find a way into these terrorists compounds and take them down....I'm calling for Norm and

Dave to join us.... I think we've found what we've been searching for.'

Roberto asks, 'We letting Scott and his boy's know, Joe?'

Joe, 'Yes, but Scott will have to work on an observation plan for flying his little birds across Montana....Maybe a little crop dusting to take suspicion away.'

Lenny points to Ryona and Roberto, asking.

'What about Ryona and Roberto, Joe...The Afghan will still be wanting to know why they're here?'

Joe nods. 'I've got it Lenny...Why they're in Montana.'

The three look for him to continue, with Ryona smiling, saying. 'Why's that, Joe, What are we doing in Montana?'

Joe smiles.'Why you're taking a small break from your business by calling to see the wonderful Rocky Mountains, before getting down to your main task, that's up in Seattle, Washington.'

Roberto laughs. 'Come on, Joe, What's with this Seattle episode?'

Joe holds out a hand to them before going on to explain that he had read in a local rag that Seattle were thinking of putting in a bid for the next but one summer Olympic Games.

'Who's not to know that Ryona, who was well known for her athletic abilities, was doing a survey on the Seattle possibilities of winning the bid. Of course she was being assisted by husband Roberto. Again it would be left to General Porter to do the necessary requirements with a legit sports association...As for the rest of us we would remain as simple tourists from the UK, members of a London Photographic Club. That would fall into Anton:s capabilities.'

The three stood amazed and began in unison to agree to Joe's plan.

Ryona smiles before blowing Joe a kiss, turning to Roberto and Lenny, she says, 'Now that's what I call genius, and could well work.'

She turns back to Joe and winks. 'Nice one, Joe.'

Joe smiles at her before saying in a more serious tone, 'You know there's a chance that we may have to kill this old school mate of yours, Ryona.....Think you can live with that?'

He adds. 'Don't hesitate, if it's you, that's left with the job....Remember you mean nothing to him.'

Ryona sighs. 'What you're trying to tell me, Joe, is that I may hold back, look back on our past friendship, think twice on killing a torturous devil? He is what he's become , Joe, a destroyer of innocence...Where I'm one who fights this sickness. Our reasons for killing differ. He gets what he deserves, as do all who sail with him.'

Roberto interrupts. 'You know my woman, her history, her family.'

He nods to her. 'She lost her whole fucking kin to such as Shadeer.' Joe holds up a hand.

'We know,Roberto, and I apologise if my conversation just now gave the impression that I doubted Ryona...The reason that I brought it up...Was, I'd once had to make a similar decision on a past friendship.'

He sighs. 'I had a moment's hesitation and it nearly cost me my life...It doesn't happen very often, thank God.'

Lenny who's be listening to Ryona said.

'That incident Joe talks of I know about. A good friend turned bad, but it happened ...The friend surprised Joe by pulling a pistol on him, he pulled the trigger and the pistol jammed...It was Joe's hesitation that allowed this play.' He looks at Joe and smiles, A lesson learnt, Joe?...Ain Salah , Algeria 2016...Brough Formby.'

'That's correct Lenny ...You were in Johnny Talbot's team.'

Ryona smiles. 'Sorry, Joe. I..'

She looks to Roberto. 'We ..didn't know.'

Joe, 'let's forget it...try putting our heads around how we're going to find the Afghan's army, it's strength...Not forgetting the Wolverines that are around here somewhere, laying low in a similar situation...So give it some thought team...I need to get Scott here to sit in with us...This time tomorrow we should have Norm and Dave with us. ..Best we're all at the table, Delta included on this.'

Bratski looks out of the head lad's house window at Alex, who looks to be in good cheer, approaching the house. Moments later the Angel's aid enters and is greeted by Bratski handing him a double vodka.

Bratski smiles. 'I take it Alfredos present was delivered, Alex, with no problems?'

Alex winks, 'I left it with the stable lad to deliver, he didn't want to do the delivery, but a little unfriendly persuasion and the little shit was away with the silver salver....not forgetting your message tied with a red ribbon my master.'

Bratski pats his aid's shoulder, As soon as that old Don is in Kentucky then I will breath a little easier.'

He nods, walks back over to the window.

'Whoever picked this ranch as our hideaway should be castrated just like old War Bonnet.'

Alex shakes his head, answering,

'I don't think the Pakham would like his balls chopped off, Bratski.'

Bratski dumbfounded, 'You don't mean to tell me?...no.'

Alex laughs, nod of his head.

'Afraid so, master. After putting out a few million as a sprat to catch a mackerel...our friend, Ricardo Alfredo, took the bait and offered his father's ranch for one month.'

Bratski, nodding. 'It's no wonder the old Don went through the roof with his idiot son; his going ahead on a deal here without his father's permission...No we cannot blame the old man for being angry...Let's just hope he takes the Kentucky vacation and in so doing avoids any more upset.'

He shrugs. 'I'm afraid we're in this mission too far now to exit.'

Alex asks, 'What if he doesn't, master?'

Bratski waves a hand, shrugs, 'Then he's a dead man, Alex...as dead as that Israeli sea. '

Alex nodding. 'His son Ricardo..what of him?'

Bratski smiles, 'Do I need to tell you, it would be a family double, Alex, their deaths kept undercover...Hadn't they gone to the horse sales in Kentucky?'

He winks at Alex. 'We couldn't allow the other families of the Mafia to hear of our executions.'

Putting up a wagging finger. 'These Sicilian bastards are has hard as barn door nails, brothers, a close knit organisation...they would take action...This we cannot allow.'

Jahaad hadn't slept too well, he'd been thinking on the woman Mari Bambella an old Cambridge associate. What was she doing in the Rocky Mountains? The guy with her, apparently her husband. Surely on vacation being the most likely explanation. Still he needed to find out...it troubled him not knowing their position.

He'd gone so far as to send a couple of his English speaking Scarabs out on a 100 mile radius search. Mainly to ease his mind. They would take in areas around Hardin, Lewistown. Maybe Miles City, and what he thought the most likely, Butte. There was of course always the chance that they'd move on through Yellowstone National Park, America's premier tourist attraction.

It would not have been as bad if the dumb idiot Pascal had taken the number plate of what he thought might have been a dark blue Buick 4x4, but he couldn't be sure. Knowing that plate number and State name was gone with the wind.

Why is it these so called bodyguards come bouncers all seemed to carry a brain hung between their loins. If you want a job done right then best do it yourself.

Rahaad had got that well known saying from his grandfather, a wise man who lived a nomadic life in the Paropamisus region of east Afganistan.

As a young boy he'd listened to his grandfather with an awe of his knowledge of world-wide issues. That would become a most precious guide. He was only twelve years old when introduced to the most influential person he'd ever met, a great genius of a futuristic, forward looking man. He went by the name of Zahbah. A man with a trained memory like no other. Zahbah would give Rahaad that gift. The great scholar was a complete encyclopaedia. Although Rahaad had tried many times to ask Zahbah a question he thought he couldn't answer he was totally amazed how quick he'd reply back with the correct answer.

It was Zahbah that taught him about his God, the Sun. that it was that great ball of fire in the sky that controlled all life on earth. It was Zahbah who'd said with a wink and a smile. 'When the Sun dies, so do we all Rahaad, for he is God.'

Wether the great man would endorse what Jahaad was doing with his army of Scarabs he would never know.

For Zahbah...Jahaad was told, left his hole in the mountain one bright sunny morning and never returned. Some seven years had passed since that day, with Jahaad keeping the great scholar's home vacant and a night candle burning, awaiting his return. If ever a man was loved other than ones own father, then Zahbah would be that man.

Jahaad had felt a little down by his thoughts that Zahbah would never ever take a man's life. ...Life was a beautiful and precious gift he'd once told him, but one needs to have a heavy lock on one's door to keep death from making an entrance ..No, no, no. he came to the decision...Zahbah would not like what he was doing with his life, that of a terrorist, a killer.

'What's this I'm seeing...Just what have we here?'

Bratski's voice having taken on a comical tone as he gazed out through the house window at the approaching figures of Ricardo and Carlotto Alfredo, walking briskly, heading towards its front door. Carlotto seems to be limping slightly and is using a cane for support, trying to keep pace with his son.

Bratski laughs and turns to Alex who's obviously wondering what his chief is talking about. Bratski waving a hand before enlightening him,

'I just knew that our little ploy would alter that old fool's mind.' He smiles.

'Come look, see, Alex...The bastards are coming to ask for my forgiveness.'

Alex nods saying. 'While they've still got the balls, Master.'

They both laugh with Bratski pointing to the door.

'Go let them in Alex...but give nothing away...I'm wanting that old bastard to get down on his fucking knees and beg my forgiveness.'

Alex muffles his laugh, proceeding to the door. He opens it wide for the Alfredos to enter.

Bratski is now sitting cross legged on the lounge sofa. He doesn't rise but simply waves the two to sit in the facing armchairs. He speaks, looking mainly into a face of one angry Don Carlotto.

'I'm hearing your stallion, War Bonnet...he's been put out to grass Carlotto...Retired you might say.'

He looks at Alex who's giggling.

Carlotto, scowling. 'So why didn't you shoot the horse..Ain't that what your fucking known for Black Angel?'

Ricardo sees fire in Bratski's eyes and interrupts, saying.

'My father, his horse, War Bonnet...it hurts him Bratski.'

Bratski smiles. 'I'm betting a sweet silver dollar that it's hurting the fucking horse more.'

He laughs. 'What with no more mares to give his time too.'

Alex sniggering, 'Must have come as quite a shock to old War Bonnet, to smell the mares on heat and his tool no longer rising.'

Bratski goes on to say. 'I've been sitting here wondering if it's a good thing to let you go on a little vacation to Kentucky...Of course you couldn't go alone.' He points to Alex.

'Why my aid Alex would need to be with you...just as a security you know.'

He shouts at Carlotto.' So you don't go opening that big fat mouth of yours Don Alfredo because you, mister ranch owner, are not to be fucking trusted.'

He looks to Ricardo. 'But in saying that I cannot have the worry of having you around with your silly interruptions... Like you've already reminded me...I'm a killer, so the choice is yours Carlotto...Your life, or being a good boy in Kentucky?'

Carlotto jumps up from his seat taking all but Ricardo by surprise. He points his cane into the face of Bratski, who immediately begins perspiring on seeing the cane is a shooting stick with a trigger attachment, Ricardo pulls out a pistol with silencer attached and puts it to Alex's head. He fires and Alex falls with a hole between his eyes. He nods to his father who puts the barrel of the cane hard against the Black Angel's head.

He smiles saying. 'You think death worries me Bratski? ...I've faced his shadow so many times in my lifetime, just as you are doing now. But as you can see I'm still alive, a little older, a little wiser. ...You Bratski are at the end of yours as was your giggling aid.'

He grins. 'So who the fuck's begging now...Come on you fucking evil bastard of a man ...Let me hear you beg for your life.'

Bratski spits at Carlotto saying. 'You're a fucking dead man Alfredo, your son too...So do your worst.'

With that the old Don pulls the trigger and the Black Angels skull is shattered. He looks to Ricardo and smiles saying.

'Today I got my son back, the one I thought a whelp became a man, a Sicilian.'

Ricardo shrugs, he goes to Carlotto and hugs him. 'When it came to choose between the millions and your life father... there was never any choice.'

He whispers in his fathers ear. 'But now we have started a war father, the remaining aids must die too...We must call on Don Nero of the Leone family...Don Piero of the Cosavenellos These we can trust...Tell them of our situation here.'

He sighs shaking his head.

'We're going to need their help father, having taken the life of a Black Angel.'

The old Don nods replying. 'This I will do Ricardo...But first things first, we take out Bratski's aids. Without leadership the Wolverines will disperse and leave America....You know these killers. OK, it will be messy...but if we open the dam on the river the fish will be washed to the sea.'

He rubs Ricardo's shoulder, 'I'm thinking you're forgetting we're in America, and the power of our families, with connections worldwide. Where even the Black Angels fear to tread without permit....Believe me my son, their journey stops here, now!'

Ricardo gives a weak smile then sighs. 'Im praying it does father.'

He, clasping his hands looking up to the ceiling.

'I'm praying it does.'

Carlotto, wagging,his finger smiles, 'You're a fucking Alfredo, a Don. You must take charge, have better control of your empire, without fear, or you will sink like the the great Titanic.'

Carlotto spreads his arms out wide saying.

'This land, West, running through Washington State to Oregon is Alfredo country....Here's where you control, here you have the final say.' He jesters, shaking a fist,

'Get hold of Jack.' He nods at the bodies of Bratski and Alex.

Tell Staines to summon his staff to strip their bodies to the pigs.' He giggles. Ricardo smiles. 'What with the remaining Alphas, father?'

Carlotto grins holding out a palm.'We take them out as soon as possible ...ASP means immediately Ricardo.'

Ricardo nods. 'And the soldiers, father?'

Carlotto, shrugs, saying. 'Let's hope they run my son.'....They stay, then they die...That new Drizen Cooperative tower block. It's foundations will have quite a few bones going in its cement pores.'

Ricardo smiles. 'Don Nero has foundations ready also father...the new east of Seattle Ice Stadium....The parking lot, it's one giant of a project, when finished said to hold a few thousand vehicles.'

'Ah that's good Ricardo, let's give them a little taste of sweet death added to their supper.'

He grins, winks. 'A little instant death to their food is all it takes.'

He wags a finger, 'Get the chemist Raymond, he owes us...tell him to mix us a lethal death cyanide potion.'

Carlotto smiles. 'A large Bordeaux Jeroboam....No, six Bordeaux Jeroboams.'

He nips Ricardo's cheek, 'Tonight my son...Give them no time to think.' Ricardo stares at Carlotto and says.

'You sure father, tonight?' Carlotto. 'A thinking man can solve problems....A drunken becomes foolish and makes mistakes.'

Ricardo smiles. 'Even in retirement...You teach me father....Tonight all will be done.'

17
WHERE HAVE ALL THE WILD WOLVES GONE

Bright morning sunshine bathed into the bedroom of the old Don Carlotto. He sat on his bed going over the previous night,s events. The serving of the cyanide wine that caused an immediate effect on its consumer, death within minutes.

Ricardo had been instrumental in seeing the Wolves all took their drink simultaneously...by giving a toast to a successful heist...The poisoned wine its result devastating... bodies lying everywhere. With the remaining Black Angel aids accounted for had the Alfredos saved America from another nightmare?

He smiled on seeing his loyal staff throwing their bodies into dump trucks. All identification had been removed along with the arsenal of weapons they had carried. A profit after all. But in his mind the old wise Don knew it was far from over.

Not too far from the Alfredo Ranch on the Montana side of the Rocky Mountains, Jahaad sat in silence with his benefactor, oil Barron, Sadat Malik, each tying to establish what the other was thinking. It was Sadat who finally broke it by saying.

'Is it the woman....You worry about her business...why she is here?'

Jahaad makes a nonchalant wave, and replies. 'Who knows?' Sadat smiles. 'I know.'

Jahaad with a finger taps his head, saying. 'Then you must tell me, my friend....You Know?'

Sadat puts a hand out to the arm of the Scarab Chief, patting it, he winks. 'After your eagerness at the Colosseum I took it on myself to enquire, by asking of a friend, a most trusted friend I might add.'

He twiddles his fingers. 'I ask about our athletic English lady.'

Jahaad gives a suspicious look at Sadat, interrupts.

'Trusted friend, Sadat?'

Sadat nods. 'She, my friend just happens to be involved in a huge way with the Seattle Kraken.' Jahaad shrugs. Sadat smiles 'Ice hockey, my friend...She received many dollars from my company. The money helped her rise in status...The woman is in debt to me.'

He holds up a palm. 'She tells me that your lady friend is here working for the Seattle Sports Council who are trying to secure the Summer Olympic Games.' Raheed, slowly nodding his head.

'This comes to me as no surprise Sadat, she is strong in many sporting activities.' He shrugs. 'But in saying that....Mari Bambella needs to be watched....We leave nothing to chance.....But what of her partner, her husband the American, who is he ? ..another sporting God...A lover?'

Sadat shakes his head, replies. 'The man is her husband... We know very little about him...I am enquiring my brother'

Rahaad sighs. 'OK, we must concentrate on the Wolverines, their movements. How are we with that Sadat?'

Sadat shakes his head. 'I'm afraid there's nothing moving on that plain either, it's like Omerta ...silence .'

Rahaad growls, 'So we must get one of your most trusted friends to find out what the fuck's going on....who would know?'

Sadat winks. 'I know a man who could know ...but he's Mafia...He's working with the Camero family down in California...Tyrone Guest...He's an enforcer, killer, hit man....expensive heavy duty...If he doesn't know...I will be very much surprised..but if it's a Cosa Nostra involvement, then it's Omertà.'

Rahaad, snarls. 'Then pay the man, out of your lousy millions Sadat...The Wolves, their plan we badly need.' He raises a hand in a fist. 'The holiday is over, now we're on the green light for go.'

Back in the guest house Joe was feeling rather concerned about the Scarab Chief Rahaad. The report received on the Afghan was alarming, more so after his avoiding of Ryona, once a close friend in their university days. This Afghan, along with his Scarabs, an Islamic State breakaway group, were in Joe's mind the main contenders, seemingly being backed by an Arab oil billionaire. The Wolverines would make formidable opponents in a fight for the nuclear warheads with America doomed to be their battlefield.

Ryona interrupted Joe's thoughts by asking if there was any updates on the Wolves, their whereabouts, sightings. Saying surely now was the time to bring Norman and Dave in along with Scott's Delta Force.

Joe, nodding agreed, adding that it was worth Ryona remembering that Norman and Dave were, in fact, out there trying to get that very information on where the Wolves had camped. Weaving their way through woodland, forestry searching whilst making their way to the Warm Welcome guest house. He also reminded them all if the Wolves were in the vicinity, Oregon state. then Norm would find them.

Roberto began to say that he was most concerned about the safety of Ryona, especially after hearing Anton's report on the Scarab Chief.

Joe, nodding, says 'I've protected her, covered every possible leak …left nothing out to dry.'

He sighs, 'Still this man Rahaad is aware, puzzled, thinking why Ryona is in Montana.' ….He nods, puts up a finger, giving a sign he's made up his mind on something.

Ryona looks at him, shrugs, saying. 'Yes, Joe?'

Joe answers with. 'We've got to take this man out, Ryona, …he's not the friend you once had, he's terrorist, a killer…his time, like that of his mentor Bin Laden, has come.'

He sighs, jabbing a finger at his team. 'This man carries no roses for Ryona, what he's holding is a bunch of deadly nightshade.'

Lenny spouts up, 'We know where he is Joe, do you think he knows where we are?'

Ryona answers. 'If you ask me, I'd say he does…Whether Joe's cover for me has worked this we don't know, but I can assure you he'll be wanting to finding out why I'm here.' She winks going on to say, 'One thing I'm sure he doesn't know about…Apart from Roberto, is the rest of the team.'

She points at Joe, then Lenny. 'You Joe, Lenny, Norm, Dave along with Scott's Delta Force.'

Roberto nods, 'More the reason for us to strike first, hit them whilst they're cold and unprepared.'

Joe smiles. 'My very thoughts guys... Ok we do a reconnaissance tonight, that's after a few phone calls...We need to know their strengths, their weaknesses, what he's got with him in that mountain retreat.'

He gives a head shake. 'This will be difficult, we know he has full security...Cameras electrified fencing, guards walking killer dogs, and God knows what else.'

Lenny. 'The phone calls, Joe?

Joe pats Leny on the shoulder before continuing.

'The calls..I will be giving a crimson to Scott to ask the chances of getting some cover over here. Not too heavy though but his best snipers. We'll also be needing a birds eye view of the oil man's fortress. A fly over with a drone sending clear images from a night view camera would be our ace in the pack for knowing and breaking into their security systems.'

Lenny nods saying, 'There's no other way, Joe, we can't go blind on this.'

Joe, goes on.'This Cambridge Sheikh I'm thinking we take him out then his army of scarabs will be caught in a sand storm of confusion, dissociated, lost.'

Ryona says. 'Lets hope so Joe, it's going to be hell if they're not.'

Joe went on to say that, until he heard from Scott, he would reserve going any further down that road. For now let best the team gain all the information possible on these Scarab invaders. Further, this would need securing a strong cloak over themselves to avoid discovery.

Joe, 'Dont underestimate these Scarabs they are not here in the United States to learn, far from it, they are here to teach...Another nine-eleven? ...Who knows....What I do know is that if it comes to a head there will be one hell of a battle for those warheads...The Wolves will be no easy opponents.'

Lenny sighs 'Thats what's puzzling me Joe, where the fuck are they? We know they are here....Chicago's Hans Ottermanze gave us that.'

Ryona 'They won't show till the very last minute... But my moneys got to favour the Wolves...Let's look at this heist, Shadeed and his Scarabs are here and we know exactly where...Im thinking the Wolverines know too.'

Roberto gives a nod, saying. 'My wife could be right ... Norm and Dave, they've had no sightings and knowing Major Aimes, they've not trod lightly in their search.'

Joe. 'So you're saying we can cross off all areas coming up from the basin?'

Roberto shrugs. 'That's blowing in the wind, Joe...There must be a lot of rabbit holes. Ghost towns, abandoned gold and silver mines...Norman wouldn't have been able to cover them all...That would take months.'

Lenny pipes up with 'Norm would have hit the majors, places that could conceal an army of over 200 men...If he's drawing blanks then they're nearer Seattle.' He shrugs.

'They're close, Joe, not too far away.'

Joe smiles. 'I agree Lenny, they need to be able to take and clear by the fastest possible route, it's got to be a late night snatch, with complete concealment. They have to block any resistance, foil the police, the National Guard...This will be essential if they're going to succeed.'He shrugs.' Then it's down to their destination...Russia, Iraq, North Korea?'

Lenny says 'If it's Wolves....Its got to be The Soviet Union..through Alaska..not by road, they'd sail them up the Bering Strait

Roberto shakes his head. 'Thats a hell of a bowl of water to cover unnoticed...up the Pacific, through or around the Aleutian Islands then into the Bering.' He sighs. 'Sorry Lenny but I don't think so...You're looking at well over a thousand mile haul.'

Joe, 'They wouldn't dare move those warheads, that's always assuming they make the heist.' Holds up a palm.

'Im leaning towards storage, a hideaway, a workshop where they'd strip them down, before safely moving them when the time is right.'

Ryona smiles, 'Joe's right, storage...like in an abandoned mine.'

Joe. 'Or maybe a highly secure enclosure with guards and electric fencing.'

He laughs. 'I think we all know where that might be.. that's when the Scarabs take the prize...Ryona's Afgan isn't here to take the silver medal....he's for the gold.'

Roberto raises a question, 'So how we going to play this, Joe?'

Joe, deep in thought, comes to the conclusion that to allow the Scarabs to exit their benefactor's enclosure would cause havoc. One God almighty battle that could well take the lives of innocent people. They must ensure never happens. That they must be contained on the Sadat Malik reservation. He felt sure Scott's Delta Force would oversee that.

It was 3am Sunday morning on the Alfredo ranch and Carlotto stood smiling at the four large refrigerator trucks being loaded with the nearly 200 dead wolverines all as naked as the day they were born and stacked like sardines. He'd left the bodies of Bratski and Alex til last and given instructions that they were to be castrated and their balls parcelled and sent to the Moscow Mansion of one Ivor Stenenski.

Ricardo had asked his father if he was sure of this action, saying the Pakham would retaliate. Carlotto just shrugged saying. 'Yesterday you became a man my son, don't you ever show fear to our enemies, our families would never let you live it down. You are an Alfredo. You have all the strength of the west coast Godfathers ...whose blood veins run all across America to Chicago and New York.'

He wags a finger. 'Do not shame me Ricardo by showing fear. I have spoken to Don Nero, who's company are about to pour the foundations for the new super ice stadium east of Seattle.' He smiles. 'The bodies of the Wolves will rest beneath the underground car park....Alas there will be no religious service, so sad....It makes me want to cry.'

18
CONFUSION

Over in Moscow a raging Ivor Stenenski was pacing his estate like a caged tiger. Before him stood his most loyal servant and head of his Bratski army Karl Somanoff.

"What the fuck's going down in Yankee land...No news....No fucking news. You said you'd got one of your best over there...A fucking black Angel for God's sake.' He snarls. 'Have you any fucking idea how much this heist is costing me?'

He bangs a hard fist into Sovmanoff's chest. 'We'll have you? ...Well I'll tell you ...fucking million's.' He spits into the face of his servant. 'I'm becoming a fucking laughing stock.'

He again prods Karl's chest.

'So you listen to me good, my friend, you get that comfy arse of yours over there, I want to know what the fucks going on.'

He taps Karl's shoulder and whispers. 'And don't you dare come back here with no fucking news. ..Now get out of my sight.'

Karl leaves, shaking his head whilst hearing the screaming voice of the Pakham shouting out. 'Two hundred fucking men and hearing fucking nothing. Can somebody tell me what the fuck is going on?'

There was confusion too at the breakfast table in the Warm Welcome. Joe and his team sat with their thoughts on the Wolves and their whereabouts when Norm and Dave entered. Frazier pointed at the empty food plates. 'Hope we ain't too late for the breakfast scran, Joe?'

Joe smiled, gave a wink to the others. 'I'm sure they'll always be an exception made for you Dave, especially with Sandra having a sort of, let's say schoolgirl crush on you.'

Dave totally gobsmacked. 'Sandra..she's here?'

Dave can be seen to blush with the rest of the team sniggering. Joe tells him that she came in this morning, took a seat on a little bird with Scott. Seems the lady's in love with our Scottish thistle. Dave throws back his head...'Oh, it's so fucking obvious, you set of wankers.'

They all laugh, it's then Sandra Petersen enters.

'So what's tickled my fellow guests ...Come on now....Let's be knowing?

Norm utters . 'Joke about that Shakespeare couple Romero and Juliette...something like how true love can become a killer.'

She can see the team are ready to burst into laughter. She sighs, 'Like shite it was.'

She rubs Dave's arm, 'I'll get it out of my Davie boy later....So watch out all of you.'

She pulls back a chair and motions Dave to sit, whispering into his ear. 'I'm helping Mary Beth, the owner out in the kitchen....You get an extra sausage my sweet.' Again Dave colours up with the team smirking and nudging each other.

Over on the Sadat estate Rahaad sits with Koo discussing their plans on finding anything at all on the Wolverines, hideaway. Koo tells of his scouts that had been sent out and had information that they, the Wolves, were hiding out on the Don Carlotto Alfredo Ranch. But after many hours of observation neither could give an answer for or against confirmation of this report.

Rahaad shakes is head, 'So let's assume we are no longer any way near into knowing their whereabouts.'

He sighs, 'This information, Koo who supplied you with it?'

Koo holds up a palm. 'From a good sauce, Rahaad, an Arab horse buyer who had a call to the ranch cancelled.'

'But that's not unusual surely.' Koo shrugs. 'I'd say it was. Sheikh Al Kahad had brought along six of his mares to the Alfredos prize stallion War Bonnet, at 50,000 dollars a service.'

He shrugs. 'To cancel, that's the death of any breeding ranch. I asked Sadat to keep the ranch covered should there be news.'

'Then we must look elsewhere my friend...We cannot move without knowing their plans, Remember, cash is king to a begger. Don't be afraid to spread a little if it gets us what we seek...I wonder if our oil billionaire has a friend who could get us into that ranch.'

Koo smiles. 'Like some oil baron who's looking to buy some horse flesh, Rahaad?'

Rahaad nods, patting the arm of his chair. 'You took the words right out of my mouth my friend...Let us see if Sadat can book himself an appointment to see this horse breeder.'

Norman had explained to them all that, and he had missed nothing in their zig-zag journey across the western coast of

America, saying that a hideout for 200 Wolves must be somewhere in the heart of no man's land, like a desert.

Ryona came in with Death Valley? Norman said not to rule that out as a maybe, but then it's anyone guess. Norm was more steered to some hole in the ground, something like Colin's abandoned iron ore mine.

Joe said the need to discover was a race against the clock. That time was running out, that Scott had been informed by Naval Command that the warheads would be hitting the road in three days, under heavy armed escort. Four trailer adapted juggernauts heading out on a last minute disclosed route only given to the drivers on exiting the plant.

Scott had informed Joe that it was a lucky dip situation. Out of six selected routes one would be drawn out of a bag and the go would fall with the one selected. That he would only know that route when his assigned officer for the Delta Force, a Major John Shaw, knew. Shaw had been given a full protection detail of the warheads convoy, with 70 stormtroopers, an elite selection of some of Delta's finest.

Scott was concerned for his men knowing very little of how these wolverines would throw their attack on the crawling possession.

All he knew was it would start on the midnight hour this coming Saturday and with an estimated speed of 25 to a top speed of 40 miles an hour having to cover an estimated 1800 miles. That's going to be taking the convoy over two days to hit that Naval Base. Scott went on to say that his estimate was not including a break. That they would need to stop. Where drivers could change, driving a big heavy for six hours would need to be on a rotation system. That's not forgetting their rest room services and canteen facilities. He sighed saying, 'That's a hell of a time to be out in the open.'

Ryona asked Scott why the warheads weren't flown to Seattle, saving all this. Scott smiled saying 'Good question, truth is I just don't know...Maybe an accident happening on the road is far less worrisome than a plane falling out of the sky.'

Joe had suggested that any stop could be the battleground but Montana was the most likely, with the team all nodding their agreement.

Ryona thought the Wolverine tactics ludicrous saying there was no way the infidels could succeed. Roberto also had thoughts on how they, these Wolves could take on America in its own back garden. A most unlikely and impossible task. There had got to be something more to this heist but what?

Lenny, who had listened intently to the teams conversation, looks to Joe,

'I'm in full agreement with Ryona and Roberto...There has to be something we're all missing, Joe....Fuck me if these Wolves aren't all a crazy Kamikaze rebirth. Besides, we've not seen a squirrel's tail of one since Minnesota.'

Joe nodding deep in thought, Norman sighed saying, 'You would have thought someone would know their whereabouts, let's face it, 200 or so wolverines, would need to be fed...and I can tell you all now ...these boys ain't dieting. If there's a den then it's a big old hole. ...I'm thinking, Joe, they won't be sitting in some field eating cabbages, Maybe, just maybe this Afghan Raheed and his billionaire buddy have formed a partnership with the two armies tucked away behind that estate's fencing.'

Joe says, 'Norm could be right, and that's why we've got to get into that compound.' It's Roberto who adds. 'It's not going to be easy Joe ...Maybe we could borrow one of those 500 drones we recovered off the Fly.'

Ryona gives her man a smile of satisfaction, saying. 'You know, Joe what my man here says ain't such a bad idea. A flight over that Barron's estate could help us just get lucky.'

Lenny adds. 'Especially if we do a night flight ...with a little bird's rotaries drowning out any noise from the drone. I've noted there's quite a lot of air traffic in and around Washington, Oregon, Montana....A chopper flying in unison with the drone I'm sure would not be noticed.'

Joe smiles. 'Let's see if we can do that Scott?'

It took less than an hour to get a thumbs-up from Scott, courtesy of Tom Hawks. One hour later and Scott and the team watched the little bird land with a member of the 'Eye in the Sky' Delta task force step out of the chopper with one drone control expert, Vincent Gates, who'd brought along with him the very latest development from the Fort Worth plant.

Joe stretched out the map and gave Gates the area he wanted to cover. Gates tapped the table and said, 'No problem Colonel.'

Joe then asked how close the drone could get to its target. Gates smiled saying he could put it down on a window ledge looking in and listening to any ongoing conversation being uttered in that room. But its zoom camera and transmission recorder should be more than sufficient to meet its task.

Gates went on to say that the weather would play a part in success or failure.

Joe said,' Well what's the forecast likely to be for tonight? ....green for go?'

Scott came in with, 'With no heavy mist or rain just a slight gentle breeze, and believe it or not we have a full moon tonight. I'd say we are on green, Joe'

Joe. 'So let's go pay the Sadat estate an uninvited visit....Scott, Vincent, you all set?'

Scott looks to Vincent who nods, 'Just blow the whistle Joe... I have my pilot Stan Conway on the ready. I'll go with him ...You and yours can stand by Vincent...oh and do remember guys he's not military...So look after him.'

19

MOON OVER MONTANA

Luckily for Joe and the team the sky was cloudless and, with the full moon Montana was lit like a baseball stadium with the majestic Rocky Mountains as its back cloth. Joe had insisted on full military black out, arms and faces masked along with full camouflaged battle dress. Vincent too was dressed accordingly and seemed rather chuffed at being a soldier. He smirked like a child when Dave did his face masking, with grease dubbing, and with Frazier saying 'Nice set of noshers a sniper could pick them out from a mile away...Best you wear a face mask too.' Then handed one over to him.

Joe went through the team seeing that there were no light reflections. He checked his watch.

'Ok, I've got 23.59 ...We need to find out how long Vincent here, needs to set up.' Ryona gently gives Vince a nudge. 'How long Vinny?'

Vince shrugs. 'All depends on the time it'll take to reach this compound, I have to work out the coordinates, then it's go .....I could launch from here but the nearer the better. Got to consider any obstructions that could crash the flight.' He gives Joe an enquiring look.

'You are wanting a low fly rest and retrieve Colonel Delph?'

Joe, 'I want anything and all that little bird can give us Vincent, ...but I want it undiscovered, a bit like my man Lenny over there.'

He nods over at Lenny.

Frazier asks. 'Lenny?'

Lenny, whispering, answers, 'Joe, he means undercover, a ghost.' Joe turns to Norman. 'Norm?'

'I've got our midnight crawl to that estate worked out to a forest pull in around an hour and a quarter. Then we have another uphill mile hike before Vinny.' He smiles, 'Err Vincent gets set up.'....Vincent interrupts. '15 minutes at the most.'

Joe nods. 'Ok, in that case we're looking at a safe time of an 2.30 launch, can I give that to Scott as a go?'

Norman looks to Vincent and they both nod.

Ryona asks, 'Say Norm, that's looking at this mile hike of a time of around 30 minutes. You sure on the terrain...like we're not hacking our way up through some overgrown woodland scrub?'

Norman laughs, 'Silly me, thinking that after climbing Everest in a day and a half.'

They all burst into laughter when Ryona puts up a finger at Norm. Joe pats her shoulder. 'You asked for that girl.'

'Men! I fucking hate em.'

Roberto looks at her with a saddened expression. 'Hate, Ryona?' She smiles at him, 'Oh not you babe, you I can handle.'

It's near on the exact time Norm had given, 02.20, when the team gather around Vincent as he tests out his equipment. Apart from some frustrated birds and a few scurrying creatures of the night their journey had been quite and uneventful.

Vincent turned to Joe. 'I'm ready Colonel, it's on your call. The target is a quarter mile north of us, slight breeze blowing north-east making it a perfect night for our mission.'

Joe took out his crimson and put in Scott's receiver code. He then gave it three bleeps before shutting off. He'd no sooner done that when the drone suddenly lifted in a vertical to some 40 feet and held its position, not unlike some over a field skylark,with Vincent smiling, saying. 'Now we await the little bird.'

Joe looks to the monitor screen that Vince brings up to power, it's showing a wide panoramic view of the team standing, gazing up at the drone, Then back to the monitor with Vince bringing up an unbelievable clear image.

Joe turns to his team saying. 'I think we're ready and Scott's on his way.'

Over in a large mansion in Las Vagas a meeting had been called for the west coast Mafia families to meet and discuss the recent requirements that the son of Don Alfredo had asked for which was the complete protection of his father's ranch and life in regard to possible infiltration by the Russians.

The San Deago head, one Don Santana, held up a hand before being invited to address the gathering that was being chaired by the Las Vagas Don Piero.

Santana spoke with deliberation.

'I find the young Ricardo's recent endeavour's was one of a fool. He thought nothing of the consequences that could explode in his initial agreements with this pack of Pakham Wolves, no thoughts whatever about asking my good friend the retired Don Carlotto for his advice.'

He slowly shakes his head. 'Now I'm hearing he's wanting our help to shovel the shit....I ask you, do we need this? ...I think not.'

Santana sits, with those gathered mumbling amongst themselves.

Don Tristaneno rose from his chair and was given the nod from Don Piero.

Tristaneno shrugged and held out his arms before addressing the table, 'OK, the boy Ricardo has made an error but I for one can forgive him for that...He has not the brain of his father Don Carlotto...He had tried to bring money into the family...Not thinking of what that money would cost our adopted country of North America. Another 9/11? no, but the start of one hell of a nuclear war..for fuck's sake.'

He gave a deep sigh then ended by a fist down onto the table.

'My brothers, fellow Dons, we must help the Alfredos by stopping the oncoming hurricane that I fear is coming.'

Don Nero Leone coughs and stands. 'I repay a long overdue debt to my great friend Don Carlotto by putting 150 wolverines under my car park on the development of the Washington Rangers Ice Stadium.' He turns to Don Piero. 'I know that you yourself added fifty or so more to the tower block foundations.' He looks to them all.

'Are we not a family? has Don Carlotto ever refused your cries for help? ...I think not ...Yes he's retired but is still breathing the fire of the dragon. He's not only helping us ... but all America.

He raises a wagging finger. 'I have spoken to the New York and Chicago families and can tell you that they want no truce with the Russian Pakham. In fact they're actually saying Don Carlotto wants a fucking medal.'

Don Piero nods, 'Exactly my thoughts Nero, but Ricardo Alfredo, he takes a warning, he makes no more major decisions without first consulting his father. ..Can I therefore take a vote here and now at the table. Do we stay strong by strengthening our families? with a raised hand I ask for your vote.'

With that came a unanimous decision with every hand raised.

'I will inform Don Carlotto that we are as one and give him our support.' They all began to tap the table top. Don Piero closed the meeting.

Over on the Sadat Malik estate the fluttering sound of an overflying little bird was having hardly any reaction. Whilst the drone was making for its intended target of any suitable landing pad that would be both unseen and secure. Its camera was relating back to the monitor its search patten. Vincent brought it down a little lower and landed on what appeared to be a sheltered overhang on a large window lit building.

Its sound recorder was picking up on a joyous sing song with shouts in Arabic for more beer. Its camera then positioned itself to zoom into a window and for the watching team to witnessing rows of what appeared to be an Afghan army dressed in black.

Joe asked Vincent to zoom in on an emblem that was displayed on each uniform. The camera could have been no more than 6 feet away when the emblem displayed showed a Scarab Beetle.

Roberto hissed. 'What's to do with the scarabs. Joe?'

Joe shook his head. 'You tell me man, I'm getting a little confused, we cannot find the Wolves but an army of Scarabs suddenly enter the arena.'

He pats Vincent on the shoulder, 'Let's put this to bed, Vince, I've seen enough.'

He looks to his team, 'We need to get our heads around this ...the situation has suddenly changed. With another anonymous problem falling down on us.'

Ryona said, 'Let's go it one step at a time Joe. You know what they say, more cooks spoil the broth.'

Norma reacts with. 'Only one problem girl, those guys in that house ain't cooks...but natural born killers, That have held a AK.since being ten years old. We know them and what we know ain't good, Ryona....That right Joe?'

Joe gives a nod saying. 'What Norman's saying is true... I've never come across Rahaad Scarabs but they're all ex IS. Islamic State...Hit and run, then leaving a mine trail behind them. I'd say heavy Taliban...It's worth remembering, with no disrespect to Roberto, but they've held off the Russians, French, Brits, and Americans in their fight to protect their homeland. Like the army of Vietnam they're in it to win it. And they've not lost yet.'

Lenny said, 'What beats me Joe is how the fuck did an army of fucking Afghans get let into America.'

Dave added. 'It's easily done with a billionaire's backing...Even the States has their easy Bought and Sold department ...Cash is king in any language.'

Norman said, 'Dave's right ..this fucking oil Barron's paid their entrance fee..that's for sure.'

Joe, 'Let's get the fuck out of here I've a few stressful calls to make, we've now got two fucking armies after those warheads.'

Ryona comes out with. 'Maybe we have three players, Me, I'm not for dismissing the Fly.'

Joe, 'Now that would be a kick up the arse, girl, let's just hope not.'

20

KARL SOMANOFF

Somanoff's arrival at Chicago's O'Hare felt strange, he had expected some kind of welcoming party but there was none.

Fuck, if he didn't feel depressed, with the shadow of Ivor the Pakham on his back and watching his every move. One thing for sure there was going to be one almighty showdown when he caught up with the bungling clowns.

How can just over 200 men, born killers just like himself and furthermore, hand selected by himself...all be unaccounted for...with no given word to their families.? He asked himself what the hell had gone down here in America.

He stood on one of the thresholds of America Chicago and hailed a taxi. It's driver looking a middle aged Spanish hombre, asked him his destination. Karl gave him the address of Ottermanze and his crew's last known one. 'Hotel Templeman'. He then sat back half taking in the sights on his journey into central Chicago and pondering on whether Ottermanze could enlighten him on the whereabouts of the black Angel Bratski.

He noted the taxi passing various sights like the Trump Tower which sat on the shoulder of the East River, before the long drive finally ended at the Templeman. He exited and took in the street and not surprisingly one hundred yards from, yes he'd guessed it, the fucking Trump Tower.

'What's the damage?'

The driver pointed at the meter. 'That's 50. 15. Sir'

He gave the driver his most threatening look and said.

'I hope that's the time your giving me. I didn't ask for a fucking tour of this city.... For your cheek you get 20 and no tip, and don't you dare fucking argue with me...you do, you lose the 20.'

The driver looked at the muscular 6-3 square jawed, 50 year old and said. 'I'll take your twenty Sir.'

Karl winked saying 'I thought you would.'

He found a hand being held out to him by a yellow and blue uniformed porter who said. 'Your case, sir. Let me take that.'

Karl smiled, saying. 'I hope it's not going to cost me. 50 .15 ?'

The Porter laughed, 'You don't have to tip, sir...reception is straight ahead.'

Karl at that moment in time was the only one booking in to what looked like a fine establishment.

The receptionist a small bespectacled lady, asked 'You have a reservation, sir?'

Karl nodded. 'That's if you have my call...names, Dieter Noss.' She smiled. 'I have you for two nights Mr Noss.'

She peeped over her her glasses at him. 'Two nights is that correct, sir?' Karl nodded.

'Could I take a look at any documentation in your name, sir...it's become a part of keeping a check on our arrivals due to the terrorist activities.'

Karl produced a passport with the name Dieter Noss and was listed as a German wine producer, with an Heidelberg address. She handed it back to him quite satisfied.

Karl asked of her 'I wonder if you could inform Mr. Ottermanze that I'm here...I don't know what room he's in?'

The receptionist ran down the ledger turning page after page. 'I'm sorry Mr. Noss, but I don't have a man of that name staying with us.'

'Your sure, he came here about a week ago with ten other members of our party, an annual get together?'

'I'm sure sir.' She turned the ledger towards him and it showed no sign of Alpha Hans Ottermanze. 'Do you still require a room, sir?' Karl shrugged and nodded.

She called the Porter telling him to take Karl and his luggage up to room 41, adding that the restaurant opened at 7 for dinner and would he like her to book him a table. He looked at his watch which was showing 16.20, before telling her yes and to make it an early booking for 7pm.

Hans tipped the Porter with a 20 euro bill, thinking it's always better to get on the top side of the staff. The Porter gave him a tip of his hat then, before leaving the room, he suddenly turned and said.

'Those friends of yours Mr. Noss, I think they were here about a week or so ago. Then, how can I forget, they were taken away by the uniforms.'

Karl asks, 'The uniforms ..the police?'

The Porter shook his head, not the police ...the Military, sir.' With that he left the room.

Back at reception the hostess was on the phone saying,

'I've a German just booked in looking for those men...No I told him nothing, shown him the dummy ledger.....I don't know if he believes me.' She laughs, 'What's that? ...Why the man's huge....built like a dam wall...Yes..phone you later.'

Karl lay back on his bed having showered and was waiting for dinner.He had two urgent calls to make; one to his Lordship the Pakham…and the other to Olga Kavich a very old friend who happened to work in the Russian Embassy. He would phone Olga first. If anything had gone down that she'd not known about then it wasn't worth investigating.

He made the call. She was on the answer phone's 'leave a message.'

He simply said 'It's Karl, I'm in Chicago.' Before hanging up. It took less than a minute before he received a text message, 'Cafe Napoleon 8pm….Buy me dinner.'

He smiled thinking did that woman ever spend a Ruble, still he needed her company …one part of his past life not owned by the Pakham. That would help him relax and more than likely have him come away with some answers.

The Porter had told him of a military intervention. What had that clown Ottermanze got himself into?

It was a little before 8 when Somanoff found himself entering the Cafe Napoleon, a restaurant that was, as its title implied, serving French cuisine and, as he later would find, asking top dollar. She had already booked a table in a private archive area.

Olga arrived some10 minutes late, making an entrance like a queen..her hour-glass frame and long flowing black hair causing quite a few scowls from some already seated ladies, with their men staring goggle eyed at the 40 year old Prima-Donna, she looked like she'd just come out of Swan Lake. He didn't think the American security system was all that tight because Olga in her youthful years had been an active member of the KGB. But times change as do the people and finding herself wrapped up in government policy had brought her a more satisfying life working in the land of the free.

Karl stood up with a bow and kissed the back of her hand before guiding her to her seat. She waved over to the waiter who seemed to know her, like she was a .regular customer.

'Gavin, my heart, this gentleman is a very old friend who has come over the pond. His name is ....Karl sprang and held out a hand, saying Dieter..Dieter Noss ... The waiter smiled, saying any friend of Miss Olga's is welcome to the Cafe Napoleon....Would you like to choose the wine, sir?

Olga broke in with we'll have the Dom .. Gavin dear, this is a special night for me.' Gavin gave a bow and a heel click leaving them to study the menus.

Olga leaned over to Karl and asked. 'What's with this Dieter Noss my sweet...Your not a wanted man are you?'

Karl whispered. 'If only...I've the Pakham on my back clinging on so tight it's if I'm more than wanted....But let's eat, your choice before I explain.'

She looked at him suspiciously.

'If it's waxed then I'll be afraid to hear your coming tale of woe. My cloak and dagger days are over, I feel I can walk the streets again, so please to God don't get me involved in any shit...I'm happy working here Karl' ....She sighs.

'Moscow and its lights went out a long time ago for me darling I'm afraid to say, and I'm not for them to be re-lit. I thought the Iron Curtain had been pulled down, but I know through my everyday work that the old establishment still exists. Like I know you are here, not to see me, but here on a mission.'

Karl takes her hand. 'Yes I'm here on a mission ...but I'm also here to see you. If I could change what's required of me ...then believe me I would... Moscow, the Pakham could all go to hell, but I'm afraid that can, as you well know, never be.'

He squeezes her hand, gives a deep sigh.

'I'm here to ask for your help, Olga. It's a question of you either know or you don't...I can only promise that whatever you give will never be revealed in that it came from you, this on my mother's grave.'

She patted his hand and turned to the menu.

'My choice you say? ...OK, let's start with the escargot, the Duck all Orange as our main and the Apple Tart Tatar to finish.'

She gave him a wayward look. 'Why is it, whenever you call, there's a hanging man tarot card falling out of the pack?'.

She shrugs. 'So let's have the real reason you're here, I know you've not come to see me...and don't you shit me Somanoff . Remember I fucking know you too well.'

Karl went on to explain the reason for his sudden appearance. Leaving out the Black Angel who was somewhere on the west coast there was no way he was going to give out the real reason of the Wolverine's mission. Knowing the whereabouts of Ottermanze and his crew would be sufficient.

Olga told him she would ask a fellow friend in confidence, saying that he would know of any central Chicago arrests on the military side. She was amazed that nothing, no news, had come of the taking of eleven German Wolves. Such an occurrence should have made news headlines. But no TV or press reports. She added that what he was asking was heavy duty.

She ended by offering a little advice to her old friend which was, Be careful where you're treading.

'You are a wanted man and in no way safe in the land of the free....If I have anything for you then I will call. Please Karl, do not try to contact me.'

He nodded that he understood and watched her walk off into the night.

Whilst over on the west coast, Rahaad sat with Woo and Sergio awaiting the return of Sadat, hoping he had news of the elusive Wolverine army. They were sitting, sharing the bubble-pipe of Afghanistan gold hash. Floating high in the clouds, it's power releasing the dreams of the Gods, standing them high looking down on the untameable oceans, then giving them the lifting wings of the falcon.

Sadat Malik had arrived back without any news on the Pakham army. He had seen nothing of there being any indication that the Wolves had been on the Alfredo ranch ... Don Carlotto told him to wait until after the Kentucky horse sales before returning, adding that the old Don had his eyes fixed on bidding against the Saudi princes for one of three two year olds that had been sired by the great American Phoenix...that he was talking over a million or so bucks, he then asked if Sadat would be interested in a partnership.

The oil Barron had left with a Maybe ...Sadat had come to the conclusion that the Wolverines were no longer in the game and that they, for some unknown reason had left the United States.

Why, was anyone's guess. Would Rahaad and his Scarabs take up the gauntlet, he thought not. That all would be decided come the morrow when everyone had a clear head.

21
A CHANGE OF PLAN

The weekend had finally arrived when the convoy of warheads were due to leave Amarillo. Joe sat with his team, along with Scott Brady Jones. They'd been discussing the none sighting of the Wolverines, asking how on earth could over 200 souls suddenly disappear. Scott reported that he'd had his men into every state, LA up to Washington searching like no man's business. They'd come back with zilch. There had been nothing coming from customs in both air and sea departments on any sudden mass withdrawal.

It was Lenny who suggested that it could be another incident. Like the one that had happened ten years ago when a the pilot, one kamikaze from Palestine had somehow managed to get to fly over 250 Israeli football supporters, destined for Egypt, into the Red Sea. Lenny's thoughts were that something similar could have happened.

Joe shook his head saying he doubted this being the cause of their disappearance. Who would have it in for the Pakham's army?

Ryona said.'So they're not around anymore, that's got to be good news hasn't it?...we've now got to concentrate on the movement of the Afghans. We cannot allow them to leave that estate.'

Scott nodded. 'Ryonas right, that's why I've got 80 of Delta surrounding that compound. They leave, my boys take them down.'

He turns to Joe, 'With no exceptions Joe, Those Scarab leaders, they fall too.'

Norman. 'And the Baron?'   Scott nods.'And the Baron, Norm.'

Roberto shrugs, 'I've a feeling we are in for a messy night...just let's keep those warheads safe on American soil.'

Whilst over in the safety of the compound the Scarabs were beginning to stir. Dressed in their long black flowing kaftans with hood...They now looked like an army of Japanese Ninjas, nothing showed to give any sightings to the enemy.

Rahaad had envisaged a platoon of National Guard, with no more than twenty men, but in the back of his mind he was still worried about Mari Bambella. Somehow he didn't get this unusual and sudden appearance. Surely she'd have noticed him in the Colosseum restaurant and if so, why hadn't she come over to his table. Come to that, why didn't he approach her, like old friends were supposed to do. He certainly wasn't convinced of this Olympic Games shit.

Enough for now, he had a final decision to make. Was he to take on the warheads heist? Had the wolverines withdrawn knowing that they'd been discovered? His mind was going through the ifs and buts of this operation. The Fly in his comfy French mansion house needed to be told by his runaround slave, Sergio, of the position here in Montana. What with the millions of dollars already invested, some final decision would have to be made.

The discussion was getting to the point of calling it a day by his uncle Woo. He was a fighter, if he was given orders then he would find the way to victory, he wasn't a loser, nor was he a fool. He was against taking his men into a no-win operation.

He told Rahaad in his Arabic language.

'I fear we are walking into a trap. We are going off our original plan,...These Wolves having withdrawn. ..Maybe they wait..maybe they know of us being here and therefore take up a plan. ..

A plan that is not unlike that of our own. They wait for our attack, then hope to take the spoils.' Raheed translates. Sadat concludes with the shake of his head,

'You must remember this my good friends, I too have put a lot of dollars into your plan, I have taken an old silver mine that lays in my estate and converted into a hold bigger than any aircraft hanger. With all the facilities, food, accommodations for the whole Scarab army. All concealed and camouflaged behind steel coded entrance doors. That requires a series of letters and numbers that any computerised brain would find impossible to break. This again I remind you did not come cheap.'

He points a serious finger at the Scarab number two.

'So Woo, you are telling me it's a no go?' Raheed once again translates.

Woo shrugs, replying to Rahaad, 'Tell our host, our benefactor that it is not my decision to take, one way or the other. that I can understand the lengthy road he has gone down to secure a successful ending to this operation.

His plans have been done and a great finish achieved. Tell him I wish only for the same, those warheads shut in his shed, his Judas hole. But like him, I like to be sure of success.'

Sadat puts his hands together in a prayer gesture and bows to Woo.

Sergio says. 'Let's hear what Conrad has to say. Allow me.'

He puts through a call to the Fly. They speak in French. Rahaad, putting up a hand, shouts. 'No, no, no.....English, Sergio if you please.' Sergio responds.

Conrad is dumbfounded with what he's hearing and asks for a moment, before responding to this last minute news.

In the Colmar mansion Conrad tells his personal aid, Ferdinand Cortez, of the problem. Ferdinand gives his answer to what evidently must give a change of plans.

'First can we afford to lose once again Conrad? It's a poor army that doesn't know it's enemy...Sergio tells of a 200 strong pack that have vanished from the face of the earth, without trace, erased, becoming extinct. The Pakham, like the dinosaur, will find he cannot exist...Making you, Conrad, the new born giant in the underworld of crime. He goes on....'We must, to ensure such a crowning glory, insult the Russian by taking the prize. Sadat has the storage till the cash register rings. The rebellious fiends of the Middle East are eager for these warheads, eager to give them back to the USA, as cascading heavy rain, a shower like no other. America left in a state of obliteration.'

He puts up a palm. 'But Conrad we must be sure of success or otherwise withdraw.'

The Fly nods. 'I think we go, give Sergio the green light.' Ferdinand gives a shrug. 'Consider it done Conrad. One Scarab is far superior to any ten National Guards.'

'Yes, yes, we go for the prize......The crown.'

The news came as no surprise to Rahaad, he could read Conrad Wolff like a book, it was never about the dollar, more of the glory. He asked Sergio to leave whilst he talked over, with Woo and Sadat, Conrad's decision to carry on, with Ferdinand saying the taking of the Missiles should be a far easier task against a National Guard unit than if they'd have had to take on a pack of wolves.

Woo wasn't convinced and so spoke against the attack. Sadat abstained saying there was some reason the Wolves had withdrawn . He wanted to know why. It was therefore left for Rahaad to make the final decision.

Rahaad said 'Let's go get those GM's, are we not the deadliest fighting machine on the planet? and Conrad gives us 10% of our catch. ...We hold till we're paid, and we accept only payment in gold.' He brings back Sergio and gives him his ultimatum. 'Ask the Fly if it's still green for go?'

Sergio relays to Conrad. He turns to Rahaad and says. 'The Fly says yes, it's still green .'

Meanwhile a report comes in to Scott telling him that all men are in position and that there much is activity going on in the compound. This he gives out to Joe and the team. He adds that Delta have more of the advantage in an all out gun battle having the superior weapons and night view goggles. The snipers had reported no goggles being seen on the enemy's attire. They seemed to be relying on their all black uniforms as more of a deterrent.

Sadat had taken the three principles up to the Judas hole and after, keying in the code and a camera flash the great steel doors slid open to a series of overhead floodlighting that showed a vast unbelievable cavern of some ten meters in hight and width far greater. It was so big it could have stored the Titanic.

It simply was a sight that took the breath away. The Cave ran in for some hundred metres.

Sadat looked at his guests and could see the amazement showing on their faces.

He spoke to them and his voice seemed to bellow in the great arena.

'If you were to venture on down some mile and a half through the tunnel over there.' He pointed to the section.

'Then my friends you would emerge out onto the other side of the mountain...This I had built as an escape route... Oh ,by the way, it also has a steel door, that has to be coded to open...Completely camouflaged of course.'

Rahaad had to take Sadat's hand and shake it.

'Sadat what you have here.....He spreads his arms fully, spinning in the great auditorium.

.....Is the most fantastic of all shelters ever built on earth. I congratulate you on a magnificent achievement.' He shakes his head, 'Fucking unbelievable.'

He turns to Woo and Sergio. 'Such an achievement deserves to hide its prize, let's go get those warheads.'

Sergio nods in agreement while Woo just shrugs.

Two phones began to vibrate One was being answered by Colonel Scott, whilst not too far away a call was being received by Oil Barron Sadat. Both calls were giving out information as to the convoy's route, which was via Denver on through Casper, Wyoming, Billings, Spokane and on to the Seawolf submarine base.

Sadat put down his phone and smiled at his three guests. 'It must be our lucky day, the Convoy's passing our doorstep, Billings ..we can strike after Billings...We are but a stone throw off their route.'

Rahaad turning to Woo. 'Your thoughts my General?'

Woo replies, still a little uncertain. 'The route Rahaad, yes, it is good that it falls within our grasp but I wish to ride and take in our ambush point. My heart cries, Yes....but my head...my mind, my brother it is not fully liking this operation. We have with us our finest beetles...veterans of hit and run tactics as you well know, it's just that, when we leave this God forsaken land I want it to be with my men.'

Rahaad nods, 'Ok. You can take a ride but you will take Sergio with you, he speaks the language, the convoy will not reach us till tomorrow's night...I'm like you my brother still carrying thoughts on those missing Wolverines.'

Sergio says. 'But it's going to be difficult finding the right vantage point. Night is here already and we should really be looking to view in daylight.'

Rahaad nods, 'Yes,yes, Sergio I'm thinking of sending Yatish who speaks the English to pick up on that convoy strength, it's weaknesses.'

Rahaad conveys the conversation to Woo.

Woo asks if one of his top warriors, Yatish speaks the English, then he should accompany him and let Sergio do the convoy....surely that would be better with Yatish speaking both languages. Sergio does no have my tongue.'

Rahaad said. 'Yes you are right Woo, I wasn't thinking, consider it done.'

Joe, when he heard the route the convoy was taking, thought of only one thing and that was relief, that there would be little chance of an inner city shootout. Denver was a bypass. The Wolves had fled. Only the Scarabs remained and if Scott and his Deltas his own team had their way, they wouldn't make it.

Tom Hawks had also enquired, offering an extra platoon of Seals which Scott had welcomed. A commander Ernest Levin, would bring in his specialist unit, after being informed that the infiltrators were after the Navy's ultimate deterrents, the sea to air nuclear missiles. And so the clock was ticking and the compound at Malik's estate was completely surrounded. There was no way that convoy was going down. If anything it would continue its journey without events. It would only travel the ordered non-stop, with each tractor trailer having a relief driver to ensure this rolling movement was contained. They would make Wyoming and skirt Montana.

Rahaad and his army were in for quite a surprise. The Baron and his invited guests were prime targets who were wanted alive if possible but there would be no set rules to fallow into. Kill or be killed was the order that would be given. A take off the mittens and pull on the iron gauntlet attitude was fed into each defender's mind.

Joe gathered his team and along with Colonel Scott and Commander Ernest Levin spoke saying that tomorrow was going to be a long day and now was the time to rest up, that Scott had already given Ernest the story so far so there was no need to tell them the drill; if it moves hit it. It seemed there was only one team left on the park, Raheed and his Scarab army.

Ryona was at a loss at the vanishing act that had been performed by the Wolves.

Still how do you evacuate your 200 plus Wolverines without some notice? No, Ryona believing there was some other explanation for this exodus. Could

her old school Buddy Rahaad have infiltrated and ended their race for the booty?

It was Commander Levin who spoke up.

'You know Ryona those,or similar thoughts, were in my head too.' He turned and addressed the gathered.

'Men, troops, people I came to the conclusion that this operation could be what you might call a Tom, Dick, and Harry ploy.'

Joe asks him to explain,

'Well let's just say, and I'm only surmising, ..that the Wolves know of the Scarabs being around and are taking more than an interest of the cargo of 'Naughty Boys. Thats on the road to Sea Base.'

Ryona. 'Naughty Boys, Commander?'

'That's what's stamped on the body of the torpedoes Ryona......., Naughty Boy USA.'

Joe, 'So what's with this Tom, Dick, and Harry?'

Ernest smiles. 'Tom is the wolf, watching the scarab, who is Dick, and Harry is the prize Naughty Boy.'

Lenny says. 'I see a little bit of deception that could well be a goer Commander.'

He smiles before going on to say, 'The Scarabs are made to believe that the Wolf has retreated back into Europe... whilst the truth is they're just waiting for the result of a Scarab attack...Then, and only then, will they counter to take the Naughty Boys into their den.'

Joe looks to Scott who's thinking whilst slowly nodding, he shrugs before saying.

'Scott, your thoughts on the Commander and Lenny's suggestions?'

Scott replies, ' The Tom Dick and Harry is a possible explanation for the missing Wolves. ..and if we, after countless hours, cannot find their lair then I'm sure the Scarabs will hit the same difficulty...We must be aware of such an event happening. ..I'm thinking we could well be looking at a Delta Tom Dick and Harry main event. ...I must inform headquarters of this and get some little bird's view of any Wolverine movement....In the meantime my men, along with Ernest and his Seals will make a frontline and rear parallel observation post.'

Ernest nods saying, 'We must do this Scott ...protect our back door.'

Meanwhile, back in Chicago, Olga Kavich had phoned Karl with no news. Her friend having informed her that what she was wanting was held in higher office and that any questions on that subject was liable for further investigation and for him to go over the fence. An action he was not going to risk. She did say that a little money thrown in the right direction could maybe give him the info. but that too would carry some risk.

He replied, asking for direction as he too, was getting an uneasiness from the man in Moscow.

She told him to try the Bear Cave a bar on the eastern side of Chicago, well known for its celebratory clientele and where you'd find the home of football's Chicago Bears big money supporters.

He'd to ask, discreetly mind, for Ziggy Moore and to be sure to take plenty of dollar bills along with him. Ziggy gave nothing for nothing. He could say discreetly of course, that Olga had sent him. She ended by saying that's the best she could do, and to please be careful.

It was some hours later that Karl left the Bears Cave with a tiny bit of information, information, that cost a few thousand dollars. He carried with him the name of a taxi driver who had taken the Alpha Bratski and the Mobster boss Ricardo Alfredo to the train station and had heard them speaking of their ongoing journey to some horse farm near Portland Oregon . He was also told by Ziggy that, as far as the locations of Alpha Hans Ottermanze and his crew, he knew nothing more than what the hotel Porter had already told him. That it was a military pickup.

So it was early evening when Karl found himself riding the Transam that would eventually take him to Portland, on the west coast of America.

22
GUNFIGHT AT THE MALIK CORRAL

Night was closing in and a little bird had reported in that the convoy was passing through Wyoming.
Scott turned to the team saying if the Scarabs were going to strike it was time they were moving into position.

'I'm thinking it's going to be Eagles Rock. Joe and I have done a survey of the area and it's an ideal vantage point for an ambush.'

Joe nods.'But we ain't going to let that happen…Why?' He smiles. 'Because there ain't no way we're letting them out of the estate. We hit them with everything we've got, a crossfire-power assault and if there's one left moving then I want to know why.'

Same goes for Rahaad and the mighty oil Barron Sadat Malik.'

Commander Levin adds, 'My Seals and I will be watching your rear door so concentrate on forward movement.'

Scott, 'Both of our units Delta Force and Ernest's Seals have been issued with the battle plan, and believe me they know their jobs.'

He sighs, shakes his head. 'They remember 9/11 so it ain't gonna happen. Those Scarabs are going down.'

The team sit huddled up behind a monitor that's filming the estate from a high flying drone. It's just after midnight when it zooms in on Woo, who can be seen marshalling the Scarabs, who have assembled at the gates of the estate, into rows of four groups of 50 assassins. The little bird tells Scott that there are four coaches on the road that leads up to the Malik estate.

Joe turns to Ryona saying 'Looks like transport has arrived.'

Ryona smiles, 'I'd say that was a bonus for us Joe...We take out the buses and it's not a messy screaming onslaught.'

Scott is already on to his Delta commandos. He's telling them to take out the coaches with a few rocket launchers. Then hit any Scarab thats fortunate to scramble out.

They view Woo boarding the last bus along with 50 Scarabs plus one extra, a man who had been standing alongside Rahaad and Malik. It's Lenny who points at the addition.saying. 'I know that face, I've seen it before.'

Joe asks. 'Where Lenny? Think man.'

Lenny rubbing his chin, smiles. 'Why he's the man who's wanted by the mob. Those murders in Sicily, he's the fucker that poisoned them all. ..Fuck me if there's not a million dollars on his head.' Ryona remembers, 'His name is Sergio Romano.'

She pushes Joe's shoulder, 'But he worked for the Fly...I just knew it.'

Lenny tugs her sleeves. 'Knew what, Ryona?'

..Roberto answers for her. 'That the Fly would be involved in all this heist business, Lenny.....and I'm thinking my girl is right.'

Joe looks at Ryona, then Lenny. 'You sure Lenny? Err don't answer that..of course your sure....So our old enemy returns.'

Ryona winks. 'Gives us the chance to find and really close the curtain on the elusive Fly.'

Roberto shrugs. 'Sergio, he'd never talk, and no disrespect but I can't see you breaking him.'

Joe says 'You never know until you've tried, Roberto.'

Ryona adds, 'He's not failed yet Roberto.'

Roberto nods. 'True, maybe I should learn to keep my big mouth shuts .'

It was at that moment the gates began to open and the coach engines started. The team could see the two figures of Rahaad and Sadat walking back towards the main lodge. As for the coaches, they'd travelled a little under a mile before they were hit by Delta rockets.

Out of the last bus came the scrambling figures of Woo and Sergio, firing their Kalashnikov's at nothing. Woo fell to his knees after a Delta bullet took away his right knee cap, he looked at Sergio for help. The Sicilian shrugged and turned to run but not before Woo had put a spray of bullets down his spine. Sergio the Sicilian was dead before hitting the ground. Woo looked around, and saw no resistance coming fom the burning coaches, along with the bodies of his army scattered on each side of the road. More explosions the flames hit the coach's fuel tanks. He raised his hands in surrender. A crescendo of sound rings into his ears as machine gun automatics trace their bullets into the coaches. Tears came streaming down his face on seeing his men falling like autumn leaves, cut down as they tried to escape a no hope violent slaughter. One of his youngest, one he had marked as a future captain, Zakir lay dead with his eyes blackened in their sockets. Once shining, smiling eyes that now shone no more. He shook his head and cursed the day they ever met the Frenchman and the Fly, a man that now must be put down to another failure. His cowardly aid, Sergio, he nods with the thought of him lying out there, dead by his making, one huge satisfactory result.

He could see them now the assassins walking steadily towards him. treading carefully avoiding the dead. So the killers were Americans not what he'd expected. His thoughts had been on the Wolverines. So what had happened to mark them down as a no show? Had they too fallen to the US armed forces?

Lucky that his nephew was safe ...The Judas Hole...if Allah was good he along with Sadat would make their escape...But what of himself. Would they stand over him and shoot him like a crazed dog?...Now was the time to find out as two of the soldiers approached. One of which bore the crown of a major.

He said something, pointing down at him Woo thought, not knowing the English that the words could have been. 'He's their leader, take him and bring him in. Thats exactly what they did. with Woo hopping in agony and given no pain relief.

Back at the estate, Rahaad found himself running along with Sadat to the Judas Hole..and the safety of the old silver mine. Jahaad is snarling, shouting to nobody but Sadat who seems, beside himself, the only man left standing. His army has been annihilated, caught cold by an unknown force, some army that had probably taken the Wolves out. He shouted, shaking a fist at the heavens.

'I'm sorry my uncle, my life's provider, I should have listened to you, your doubts, that Fly's greed. We will find these killers, we shall have our day, forgive me for leaving your body to scavengers. Your name will be taken to the great cave house of Maphinda. To be martyred by our people. You will live in the broken heart of Jahaad for all times.'

Sadat calls for Rahaad to hurry, saying the infidels will soon be into the estate. 'We shall live on my brother, they will pay a heavy cost for this day.'

They reach the great door of the Judas Hole and Sadat puts in the code, a camera clicks and the door slides open. On entering the vast cathedral like dome the door shuts and an array of lights cuts into the darkness.

'What now Sadat, do we go to exit this fortress?'

Sadat smiles. He pats Rahaad on his shoulder. 'Tonight has not been fruitful my brother but remember this. tomorrow brings a new day, a new season, fresh buds that will produce fruit once more, to a wiser tree, and...' He wags a finger, 'A fruit not left to go rotten...picked only when it's fully ripened.'

Rahaad forces a smile saying, 'You know I've never heard that saying,...the fruit...It's not of my tongue. ..but it holds in the heart a satisfying beat Sadat.'

Sadat replies. 'It comes from one of my father's books of verse, by the great Arabian philologist, Shamah Mohammed...There in Riyadh lived a man of great mind.'

'You have lost a lot of Afghani in this operation Sadat and you must be repaid.'

'My brother,' He hugs Rahaad, 'Sadat Malik came into this world with nothing, he will one day leave with nothing. He would sooner lose all his millions of dollars than his blood...Remember my friend, life is a gift more precious than all the gold on earth. So live your life to its full.'

Rahaad smiles, 'Is that another saying from your fathers book of verse?'

'No, it is mine.' They laugh as they take to the hollowed out escape tunnel.

23
BRUSH AND PAN

Joe stood with arms folded surveying the main compound of the Malik estate. Scott's Delta boys were busy hunting the whereabouts of the main men, Rahaad and his benefactor Sadat.

Suddenly a cry came out of a dense woodland area of pine, with under bush gorse, that lay beneath the mountains face.

' Over here ' A voice was calling out.

Ryona, 'Looks like they've found something.'

Joe smiled as he looked at his team, all still with him and showing not a scratch from a most bloody encounter.

'So let's go take a look-see shall we?'

Frazier 'Still better to be a bit wary, guys ..those fuckers are still close, who knows could be looking right at us.'

Roberto nods his head towards the wood. 'I think we're needed, Joe.'

Two of Delta's finest stood with Scott pointing at the great steel door that covered the oil Barron's Judas Hole.

Joe and the team approached with Joe asking, 'So what's lying behind the steel, Scott, some kind of storage depots?' Scott, taking off his helmet, scratches his head. 'Your guess is as good a one as mine Joe. We're going to have to open it ….to know what's what.'

Ryona says, 'With his kind of bank roll, that of a billionaire...it could well contain anything, that door was put there to house something special.'

Norman says, 'Something like a Naughty Boy missile, Ryona?'

Joe says. 'We'll there's only one way we're ever going to find out...and that's to open the fucker.'

Roberto, pointing to its code entry box, 'Looks like it's got a numbered entry code that if we can't break, it will stay shut.'

Ryona asks, 'What about that dumb looking Afghan prisoner, he was sat at that restaurant table with Rahaad and the oilman, think he knows?'

Lenny comes in with. 'If he does he's not going to tell us... and he don't speak'a the English just some muddled Afghani tribal language that you wouldn't find in any Middle Eastern jargon.'

Joe nods, 'Lenny's right, I know a little Arabic ...but not the sort he speaks. ...The code to that door, it's going to be a huge problem.'

Scott who's been patiently listening, interrupts saying

'That ain't no problem for a tank, it would, I'm sure would blast a hole in the fucker.'

Joe said. 'I'm thinking that's the only way we're going to get into what's behind. By getting the heavy demolition crew in.'

He smiles.'That of course is providing non of our super brains here have some other idea.'

Frazier looks back at the black smoke that's darkening the dawn sky. He turns and says, looks like Delta are burning the dead, there are was a whole lot of meat lying on the road back there.'

Scott says, 'We too, have what you call a cleaning team... ours is a part of Delta Force Dave, known as the B and P's unit. ..That's Brush and Pan. We have no problem, when we need a clean up, they respond.'

Ryona asks. 'That door, wouldn't it be better to contact the installers...Surely they'd have it in their books.'

Roberto says. 'That's always surmising they have such knowledge..I'd think Sadat would not want the code known to anyone but himself. What's the use of having such a fortress with another holding the key?'

Scott, 'By the time we get someone over from the installation crew, we'd be losing time, a few heavy mortars would bring that down.'

Scott calls in on his field phone. 'Kenny ...get me some heavy duties up to me, I've got a heavy steel enormous door I need opening. What's that you say?...

'Yes, yes....One hour...do it in half and I'll get you a bottle of KB...Good man.'

He turns to the team and a few of Delta that have assembled around him. He looks to a sergeant.

'So what you got for me Bill?' The sergeant shrugs, 'Not a lot Sir....one thing I can say for sure is that pair of Afghans ..Well,, they ain't on this compound, no sir, they've hitched a lift skywards or dug a damn hole into Wyoming.'

Ryona says 'Or hiding inside of this mountain behind that door.'

Norman, 'If I was a gambling man of which I'm not, I'd go with Ryona on the door.'

Joe, 'I think we all have come to that conclusion.'

Not too far away sitting in an early morning Taxi, Karl Somanoff is hoping there's going to be no further tour of America. For the umpteenth time his phone was beeping. The screen lit up with a Moscow number. Karl, forgetting himself cries out 'Fuck man can't you let me do my fucking job?'

The driver shouts to him. 'You OK back there.'

'I'm fine just get me to this horse ranch then I'll feel better.'

The driver replies, 'Another twenty should see us at the gates.'

Back on the Malik estate and the doors were down after taking six cannon shells into the bedrock. The team waited for the all clear before finally stepping into the great arena.

Joe gave a low whistle on its vast spaciousness, it's grandeur.

'Now this cave could well hide those warheads,what you think Scott?'

Scott gives a shake of his head. 'I think you could have put the the White House in here, with those naughty boys, no trouble at all, Joe.'

Ryona adds, 'That means this heist had been planned for quite some time..maybe three years or more.'

Roberto says. 'It certainly wasn't done in a day, that's for sure.'

Norman. 'They would need a good year to get all this equipment in.' He points to the large generator, the lighting, the row of monitors that are now lit up ...The words Judas Hole every screen. Freezer doors along with all the facilities for living a lifetime here. Like some gigantic nuclear fallout shelter. It had an inbuilt toilet and shower, a food storage section

Joe says, 'This hollow certainty could be used for not only the storage of those warheads ...but for sanctuary in a the event of a nuclear attack on America.

He shakes his head as Scott approached from his inner search of the Hole. Scott tells Joe and the team. 'Looks like they got away, I've got men searching a concealed tunnel that seems to be cutting through the mountain, I fear the Afghans must have made their escape along it.'

Ryona gives him a little satisfaction in saying 'At least you've got the Naughty Boys safe and into Bremerton base, Colonel, those Seawolves can load and make our world a whole lot safer.'

Scott nods.'That has always been the objective Ryona, with only three Seawolves left in commission, each with a torpedo load of 50 missiles and eight firing tubes, I think we did well to come away with a couple of my men receiving non life threatening injuries, but other than that, we're burying around 200 Scarabs.' He winks, 'Things get even better when their ashes fill a hole deep inside an old silver mine called the Judas Hole.'

Ryona. 'You mean to say.....oh..the Brush and Pan detail; they haven't far to sweep-up and bury the rubbish.'

Joe, 'That would be the perfect ending to a most eventful day. Get the boys to pack out that escape hole and then bury the lot of them with a couple of grenades from a FGM javelin. That's enough to bring a cave in and so into history.'

Roberto asks, 'So what do you think's going to happen to this auditorium Scott?'

'Not our worry Robby...but if they were to ask me...Then I'd refit them doors, then I'm thinking it would make one hell of a sports arena, concert hall...something on the same lines as New York's Madison Square Garden.'

'You ever been there?'

Roberto shakes his head, 'Can't say that I have..but I know a man who has, Joe.'

Joe gives a half smile in remembering when Stacy Kilmer and he, went to see the world middleweight boxing championship. He says, 'I don't know of any boxer who wouldn't dream of fighting there. It's the Mecca.'

Karl had just finished answering the phone call from Ivor the Pakham telling him of his every move made so far. He told him he was on his way to a horse breeding ranch that was supposedly the place where the wolves had bought their privacy and that it was owned by a retired mafia boss Carlotto Alfredo.. He was hoping that this was his final call.

He also informed the Pakham that the Alpha and his crew were no longer in the play after being seized by the military. Ivor's reply was a long ear burning abuse, Karl had to hold away the earpiece while his non-stop raging venomous words subsided.

It was then that the taxi stopped at the main gate of what looked to be a long tree lined driveway where chipmunks could be seen racing up near on every available tree seeking a place of safety. The driveway gates demanded a name and a reason for the call. Meanwhile a camera looked down from a high telegraph pole, giving a full panoramic view.

A rough sounding Italian voice came out of the speaker box which was embedded into one of the gates stone pillars.

'What is your name, your business with the Alfredo Ranch?'

Karl replied with a strong verbal counter...

'My name is Deiter Noss and I wish to speak with one Carlotto Alfredo on some urgent and private business in regards to the whereabouts of one Bratski Onasskikoff and 200 of his men. I represent the Pakham of Moscow. And await your gates to open.'

Inside the Alfredo lodge Ricardo was pacing the floor wringing his hands on the news of a Pakham representative's arrival. While Carlotto sat smiling, looking as if he hadn't a care in the world.

Ricardo gasps. 'Holy shit father, you fucking hear the man ? ..fuck if we ain't in a mess.'

Carlotto growls at his son, 'Keep acting like you know something and we will be. Not in a mess but having to put another fucking terrorist arse into that parking lot....So open the gates and let the inquisitive fucker in...Dieter Noss, my arse.'

The taxi cab entered and slowly drove down the long, half mile driveway at the indicated speed limit of 15 mph. Karl could see that the Alfredo Ranch was somewhat special. It's lines of freshly painted white wicker fencing was far superior to any he'd seen anywhere. The cross road sign post with its arrow heads clearly indicating the various areas of the farm; Stables, Office, Lodge, Gallops, Staff Only.

The driver whose name and photo ID hung from the windscreen inner mirror was called Frank Zapatta. He turned to his client and asked. 'Which one?'

'Let's try the Office as I'm thinking to make for the Lodge might be an unwelcoming choice.'

'Will you be wanting me to wait, sir?'

' Let's give it one half hour and if I'm not back by then you can say your no longer required...best I settle your account now, just in case.'

Frank looked at his meter showing 70 dollar 60. He then calculated the waiting time of 30 minutes before saying 'That'll be a cool 100 dollars, sir.'

Karl, nodding, had expected more, so this driver wasn't a robbing son of a bitch like most others tended to be, so for his honesty Karl passed him two crisp 100 dollar bills. Frank touched the Seahawks hat he was wearing and said a much appreciated 'Thank you, sir.'

Karl, on getting out of the cab said, 'Half an hour, Frank.'

As Frank watched Karl making for the office he noticed a movement in the office window blinds. One other thing about his client, who was built like a brick shit house, gave an impression that he looked nor spoke like a horse person, more like a boxing wrestling impresario, one tough looking cookie you'd make sure to avoid, least of all argue with.

Karl entered the office and came face to face with an old, in his late sixties looking, white haired man who sat nursing a silver cane. Standing a little over to the man's left was a younger man who seemed to be avoiding looking at Karl.

Carlotto spoke. 'Mr. Noss I presume?' Karl bowed a yes.

'So you want to meet up with this Bratski character and his merry men?'

Karl shrugs, looks all around before replying. 'I was told he is here, on your farm, he and 200 of his men.' he holds up a palm. 'But I can see neither. Is he hiding, or has he left for some unknown reason?'

He smiles. 'Then I'm sure you'd know the answer to that...Am I right?'

Carlotto smiles, holds up a hand. 'He was here mister Noss but packed up and left for reasons unknown to me or my son.' He points to Ricardo. 'He didn't pay the full accommodation price. I'm thinking he was disappointed with the lack of facilities here, Could we'll be he was missing the sleazy underground dives that he and his motley crew came out from.'

'Am I taking it that he left no forwarding address?'

Carlotto looks to Ricardo who is shaking his head. 'Not a whisper.'

Karl, 'Mind if I look around?'

'Do I take it that you don't believe me?'

Karl smiles. 'No, it's just that maybe some of your staff may have some information that could help me find them.'

'In that case you may, but not without being accompanied. I will personally give you a full tour.'

24
A TABLE FOR EIGHT

Rahaad and Sadat, having safely made their escape out of the Judas Hole, were met by Sadat's younger brother Memet. who guided them down the mountain to the waiting chopper, Memet its pilot with the instruction to fly to the Colosseum where Giovanni had a room ready that would keep the three safe till a Sadat super tanker could ship them to Kuwait.

They had only three days to stick out their luxurious apartment which was part of the restaurant's fine hotel facilities. Giovanni had insisted that they kept to their room, that he would supply all their needs for what would be a short stay. Of course he would be well compensated for this service.

If the truth be known. Giovanni would be glad to see the back of them thinking fucking terrorists taking on America. Hadn't it provided his family with a good living, his friendship with the west coast mob. Over a nine year period it had given him protection at the cost of a few annual weekend meetings. On the whole he was making a good profit. He would miss Sadat Malik digging into his pocket but that wouldn't be the end of the world, not after Sadat had told him to look after the Malik estate. At a price of course.

All that was needed were a few guards with dogs. Easy money, nbringing in a large profit. He'd already got plans on that action.

Over on the Alfredo ranch. Carlotto walked the Pakham envoy all around the farm telling him he was free to ask questions. He did, getting nothing but negative replies. A repeated 'They just packed up and left....Where? ...we have no idea, they weren't very talkative.'

One thing caught his eye and that was a stable hand smoking a cigarette from a Red Hand pack. Now what was he doing with a packet of German ciggys? Strange, wouldn't expect to find that label being sold in Oregon.

Carlotto noticed the error too with the feeling that it could quite easily be accounted for, say if one of the Wolverines had left them lying around. He waited for this Noss to ask. but he didn't. Still it was best to take him out. Like in the old days. A dead head can't talk. With that Carlotto put his stick to the back of Karl's head and pulled the trigger, the envoy was no more.

He looked at the stable lad and shouted. 'Get rid of those fucking smokes, you got any more?'

The lad shook his head saying. 'I'm sorry mister Alfredo.'

'And so you should be.' He points to the still body of Karl. 'Get some help, wrap him up ready for a midnight disposal, he goes in the wood chipper.' He walks away, stops and suddenly turns to shout back.'All of him, in the chipper. If he's got dollars on him buy yourself some fucking American smokes. You hearing me?'

'Yes Sir, mister Alfredo. I'm hearing you good.'

Joe sat with his team around the Shady Nook TV set watching the news on CNN.

Ryona said. 'Looks like Tom Hawks has shut down the news media.'

Roberto, 'That's not Toms doing my sweet, that's got an all Presidential look about it..J. Mac. I'd say that's come right from the top.'

Joe, 'I think you could be right about it coming from the President.'

Norman said. 'I don't know Joe, would he be looking for another Watergate holding back from the press?'

Frazier. 'I'd think it more of a National Security question, Norm, such news could stir up the country.That's the last thing he'd want happening, causing panic, telling America there's terrorists in the country, remember we've heard nothing of an army of Wolverines, who could be out there.'

Lenny. 'Dave could be right, let's suppose they had information on the Scarab attack. Could have called for a change of plan...Like check-mate.'

Ryona. 'So what's our next move.?'

Joe smiles. 'I'm thinking of treating you all to a nice dinner, I've already invited Scott and Ernest along.' He turns to Frazier, 'And Miss Sandra Peterson. ..to keep Ryona company.'

Frazier smiles. 'That's about the best news I've heard all day Joe.'

They all burst into laughter and cheer.

Lenny winks saying, 'What I can't understand, Joe, is after looking around this handsome group of chaps, how she came to pick Dave.' Dave throws a place mat at him.

Ryona says, 'So's where this fine dining going to take place Joe?....Hope your not thinking of having Sandra and me doing the cooking.'

Joe laughs, 'Wouldn't dream of it girl although, you'd both do us proud.'

He looks to Roberto, 'I was thinking of paying a visit to that hot shot restaurant that you and Ryona called on. The Colosseum...your brief encounter with our runaways Shadeed and his partner in crime Malik...I think I'd be right into thinking that the owner could have something to tell us.'

Ryona nods, 'Good thinking Batman...he certainly knows something, especially after putting that peeping Tom on us.'

Roberto, 'I totally agree but let's go carefully on this Joe.' ...he sighs. 'I think one shootout at the OK Corral is enough. We came out with scratches on our first duel, not sure we'd be so lucky a second time. This owner ...Giovanni...he's a sly customer and it's better to have our dinner, then, and only after dinner, We take him in.'

Lenny says, 'I'll go with that Roberto, Joe?'

Joe, 'Ok, it's feasible that something could go amiss. In saying that, I'm thinking of the Sicilian poisonings,'

Ryan. 'So how are we going to know, Joe, If it's been poisoned, give some to a pussy cat?'

She winks to the team, 'Cats won't eat if it's poisoned.'

Joe said, 'That's a risk one of us will have to take by sampling the food first.' He looks at their unsure faces, 'Oh, don't worry, I'm going to be our food tester.'

Norman who's been somewhat quiet, finally puts his pennyworth in,

'I'm going to be our tester...can't risk losing Joe to a bowl of minestrone soup, now can we?..he's more important to this operation than I am,'

Dave coughs, 'In that case, I'm the lowest ranked here so it should be me.'

Lenny 'What! and have Sandra poising the bloody Lot of us...No way Kincade. '

They all turn and look at Dave's face, that's illuminating his shyness, before breaking into laughter.

Dave bangs a fist down shouting, 'You can all bollocks.'

It's then, that Sandra who has been helping Mary Beth in the kitchen enters with coffee. She looks at Dave who's trying to force a smile.

'Did I hear my Scottish flower swearing just then?'

They can't hold it back and have to turn away and giggle.

Sandra says, 'Did I say something funny?'

Joe goes over and puts his arm around her, saying. 'No, you did not ...Your Scottish flower might have done though.'

They all laugh including Dave who's slowly shaking his head.

Over in the hot shot restaurant, Rahaad had arrived along with the two Malik brothers Sadat and Memet. They've used the company's own 6 seater, FlyMalik chopper.

Memet, its pilot, on receiving the urgency call from Sadat, had already been there to receive them, Sadat had told his brother to make for the safety of the Colosseum.

On their arrival at the Colosseum a waiting Giovanni had rushed them into one of his most exclusive apartments, situated some distance away from the main hotel restaurant area. For their stay, their needs would be met by himself.

Sadat Malik had told him their stay was for two nights, and that they would be leaving once his cargo ship the 'Annoyance' left port for Kuwait.

Joe had phoned reception and asked for a table that would have seating for 8, adding a time of 7.30 pm. He was asked for his name, he gave a false ID. Using the old alias Clyde Barrow adding that he would want the table for this evening.

A reply of Just one moment Mister Barrow was followed by a yes and a request for his phone number. Again he gave a false number that was now no longer in use, he gave Stacy Kilmer's which was in the UK, High Melton near Doncaster.

He was asked if the code was one of a foreign country. Joe replied that it was the United Kingdom's. He asked if they wanted his mother's name, they answered that his mother's name wasn't required. They finished with.

'You have a booking for 8 people for 7.30pm tonight Mister Barrow. Please try to be punctual as we may have others waiting, thank you.'

Joe turned to his team. 'OK guys we're in 7.30pm the Colosseum...Don't lose your vigilance...It's important we keep awake on what might happen.'

Norman asks, 'We taking our small arms with us Joe?, ..you did say something might happen.'

Ryona answered, 'I'm taking mine in my purse, I'd feel kinda lost without it.'

It was 7.35 when the two vehicles entered the Colosseum parking lot. Joe noticed a surprised look coming from the face of owner Giovanni. He made straight for Ryona saying, 'Welcome..welcome madam, and I see you've brought some new customers to the Colosseum. The first bottle of your choice will be taken to your table...No charge of course, compliments of Giovanni your grateful host.'

He bows, then begins his hand shaking, Asking 'Who is mister Barrow?' Joe nods. 'I have selected a special table for you, sir, so the two ladies can have a magnificent view of the Rainer Mountains, see the wonderful sunset. ...it's due in the next half hour.'

He sighs, 'You will excuse while send my man Piero over with the menus and the wine list. wines we have Imported from all over the world.'

He backs away with a continuous bowing motion. After sending Piero to their table with the wine lists and menu's he went into his office and picked up the phone. He phones number 4. on the internal line.

Sadat answered 'Yes..... , your sure?.....OK I'll tell him.'

Rahaad looked at the smirking face of Sadat, who had just returned from making arrangements for the three to leave America.

'Who was that?'

'Giovanni.'

'What did he want?'

Sadat winks. Rahaad throws up his arms .

'Don't I ever get to know anything?'

'Yes'

'So come on my friend, let's be hearing.'

Sadat smiles 'First and most important, Rahaad ....My lady friend told me something that will make the flies on a camel's arse buzz with glee.'

'That good ....So let's be knowing, my benevolent brother?'

'It's Woo.'

'My Woo? ...'

'He's alive and in a military prison somewhere in Texas.'

Rahaad eyes light up at this fantastic news. 'My Woos alive!'

Sadat wags his finger. 'Yes he's alive...but his right knee, it's shattered. He's hospitalised, hoping, waiting for a replacement.'

Rahaad dances with Memet...'He's alive Memet...Woo, I thought him dead. ..He's unbreakable ...He'll live forever.'

He turns to Sadat, 'Sadat my brother....You..you must get him out ...I don't care how many millions of dollars it costs.'

Sadat nods, 'Yes, of course Raheed, and my friend brings to me my second piece of good news.'

Memet. 'Tell us my brother?'

Rahaad . 'Don't keep us in suspense Sadat...I'm so excited ...tell us.'

'Giovanni was on the phone just now.'

Rahaad 'Yes, yes.' Sadat smiles and pretends to polish his nails.

Rahaad pushes him on the shoulder. 'You going to tell us or not?'

'Giovanni has told me your lady and her husband have just walked into the Colosseum with six others. That they have a table on the outer rim with all the views of sunset and stars. He thought you'd want to know.'

Rahaad.'So what's the plan?'

Sadat, 'This is what I'm thinking Raheed...Woo is in a military prison, a problem to get him out,..even me paying my dollars it would be hard and could quite easily go foul.'

Rahaad, 'So, Sadat?'

'I'm thinking of us doing an exchange, Woo for the woman, if you get my drift... We grab her tonight when she gets up to visit the rest room.'

Rahaad 'Then what ...If we do this we have to move her somewhere fast, not here.'

'I have such a place in mind, my office and storage house in Coo's Bay, it's a family house that's private, a place where records are kept away from a tax inspector's eyes. My main office in Eugene they would know of.'

He shrugs, 'You must remember Raheed I'm now a wanted man, a man they would class as a terrorist. The FBI will search for us both this minute.' He looks to Memet.

'My brother Memet is safe for a while until we take our cruise to Kuwait. Then we are all on their most wanted list.'

Suddenly theres a rap on their door and each stand with pistols drawn. Sadat takes to the doors spy-hole. smiles and opens he door to an anxious Giovanni who's excitedly rushing by Sadat into the room.

'I have them seated, you can view from the stage's lighting box, it's high above the arena and a most perfect unseen spot.' He rubs his hands. 'Eight people in all, 2 of them women. The men all look to be in their 30's to fifties with a military look about them.

Sadat taps Giovani's shoulder. 'You have a bonus to come my friend, so when either of the two, the woman or her husband, pay a visit to the rest room we take them. Giovanni you have the men for a successful job?'

Giovanni nods 'No problem, Sadat.'

Rahaad gives him an untrusting look. 'I hope you've not got that imbecile Pascal involved?'

'Oh, him...He's no longer with us. I give him his bladders...This I see to personally.'

'Good man.'

Sadat puts up a finger to Giovanni. 'Giovanni my friend, no mistakes.We only need the woman or her husband one of the two.'....He taps his shoulder.

'Once the job is done...we have only minutes to vacate the Colosseum and I really do mean minutes.'

Rahaad interrupts, 'You don't bring anyone here, take to the helicopter. We shall already be on board waiting, and Giovanni! I don't want to see you if things go wrong.'

The statement made by Rahaad sent a cold shiver down the spine of the restaurant owner.

The restaurant was beginning to fill with cars piling in from all parts of the State While the girls sat drinking martinis, and, were taking in the most beautiful panoramic views of the Rocky Mountain range and the sun finally leaving Montana for another day, the boys were all eyes on the clientele that had entered, a crowd that just reeked of money with gold hanging from all wrists, and Diamonds dazzling under the red sombre lighting of the table lamps.

They'd allowed Roberto to order, his knowledge of Italian cuisine was accepted as classified A, he felt so proud to be able to give his friends a taste of his country's best known dishes.

Even the waiter on receiving the order had to admire Roberto's knowledge of the finer points of Italian fine wines and dining.

Lenny just had to comment. 'Your a man, who to me, knows the best table Roberto...But for me, personally...I'm a mug of tea, with a plate of buttery mash potato, sausage and fried Union lover. Thick Oxo gravy and a slice of crusty bread to dip into.'

Roberto smiled. 'I'd love that too Lenny but I'm sorry you ain't got a chance in this joint....or anywhere in America for that matter!'

Sandra smiles saying. 'You know something Lenny that's what I'll cook up for you tomorrow if that's fine with the rest of you.'

Joe grins, 'Sounds like what I used to get for school dinners. A little Yorkshire pud and you've got a meal set for kings.'

Roberto rises saying. 'Excuse me guys but I'm away to the rest room, duty calls.'

Giovanni, back stage, gives his awaiting kidnappers the nod. He then calls Sadat, telling him it's the husband and that he's got five minutes to get him and his entourage off the premises.

Sadat, Rahaad and Memet are already in the chopper with the blades whirling. Rahaad opens the door and the slump body of Roberto is passed to him with Sadat unceremoniously dragging the CIA agent to the floor of the air bus. He salutes the four kidnappers telling them to high tail it away from the Colosseum, he then throws a wad of dollars at them.

Back at the table Ryona is looking down at her watch then in the direction of the mens rest room. Joe looks at her seeing a look of concern on her beautiful face. He says 'Ryona it's Okay, I'm on to the rest room myself, I'll give him a prod,'

'If you would Joe, starters are coming out, for Dave to test.'

Sandra almost spills her drink, 'Dave's testing what Ryona?'

She pats Sandra's hand . The food, errr, seeing if it's fit for human consumption .'

Sandra 'You are joking of course, Ryona?'

Ryona smiles.'Of course silly, ...they'll be serving the two of us ladies first, so it's I who will be doctor Jekyll.'

They whole table laughed.

'You won't be laughing if I turn into Ryona Hide now will you?'

Joe comes racing back to the table knocking the waiter and the tray of starters up into the air before crashing down onto the arena floor. Women are screaming men standing showing contempt and hatred to Joe Delph.

Scott, 'Jesus, Joe ..What the fuck's going on?'

Joe gasps, 'Come on we're out of here ...Roberto's missing ...They must have snatched him in the rest room.'

Ryona screaming. 'Get me that Giovanni ...get me that fucking owner ...He fucking damn well knows what's gone down here. ...Robby and I , we had a spy watching us last time we were here and I don't see the creep around.'

Joe, 'Ok, we search this joint, every damn cupboard in the joint...no fucker leaves.'

Ernest Levin says, 'Funny I did hear a faint sound of a whirlybird taking off Flying West ...What with the clientele here it didn't seem important. ...But by God it does now.'

Norman shouts 'Come on guys we're losing vital seconds.' He looks at Ryona who's looking shell- shocked.

'Let's get our man back, for our sister here.'

Joe rubs Ryona's arm, 'Come on baby let's go get that sneaky bastard, Giovanni...like you said, he knows....and I promise you this girl. Before this night is over we will too.'

Ryona's voice shakes. 'They better not fucking harm him or they're dead Joe.'

Joe grips her hand, 'They're fucking dead whether they harm him or not.'

They gave it a full two hours of interrogations wth the customers and staff. Before eventually coming across a frightened Giovanni. Whose excuse was that he'd been busy over at a neighbour's house arranging a couple's wedding reception for their daughter.

Joe told Norman and Dave to go check it out. He turned to Giovanni who was constantly mopping his brow.

Joe said.' Do you know what we do with lying bastards like you?'

'It seems you don't, so l will tell you. We take them out to some shitty swamp and watch the concrete blocks that have been attached to their feet slowly sink, taking all to a dark messy grave....Oh, and if the victim struggles then the swamp takes him under faster, virtually seconds not even a minute. I want their fucking names, the men who have Roberto my good friend, her husband.' He taps Ryona, 'You tried once before, so not only you, but your wife Claudette and your two little boys I'm afraid will have to suffer for their stupid father's greed and his part in taking the government agent to God Knows where, but little Giovanni knows. I'm giving you one minute by my watch to satisfy me with your answers to my question.

If you still remain adamant that you know nothing ..then you and your family are finished...like the poor old dodo bird extinct ....

Giovanni sobs 'I was threatened, told what to do by Sadat Malik.'   He continued to try and lie his way out of the abduction of Roberto.

Joe shook his head and said. 'I don't belive you and the time is running out for you.'

He turns to Norman who has just entered. 'Go pick up the wife Claudette and the boys ..you know what to do.'

Giovanni screams. 'Stop, stop, ..please, it was Rahaad Shadeed that noticed the wife here with you...he asked me to keep a look out for her.'

Joe, 'Why didn't he walk over and talk with her instead of this fucking cloak and dagger business, going around the fucking playground?'

'Believe me I don't know, then when I see the good lady tonight I tell him that she is here with yourself and six others.' He then tells me to say immediately if either of the two, the lady or her husband, visit our rest room.'

' I tell him the husband has gone.'

Scott snarls, 'Where have they taken him.?'

'Memet takes them in the chopper, where to I don't know.' Ryona snarls. 'Who is Memet?'

'Sadat's brother, he's the pilot.'

'So you help two terrorists in the abduction of a high rated agent of the CIA?'

' I was under pressure.'

Joe, 'Under pressure my arse, you were all fucking loves doves with us when we came into your mob infested place.'

Scott, 'You're in for a long time prison term ...oh, the inmates are going to love having you, a man who helps terrorist ...9-11. You're facing hell man.'

Giovanni now becomes desperate in an attempt to seek forgiveness not for himself but his vulnerable family.

'They took him for an exchange.'

Ryona. 'An exchange ..what are you taking about?'

'They said that Rahaads Uncle Woo...who was captured on the attack on Sadat's estate...They are thinking to exchange. Woo for your husband...They said he was hospitalised in a high security military unit.'

Joe, 'How come they got this information?..who?'

Giovanni shrugs. 'This I don't know...but you must remember mister Barrow, that Sadat, he has friends in high places, even the Mafia . He pays their asking price...money talks and he's got plenty...need I say more?'

'If you want to knock a few years of your prison sentence then I'd be giving us all you've got.'   Shouted an angry Ryona, 'If any harm comes to my husband then you wont be serving any fucking prison sentence, you get me mister Giovanni Colosseum? You'll be in that arena of yours facing more than a gladiator or lions. Am I getting through to that fucking greedy brain of yours? how much were you due from the pocket of Malik your none taxable service?'

Trying to soothe the depressed state of Ryona, Giovanni utters.

'They could have flown that sky bird to Eugene... he .Sadat...has an office there..this I know.'

Ryona snarls into his ear, 'You better hope my husbands Ok...because, mister Colosseum, If he dies ...So do you.'

25

THE LONE ASSASSIN

It was some time later that Ivor Stravinsky heard of an informer in the Russian USA embassy, Olga Kavich, she seemed to know a little of what had occurred in regards to Karl Somanoff and so gave the Pakham Karl's destination as being Portland Oregon. That this is all she knew, and that he'd already left Chicago.

Stravinsky roared like a wounded lion, he threw a paperweight at the door with such force it split the fine chestnut panelling.

'Why is it I have over two hundred fucking fighters over on that west coast and get to hear nothing of our operation. Now fucking Somanoff goes on a fucking walkabout.'

His aid Gorky Zimanoff was standing to attention, taking a silent view of a raging Pakham, and knowing only to well not to interrupt the storm that was coming from his master.

Ivor shouts at him. 'Get me those fucking Black Angels in here. Am I going crazy or what? I'm fucking losing millions of dollars on this shite of an heist.'

Gorky shrugs, 'I thought they were the best silent assassins on the planet my master. Now I hear it being spoken openly, that the Black Angels have been broken, are not feared anymore, their once great dominance gone.'

The Pakham takes time to think, the room exuding a deathly silence. He turns to Gorky, shaking his head with a tormented mind and a heavy heart. He cries out.

'Then who?...who is this destroyer of our plans ..our armies?...who Gorky?'

Gorky sighs, 'Maybe my master should be looking at a more recent enemy, one that we thought was finished...the one they call the Fly.'

He holds out his hands to Ivor, 'Who is the one to ever challenge you...to kill our brigadiers, the Sicilian poisoning's? ..The Fly, my master.'

Ivor looks to the ceiling, his head now furiously nodding.

'Of course, Gorky, who else?... But it is I who took over the Wolverines along with the Angels....The Albanians, he no longer has their support...So who Gorky..who the fuck's climbing his mountain?'

Gorky, 'Didn't he have great ties with the Middle East ..the Afghans, the Islamic State....or maybe the IS. breakaway group, the Scarabs?'

Again there comes a period of silence. 'I'm thinking you could be right Gorky..He must have found support from the Middle East, a far superior force being led by a five star general.'

He sighs, 'Those warheads are no longer the prize, they're now safe in the submarine base.' Again he turns to Gorky 'So where are my 200 plus warriors..Where are Ottermanze, Bratski and Stormanof?...Not one but three fucking fighting generals.'

'If we knew that my Pakham then we'd know our enemy. I say it's that Fly.'

Ivor kicks out at the round global paperweight.

He snarls. 'Find this fly ..I don't care about the cost... somebody knows, and believe me they'll sing if the price is right.'

He smiles. 'Cash is king Gorky.' He slams a fist down hard onto a side table.

'Go Gorky, go before I blow some fucker's brains out..Put the word out, I want that Fly's name.'

Gorky leaves the Packham lying with his head back on a lounge chair with a damp towel over his head.

If only Ivor Stravinsky could have seen into the large fortress of a house in Colmar then he would have realised that the man, Conrad Wolff, was pacing his library in an angry mood. News had come through on his crime grapevine of the loss of the Scarab Army that included Sergio Ramero, with the nuclear Naughty Boys safe, in their US base.

He didn't want to know what Rahaad, must be thinking, especially after him giving the green light to go, thus changing the plans of the heist. He'd just had the news from Ferdinand Cortez that there were no Wolverines involved, they didn't show, and that the Wolverines had more than likely been exterminated by Delta Force along with that thorn in his side, Joe Delph.

He turns to Ferdinand,sighs. 'Another fuck up Ferdinand, soon no one will entertain us, they see us good as finished.'

He shakes his head.'We must kill that Delph once and for all...Put a contract out on him Ferdinand...1,000.000 Euros for his head in a basket and brought to my door.'

Ferdinand nods.'I have just the very man, Conrad an evil killing machine who will work for much less than you're offering. This man would kill the fucking President of the United States for half of what you're offering..his name is Klasso, the underworld know him as KO...I think we'd get him for 200,000, Conrad.'

Conrad shrugs 'Ok, 500,000 on completion, no mistakes, if he fails he gets nothing.'

'You sure Conrad?..still seems a heavy load for what to Klasso would be a simple job.'

'When we're down 40 million to this Delph then believe me brother it's chicken feed.'

'Then consider it done Conrad…Klasso is a perfectionist..He has to have everything put before him about Delph…He will tell us nothing, only when it is done, when Delph is dead.

Meanwhile Joe and his team had been given a military Chinoook ride over to Eugene Oregon with the intention of storming the offices of Malik Oil, in a search and rescue operation. hoping to find Roberto Veneto safe and well. He could see Ryona was stressed out. The first thing that came of notice was the helicopter pad with the company's Malik Fly-Bird sitting there being re fuelled. The Chinook was hovering, circling the company rooftops, ready to drop a free-fall ladder to the deck below.

Geoff Hogan the pilot was asking Joe, 'Where Colonel?'

Joe answers 'As near to that little bird you can get Geoff.' He turned to his team. 'We go one at a time, first take a defensive position on that decking. He's on his own once down …No fucking heroics…You see retaliation, then you take it out. This freeze and observation stays till the last man down is clear.'

The ladder falls and Ryona makes an eager move to step on it. Joe holds her back. 'Not this time baby, you go after me.' She scowls.

'And don't look at me like that..I'm looking after a woman who needs to live for Roberto. Norm will go first, he knows the play.' He taps Norman's shoulder. 'There's Cover at 12.15
'

'I see it Joe.'

'Dave, you go next, take that sheeting at 12.45. Lenny you're12 .30 ...I'm on the hour. ...Ryona follows me...Ryona you take the mechanic fuelling up.' He shouts to Geoff ...'I want you back in 30 minutes for the pick-up.'

'I'm with you Colonel.'

Joe, 'So let's move on this, remember no heroism. Take out what needs to be.'

Memet stood watching the teams dissent onto the decking. But remained motionless as the fuel continued to flow into the sky-bird's tank. Ryona approached him holding a pistol. She shouted for him to cut the fuel, to get down on his knees, with his hands on his head. He nodded and did all that was asked.

Ryona kicked him.'You the pilot?'

He answered.'Yes mam.'

Joe and the others arrived, Joe putting up a hand and inviting Ryona to press on.

'So where's your loving brother Sadat? ..you must be Memet Malik.'   Memet nodded saying. 'He didn't make the full ride here I dropped them in Portland. They took a friend of theirs home, he was a little drunk. I picked them up in Montana, dropped them in Portland.'

Ryona taps him on the head. 'Now I want to hear the truth, not this fucking bullshit..Your life right now depends on whether you're going to tell me. Or if I'm going to blow your brains out. '

He smirks.'You harm me and they'll harm him ...eye for an eye pretty woman.'

Joe steps forward. 'They won't harm him, Rahaad wants Woo more than he wants a little shit like you. They hurt him ...we hurt Woo, eye for an eye clever boy.'

This statement brings Memet into thinking. As long as his brother is safe, then he's prepared to waver a little. Just a sprat to catch a mackerel.

Memet says, 'News travels fast...So you know of the exchange...What you don't know is where....Also let me tell you this, English, my brother Sadat is a most powerful man not only in our Middle East ...but here in America ...He is owed many favours, from Oregon right up to the Senators walking the corridors of DC, If you treat me badly then expect reprisals.'

He smirks at Ryona. 'Your husband for one, he would suffer.'

Ryona throws a kick up and under, hard to the kneeling man's face resulting in a flow of blood and him rolling back on his heels. She drags him unceremoniously back to his kneeling position saying,

'Watch what you're saying clever boy...Your brother is already a dead man, along with that bastard Rahaad. You my friend will get more off me than a fucking bloody nose. ... This so called exchange, let me tell you, is just the start of a war, it will not end there ....'

Joe adds, 'Our man for the Scarab Woo and Sadat's rat of a brother...I'm sure they'll be wanting it to go down well... don't you think?'

Memet sighs, 'By the next full moon we shall know....You're a brave man English, to take on a billionaire and all his ready resources. ...but I tend to agree with the way of your thoughts, that it's not the finale.'

He again smirks. 'I only know who my money will be on... the odds on the favourite as they say in the gambling world....That's my brother.'

Joe says, 'Even a favourite can finish down the field ...as they say in the gambling world. '

Norman, who has been giving the officers of Malik Oil the once over, has returned with Dave and Lenny.

'There's no sign of anything other than what's in front of you, Joe...We've done a clean sweep of the place.'

Joe nods down at Memet. 'Clever boy here knows all the answers, he's been trying to convince us that they have our man in Portland which we all know is a load of bollocks .' He gives a deep sigh, winking to the team.

'So what do you suggest we do with this lying clever boy, brother of a billionaire.'

Norman snarls, 'Let's be rid of him ..kill the bastard.'

Lenny bends down, going face to face with a now worried looking Memet.

'Not before a little water torture...he smells, needs a bath.'

Dave cries out 'I want to use those electronic jump leads on his bollocks.'

He points to a large mobile battery charger that is part of the Sky Bird's accessory.

Ryona laughs, 'Why not use all...we can have a bet on how long he lasts out.'

Memet screams.'You wouldn't dare ...It's..its..against protocol.'

Ryona says. 'Let me have him, Joe. It's just come to me.' She smiles at the sweating Memet. ' We take him up in his Malik chopper over there and drop him out over Eugene at some 20,000 feet.'...She winks at Lenny.

'Lenny can fly that chopper...after all he's flown Chinooks.'

Lenny smiles. 'No problem....I'd drop him out over the rockiest terrain. ..give him a real crunch of the bones on impact.'

Memet. 'Ok, they've taken your man to Kuwait...on a Airstream Jet. You will hear from them soon.'

Ryona. 'Kuwait!...why Kuwait?'

Memet. 'Like I've already said, my brother has many friends,'

He kneels thinking he'd not given them anything that they wouldn't soon know, okay he threw the Kuwait bit in, hoping they'd give up their chase in Oregon, keeping them from pursuing leads in the United States. His brother was sitting snugly in his private hideaway In Coo's Bay.

'I've told you all that I know I can't say anymore than that now can I.' He laughed lifted his head and looked at Ryona smirking. 'No more kisses for you tonight, sweet lady.'

He laughs. Ryona calmly pulls out her pistol and shoots Memet with two direct head shots. She spits on his dead form, saying.

'Laugh that off, clever boy.' With her boot she rolls his dead body over onto its face and says, 'Can't hear you laughing now clever boy.'

Joe gives her a hug and tells Norman and Dave to parcel up Memet. Saying.

'Don't want Roberto getting a bullet so he goes with us as taken into custody for aiding known terrorists. We dump him with Scott's pan and brush boys. Clean up here, Geoff is due back anytime. We say nothing, you all got that?' The team nod and begin the clean up.

Sitting in his office suite some seventy miles away in Coo's Bay Sadat is trying to communicate with his brother Memet. The phone line is dead. He turns to Rahaad.

'What the fuck's up with the boy, he knows we need to know what the fuck's happening in Eugene.'

Rahaad shrugs. 'Maybe he's not in any position to answer you Sadat...maybe he's got visitors?'

Sadat. 'Visitors.'

'I'm thinking your friend Giovanni could have been pressured into giving our flight to Eugene to the military.'

'Yes and so they've arrested Memet, is that what your thinking Rahaad?..You could be right, that would seem plausible.' He looks to the unconscious Roberto who's lying bound, tied at feet and wrists in the corner of the room.

'We have to get out of America now! '

Rahaad snorts. 'But the tanker cruise to Kuwait in the next day or two....Does that mean it's off cancelled, Sadat?'

' Yes Rahaad to stay overnight would be a risk...all ports, air and sea will be watched...But I have a friend who owes will fly us out tonight, within the next hour or two.'

'Fly Sadat? I thought you said all ports would be watched.'

'They will, but not his, he has a private take-off-landing strip. His name is Jacob Passata. He has his own pilot schooling company. Albatross...it's anything from hand gliding to flying two seater Moths.'

Sadat winks. 'But I happen to know he has an eight seater executive Airstream Jet tucked away in one hanger.' He smiles. 'Our escape to Kuwait.'

26
BOWLING GREEN, KENTUCKY

Stravinsky calls for his personal aid Gorky and sits nursing a large vodka and humming a Russian folk ballad. Gorky peers around the library's open door and knocks before entering.

Ivor beckons him in before asking for news. Gorky tells the impatient Pakham that the contract has been taken on by Klasso the perfectionist, the very best of Romania's hit men. With Klasso I'm afraid you have to pay…it's the way of our world these days.'

Gorky holds out a palm. 'So do I take it he's employed Ivor?'

'Of course Gorky give him whatever he asks…But stress no swat, no pay.'

In a roadside caravan park on the outskirts of Oradea, Klasso Revakious sat studying the information he'd received from his two customers ….assessing who to hit first. The British agent….or the Fly… He had obtained from his whys and wherefores for two successful hits.

Was it to be the one, Delph, a man of cunning, a soldier, established as a highly respected and trained assassin, or the planner, the office man, who hides in the shadow of his late father Franz Wolff.

He knew Wolff had a contract of 500,000 dollars. That would be hard to get if the man was to be eliminated first. His secure fortress home in Colmar was nothing in the way of obstruction. He saw no problem in taking it on, it would be quite a challenge although he'd had many previous jobs of a similar nature that hadn't been a problem. He was born for taking risks.

He'd asked the Pakham's aid Gorky for the same amount and was in no way surprised at their acceptance. The Fly was in his soup and Ivor Stravinsky wasn't liking it anymore. He Klasso was to be the final decider on who would wear the crown of international crime.

Taking out the Fly would certainly help get him that status as King of the streets again but then Klasso wasn't involved in the political side of things. He was a tradesman a man who took risks with his life. A man who set a price for his deeds. A man to be feared. He worked alone. If there was a mistake then it was his to sort. He finally decided on Joe Delph.

He would move into one of his many rented caravans that he'd set up around the globe. England, yes he'd not been there for quite some time, destination Vauxhall, London. He knew of an ideal quiet place to stay outside Canterbury... Perfect.

Where was Delph now?..The United States...too risky .....He didn't do the States. No, it would have to be London England. If Conrad Wolff didn't like it then he could get someone else to do his job, wouldn't matter much to him because he'd still have the contract for his life riding in his pocket worth 500,000 American dollars.

It was over a week and still no word, from Scott and his Delta boys of any sightings of Roberto or the terrorist Rahaad.

Sadat, they had been told by Malik Oil, was taking a long vacation. They did not expect him back till the New Year.

Then only a few days later news came through to Joe of the exchange; Woo for Roberto ....The date November the 16th...the time six am. The place Kandahar, Afghanistan.

The news gave Joe and the team time to consult with Scott and plan the requirements that would be needed to make for a safe transaction. They had four days to prepare. Tom Hawks the President's aid would give the final word on the play, after having the all-clear from the White House.

Joe was concerned about Ryona and would have liked her to come up only after the job was done and dusted, he knew it was no use ordering her to stand down. Would he, had if he'd been given the same order for Stacy? ....No way. He told Norman to keep a protective eye on her.

For Ryona the four days couldn't come fast enough. She was desperate to see Roberto, to see that he was alive and well. One thing for sure, there would be no extension to her SIS career or his CIA one once this was over....Chasing the quiet company fraud investigations they would revert back to.

Having him back for Christmas? what more could a girl ask for, the perfect Christmas gift. Roberto home with her and the girls.

And so the day had arrived. The team along with Scott and four of his best Delta squad, along with the limping Woo. They'd flown into Pakistan and crossed the border at Charman into Afghanistan. It seemed to Joe that a thousand eyes were watching their drive towards Kandahar. The exchange had been set to take place on the side banks of a dry river bed. Each party to occupy one side of the banking facing each other. Two representatives were allowed to escort their exchange man, showing themselves to be unarmed, bearing no weapons of any kind. Vehicles were to sit more than a half mile from the designated area.

Colonel Scott Brady Jones along with Colonel Joe Delph would escort the Afghan Terrorist Woo. Whilst Scarab leader Rahaad Shadeed along with Sadat Malik would bring Roberto up to the point of exchange, a near central position on the floor of the riverbed.

Ryona walked up and whispered to Joe, 'Check Roberto out Joe, if there are signs of heavy deterioration, then put both hands up high and the team and I will finish the bastards so Scott, Roberto and yourself hit the deck.'

Joe replied, 'Hit those attending on the far bank. leave me and Scott to see to the principals. I'm hoping it won't come down to that. ..but whatever, be prepared. These are not known for being nice men. ..in fact the nearest thing to evil you're ever likely to meet. Then again you've already met the Impala and his goon Woo.' He gives a deep sigh. 'Let's be sure we get our man home Ryona, that's what we're here for.' He turns to Norman.

'Norm. You see to the team position and any rapid fire and keep Ryona safe.'

Norman nods, 'Understood boss.'

The morning dawn had broken through with a great ball of sunshine, bringing the terrain steaming like some giant iron wavering over the sandy landscape.

It was on the 6th hour that Scott and Joe walked a limping Woo down into the river basin. He could see Roberto being led like some zombie from a George A. Romero movie, being supported by his arms but moving, not limping, like a clockwork soldier. They stopped, with each party eyeing the other up.

Rahaad spoke in a strange Arabic language, Rahaad asking Woo if he was good…Woo nodding and said he'd been treated better than he'd expected.

Joe looked at a dazed figure of Roberto, who for some unknown reason seemed to be as though he was trying to read what was happening in his mind. He looked to be distant not of this world.

Scott nudged Joe and said, 'He don't look good, Joe…He's been loaded with pick me ups, we need to get him hospitalised, let our medics take a look at him.'

Joe nods, and says to a joyful looking Rahaad.

'I don't think you've taken care of my man but I will tell you this, Cambridge, Harvard offspring, if you messed with his mind, then watch every step you take, look into every shadow, from now on…I'll be coming for you.'

Rahaad replied. 'After you cut down the Wolverines …My Scarabs it's you who must sleep with one eye open, you who will feel the Afghan sand storm hitting and burying you deep into a grave. Your time is near…Tell the beautiful Mari Bambella that one who plays with fire can expect to be burnt. It is written that you've played your last game Delph …You have picked the wrong opponent. You cannot win with a losing hand my enemy.'

Rahaad opens his arms displaying the land around them. 'We leave today as men of honour…tomorrow we are at war you and I.'

Joe wanted so much to raise his hands but now after meeting the Scarab Rahaad he'd decided getting Roberto home could not be done without a blood bath. He didn't know what heavy gunfire would do to his seemingly traumatised mind. He gave a final nod to Rahaad and was about to leave when Sadat Malik asked. 'My brother…Delph …where is he, what prison?'

Joe smiled, 'Why are you thinking of paying him a visit? ..Then you would be immediately arrested on arrival back to the States....You're finished there Malik your as dead as your sea.'

Malik winks. 'You forget money talks Delph, I've yet to know a man that can't be bought.'

'Then I'd say your travels must have been limited Malik ... There's quite a few honourable men left in the world....pity you mix with the shite, you're has thick as your oil.'

Scott adds. 'By all means pay us a visit Malik...we can always make room to accommodate you....like San Quentin, Folsom, Rikers Island...take your pick. You'll spend a lifetime in anyone of them....Maybe your brother Memet awaits you I might add. that none of those mentioned have a love for terrorists.'

And so the exchanged was done, with a smiling Woo limping into the land of sand and Roberto staggering like the living dead, heading for Bowling Green Kentucky. But not before a two week hospitalised check into the clinic of Professor Paul Reid in Bakersfield California. The clinic was renowned for its celebrity clientele. Stars from stage and screen with psychological problems called on Paul Reid to work his magic. Now a desperate Ryona was praying the professor could bring Roberto's memory back.

She sat along with Joe in the professor's outer office awaiting her appointment, Joe hadn't left her side for the two whole weeks of treatment. Today she would be given a full report.

Ryona had been sharing the bedside of Roberto with Joe. They'd been playing his music hoping for the slightest improvement of Roberto's lips moving with the sounds.....Hadn't he always hummed along to his favourites, Pink Floyd, the Rolling Stones to name just two. But he didn't respond. She squeezed his hand hoping for a squeeze back. But to no avail, she shook it saying.

'It's me sweetheart Ryona...Mari.' Nothing.

She turned to Joe. 'What the fuck have they done to my man, Joe?'

She sobs. 'I'm a complete stranger to him ...what have those bastards given him?'

Joe gave her a gentle hug and said. 'That's what we're here to find out baby...we should know something today.'

He hears the footsteps of the staff nurse approaching and adds. 'I'm thinking in the next half hour or so.'

The staff smiles and says 'If you would kindly follow me Mrs Veneto, Mr. Delph, the professor will see you now, I will be bringing in coffee, would you like some.?'

They both declined. 'As you wish if you change your mind there's no problem just let me know.'

They entered the office of a well organised man. Everything in there was in place as it should be, spotlessly clean and files in cabinets of all Reid's previous clents listed in alphabetical order with year indications .

The professor, a fit looking man of some 60 years, pretty tall at six-three. Immaculately dressed in suit and tie. He sort of reminded Joe of the musician, country music star Kenny Rodger's he rose from his chair and offered his hand before inviting them to be seated.

He picked up the x-Ray taken of Roberto's brain and pinned it to the light screen box. He pointed out to them an area that was damaged.

'This my dear Mrs. Veneto is where the problem lies. He taps with a finger and sits back down. Ryona and Joe stare at the dark area that the professor has indicated.

Ryona asks 'What exactly are we looking at Professor... the dark area?'

Joe, 'What I'm wanting to know is can it be cured, can we have Roberto back to some normality?'

The Professor sighs saying 'Roberto has been injected with a powerful mind stimulating drug....A drug that, in my working career, have only come across three times. It's called DMS 51. otherwise known to a few surgeons as Black Rain. Once administered it has a kick like a mule, it's strength is on a scale that leaves Heroin, Chemical Meth all the other dream makers far behind LSD but with a 50 times more powerful mind bender.'

He taps his desk and sighs before continuing.

'I'm not here to take money from you and I want to be quite clear in telling you that Roberto has been administered with a colossal dose....To bring him back to some kind of normality could take years costing thousands of dollars..Oh I know what you're going to say ...the money, it doesn't matter..he's insured ..but believe me it does.'

Joe . 'So these three cases ,..the ones you've come across before....did they return back to normality?'

Ryona. 'Yes Professor, what happened with those three?'

The Professor shakes his head and looks at them both. 'You really want to know?'

Joe, 'If you don't mind, Yes sir I think we'd like to.'

'They, all three, two males and a woman committed suicide.' He shakes his head. 'What people don't realise is this is not a dreamer, a float with the clouds kind of drug, this drug brings unbearable pain to the receiver...it's one continuing nightmare.'

'So what has been done in getting rid of this pain, sir?' Ryona at a loss knowing Roberto is in pain.

'In our most recent attempts to find relief for the patient we have put the patient into a coma. Then injected ...and I'll try to simplify the treatment....a boss bubble into the damaged brain area. ...this is a bubble that contains one of the strongest anti-virus known to man . Each time the black rain runs into the bubble our virus known as Klotch 841. attacks and kills it.'

Ryona interrupts. 'Then you must give Roberto this Klotch ..whatever its name is....kill this pain that he's suffering.'

'Please, if you will let me finish Mrs Veneto...We are only in the early stages of testing and have found that, in Klotch clearing the black rain, it's bringing in a multitude of cancer cells. We have unfortunately after discussion with SRC ... Scientific Research Council deciding to halt the program.'

Ryona .'So my husband suffers whilst he waits for some kind voice of authority to get this testing restarted,'

The Professor nods. 'That's just about it I'm afraid .'

'So I can take Roberto home?'

'I can give you our strongest pain reduction tablets. That's about the best I can do, a brain operation is a definite no go....it would surely end his life.'

Ryona stands and says. 'I think his life's already ended Professor, but thank you for your honesty.'

Professor Reid stands and says 'I just wish I could have given you better news Mrs Veneto, I feel for you, if there's any other way I can help! '

He holds up a hand....'I will have nurse prepare Roberto for his journey to Kentucky.'

Christmas had finally arrived. In the weeks leading up to it Roberto had made no sign of any recovery, If anything he'd gone the other way, with Ryona noticing an increase in him showing pain. The tablets she administered from Professor Reid seemed to have no effect and his condition had quickly deteriorated.

It was 2pm. Christmas eve and Ryona was lying half asleep at Roberto's bedside She awoke listening to the loud moans coming from him. The violent shaking of his head along with his heavy perspiring body really worried her.

She mopped his brow, sobbing and thought of 'Please God help him or take him....enough is enough.'

The bell to the front entrance rang, she kissed him gently straightening his hair once jet black and now showing increasing amounts of grey. She left him to see to the door.

She opened it to see Joe and the girls Katrina and Juliet with armfuls of presents, Joe having flown the girls over from their Christmas break in North Yorkshire. Ryona kissed and hugged them, happy that they were here to help her get through a difficult Christmas period.

Joe, stroking her arm said, 'How's things girl, You look tired out....Roberto?' She gave a deep sigh.

'That bad, baby?...I know.'

Tears begin to swim in her eyes...the girls hugged her tighter clinging to their adopted mother, never wanting to let go.

'He's not good Joe, I'm worried.'

Joe nods and indicates upstairs. 'Mind if I take a look?'

'Go ahead while I see to the girls ..I'll put the coffee on, shall I ?'

She ruffles the girls hair...You two eaten since the flight. ...No...well you know where everything is..It's not changed since you were last here...Now how can I say that... Everything's change ...Roberto. ..Sorry.'

Katrina said, 'We know mum ...we know.'

'So let's get organised...How long have I got you for?'

'Till forever ' smiles Juliet.

Joe sat down slowly shaking his head at a deteriorating Roberto ...he'd aged another 10 to 20 years and was showing so much pain, his eyes staring into another world, his tee shirt soaked and stuck to his body. With his head shakes and moans Joe felt helpless. He stood and walked into the bathroom and came out with a towel. From a set of nearby draws he took out a fresh dry tee shirt and began to wipe down the body of his dear friend.

He bent over him and spoke in his ear. 'If you can hear me buddy, give me a sign ...It's Joe, Roberto.'

There was no reaction coming from his friend. Joe began to tidy up making him look more presentable for the girls. He tapped Roberto's arm.

'I won't be long buddy, I'll see Ryona...then get back to you.'

It was then and only then Joe got the feeling Roberto had heard him. Was it so or just Joe's mind wishing he had. He left the bedroom with nothing coming from Roberto in regards to any eye movement just a blank stare remained.

Joe returned to the living trying hard to bring out a smile. Coffee was on the go and the girls were busy telling Ryona about their schooling and how they had missed her and Roberto's company.

'Have some coffee Joe...while I go and see to Roberto.'

Joe said 'Just you take a break girl, I've seen to his immediate needs.... How long has he been like that, moaning and sweating?'

'First time I noticed was yesterday I'm giving him liquid foods, high multi vitamin content. Solids, he doesn't move his jaws, if I try to force it...he damn near chokes.'

She shakes her head. 'His weight loss ...He's lost near 3 stone in as many weeks.'

Joe. 'I'm not going to lie by saying he looks fine, truth be known Ryona he looks ghastly.'

With a shrug he tells her. 'You gotta get some help girl ... and until you do I'm staying with you and so are the girls.' The girls nod.

Over the next few days the decline in Roberto's health got worse going from moans to screaming sessions.. His head shaking came to the point needing to hold him while he was being fed. His toilet needs an ongoing disaster. His lower body having been wrapped in waterproof nappies, his upper in large bibs to absorb the vomit that was now coming out at constant intervals unlimited interval's.

Roberto's brother the priest had arrived from Botswana. Father Stefano and Ryona's hope of some reaction from Roberto at the presence of his brother sadly was not to come. Father Stefano told Ryona that if Roberto's condition worsened she was to call him. He gave her father Michael's number at the small church of St.Paul's. She'd asked how long he was likely to be around….away from his church in Botswana?

He answered saying. ' Till the high father decides my brother's fate.' I shall pray for his relief from all pain Mari.'

He held her hand whilst giving the sign of the cross to his brother. 'You must stay strong, if death comes then think only of t as relief. It's plain to see that he's functioning with no mind. When he leaves us he leaves his pain with us, we suffer….Just remember, Mari, death is not the end.'

Christmas had by-passed the Veneto home in Bowling Green, Kentucky. The festive occasion was lost in what was to be Roberto's final days. He had fallen into a deep sleep that he didn't come out of, and so it was the full team had gathered in the Catholic Church of St Paul's to hear the service for the dead, which was being given by Roberto's brother Father Stefano.

The coffin was carried out by Joe, Norman, Dave and Lenny. Colonel Scott had brought with him six of his Delta Force for the final salute. A six round volley over the Medal of Honour holder Roberto. Joe was not surprised that General Porter and Pat Taylor had flown in from Berlin. He looked over the cemetery at numerous agents, all dressed in black. They were there, not only as a mark of respect, but as a protective bodyguard for the attendance of the President of the United States John S MacArthur and his long time aid and advisor Tom Hawks. There were so many in attendance that it seemed all of Kentucky had a come to pay their last respects. Joe noted a group of New York City Firefighters solemnly standing, heads bowed, as the casket was slowly lowered into its final resting place. He could see that Ryona was in danger of following it so he held on tightly to her arm. The girls Katrina and Juliet had sobbed all throughout the service. They had truly lost a father.

Ryona herself had simply run out of tears and for the first time of Joe's four year association with her he sensed a crack in that heart of stone. She, like his love for Stacy Kilmer, had now to carry the pain, a pain that would be forever, never to leave. The cruelest pain of all, the one of lost love.

Ryona had thanked everyone who had attended and pointed out to Joe the many sympathy cards from all over America and Europe...many coming from the lives Roberto had saved in his heroic 9/11 trauma. She told Joe that she would reply to everyone. Joe suggested she put a column in the Washington Post. Thinking the individual effort would be too much of a trial, that she should take a little time with the girls to get anywhere near to normal functioning again.

She nodded then pulled Joe to her and said defiantly,

'I'm coming back Joe....I've one hell of a job to take on in the land of sand...He's going to die, that Scarab...and all who sail with him.'

She gives a deep sigh. 'I won't rest till Roberto's avenged.' She gives a sickening smile. 'You know what Joe, he's going to die the same way as Roberto, only ten times the fucking dose.'

Joe pats her hand. 'I know how you feel it's like Stacy all over again....You were with me then....I shall be with you now…You take a rest… meanwhile I'll get working on the Scarab….When I know it's a go, then so will you.'

He sighs. 'I've got to get back to Vauxhall..Go

through a few things with Anton….Then we go.'

Ryona smiles, 'Thanks Joe ..for being more than a boss… for being my best friend.'

27

THE BLACK LION

Say it was pure luck being in the right place at the right time, but Lenny Jameson spotted a face that he'd not seen in 12 years, the face of the Romanian contract killer Klasso Revakious. Now what would this Romanian gangster be doing in London casually drinking a glass of Stella lager in a pub across from Vauxhall Bridge, The Black Lion.

Lenny knew him as a sleeper...12 years ago he'd been highly involved with the Russian KGB. A known silent killer who was wanted world wide for a string of murders. He, like Lenny, lived in the shadows, making an appearance when called for. Lenny had heard that KO, as he was known, had strayed, going underground, solo. This after numerous attempts on his life, but Klasso had lived through them all like some lone unattached creditor, he was a hard fish to net.

12 years ago, Lenny sighs. In those days he himself had crawled the gutters slept in alleyways, to watch to listen and report back to MI5/6, dressed like some destitute wandering tramp complete with beard and long unkept hair.

Klasso sat near the pub's main Street window seemingly looking at the news stand and coffee cabin across the street, or was he having a look down a little further at Ronnie's barge restaurant. Lenny himself was now a blue Jean sweater man with short managed hair, clean shaven, not the Lenny of old.

He was scheduled to meet Joe and the remains of the team, Norman and Dave for lunch at Ronnie's. There was a new operation on the books and after Roberto's funeral things had gone a little sour regarding the eagerness to pursue a new adventure.

Ryona was still on sick leave and Lenny was wondering if she'd be coming back. She was one heck of a hell-fire lady to survive after what she had been through.

No one would blame her if she called it a day but somehow Lenny knew she'd be back ...The Scarab would be burning inside of her and she'd be back to put that fire out... revenge for Roberto.

Joe had told him that she'd let the house in Bowling Green Kentucky go. And the one in Yorkshire also ...too many memories ..Ghosts...she'd moved to a country place near Pickering, still in North Yorkshire,which she'd come to love.

Besides, the girls were studying at York university and had loads of friends. Joe was giving her time to mourn the loss of Roberto, something that he too was still trying to get over with his beloved Stacy.

Pain, it never goes away and when you think its gone, then there's always something that comes up to remind you. A spoken word, a name, something read, something seen. It's there for the rest of your days.

It's a lucky day for Joe, lucky that Lenny knows the assassin, because it's suddenly struck him that Klasso is here for Joe. He decides to give the Romanian a full observation job. Lenny has more experience than any man on reading situations. He decides to phone Joe and give him the news. He walks over to the gents toilet and phones whilst eyeing Klassso through a slightly open door.

Lenny tells him he is in the Black Lion. Joe then asks if he should call in a get a look at him. What is he wearing? Lenny says there's only five of us in, he's unmissable dressed in black, with a scar down his left hand side of his face ... Believed to be put there by a woman.

Joe asks 'You sure it's him ?'

Lenny answers 'Like I know my own mother.'

'Think he knows you?'

'It's a face I'll never forget …the scar does it …he knew me when I was a tramp, Joe …He don't know me now …looking like I've just walked out of a fucking fashion show.'

Joe. 'That sure, eh, Lenny?'

'Joe listen to me, this man's a fucking killer, an expert at his trade, if he's got the opportunity he's going to have you… he's a lover of the knife…he likes to cut throats.'

'So here's what I'm thinking Lenny I take a stroll down to the Lion…is Chris behind the bar?'

Lenny 'Yes.'

'OK, I'll enter and ask for Billy Harrison… say I want a word about something.'

Lenny, 'Billy Harrison?'

'Yes, Remember I don't know you, but keep me covered ..I'll be with you in ten.'

'Billy Harrison, Joe?'

'Yes, Billy, because I know he's not going to be in , …its Saturday, Billy's not one to miss his TV seven bet at William Hills….he's at the bookies. Chris will remind me of that….So I leave, and give your man his opportunity to follow. I shall be armed, safety off, silencer on, fully loaded.'

Lenny comes back and takes his seat at the bar taking casual glance into the back bar mirror. He watches Klasso as Joe entered. The assassin taken by surprise, goes into his pocket and fiddles for something, but brings nothing out.

Joe asks Chris about Billy and got the answer he'd expected.

Chris telling him to try William Hills. Joe waves a thank you and turns and leaves. Klasso leaves his Lager and followed him out .

Joe strolled casually down the street, it was Saturday and the shops were busy. The assassin Klasso could see there was too many people around including children. So he kept a fair distance from his contract victim. He was hoping for a nice quite spot to make his half million dollar hit.

Joe too was deep in thought of how the Romanian was going to play his cards. He expected a rush and hit with his cut-throat or what ever weapon he was carrying. So Joe decided on taking him down to the park where the opportunity would be ideal for the killers move.

A slash and exit through one of the many side gateways. Joe was taking him to the ideal killing ground that lay a short distance ahead. Joe, already prepared, his pistol with suppressor, safety off held to his chest.

He reached the expected spot and turned to meet the charging Klasso who was holding a cut-throat razor held high in one hand. The assassin stopped, his face totally shocked at the pistol now pointing at him. Then it happened, with Joe firing two shots, direct hits between the eyes of the would be killer.

Lenny, who had been following, helped Joe pull the lifeless Klasso into the park and push him under some heavy shrubbery. Joe called the cleaners and was told to stand by that they'd be there in no more than 15 minutes.

Joe looked at Lenny and said 'I owe you for that Lenny, wonder who called the hit?'

Lenny smiled, 'Buy me a pint and we're even, remember Tehran?..you pulled me out of some shit there.' Joe nodded saying 'Thanks buddy anyway.'

Lenny, 'Think it could have been the Scarab or Malik? more likely Malik, I've heard he's been spending big bucks on trying to find his brother.'

Joe 'Let's get on down to Ronnie's, I've got Norm and Dave coming for lunch.'

'Better make that tea Joe, It's half past four.'

Joe, 'So it is, I'd better phone Norm, tell him to make it five fifteen, can't leave here till the cleaners have done their bit.'

It was exactly 15 minutes later when the cleaners arrived, two highly trained members of Harry Parker's team. Harry had units all over the UK working only for SIS . The London outfit had come in a 4x4 two patient Ambulance transporter with accurate NHS markings. Harry's team were all in hospital uniform. Nothing was left out that could deny their profession being what it said. So the body of Klasso was taken to one of the company's many wood chip incinerator yards.....History.

Lenny remarked, as the ambulance left, 'At least we have no John Barlow to worry about...I'd say this episode was now dead and buried.'

Joe shook his head. 'I'm not so sure about that, the contract on me will remain ....I'm thinking Sadat Malik the most likely.'

'That damn Fly, Joe?...he's still buzzing somewhere... Jesus, Joe, you're a wanted man. ..Don't that worry you?'

'I thought after the Gordon Cummings exchange and Norman's wipe out of the Russians, That they'd be wanting to take me out, but a lot of water has passed under the bridge since then...and believe me Lenny it's not like the Soviets to forgive and forget...but somehow I'm thinking it's not them although you say our friend Klasso was ex KGB...He'd left them, going on his lonesome for a higher wage packet.'

Lenny nods, 'I wonder what your going price is now, ..especially after Klasso's exit.'

Joe laughs, 'To employ Klasso had to cost. ...You we're saying, Lenny, that he was rated number one in Europe. ... it's frightening to think what the asking price for me will be now.'

'I'd say a couple of million...Next time the assassin could be the assassins, maybe four ...500.000 a man, that's very likely.'

' Now you're really worrying me Lenny.... Making me feel like it's not safe to go outside.'

It was after six and London was coming alive with people filling the streets, commuters racing to get home, tourists heading for the West End, mixing with the theatre going multitude. How long has the Mousetrap been bringing them in?

The team of Joe, Lenny, Norman and Dave had all tucked into a most enjoyable dinner at Ronnie's. They were all talking of their new mission. The Drug infested world having a new man on the street....The Dream-Seller.

A man yes who was bringing to the young people a new kind of devilish mind bender like a Salvador Dali painting taking them into a surrealist dream world a moment of supreme bliss followed by a coming down of excruciating pain, so damaging it was causing the partaker a drive down the road to eventual suicide. The Meth Black Rain was filling Europe's city morgues.

Lenny had through his underground connections said all roads were pointing to Iraq, that this evil tablet was being produced in some part of Iraq's Al-Hijarah desert west of Basra, before crossing its southern borders into Kuwait.

Joe. 'Now isn't that a coincidence, our fucking most wanted, the Scarab Rahaad was last seen by ourselves in Kuwait.'

Norman. 'His big buddy Malik must be down a few million on their failed heist operation...Maybe it's their way of taking back a little of their loss, cash and lives.'

Dave. 'Dream-Seller's...Rahaad   and Malik...it's more than possible.'

Joe's phone beeps, it's Anton Spicer.

'Hi Ant, what's to do?'

'Are you done with the meeting...because if you are Well I'd like you all to visit my office...I know it's late but I've a late arrival here who wants to see you all.'

'Now who would that be, Ant?'

'Why don't you all pop along and find out is all I'm saying.'

15 minutes later Joe walked in to Anton's office followed by Norman, Lenny and Dave. He looks at Ant who's smiling

Joe, 'So what's with the surprise, chief ?'

Anton shouts over at the rest room door. 'Come on out and meet the team.'

The door opens and a smiling Ryona enters, hands on hips, saying.

'So is this the crazy crew you want me with chief Spicer?'

They all rush over to her and hug and kiss her. She looks at Joe saying. 'We ready to rock and roll, Joe?'

Joe smiles and a nods 'We missed you girl ...if you're ready ..we're ready. ..Good to have you back. 'With the team all nodding their heads in agreement

Norm, barely able to speak croaks through watering eyes.

'Come here baby and give us a hug....God knows we've all missed you baby.'

Ryona gives Norman a big kiss saying 'Thank you Norm, all of you have never been out of my thoughts...You're my family and besides I've still a job to do.'

She sighs, 'Them Afghan bastards ..it's not finished.'

Joe puts his arm around her saying 'We are going to base, then you may be surprised what we're on with....But we'll talk later on the journey.'

'We going to Donny, Joe?'

Joe laughs at Ryona's reference to Doncaster as Donny. He looks at the team and says 'Donny ..can't get nearer to being a Yorkshire girl than that, guys.'

28
LAND OF SAND

It was late that evening when the team, with Ryona back finally arrived in Doncaster.

Joe, on the journey, had put Ryona in the picture about on their forthcoming operation, Dream-Seller. Her interest in this mission Joe could see was lighting up her face. The loss of Roberto was hurting, he knew, like his own feeling the tragic loss of Stacy Kilmer. It would only ease slightly with the deaths of Rahaad, Sadat and Koo. Revenge was sweet but the hurt would never go away.

There's a hole in her breast where the heart should be. She, Joe knew, was putting on a brave front. The team had all gone to bed leaving Joe and Ryona sitting by a burning log fire nursing mugs of hot chocolate.

Joe knew she was somewhat distressed about something. So he asked her if there was anything he could help her with.

She began to shed tears. She nodded, 'I did it Joe, ..I'm a fucking murderer.'

Joe leans over taking her hand, a little.confused.

'What you trying to say baby...did what...murdered who?'

'She squeezed his hand, 'Roberto, Joe ...I couldn't see him take anymore pain...I put a pillow over his face..I had to do it...it was hurting me so much to see the pain, the suffering....I couldn't let him go on screaming like that running with perspiration. What he was going through wasn't living a life, Joe..He...he..'

She broke down, finding it hard to continue. What she had done was put her love to sleep. She'd wept all through that night, holding his hand as she lay on the bed beside him, hugging and seeing a face all dereft of the pain. She even thought Roberto was smiling, whispering goodbye my love.

'If that had been me baby, I'd have wanted you to do the same....That's not murder girl ..that's love, that's one of the hardest things you'll ever have to forgive yourself for.'

He squeezes her hand. 'But Professor Reid did say Roberto was brain dead, that there was nothing there baby, he didn't recognise any of us....You, me, his own brother Stefano.'

Ryona said 'In the final end ...he did come back to me, I swear I saw him smile, and whisper.'

Joe again squeezes her hand, 'That's so nice to know Ryona..so beautiful.'

Ryona said. 'So you think the drug they gave my Roberto...They got from this Dream-Seller...That it's the Scarabs who are bringing it into Europe, Joe?'

Joe shrugs. 'That bastard of a man Malik ...he's lost his business in the West. He's now a wanted man Ryona, losing millions of dollars. All his assets are frozen. He wants revenge...he wants us, our team dead.'

They turn to the door at the sound of footsteps approaching. The door opens and Norman pops his head round.

'You two still up ...I can't seem to sleep either, old war wound catching up on me.' He points to their mugs. 'What you got there?'

Ryona holding up her mug. 'Hot Chocolate...you want a cup, Norm?'

He nods, turning to Joe. 'Ain't had hot chocolate since I was a kid.'

Joe pulls back looking at him with suspicion.

Norman continues. 'I was brought up on Ovaltine. ..My Grandma...now she was the one for hot chocolate, coco, that sort of thing.'

Ryona shouts whilst making his drink. 'What's with this old war wound Norm?'

Joe laughs. 'Now this is going to be interesting.'

'You can laugh, but my knee gives me a bit of Wally sometimes, with crawling in all the shit and bogs...marshes.'

He puts up a finger, saying 'Where we're going Iraq, Basra, western desert, the marsh fields. ...you'll soon know about Wally knee. That nutter Hussein he drained them...but from what I gather they're back, bloody boggy as ever.'

Joe. 'I missed that...Basra that is.'

Norm. 'I was with SAS special search and recover unit..our team busted down the prison wall In Basra, got two of our boys out. Left what you might call police, with egg on the face.'

Joe. 'Wasn't it a mess Norm, what with the inner sectarian clashes, Shia, Mehdi army, against the ruling government forces?'

He sighs, 'What was the real kick up the arse were these so called forces who were using weapons given to them by Uncle Sam, an army full of insurgents...what a fucking nightmare that was.'

He shook his head, thanking Ryona as she handed him his chocolate drink.

'You say you didn't get to do Basra, Joe?'

Joe shrugs, 'No, I was supposed to get involved with some Shia kidnapping of three British oil workers, engineers…But it was cancelled…I never got to know why,'

'There was a lot of that going on Joe, the Yanks were targeted more than our lot.'

Ryona asked,'What about the drugs Norm, you catch anything on that?'

'There's always yeh weed floating about everywhere …the serious stuff your class A. Never was an issue. Most crime was pointing in the direction of our friend oil Barron Sadat Malik. At one time it was said that around 100,000 to 300,000 barrels of oil were being smuggled every day, worth around 5 to 15 million dollars….insurgents, through corrupt government officials were making. 25 to 100 million a year through oil smuggling.'

Joe, 'So that's how our Sadat Malik came into his millions.'

Ryona, 'So I'm thinking that's why he's funded Shadeed. ..to protect his little nest egg.'

Norman shrugs. 'Your guess is as good as mine girl but its sure looking something like that.'

Ryona says 'That country Iraq, along with a few others are never going to come to a peaceful conclusion…some of which are sadly nearer to home.'

Joe 'Your referring to Ireland.'

She nods, 'Why is it, when wars like these happen, it's always the innocent that suffer?'

Norman. 'It's been going on since the beginning of time, the list of greedy war mongers we fill Wembley Stadium and is never ending.'

Joe, 'It's good that you're onboard for this mission Norm, sorry to bring the pain in the knee back.'

They all burst into a bout of laughter.

Two days later and all that was planned was now ready to be executed. They would come in as tourists from Saudi Arabia into the Al- Hijarah desert. Everything had been gone over and Anton had secured a sound undercover link with one Mustafa Assad, who had helped the British army in their taking of Basra Palace...He had fought, along with many of his brothers, against The Sadam Hussain regime. Without a surname, for his family members protection, if ever he fell into hands of the death squads, a hand picked evil army of slaughterers controlled by Qusay Hussain, his son, who was head of security. Anton had asked about the Scarabs and was told they would not be able to function in Iraq, Shia, after having some foothold in the major towns, were keeping a close eye on the Kurd forces who had dug many a grave in their fight for equal representation presentation in the ruling of Iraq.

Diwaniya was the start of the opium trade were the drug had replaced rice irrigation in the fields towns now run by gangster smugglers. These were a no area go for any foreign face, mainly because government officials were filling their pockets with the exported Heroin that was running through their open door, Saudi Arabia and the Gulf and back out the other, up the Mediterranean Sea into Turkey and suppling areas all over Europe.Mafia gangs had replaced Sadams Baath party. The Shia forces were finding it hard to be accepted.

This knowledge was given by Joe to his team... with the concluding thought that if caught expect no mercy, because if caught your finished. After being tortured your death will be Satanic never go solo. It's the land of bloodstained sand. Norman added that they'd have no friends where they were going that the minds of the Iraqi people were filled with thoughts of mistrust. After years of ongoing wars who could blame them. Human remains had been found estimated at

150.000 years old. And there had never been was never a period of peaceful living.

Three days later Joe was standing face to face with Anton's Mustafa Assad. The agent looked a lot older than the 40 years Joe had been given, Assad looked to be nearer sixty.

He walked with a crouched hobble like a man with a pebble in his shoe, He'd stand a good six feet tall if he ever came out of this bent posture. He had a beard that was black, already showing strands of grey. One thing he had going for him was a good knowledge of English he spoke it fluently.

He explained to the team what they'd come to already know. That they were entering a battlefield, so it was not a good idea to stray. True, he told them the war with Sadam Hussain was over but there were many of its participants still prowling the hills and plains. Now there were Mafia like gangs that showed no mercy in their day in, day out plundering, human trafficking mostly girls and children was causing mass family exits out of Iraq. With Saudi Arabia, Syria and Turkey taking the bulk of the refugees.

From the Kurds in the northern mountain area to the Shia in the heart of Iraq this infighting would never end.

And so he came to their mission. He waved his arms around himself like a fairground carousel,

Then said. 'This is the Al- Hijarah desert...A harsh land that still has its inhabitants.'

He smiled, 'North of here is where the opium fields are, also where the gangsters are manufacturing the Black Rain. A chemical additive, some sort of Methamphetamine, is being added to the purest of Heroin.'

Again gave a wave of his hand, 'This is to the farmers who have forsaken their rice crops, an area most guarded. As bad as its product may be it's their way of making life easier.'

Ryona asks, 'So it's a mix, this chemical and these meths added into the opium?'

Assad nods, 'It's Heroin that delivers the dream...it's the kick in chemical that electrifies the mind, taking the participants into a world of surrealism.' He sighs, 'For a while it's fantasyland, paradise. Then its a horror show driving the mind into an insensate condition. Slowly burning the brain cells into a suicidal death state...There is no coming back. No known cure.'

Joe 'So how do we know all about this, knowing there's never been a survivor?'

'One time, and only once did a participant come out of a coma. She lasted exactly 60 minutes in that time she gave a doctor the information then had a sudden heart seizure and died.'

'So do you know where this drug lab is?'

'I know just about everything there is to know, Joe Delph, that's why I'm still on this earth, knowledge is surviving, without it you're a nobody with a life that's not worth living....My English brother Anton gets what I give and gives what I want. We have an understanding about loyalty.' He shrugs. 'My life is not unlike that of yours Joe Delph. We share a similar situation in putting our necks on the line, both sharing a love for our countries.'

Norman says, 'Its people like yourself Assad that need to govern, bring the clans together and stability to these inside infringements.'

Assad smiles, 'There is a vast difference in our cultures, my brother, In the UK people of many religions are living a non violent existence with what you call neighbouring clans. ...OK, a spark here and there but non-violent. Here in Iraq my brother...it's guns and bloodshed...suicide bombings and market square executions, watched over by young children who haven't been given time to grow up before, like their fathers, they join the Mehdi army or some other arms carrying group or Clan.' He smiles and pats Norma's back.

'Clans, I think I like that introduction to the many Mafia gangsters that no longer herd the goats or harvest the rice fields. That, after giving a violent beating to their opium workers. Working every hour Mohammed brings 24/7.'

Joe, 'So the gangsters control our mission, Assad?'

Ryona, 'So you said, just a while ago, that you knew everything that was going on, in regards to Iraq, Assad...So who is the Dream-Seller.?'

'The Dream-Seller, sweet lady, happens to be one who does not walk the sand of the Middle East. He is European he is French.'

Joe, 'Hs name Assad..give us his name?'

Assad holds them all in suspense as they wait a name. 'He is known only to a handful of people. Me along with Scarab leaders Rahaad Shadeed, His uncle Woo the axeman. Sadat Malik, and two more Frenchman Cortez, and Italian Romero. This information was given to me at the cost of a man's life.'

Dave whispers, 'His nameAssad?'

'I only know he's called the Fly.'

Lenny shakes his head, 'Didn't I say that the most wanted was somehow involved with the warhead heist. This Fly is becoming a nuisance. ...So we're getting closer.

'Closer .' Utters Norman. Lenny nods. 'Now we know he's French.'

Joe. 'How come you know all this, that the Fly is French, the names of our most wanted, the Scarabs?'

Assad puts up a finger, 'How, why, because that's what I'm about Joe, I'm a ghost, I put my trust in none, that's why I'm alive. Secrets should never be shared. To share a secret, then it becomes no longer a secret.'

He smiles, 'I try not to keep a calendar of events, past and future are the only terms I live by.'

He shrugs, 'One member of my scattered family came to my abode and we had tea. His name was Zakir...so young, but with the brain of a college don. He spoke of his being accepted into this Scarab army...He had at an even younger age, along with his father given their alliance to the Mehdi army but sadly he broke away for the, then new, Scarab brigade.'

He looks at Norman, smiles with a bow.

'Or should I say Scarab clan, I tell you this knowing Zakir is dead along with the many Scarab assassins who attempted to take on America. Whilst having tea with the sixteen year old he spoke of its leader Rahaad Shadeed, away in France, adding that a big play was going down which would make him a very rich man, so rich his father and mother would no longer need to toil everyday from Sun-up to Sun-down for this wealth would be for them.'

Ryona, 'So he met his end in the American heist failure.'

Assad nods, 'But what he did tell me was that his General Woo was going to talk with a Fly, he was to accompany Rahaad on a journey to France.'

He waves his hand. 'So there you have it.'

Ryona turns to Joe saying.'That's just where our twins came from, Joe...The Fly's never been out of the picture and let's face it who is more evil than the Fly to want our people to sample a little Black Rain.'

Four hours later Assad drove the beaten up Volkswagen passing the wester harbour on the Ur city wall. He turned to the team telling them that the true tourist would want to see Ur with it's royal tombs and places of interest, but when it came to the British the city dwellers wouldn't take too kindly to their presence of their looking at tombs that they had once plundered of silver and gold, lost Iraqi treasure, probably somewhere in the British museum or so it was thought.

Norman sighed, 'I never knew that Assad but I felt this unfriendliness when I was here in 2007...Now I know why.'

Assad, 'You we're here then Norman?...then you were lucky to keep your life.'

Norman nodded, saying. 'I had my moments, but then I was riding in a Half- track.dragging a cannon. The danger wasn't the snipers but the land mines that were every 200 metres or so.'

Assad smiled 'They're still there Norman but my people they know the signs, the markers left, little pyramids of pebbles.'

Joe, 'But at night Assad?'

The ghost laughs, 'We never travel without the moon, Joe.'

Ryona, 'But there's no moon tonight Assad.' Again he laughs, 'Then we're so lucky...You have a driver who knows the road....Like your Lewis Hamilton yes! '

Dave who's laying his head on Lenny's shoulder yawns saying. 'When's our tea break Assad?'

Assad, 'When we get well clear of Ur...then we bivouac....one more hour I'm thinking.'

Lenny says. 'It good we're not working to union rules.'

Assad, 'What's with this union rules?'

Joe smiles, 'What Lenny's trying to say is if we miss a tea break then we'd be out on strike.'

Assad. 'You British are so taken to rules...That at times is not a good thing, No?'

Norman says. 'Those signs Assad...little pebble pyramids.'

'Yes Norman?' Norm says, 'Well you've just passed one.'

Assad cries, 'Bugger me. ....Just, Norman?'

'I'd say fifty metres back.' Norman winks to the team,

'Bloody hell ...which way was stalk of its pear shaped base pointing...did you see? ...you must tell me.' Again Norman winks.

'I thought it was pointing'. ..leaning over he points a finger. Twirling it before jabbing it into Assad's chest.' The team burstout laughing. Assad slaps his hand down on the dash, hitting the horn which gives a sharp beep. He puts a finger up to his lips in the sign of silence. The team fall quiet before Assad gives it a couple more beeps and begins to laugh.

'You fucking British ...You make fun of Assad...But I'm now driving blind...I look for the pebbles. If you blow up boom ,boom. Then we all die.'

Lenny said. 'Norm, take front left ...I'm on front right... he's not joking about those signs.' He winks at Joe...They all catch on, with Norm straining to see into the dipped headlights. His face inches away from the wagons windscreen. Norman turns to tell Assad to slow down and sees the team all holding back their laughter. He points a finger at Lenny.

'Nice one Lenny baby ...Keep it up sunshine ...You were once a ghost...be prepared to be one again you bastard.' They all fall about laughing, even Norman, after taking a deep breath, joins in.

Assad shakes his head, saying. 'Crazy English ...You'll all die fucking laughing.' He too joins in.

It's dawn and the Sun is beginning to warm up the earth over Iraq after a cold night with temperatures dropping well below zero. The team have breakfast and are prepared for any action. Assad, Joe noted, had been showing more concern over the past hour or so. Acting like a caged tiger waiting impatiently for a gate to open. Joe asks.

'You OK Assad ...Are we all good?'

Assad with a half smile. 'This road, it's not as it should be ..We have no travellers ..There should be farmers coming from the north, bringing their wares to market at Ur.' He shrugs. 'But I see none...this is not good Joe Delph.'

Joe, 'So you think there's a hold up ahead?'

'Look a the time..it's 4.15...early morning travelling is a must for a profitable good day. Only time I have seen the road from Uruk to Ur empty was in the days of Saddam Hussein when the farmer's were openly stopped and their goods and livestock were taken by the Hussein bandits...I fear something is amiss.'

Joe turns to the team. 'You heard Assad there may be trouble ahead....Lock and load.'

The VW's windows because of the suns heat had been taken out and replaced with a rolled-up colourful curtain, this being pulled down as a night-time replacement. Joe suggested that they let the curtain down. If there was troubled ahead, like gangsters, then they had to be shot, gunned down, exterminated. This mission wasn't to be held up by a bunch of Dick Turpin, highwaymen. So he gave the order silencers on and be prepared for anything.

It was as Assad had imagined ...A road block. Six armed gangsters could be viewed through Joe's binoculars. One holding up the oncoming traffic, whilst we're three ravaging the unfortunate farmers. The two others were firing their Kalashnikov's into the air at the farmers who were trying desperately to turn their trucks and carts that were being pulled by snorting water buffaloes, around and back to Uruk. There was little resistance, especially after seeing one farmer being shot and dragged to the side of the road.

These gangsters, Assad told them were high on Captagon, a Mind stimulation drug that induced bravery and mind to fight. As far as the opium trade went, it was on a never ending course that was coming in from other Middle Eastern countries into the heart of Iraq and Iraq Kurdistan.

Joe handed the field glasses over to Norman saying. 'Six. We have one each.'

Assad smiled, 'I think the farmers will be grateful.' Norman, passing him the glasses, says. 'I'm for the one who put the farmer down. He's at 100 meters. I'll take the fucker's head off.'

Joe, 'OK. Assad takes the one stopping the traffic. Let him close on us then take him out.' He looks to Ryona, Lenny and Dave. ...I'm taking the one next down to Norm's hit, ..You three hit the ravagers When Assad takes his man we follow with an immediate action...and for fuck's sake don't hit the farmers.'

Moments later Assad pops the traffic stop-go man as he approaches his window. There followed a pop, pop, popping of accurate gun fire..six gangsters lay dead ...the farmers all cheer as the VW drives past.

Ryona. Rolling up her curtain looks out on a young boy knelt by the shot farmer's body. He puts up a hand in a thank you salute as the wagon picks up speed with Assad eager to leave the scene.

Dave said 'I've a feeling those poor farmers are going to suffer for our executions... but there again it was either the gangsters or us.'

Assad turns to him, saying. 'It's us, my friend, who will be searched for. One of those farmers will talk of a dark blue VW and a burst of fire coming from it.'

Ryona. 'So how long before we get to our destination?'

Assad replies, '150 miles to Najaf...on this road a good four hours.'

Joe, 'This Najaf, is where they do the mix, Assad?'

'I have never been into the area where they do the mix ... it's off the town of Najaf.. some ten miles west. A spot in the desert…it's highly guarded, and I've been told with warnings of electrified fences… There are four tower lookout nests with search lights …I knew it as at one other time, being a prison.'

Ryona in her eagerness asks, 'Are we likely to find any of the principals there the likes of Shadeed..Malik…Woo?'

'If I was to guess then it would be Woo, My man had told me of a man with a limp taking control of shipments destination Turkey …Shadeed, Malik…they would be at the money end.'

Joe nods. 'All piled into a Swiss account.'

Assad adds, 'Don't forget our billionaire, his smuggled oil flowing out of Iraq into the scavenger's black market Europe.'

Norman, 'Or Africa.' Assad nods, 'Or Africa.'

Lenny, 'Or over to Uncle Sam he did have a big interest in the States.'

Joe, 'Does it matter?…I think not…we have to take these opponents on round after round. The drugs, round one. Shadeed, Malik, round two then the knockout punch, the Fly, round three.'

Dave. 'I think you missed out Woo.'

Joe. 'He's just a support bout…He'll go but we want to take on the top of the bill.'

Assad turns off the road into a deep dried out river bed that at one time ran into the Tigris. It was well below road level and a perfect lay-by in which to wait out the blazing sun and rest till the night and their forthcoming attack on the Meth mixing factory.

Assad spread out the area map that he'd been given by SIS. He'd also received photographs taken by a Night Hawk, a highly successful infrared drone, that had been employed for the mission, photographs showing the watch towers quite clearly having a overall view of the compound and it's inner buildings.

He pointed out to the team its vulnerable spots, like a large off-shot shed that contained the generator, the source of all the electrical feeds. Joe looked at Ryona and said 'That's your baby...for pouring a mixture of rapid setting cement into. We have the night views but I very much doubt them having any night vision.'

Ryona nodding replied 'I've still to get under the wire.'

Joe, 'Norm, and Dave will take you with them using the sand hoods and the jump over bridge on the fencing.'

The sand hoods were a simple desert cover cloak that would protect its user from any overhead view. They were some seven feet in length with a four foot width, with sealed sleeves that allowed their wearer to slowly move, making up ground like a baby turtle on its journey to the sea.

Joe said that they would be told when to proceed and when to stop. This would be done by Assad viewing the selected area's towers and giving a phone signal of two beeps to move, one to stop, on reaching the wire will fix the bridge.

He went on to say that Lenny and himself would be on the rear crawl taking on the blowing up of the Meth lab. And hoping that its prisoner workers would be given the chance to escape.

Every part of the operation would need to be run smoothly. The tower guards taken out when the electricity dies from Ryona's hit on the generator. Norm and Dave, if at all possible, would take out any inquisitive mobster with the knife...making the need for gunfire a last resort.

The Night Hawk found the building on the right was the most used by the gangsters and was their all-in- one lodging area. It also counted twelve gangsters. With Joe's caution by adding another four, making sixteen in all. Woo if in there..was to be exterminated. He turned to the team, asking if there were any questions.

Ryona said 'I'd like a sample of the most potent Black Rain...I've a couple of guinea pigs that I'm wanting to administer it into.'

She gives Joe a positive look, Joe nods, 'No problem.'

Assad said. 'Protect yourselves at all times, it's kill or be killed in there. Feel no remorse for these Iraqi gangsters... They are not my kind of people.'

They didn't have to wait too long before the sun went down. There was no moon but still a full starry, starry night sky that could have floated out of Van Gogh's masterpiece.

Assad had taken the VW as far as he dared. Shutting off the engine in another off road, out of view location, a hoofed track that was the ships of the desert's caravan route that allowed the camels a far superior crossing of the ever changing sand dune landscape.

The team, along with Assad, would have to make the further mile on foot, each sharing a heavy load that contained arms and ammunition. Their loads were checked and double checked by Joe.

Having reached their best entrance point to the electrified fencing, and consequently their last of the shaded cover, the border line of the deserts black night and the compounds searching floodlights, the team donned their sand hoods before lying down flat on their stomach's with their weapons and equipment needed, bagged and safely tied to their torso to be dragged along in a slithering snake like fashion. Their progress to be made in an arrowhead formation, only to close up on the final few metres of the operation.

Joe then signalled Assad to sound two beeps to start. Norm at the point of the arrow to lead followed by Ryona and Dave taking first flight with Lenny and Joe taking the back pull. Joe, on his estimated timing, figured the crawl to be a good twenty minuets to the wire. Another ten to make the bridge, then the cut. All would depend on the inner action; Ryona to see to the fouling of the generator allowing the guard on each tower to be taken out of play, followed by the gangster's lodging quarters. Then releasing the innocent before blowing the laboratory and it's General Woo into kingdom come.

The job in all had never been easier, all done and dusted in just under the hour with Ryona taking out a gangster who was making for the latrine. She cut his larynx pulling the body away out of sight. Two minutes later the power was deactivated leaving the compound to the stars for any possible illumination. Of course there was little. The curiosity of the tower guards brought them down from their gun nests to be taken out by the team still carrying their cutthroats.

The lodge was too easy; a couple of stun grenades then the picking off the bewildered gangsters as they came, coughing, out of the building. Their Kalashnikovs firing everywhere but on target. Rapid bursts from the team's automatics cut the gangsters down.

When it came to the laboratory, Joe and Lenny could see through their night goggles the Afghan Woo standing firing his Kalashnikov. Ryona, who had come to assist wasted no time by cutting him down putting two bullets into Woo's head. The courier was dead. The chemists and lab. Assistants all stood together, some holding their arms high on seeing the dead Afghan.

Ryan moved in on them, trying to calm down the frightened few. One woman pointed to a man in the group, shouting. 'He gangster, he bad man.'

The man tried to make a break, not knowing in the darkness which way to turn. He ran straight into the arms of

David who smiled before plunging his knife into him. The workers were told by a now disguised Assad to make their way home. He told them about the VW waiting if they needed transport.

Ryona asked Assad to get one of the chemists to bring out the most lethal of the Black Rain. .. Moments later she was holding the agony death syringes in her hand...The chemist then told Assad that in this was pure heroine mixed with Captagon and a unknown ingredient that had been brought in from North Korea call Z184D. This he told Assad was bad medicine, Black Rain and that the hypodermics Ryona held were the most deadly being 100 per cent pure.

Assad handed him the keys to the VW and told him to make his journey then fire the vehicle. It would be unwise for him to keep it. Ryona then wanted to know if other Afghans had visited the lab...Assad spoke with the man who informed him that two other chiefs had been along with Woo...Woo had remained. Of the other two, he shrugged.

There was a large fire burning in what used to be a prison. The Iraqi occupants who'd been imprisoned for no fault of their own, young chemists and attendants, who were made to work in the Meth creating laboratories turning out the devastating mind blower Black Rain. Stood watching the bodies of the dead gangsters being incinerated.

Joe decided that these unfortunates be allowed to go home, set free. They blessed the invading team.

The team having successfully fulfilled their contract, were air-lifted by Chinook on a heading for Kuwait.

While below the chemists had fourteen dead gangsters adding fuel to a grand bonfire event, didn't hang around, with a fire still crackling they'd taken everything of any value away with them. On one part of the great desert Joe had spread a flour like powder, some nine sacks worth many millions of dollars onto the forever shifting sands. Ryona smiled at the few thousand dollars worth she had in her shoulder bag…..Customs?..No problem, it being stamped and sealed, part of a diplomatic bag.

29

ROUND TWO, KUWAIT

'Another day, another dollar' Lenny remarked on touch down at the Military airport in Kuwait. The city itself was amass with people, all going like ants somewhere, all doing something.

Assad had left the team after getting another assignment back in Basra, this time ghosting for the USA. on another problem, he would be going undercover on a continuing case of oil smuggling, a most dangerous area. He had left Joe his private contact number saying for him to keep in touch.

The team all shook his hand, thanked him and wished him luck.

The one hotel in Kuwait City which, was known as the central meeting point to do business in was the St Washam. It's decor was very much in the style one would find in a Bedouin chieftains tent, flamboyant with bright mixing of colour, giving a wraparound feeling of warmth even though its ceiling was littered with highly decorated fans.

Business meetings were held in side quarters with costumed attendants looking like they'd just walked out of the Rudolph Valentino movie 'The Sheik'

Definitely a place of relaxation, a palace to come into, to escape the killing heat of a mid day sun and definitely from the least hospitable desert on earth. A place where money talks. Who's got what and who goes where could be brought for a small price from attendants that made it their business to know. A secret poker school for high stake players, an underground hen house for sexual pleasure. Where the consumption of alcohol was, along with sex and gambling strictly illegal. Where pornography was a no, but could still be obtained at ...risk. There were no, pubs, clubs or sex haunts active on the streets and alleyways of Kuwait City but with a city full to the brim with immigrant workers who were treated like vermin then in the subterranean holes they survived in, money was king, and money could buy almost anything.

Assad had already told Joe of this hotel, the St Washam, being the place to launch their search for the Afghans. If the likes of Shadeed and Malik were in town then this is where they would stay. He left the team with, 'Be careful who you trust, stay hidden in the shadows.'

Ryona asked 'So who do we trust?'

Joe, 'You trust no one...who's looking to make a buck. A man who looks nothing, knows nothing....If you've ever been on a race track there's always one who can give you a winner...My dad who was a race goer, always told them, when they approached, 'Sorry sunshine but I can back my own losers.'

Norman nods. 'I always get the best information from the man behind the bar but our ghost Lenny here, he knows better than all of us who to select.'

Dave. 'Lenny?'

Lenny nods, 'I've had information come to me from all walks of life. Some that I thought good' He shrugs, 'Turns out worthless...and so the reverse, If you want a shoe repaired, then you go to the cobbler is my advise.'

Ryona said 'We know what they look like, we're sure to find if they're here. ..If we could somehow get a look at the hotel's ledger then I think we'd know.'

Joe, 'That would tick a lot of problems getting a look at the hotel register...Lots of Kuwait's people speak English as well as Arabic...Most business is done in English ...So it should be no trouble in a five star hotel at 400 euros a night. A few dollars thrown into the night receptionist hat, maybe?'

Lenny. 'OK, here's what I think, I ask for some fictitious woman's name. Then Ryona comes and argues with me, saying something like ...Well you seeing if your tramp as turned up then?...

She then turns to the receptionist asking to see the register about whether this fictitious woman is in it or not... She snarls at me, saying if she's here or you've got her a room then I'm going home on the next flight out.'

Ryona smiles, 'You know Lenny that's a golden idea and it might just work...I might even get to slap your face.' The team giggle. She looks to Joe who nods saying, 'OK, let's go with it .' He looks to them all. 'If anyone thinks of something better then I'm all ears.'

One hour later and the team meet in Joe and Normans room.

An excited Ryona is telling them that the Scarabs are in the hotel. She even got their departure time as 12 noon Friday which was two days away.

Joe, 'So let's get our heads together on how we're going to take them out.'

Dave asks. 'What name did you use, the other woman.?'

Lenny winks unknowingly to Dave and putting a finger up says. 'Ah, that was Sandra Peterson .'

Dave, mouth agape snarls, 'You wouldn't fucking dare, Ghosty.'

They all laugh. Dave too, 'I wouldn't put anything past the ghost. It's a fucking wonder he's still alive.'

Joe puts up a hand, 'I'm thinking we get moving on this. Two days isn't that long. If they catch a glimpse of anyone of us it's game over so keep out of the main corridors. Like Assad said, stay in the shadows.'

Ryona. 'Surely they've heard of Woo's disappearance maybe they'll want to move tonight...I'm so darn lucky that I happened to glance at their room number. It's seven....room seven ground floor.'

Joe. 'Well thank you for telling us that, knowing the room makes our quest far easier....Yes now I'm thinking of a late night hit, a clobber and bind job, out through the French window, into the garden area then into our vehicle and away,..into the freezing desert with barely any clothing. ..Let's be straight about this, these pigs ain't going to tell us shite so let's give them the product they'd hope to receive, Black Rain, but ten times the fucking dose they gave Roberto, then leave them to their fate...Then it's the Fly... he's the icing on the cake.'

It's after midnight when the team finally get down to putting their plan into action. Lenny, who Joe thought was the least likely to be remembered as being at the table for eight at the Montana Coliseum restaurant, had been given the task of giving a surveillance job on apartment 7.

The ground floor, Numbered 1-20 in a full circle with three doors that led from the hotel foyer quadrant to its winding corridor was lavishly carpeted with the very finest

Arabian knit displayed anywhere in the world. The much regarded London Ritz at many thousands of pounds a night could never match this underfoot assortment of colour. In the foyer itself were two lifts that could take residents to any of its six floors.

Lenny had opted for the emergency stairs.. The hotel's lavishly produced brochure gave an insight to all floors. With the team's interest in only the one, the ground floor. Looking at the luxurious apartments on this floor was as if walking into paradise. It's twenty apartments had extended extras on having their own sauna's, outdoor private pools and a butler service who laundered and ironed the occupant's finest silk attire.

This man of all trades just happened to be the one to see for the illegal drink and games.

Lenny silently counted off the apartment numbers stopping at number 7. He heard no sound so thinking the Afghans could have retired, he pulled from his pocket a stethoscope and put it to the apartment's wall. To hear what could only be a TV...with intermittent voices. He also caught the voices of the two Afghans. He pocketed the stethoscope just as a butler came down the hallway towards him.

He spoke to Lenny in Arabic. Lenny acted like he was pissed or something. 'Me, no speak the Arabic. Irish ... Dublin...English.' The butler held a now swaying Lenny under the elbow, replying in English he said.

'You seem to have lost your way sir...What apartment number is yours?'

Lenny answered with a bit of a slur, 'Sixty two.' which was the truth.

The butler said, 'Then you must take the elevator Sir....Come along take your time..I will take you.'

Lenny gips before saying 'What a good man you are, I must put in a word with the management about your kindness.' He staggers, being led though the foyer to a waiting lift...He's then put into it and the butler points to the button saying 3rd floor. Lenny waggles his finger as the door slides shut. The waiter standing in the foyer. Watches the floor light for 3 show...The night receptionist asks. 'Where you dragged him out of ?'

The Butler laughs, 'Pissed as a fart, hey but don't look at me, he's not one of mine, floor 3, one of Abdulla's cast off's .'

Lenny entered apartment sixty two, staggering and getting strange looks from the eager awaiting team.

Norman said. 'What the fuck happened to you, man?'

Lenny smiled. 'I did the scout, they're in there, TV on it but two distinct Arabic voices over it. I was spotted in the hallway by one of the butlers, had to put the over the limit act on, he escorted me to the lift.'

Joe, 'OK, we're on go for two am...Norm and Dave will do the fire escape stairs down into the underground garage, up from there and out through the garden area, make for apartment seven. Then at precisely two thirty take the French window into their lounge area.

We, Ryona, Lenny, and myself will wait by the hallway door. Norm, make sure our prisoners are made incapable of giving any alarm. Tape their mouths shut tight, drop em the sleeper drug. ..then it's away to the vehicle.'

He smiles. 'With just their bed shifts on they're in for a freeze up in the cold desert sands, should be near ten below.

'Ryona asks . 'Excuse me for asking Joe but where the fuck's the motor coming from?'

Joe, 'Earlier this afternoon when I knew it was on, the grab. I phoned Assad and asked if there was any chance of a motor.'

Joe smiled. 'He said to leave everything to him, he'd have a man at the statue of a woman in her Muslim attire holding out a basket of fruit and rice. It's near the four fountains...

The time given was for 3 am the mans name is Shalam. he needs to be paid. 1000 euros. Assad said for Shalam the risk is great, if caught could mean his life, a market square execution.'

With watches synchronised Norman and Dave left the apartment, they had taken the stairs that led them one below ground floor level. Out and onto the hotel's picturesque gardens and began to count off the small apartments pools. From their back-packs they put on the night view goggles and could clearly now see the brass pool brass plaque, indicating the pool was for the occupants of apartment 7.

The two agents were grateful that the hotel's neon lighting that was fixed above floor six, had created a 10 foot shadow that fell over the apartment's French windows and so shaded a pool that was lit by underwater lighting, this being the only lighting in use.

Norman pointed to the doors and produced a small jemmy waving Dave up to the French doors. They listened for any sounds coming from the inner lounge area.

There was no late night TV, the apartment lay silent except for one occupant snoring and in complete darkness.

Dave whispering said. 'I wonder how long it's been since they took to their beds?'

'It makes no difference, Dave.' Norm smiled 'It's now or never.' Winks. 'Old Elvis hit...We have to be quick, You take the snorer and I'll settle the dreamer....Stun and tape, then we let Joe in to take over the Scarab and the billionaire.'

Dave looks all around the windows frame work, before pointing and whispering 'The windows, Norm, they ain't locked. They're sliders, not having caught the catch it's a lucky night for us Major.'

Norman whispers, ' Now that's what Yeh might call a golden opportunity...You ready marine?' 'Ready as I'll ever be Norm.'

Norman punches Dave's shoulder, saying. 'So let's do this.'

Five minutes later and the two wriggling bodies of the Afghans,with taped over mouths and electrical wraps binding hands and feet, were unceremoniously dragged in to the lounge. Both were trying to communicate with their kidnappers and themselves all but to no avail.

Meanwhile Norman had scurried and opened the main door to the hallway, to let Joe and the rest of the team in.

Ryona, without more ado, gave the sleeper injection into Jahaad Shadeed's neck a second needle was administered by Lenny into Malik.

Malik's head was moving none stop, side to side, up and down, trying to get to talk to their abductors. Shadeer just sat there trying to look unconcerned. They soon were soundly sleeping.

Joe said 'Ok, do a quick clean up, take anything that looks important, then it's the fountains.' He pinches Malik's cheeks, saying 'It's showtime baby.'

They all smile at Dave who's picked up Malik like a rolled up carpet and fireman's lifted him over his shoulder. Norm. shrugs 'Best I go with him as cover, Joe.'

Joe nods saying 'That knee playing yo-yo, Norm?'

Smiles. 'That's fine, you two get moving ....Go with them Lenny. Ryona and I will be right behind you with Scarab Shadeer.'

It had taken no longer than 15 minutes before they were on their way sitting in the back of an old Ford Tranny With a maybe 50 year old Shalam behind the wheel. The Arab patted the dash and said to Joe 'This good American motor Mr. Joe, yes?'

Joe, laughed at the crunching sound the gear box was making and said. 'As long as it gets us to Ground Zero, then yes, Shalam, a beautiful motor.'

Salam reminded Joe that it was his life if he was caught, that he owed many favours to Assad, that he was in fact his cousin on his fathers side.

Joe patted him saying he understood and if the truth be known, if caught it would be their lives too.

Joe had told Assad that he'd a chopper pick-up point somewhere in the the Great Nefud, where an air lift would be waiting. He'd contacted Sheikh Mohammed Al Rhatoob and called up an old favour.

Joe, at one time had along with a team of special forces, worked a search and rescue operation bringing home the Sheiks youngest daughter from some Yemen infiltrators, a band of gangsters that were seeking a ransom of several million dollars. The safe return of his most treasured possession gave Joe the key to upper north eastern Saudi Arabia. The Sheik had given Joe the place for the pick-up. saying that whatever the reason Joe had only to ask.

Joe had shown Shalam the spot asking if he knew of it and what sort of time frame they would need.

Shalam said it was a good one and a half to two hundred miles to the oasis. Yes he knew of it, but had never ventured that far north into the Saudi desert With that, Joe went on to assure the nervous Kuwaiti that there was no fear of being arrested, that all had been arranged through the power of the Sheik familie's hold on the land of Mecca.

Joe told Ryona that the Afghans get their stinger of Black Rain whatever, wherever,..They've got a full Hurricane to fight their way through.

She looks to the team who are nodding in agreement.

'I wouldn't have it any other way Joe, they'll get the most heavenly hit that's ever been shot into their Afghan arms. While we watch.'

Joe 'I was thinking of dropping them deep into no man's land,two zombies with fucked minds.'

Ryona 'I'm happy to see the terror, the pain showing in their faces, Joe...then I know that Roberto has had his Sicilian revenge...It's personal, but I'd like to see Malik with all his billions, along with his buddy in crime Shadeer, trying to buy themselves out of their tormented souls,'

Norman pressed down on her hands. 'All of us in this tin can know just where you're coming from girl...I'd think Joe would pass on to you the final say.' He looks to Joe. 'That right, Joe?'

Joe nods, shrugs . 'Our girl gets the final curtain Norm it goes without saying.'

The team had finally left Kuwait and had taken a safe crossing point over the border into Saudi Arabia.The two prisoners who had passed out with the high dosage of the sleeper were coming round.

Joes thoughts were back in the days he was last in Saudi..and his triumphant return with the daughter of Sheikh Al Mohammed Rhatoob. He remembered the Sheik had offered Joe a king's ransom but Joe declined his great offer, saying for him to give it to some children's charity. The Sheik couldn't believe that a man with the chance to set himself up for life, would calmly give it all away. But this Joe did, and many Arabian children, having gown up now, still write to him with their New Years greetings.

It took Shalam a good five hours to reach the oasis and with Joe to find out that the Sheik had been true to his word.

Standing waiting was one of his family's private helicopters. With room for eight passengers. Filled with all the desert fruit and beverages refrigerated water. The pilot topped it all by handing over a bottle of Johnny Walker Black label to the grateful Joe.

Joe had the two Scarabs tossed out of the transit I just their shifts.It was a bitterly cold morning with temperatures well below zero. He walked over to the frightened billionaire

Malik and ripped off the tape that had covered his mouth, fetching quite a few hairs out of his beard. Malik flinched whilst trying to make out what was happening.

Joe spoke. 'I have one question to ask, your one and only chance to make your peace with Allah…I want the name of the Fly.'

Malik replied. 'You tell me ..I didn't deal with him..it was Rahaad and Woo who did all the arrangements. They met him….Maybe Woo will tell you.'

Joe. 'Wrong answer…So you put money into a no-win heist…costing millions of dollars and you didn't know who the fuck you were dealing with?'

He waves his hand across his chest saying. 'Enough.'

He nods over to Ryona, saying 'Why don't you have a word with the our billionaire boy, girl.'

She holds up a syringe holding the black rain serum and walks up to Malik saying. 'This is what you fed into my husband, and this is what, on behalf of my husband, I'm giving back to you. This being ten times more potent.'

Ryona watched him scream as the needle was stabbed into his neck. He began perspiring his eyes bulged, like the balls were going to fly out of their sockets. Then they rolled. He began to cough blood before turning into a Zombie like stiff with eyes bleeding staring into nothingness. He began a series of ongoing scream's his head violently shaking.

Joe could see Shalam looking like he wanted none of this, ready to hot foot it back to Kuwait. Joe patted his shoulder saying.

'It's OK, if you want to leave, then you can go. He smiled. 'Your work here is done. I've even added an extra 500 euro's He handed Shalam a package. 'A little extra for your family.'

Shalam bowed saying 'You're a fine man Mr. Joe…thank you, may your God protect you.' He wasn't staying to see anymore of the Black Rain. He saluted the team and the old Tranny fired up and rattled its way back to Kuwait.

Ryona looked at the Scarab, his face was now showing fear as she approached him with another syringe full of the deadly venom She reached down and gripped his shoulder, she smiled, shrugged and said. 'You can see what a nice time your once powerful benefactor is having. Then people like you…well you love to see horror, people suffering.'

Rahaad is trying to say something, but Ryona continues. 'Your uncle is it, this Woo? I thought I'd tell you ….he's dead..Your buddy there Sadat, his brother…he's dead, your raging army …all dead. So that just leaves the fucking ace in the pack and it'll be game over…Such a brain Shadeer, to have been so wrongly used, but I shed not a tear for a ruthless bastard like you.'

She gives him it's an all over shrug, a wink and a smile.

'I'm not going to lower myself into asking you for a name, the team, we will find this Fly maybe we will give him a little of this Black Rain…his family too.'

She gives a now cold staring Rahaad another wink and a smile.'Oh, but I was forgetting..that you and your money loaded Malik…Neither of you will be able to tell him about the wonderful dreams he'll be having.'

She laughs, 'One hit of a lifetime I might add, his fucking last.' She holds up her hand to the heavens.

'Where is your great Sun God now Rahaad?...The great scholar I once knew is no more..You'd have made a fine voice for your people in the world's diplomatic halls.' She sighs. 'Instead you join the armies of Bin Laden and look what happened to him …You play with the fire power then expect to get burnt…I believe you one time sent me that message.'

Shadeer's eyes die in a swimming mist as Ryona plunges the needle deep into his neck and inserts the lethal dose of Rain. His eyes roll and fall back bringing the white, Black veins like some cracked saucer appear and his head rocks and shakes. She rips the tape from his mouth to hear the sound of Arabic words, crying out in loudness being carried off over the shifting sands of a cold Saudi desert. They all look down on the two terrorists that are now entering a Zombified state that's giving them non-stop pain.

Joe turns to the pilot and says 'I think we're finished here.'

The pilot asks. 'You taking them with you?'

Joe says 'Ask the lady, it's her day today.'

Ryona shugs saying. 'Sorry Joe, but I want them dead. Let them feel the pain for a while, we take them with us... Give them the cement boots, acouple of hold-alls filled with sand...Then a drop from hight into the Red Sea...Before we land in Jiddah.'

Pilot nods.'We can do that....no problem.'

Joe, looks down at the two zombies, who by now are completely out of it, he can see their faces wracked going through the pain, that he had seen with Roberto. With eyes that are opening and closing, like Belisha beacons, pupils remaining fixed in a constant stare. Blood flowing out of every possible face opening.

Joe with a nods to Norman. 'Get them aboard ...Ryona you ready?...let's do this.'

Ten minutes later and the two walking like Frankenstein monsters are taken and loaded along with two sand filled hold-alls fixed like parachutes onto their backs of the luxurious Airbus H175. It came as no surprise to Joe that Ryona sat opposite the two Scarabs. He could see the smile on her face as she watched each stab of pain that was plainly being displayed on their face and body shudders. Malik was beginning to froth at the mouth a deep yellow and blood mixed bile.

Moments later the airbus had lifted and was racing at top speed towards the Red Sea. Shadeer's injection must have contained a higher inflow of the deadly Black Rain, with his ears and eyes now seeping blood.

Ryona jabbing a finger at the Malik. 'So how's it feel to sample what you've created mister oil billionaire...you enjoying your ride into hell?' She looks to Shadeer.

'What a fuck-up you've made of your life college boy...You forgot one thing, one thing that in our business you should never forget....Never underestimate your opponent's...What you did to my husband...You should have known I'd come after you...To kill you, with more than a vengeance.'

Lenny said. 'They can't hear you girl , they've gone.'

Joe puts up a hand saying. 'Let her have her say...it doesn't matter if they can hear or not...she needs to know if there's anything left upstairs in them brains of theirs, they've heard.'

The team watched on as Ryona came to virtually throwing them out through the open door of the Airbus that had reached the Red Sea.

One thing for sure there was no screams, no frightening reaction coming from the two descending bodies as they plunged into the water.

30
NOTHING BUT BLUE SKIES

Lunch at the White House were Joe and the team sat with the President John MacArthur, who'd thanked them along with Scott Brady Jones and Tom Hawk, for giving him a full report on the safe deliverance of the Naughty Boy missiles. He was exceptionally pleased that there was very little life lost in such a delicate situation. He expressed his sorrow to Ryona on her loss of Roberto and hoped that this would close the door, put an end to any further attempts by terrorists infiltrations. His exact words being 'Make the bastards think twice, before taking on the United States.'

Tom, said. 'I think we've certainly given them a kick out of the ball park John...They woke us with 9/11...It's not going to happen again?'

The President sighed. 'Not in my term of office, Tom.' He saluted the team. 'Not with these sort of guys watching our backs, thank God.'

Joe said. 'It was a joint operation with Scott and Delta Force, Sir...couldn't have performed with out them.'

Scott winked saying. 'Thank you, Joe...Let's not forget Ernest and his Seals.'

Two days later and Joe found himself back in the UK...Given a two week furlough by Anton, and was hoping to continue the holiday in Hemingway's Havana, Cuba.....That was until Ryona asked him if he'd help out with some chores at her new home in North Yorkshire. He had answered her with a 'Why not.' With the girls away with their studies, Ryona had no close friends, Joe being in Doncaster was roughly only an hour and a half away....70 miles down the A64.

The following day Joe had arrived on the outskirts of the beautiful picturesque village of Thornton-Le-Dale. Ryona greeted him at her converted barn homestead.that was situated overlooking the village on what was once a small holding of some 3 acres of green pasture fields with a wooded copse running down and around giving a weather protection shield to the long rectangular building.

It wasn't too long before she had him painting and repairing white wicker fencing that had in parts perished. Luckily the building was sound, the barn being only converted in the last few years or so.

Ryona was sharing a period of grief with Joe, knowing he had not got over his love for Stacy Kilmer...It would take time, if ever. ...herself, hadn't she had a lifetime of grief. The murders of her family, Roberto's death, played heavy on her mind. Joe was more than being her boss, he was her only true close friend, that wasn't to say the team wouldn't be there for her. They were something special without a doubt.

It was whilst they sat in front of a blazing log fire with a glass of fine wine and going over the chasing of the Fly, that Joe's phone beeped crimson with Anton's name showing on its screen.

Joe swiped to reply. 'Yes Anton?'

Anton said. 'Sorry for disturbing your holiday Joe but something come up that I know you will be interested in.....The Fly! '

Joe. 'Do go on chief...I'm all ears.'

Best you and Ryona get yourselves back to London. The information I've received needs looking at.'

Joe said. 'Look Anton, you're forever cutting short my furlough ...This better be good.'

'Oh, it's good, Joe..Comes from a very reliable sauce.'

'OK, we're on our way...You can expect us, first thing tomorrow morning.'

It was a little after 12 noon the following day when the two agents finally arrived at SIS's Vauxhall headquarters and the office of Anton Spicer. Who was waiting with freshly brewed coffee to greet them. Joe had noticed a lady of around 45 to 50 years. Well dressed in a sort of Bohemian style outfit, that gave her a much younger appearance. Anton introduced her as a Miss Georgette Zaponi.

'Miss Zaponi was the manager of a very special young lady..I don't think you, Joe would know of her...Ryona could well have.' He looks over at Georgette.

Miss Zaponi says.'looking at Ryona ...I could well have managed her and taken her to the top, a possible Vogue front pager.'

Ryona smiles. 'Sometimes I wish, Georgette. Then again I'm not one for the spotlight.'

'Call me Georgi, Ryona...everybody else does.'

Anton. 'Georgi is a well respected manager in the worlds top fashion model agency's for both male and female. 'Papillon et Abeilles'

Joe, looking rather confused. 'Sorry, Anton ...but fashion?' '

'Wait...Let me go on ..I'll explain,, Joe.'

He sighs. 'It was around two years ago that Georgi lost one of the worlds premiere models. The outstanding beautiful Angelina Hardy in what was called a suicide. A very suspicious death for Angelina was at the hight of her career....This so called suicide happened after Angelina refused to walk the floor for the Sister Wolff fashion house. This house is owned by Simone and Rachel Wolff, daughters of Conrad Wolff. This family live on the French/German border town of Colmar '

The known Controller Franz Wolff, father of the twins also lived in Colmar, it looks like his death, criminal activity could well have passed on to brother Conrad. This we need to establish. By putting a ghost on the inside. So what do you think Ryona?'

'In regards to what Chief?'

'By walking the floor for the Sister Wolff House of Fashion.?'

Joe said 'No disrespect, Anton, or to Ryona, who's looks would compete with the best, but she's not trained for cat walking...Sorry but I'm not for pushing her into being some Kate Moss.'

'I agree, Joe and that is why I have Georgi here to train her, should she except the mission. ...Do not worry one little bit, Ryona does not enter the play without this lady's complete assurance that she's ready. It won't be happening overnight.'

Georgi said. 'I have already lost a great model to these killers, one is enough, I'm not aiming to lose Ryona.' She shrugs. 'I need the Wolff girls to come to me for her, we don't go to them....Doing that would only add to suspicion.'

Anton interrupts saying. 'Joe...Ryona she'd be on her own on this play.'

Joe 'I sort of figured that out already, Ant. That's why I'd be a little worried.'

Ryona laughs. 'I've not said that I'm going with this fashion model idea...If Conrad Wolff is the Fly, then the question is, would his girls know their father was a murderer and thief ? ...And if they did, what then?'

Anton puts up a palm and says.

'We'll it's make your mind up time, Ryona are we on a green light or red?'

looks to Georgi and asks. 'Think I can pass for a top Gucci girl Georgi?'

Georgi smiles,and replies. 'Yes, I do..but I won't let you go into that house if you don't pass the work I've got scheduled for you.' I've never ever trained a looser. My girls all have an education upstairs a super brain to match their bodies....So, if your going to go with Anton's green light....Then it's a morning nine o clock date in my Kensington studios, First lesson, is to be on time, always.....'

Ryona smiles at Joe and says. 'What the fuck am I letting myself into Joe?'

It would take a further three weeks for Georgi to get Ryona into an most excellent floor walker. She had booked her into a few photo shoots and had enquiries on her possible doing full video advertising for gymnasium equipment. It had come to Georgi's notice that the Wolff sisters were going to be attending a recruiting programme at the 'Nightingale' a premier night spot in Manchester. Ryona would appear with Georgi knowing that with her representation, Ryona would get the interest from the Sister Wolff House. She would carry a new name and passport one Ramona Flood.

Two days later with Joe and Anton relaxing over a beer in the Cricketers Arms. A small waterside pub in Richmond. Joe's phone beeped. It's screen lit up the name of Ryona.

Joe. 'How's it going girl?'

Ryona. 'Looks like we're in the Wolff's den, Joe....I'm booked along with Georgi on a flight to Paris.'

She giggle's. 'I cannot believe it I'm to walk the west wing of the Grand Palais complex..for the Wolff sisters....Everybody who's somebody is there Coco Chanel,Christian Dior, Stella McCartney, Valli, ...What a line up ..I'll be doing three changes ....Spring collection.'

Joe nods to Anton,saying ...'She's in.'

Anton gets up leans over, squeezes Joes shoulder.

'I think it's time for you to take a trip to Paris, don't you? take Lenny, the ghost with you.'

Joe shrugs. 'Why not....this Fly, Conrad Wolff ...will finally get to meet Spiderman, Joe Delph.'

Anton sighs. 'Just remember Joe, we have nothing, the guy's a genius in French eyes. His charitable events that include huge inputs into financing cancer research along with the Colmar Childrens hospital were he sits as its chairman. His money having created its new West Wing with an additional hundred beds.'

Joe shakes his head. 'That's going to be some problem... taking him through the necessary law courts...We'll it'll be a no go...I'm afraid he's got to go down.... This needs some serious thinking about.'

Anton nods. 'You thinking, same mind as me, Joe...An accidental death?'

Joe shrugs. 'Let's get over to Paris and take a look at such a possibility, chief.'

EPILOGUE

The series of heavy damaging hits given to the Fly had sadly not come without cost to Joe Delph and Ryona Steel. The last couple of years had brought the loss of Captain Tony Ford and Ryona's husband Roberto Veneto. Those along with the murders of Joe's first and only love Stacy Kilmer along with David Carter had not been easy to take.

Still this Fly was still out there, sitting in his luxurious fortress in Colmar. He and his right hand man Ferdinand Cortez,were deep into planing their next criminal activities. Mission London.

Cortez said that this agent Delph had been one hell of a thorn in their side. That putting the very best known assassin on to him at a cost of a half million dollars had been their only option.

Still they waited with no news coming out of London on completion of the contract, things didn't look good. All this whilst unknown to the Fly the Moscow Pakham had put out a contract for his death.

THE END

The third book in the *Doonata* trilogy, *Closing Time*, is due out in 2024.

Walt Oxer was born in the mining village of Denaby Main, South Yorkshire, once part of a thriving coal mining area. He now lives on the North West coastline, in Blackpool, with his wife Jan Lorraine.

Milton Keynes UK
Ingram Content Group UK Ltd.
UKHW040627170124
436182UK00001B/15